"Magic and mortals and memories, oh my! This fae-tastic fantasy novel had me in a whirlwind of emotions. Kay L. Moody really knows how to keep her readers on their toes."
–Cheyenne, @chey.enne_books

"Kay did it again by taking my heart into Crystal Thorn. The mystery of the blade and the kingdom's secrets make it so easy to fall into the romantasy of Chloe and Quintus. Epic Series." –Lianne, @lianne_the_bibliophile

"Filled with breathtakingly vivid scenes, mesmerizing moments of what comes next and a satisfying storyline, Kay has continued to out write herself. Crystalfall is a court that many readers would love to visit with imagery so beautifully described that the scenes danced from the pages. Enthralling, captivating, Kay remains a firm favorite author."
–Anita, @hermeslvfan

"Another epic installment in this amazing Fae adventure, full of quests, betrayals & forgiveness. It will leave you wanting more love after betrayal and hope for a new beginning."
–Erin, @pagesinkedinshadows

"Kay L. Moody delivers another spellbinding Romantasy filled with epic adventure and sweet stolen moments between Chloe & Quintus! Crystalfall Court opens Faerie up to new mysteries & chaos. This series is perfect for YA fantasy readers and left me in great anticipation for the next book!!"
–Kelly, @mermade.withlove

ALSO BY KAY L. MOODY

Fae and Crystal Thorns
Flame & Crystal Thorns
Shadow & Crystal Thorns
Blade & Crystal Thorns
Curse & Crystal Thorns

Standalone: Nutcracker of Crystalfall

The Fae of Bitter Thorn
Heir of Bitter Thorn
Court of Bitter Thorn
Castle of Bitter Thorn
Crown of Bitter Thorn
Queen of Bitter Thorn

The Elements of Kamdaria
The Elements of the Crown
The Elements of the Gate
The Elements of the Storm

Truth Seer Trilogy
Truth Seer
Healer
Truth Changer

Visit **kaylmoody.com/bitter** to download a prequel novella,
Heir of Bitter Thorn, for free.

KAY L. MOODY

BLADE &
CRYSTAL THORNS

FAE AND CRYSTAL THORNS 3

Blade & Crystal Thorns
Fae and Crystal Thorns, #3
By Kay L. Moody

Published by Marten Press
3731 W 10400 S Ste 102, #205
South Jordan, UT 84009

www.MartenPress.com

Cover by Angel Leya
Edited by Deborah Spencer and Justin Greer

ISBN: 978-1-954335-14-1

Dedication

For anyone still looking for their home.

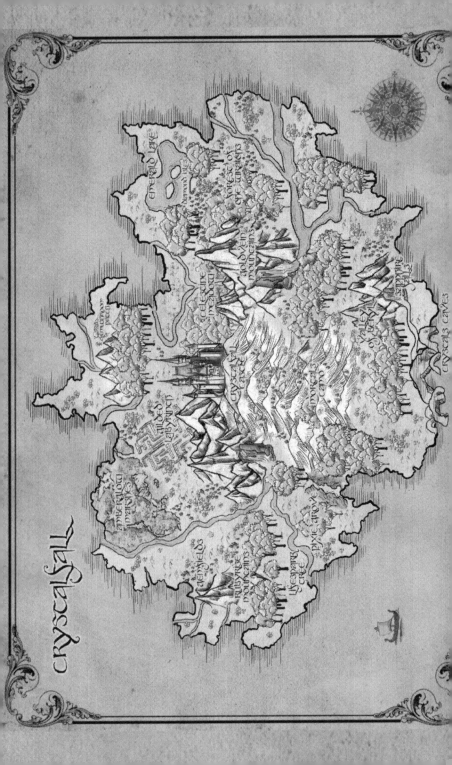

1

WITH TREES MADE OF GOLD and fruit made of jewels, how did anyone eat? Chloe stared at the ruby red apple in her hand. Soft sun rays glinted off its sparkling surface. She could have attached a golden chain to it and worn it as a necklace.

In the mortal realm, it would have been immediately the envy of every courtier and lady. It was a jewel stunning enough to break hearts, to start wars. Even in the rest of Faerie, a gem so beautiful would have been admired. But here, in a landscape of golden trees with emerald leaves, it was just an apple.

Her fingernail tapped against the ruby surface. Maybe the jeweled part could turn into a real apple somehow. Or maybe a little magic could transform it into food. There had to be some way to eat in this new court. All the other Faerie courts had food.

As she cast a look backward, her tangled and knotted blonde hair shifted across her back. A waterfall of sparkling blue glimmered nearby. Though it clearly contained liquid, it also glittered as if filled with gems. Could the water be safe to drink if it contained gems?

With each step deeper into the court, the aroma of vanilla and lilacs intensified. For a moment, she even forgot to be worried about food.

"We are almost there." Quintus followed a path of black soil and tiny pearlescent pebbles, seemingly unburdened by any of the concern plaguing Chloe's mind. Ever since they had stepped through the black caves and into this new court, his gaze had stayed fixed on the golden castle with ruby red spires ahead of them. After marching for what felt like an entire day, they had finally almost reached it.

His wool cape covered his torso. She'd given it back to him after he'd used it to help dry her off. Though it had mostly dried now, it still hung limp and awkward over his frame.

Her own clothes had mostly dried too, but the sulfur waters she had fallen into in Mistmount must not have been ideal for clothing. Her once worn-but-comfortable red dress and cream underdress now looked like the scrappy bits of fabric that sat at the bottom of a mending basket.

Once they got to the golden castle and took a breath, she'd ask Quintus to make her some new clothes.

Glancing down at the sparkling ruby in her hand again, she increased her pace and caught up to Quintus's side. She lifted the apple for him to see. "All the fruit here looks like this. Even the water seems to have gems in it." Her head tilted to the side. "How do you think we're supposed to eat in this court?"

His gaze shifted off the castle and toward her for only a flicker of a second. "Do you need to eat *right* now?"

"No." She had to nearly jog to keep up with his hurried strides. "I'm just thinking hypothetically. Obviously, we can go back to Elora's court to eat when we need to. But all the other courts have nuts and berries and animals and other naturally occurring foods. Yet everything here in this new court seems to be made of jewels. I just don't understand how anyone is supposed to eat."

Her head shook side to side as she took in the glistening waterfall again. She spoke more to herself now, since Quintus had stopped paying attention, fixating his attention on the castle instead. "This new court is breathtaking, but how is anyone supposed to live here?"

The word *new* snagged in her mind. She remembered a story her magical book had once shared with her. At some point in Faerie's history, a mortal had gotten magic and destroyed an entire court with it. She'd always assumed one of the other six courts had been destroyed and rebuilt again, but what if it hadn't been one of those courts? What if it had been this one? Perhaps this court wasn't *new* at all. Perhaps it was so old everyone in Faerie had forgotten about it. She considered dropping the ruby apple into her leather bag, but decided to just set it onto the black soil instead.

Right then, they reached the point where the black soil opened wide until it met the gleaming golden staircase leading to the castle's entrance. They had arrived.

Quintus yanked on the large golden handles that should have opened the enormous front doors. But even with his fae strength, the doors didn't budge. It wasn't that they only moved a little. It wasn't as though a lock of some sort held them mostly in place. No, these doors didn't budge at all, almost like they weren't actual doors but some sort of decoration instead. They appeared to be carved into the golden castle wall rather than having true hinges.

Quintus yanked on the handles again. They still didn't budge. Not even a smidgeon.

Chloe narrowed her eyes at them before shrugging. "Maybe you have to use magic to open them."

After a hurried nod, Quintus shot emerald-green magic from his fingertips. The magic flowed across the doors until its tendrils slithered into the edges of the doors. It took a moment before the transformation became apparent. Gradually, the doors morphed from looking as though they had been carved from a single slab of gold to having true hinges that connected them to the wall.

Once the magic had dissipated, Quintus yanked on the doors again. This time, they opened.

Nudging him with her elbow, Chloe smirked. "I told you you're the leader of this court. Who else could have opened the doors of the castle so easily?"

For the first time since he caught sight of the castle, Quintus's gaze turned away from it. His shoulders slumped, and he stared down at his feet. "And I already told you, I cannot possibly be the leader of this court. Just because I was drawn to it after you healed Faerie, does not mean… it …" He tensed, shaking his head in response. "Only High King Brannick can choose the leader for a court. Maybe this new court is my home, but that does not mean I am the leader of it."

She rolled her eyes at him, but since he had already disappeared inside the castle, he missed the expression.

He was wrong. He had to be. Just as surely as she knew she needed a new dress, she was certain Quintus would someday lead this new mysterious court that, apparently, had no real food.

On her initial step inside the castle, her mind spun. A musty, old smell clung to the air. Aged and faded paintings hung on the walls of the golden hallway. Rugs with spots and holes stretched across the ground. She inhaled deeper, studying the smell. One eyebrow arched upward. It appeared she'd been right to think this court might be old instead of new.

As her hand brushed against the golden castle wall, she felt it humming under her touch. It radiated an energy just under its surface, one that did not exist in the paintings or the rugs. Unlike all the items inside it, the castle itself didn't seem old or new. It seemed … different.

She stopped abruptly and ran her fingers along the wall, trying to make sense of the strange phrase that had just crossed her mind. When that produced nothing useful, she shook her head and caught up to Quintus. "There's something strange about this court. Everything inside this castle looks and smells old, but everything else about the court is…"

He turned to face her when she trailed off. Giving her a questioning look, he raised his eyebrows in anticipation.

She started again. "The court is gorgeous, obviously, but it's not…"

"Alive," he finished.

Uneasiness pooled in her gut when she tried to nod. Instead, she found herself tilting her head to the side. "It's not alive, but it's not dead either." She shrugged. "It's like the court is in hibernation."

He gave a slight nod, and his feet moved a little slower down the hallway. The confidence and surety he had when they were on the way to the castle seemed to have disappeared now that they were inside. Now he seemed unsure of what to do next.

Lifting her skirts and her chin, Chloe pushed past him and marched ahead. "The first thing we need to find is the library."

Even from behind her, she could hear Quintus scoff. "You want to read *now*?"

She glanced back at him, shaking her head. "When will you understand that books are the key to knowledge? And don't we need knowledge right now? If this court is new, then why is everything inside of the castle old?"

His face looked as rigid as stone for a moment, but then he slowly nodded. "I suppose you are right."

If their fae friend, Ludo, had been with them, he could have used his magic to find the library right away. But Chloe's love of books basically gave her the same magic anyway. She scanned the hallway, eyeing the doors throughout it. None of them looked grand enough to lead to a library.

When the hallway ended at a fork, she went to the right. Quintus stayed a step behind her. Each time she glanced back at him, he stared at the walls with wonder. Or perhaps it was confusion. In fact, a bit of fear may have danced in his eyes too.

It came time to choose right or left again, and this time, Chloe went left. The hallway opened to a grand hall with a throne made of rubies, sapphires, and emeralds. Originally, gold didn't seem like the most practical material for castle walls, considering it was a soft metal. But while every rug and painting had signs of age, the castle walls glinted as bright and shiny as if it they'd been created that very day.

"The throne room," Quintus breathed. His mouth dropped at seeing the great hall ahead of them. He stared at the glittering throne and then he glanced down at her hand, to the ring he had just recently given her. The golden and emerald piece of jewelry had apparently once belonged to his mother. He had never said much else about it though.

Grabbing him by the hand, she forced him past the throne room until they were moving down the hallway again. "That room will be no use to us. We need real information. The kind of information people try to hide. We'll never find that in the throne room where everyone could see it. The best information is only going to be in one place, the library."

As she turned down another hallway, it occurred to her that she could see clearly, even without candles lit. But when she glanced upward, the glowing green light of sprites that provided light to the rest of Faerie did not glow above them.

So how could she see?

Perhaps windows from other parts of the castle brought light into these hallways too. Or perhaps Faerie itself lit the way.

Her focus shifted away from that stream of thought when she spotted two grand doors with golden handles and an elaborate scroll design etched into the front. For someone who didn't frequent libraries, the doors might have seemed to lead to any number of different rooms, but she knew better.

With a smile on her lips, she pushed through the doors and immediately inhaled deeply. The rest of the castle had a mildewy, old smell, but not here. In libraries, the smell of books only got better with age.

Bookshelves made of gold stretched high toward the ceiling. A glass domed window with gilded windowpanes covered the room. Each bookshelf had a colored gem embedded into its side, probably denoting a category or a section of some sort. She'd have to study the gems and the books later to decode the system.

Her feet nearly bounced as she walked. Excitement tingled all through her. After spending so much time in the forests of Faerie, she had nearly forgotten just how magical a library could feel, especially a library like this.

Velvety chairs in rich jewel tones had been tucked into every available space. Large fireplaces stood near the chairs. Even though no fires burned today, she could still almost hear the crackling logs and feel the warmth of the flames. Best of all, each tall bookshelf had a rolling ladder attached, making it easy to reach even the highest shelves. The urge to pluck books off the shelves grew, sending a thrum through her fingertips.

She did her best to ignore the sensation as she headed to the back of the large room. Quintus eyed the library with some vague interest as he trailed through it, but he was still somewhere around the middle of the room. On the other hand, she had reached the very back of it. This time, she was certain Faerie itself guided her because she walked straight to an innocuous corner and lifted a very plain-looking vase from a crumbly wooden table.

The moment the vase left the surface of the table, a hidden door appeared in the wall ahead. When she walked through it, she found a small study with a dusty old desk, a bookshelf stuffed with books and scrolls, and a fireplace that still smelled of burnt wood. In only a few moments, she found another secret door. This one was painted to match the wall, but little ridges along the sides gave it away. Quintus still roamed the library, so he wouldn't notice her disappearing into a secret room. She'd return soon anyway.

Upon opening the door, a cold breeze swept over her. Stale air filled the large space. A rotting four-poster bed with a curtain of cobwebs stood at the center of the room. At one time, it probably looked as grand as the throne or the castle itself. Now, it looked ready to fall apart with a single touch.

Her lips turned upward into a smile. Whoever had a bedroom with a secret study that connected to the library had to be someone of importance. She must be getting close to some answers.

Turning on her heel, she intended to return to the secret study. But then her gaze snagged on a pile of fabric tossed over a golden chair. Unlike everything else in the room, the fabric appeared to be fresh and new.

She lifted it off the chair and found not just cloth but clothing. The pants with leather stitching down the side looked similar to the pants Quintus had always worn, except these pants were black instead of brown. There was also a jade-colored shirt as soft as cotton with long sleeves and golden buttons down the front. Maybe she just imagined it, but the size appeared perfect for Quintus too. Next, she lifted a sturdy vest of emerald green off the chair. It had a short, standing collar with a deep V opening at the front. It had two golden buckles that would rest just below the chest. Golden rivets decorated the bottom corners of the garment. A leather belt with a golden buckle sat at the very bottom of the pile.

With the items in her arms, she rushed back into the library. "Quintus, look. You have to try these on."

His eyes widened as he scanned the clothes. He tentatively touched the smooth fabric, taking extra care over the embellishments. His lips parted in awe as his gaze traveled from one item to the next, but he seemed unable to put to words what he felt.

Somehow, she managed to hold back her smirk. He couldn't very well claim he wasn't the ruler of this court anymore. Not if those clothes fit, anyway.

Pushing the outfit completely into his arms, she darted back to the study. Once inside, she carefully opened each drawer in the large desk. Not a single one produced anything of interest. She found empty bottles of ink and papers scribbled with numbers and short notes about locations she'd never heard of, but nothing that would explain what had happened to this mysterious court.

The final drawer had a few books on metalworking, but that remained the only somewhat interesting thing the desk had produced.

Scowling, she slumped onto the desk's chair. In that short moment, a new sight caught her eye. Sucking in a short gasp, she leaned forward and opened the very first drawer again.

This time, she removed the entire contents of the drawer. And then she smiled. The outside of the drawer definitely looked deeper than the inside of it, which meant this drawer had a false bottom.

After a few moments of poking and prodding, she managed to loosen the false bottom until she removed that too. In an instant, she knew she had found exactly what they needed. A worn leather journal sat inside the drawer. It had thin leather strings holding it closed.

Carefully, she unwound the leather strings and pulled the leather cover open. She read the first sentence and grinned.

I have just been crowned king of Crystalfall.

King. Her finger then drifted over the final word of that sentence. Crystalfall. That must have been the name of this mysterious court. And this journal belonged to the court's king. If anyone had answers about what happened to this court, the king had to be the first and best place to start.

2

EXCITEMENT BUBBLED INSIDE CHLOE'S CHEST at her discovery. When a shadow appeared in the doorway, and she saw Quintus standing there. The excitement only grew. "The clothes fit you perfectly, do they? It almost seems like they were made just for you."

She paused, tapping one finger against her chin. "But what magical force could have the power to create new clothes, tailored to your exact size, and in a place you just happened to stumble across? Would Faerie itself, by chance, have that sort of power?"

He pinched the bridge of his nose, letting out a long sigh. "It does not mean I am the ruler of this court." He even huffed at the end of his sentence—and probably didn't appreciate that it made her chuckle.

"What is that book you are playing with?" He said the words as icily as he could, but it didn't hide the spark of curiosity in his eyes.

"This place is old, just like I guessed. It has to be, because this journal once belonged to the king of this court. At least this journal can tell us what happened to it. No one else in Faerie seems to even be aware of this seventh court's existence."

The moment the words left her mouth, a memory ignited in her mind. In the span of one breath, her mouth unconsciously fell open and her fingers released the journal, which fell softly into her lap.

Quintus's eyebrows lowered at her.

Before he could open his mouth, she shrugged off the strap of her leather bag and dug into it. With the journal still on her lap, she placed her favorite book in the realm right on top. Her magical book from Faerie opened easily. The pages started flipping on their own, even before she could touch them. Chloe's chest filled with awe as tiny glowing sparkles rose from the flipping pages.

Nothing was better than books, and magical books were best of all.

When the pages stopped turning, the parchment in front of her had exactly the story she had been hoping to find. Faerie had shared this story with her before, but the words were slightly different now.

A mortal man once lived in Faerie. He walked its paths and made it his home.

He learned of the creation magic left behind when Nouvel, the first fae, formed Faerie. After searching long and hard, he discovered this creation magic. A single touch gave him abilities like he had never experienced before.

He immediately harnessed his new magic for evil, killing anyone who stood in his way and destroying the entire Court of Crystalfall.

The more she read, the faster her breathing became until only short and shallow breaths moved through her mouth. Her finger traced the final word, her second time seeing it now.

Crystalfall. The Court of Crystalfall.

Before she could tell Quintus to look, she glanced up and found his gaze already fixated on the page. His lips moved, forming the same word she had just traced. *Crystalfall.*

Her breathing turned steady and sure in that moment. There were still more questions they needed answered, but this already explained so much. Opening her mouth, she intended to say as much.

But Quintus spoke first. "No." He shook his head and turned away. "This court cannot be called Crystalfall. The high court is already called Crystal Thorn. Faerie itself would never allow there to be a Crystalfall and a Crystal Thorn."

Chloe raised an eyebrow, already guessing the next part of his argument.

"It is not our place to name this court. And it is certainly not our place to presume who the new leader might be. Only High King Brannick can choose the ruler for this court."

Rolling her eyes, Chloe pulled the king's journal out from under her magical book. "You have to admit the name fits though. The land is filled with gems and jewels. The fruits and berries and even the birds are made of crystals."

Quintus stared down at his clothes, examining them carefully. He probably searched for evidence that the clothes had not been magically made just for him. To her immense satisfaction, he grimaced and turned away in defeat.

"Besides," Chloe said, lifting her nose in the air. "The *fall* part is appropriate too, considering all the waterfalls filled with sparkling liquid that looks more like crystals than actual water."

Her heart skipped as a new idea occurred to her. Since the entire court had once been destroyed by a power-hungry mortal, the *fall* in Crystalfall fit even better. It indicated the court's destruction.

Huffing loudly, Quintus opened his mouth, clearly eager to keep arguing his position. But what could he say now that could possibly dispute the evidence she had already found? Letting him argue would only slow her down. She'd much rather start reading the king's journal to see what she could glean from it about the history of this mysterious court.

Lifting her head sweetly, she batted her eyes at Quintus. "Have you noticed how faded and threadbare my clothes have turned ever since I fell into those sulfur waters in Mistmount?" She bit her bottom lip and turned her gaze downward. "I wondered if maybe you could make a new dress for me. Since I did just save Faerie from iron poisoning and all."

His expression resisted her words at first, but that last part got him. He let out a long sigh and stomped toward the library exit. "Stay here. I want you safe while I go look for fabric."

"Of course, of course." She flicked her fingers toward the exit, urging him to leave. "I'll be right here reading the whole time."

The sound of his boots echoed through the library, but her focus had already turned so completely to the king's journal, she hardly noticed it at all.

First, she wanted to know what happened to the power-hungry mortal after Crystalfall got destroyed. Did the mortal get destroyed too? Back when she bonded with Quintus and they both received their moon and stars tattoos, she learned that Faerie could not take the magic away from the mortal man,

20

but Faerie did find a way to set a block inside him so he could not access his magic anymore.

She had a similar block, but her bond with Quintus allowed her access to her magic—but only when their skin touched.

For the most complete and accurate information, she should go through the king's entire journal from start to finish. She'd do that eventually, but for now, she'd skip ahead to the last entry. Then at least she'd know what was happening at the time the king stopped writing in his journal.

Just as she suspected, the journal did not fill all the pages of the book. Several pages had been left blank, proving the king had unexpectedly stopped writing. The last page gave more answers than she could have dreamed for.

They are after me. They want to kill me. I let them stay in my court, and now they want to rip away my crown. If they manage to kill me, all the power inside my crown will be given to whoever wears the crown next.

I won't let that happen.

If I hide my crown, they will certainly stop trying to kill me. No one else can become ruler without my crown. And if there is no crown to steal, then there is no reason to kill me.

It's a good thing I have studied metal-working so diligently. I have studied how the crown magic works, and I am certain that even if I break the crown apart, melt the gold, rearrange the jewels, and turn my crown into items that do not resemble a crown at all, the magic will be retained.

I will keep my power, but others will not be able to kill me and get that power for themselves unless they somehow manage to find all the pieces and put the crown back in its original form. My work begins tonight. In only a few days, I will no longer have a crown on my head, and my enemies will no longer have a way to steal my power.

If the journal had ended there, she might have assumed the king had been killed before he could do anything with his crown. But even though the journal didn't have another entry, it did have a map on the next page.

Her gaze trailed over to that detailed drawing. A castle had been drawn at the center of it. She recognized the waterfall she and Quintus had passed on their way to the castle, but she didn't recognize any of the other land features. It might take some traveling to find the different pieces of the crown, but at least she knew what the first item was.

In the top right corner, someone—presumably the king—had drawn a detailed dagger. In the other three corners, decorative question marks had been drawn. That made it clear then, the first item they had to find was a dagger. And apparently, there would be three more items to find as well.

As she studied the map further, her excitement wore off. The map had no clues or paths or anything specifying where the dagger had been hidden. It only portrayed the landscape of Crystalfall. A few areas of the map had more detail than others, but there were too many spots like that to go searching through all of them. In frustration, she huffed.

That was all it took. One huff, and everything in front of her changed when her breath reacted with the parchment. A blue faded line appeared on the map, drawing a course to a cluster of trees with tiny, winged creatures flying around them. The blue line ended in a blue X.

Anticipation rose within her as the faint blue line slowly disappeared from the page of the journal. Holding her breath, she leaned closer and exhaled with a wide, warm breath.

The line appeared again, an even clearer and darker blue than before. Even more astonishing, blue words appeared just under the X.

The dagger is hidden under a rock that is not a rock.

Nothing could stop her from grinning now. She had found her first clue to obtaining the crown of Crystalfall.

As if on signal, Quintus came trailing into the library holding a bundle of red-and-gold fabric. Even from far away, he must have seen scheming on her face. After catching sight of her, his expression hardened. "Let me guess. You just read some passage that somehow proves I am the true ruler of this court."

"No." She raised her eyebrows. "But I did find us a quest. We must find four items, including a dagger, and then put them all together to make the crown of Crystalfall. Then High King Brannick can crown someone—probably you, but maybe someone else—as leader of this court."

Quintus rolled his eyes. "A quest. Have you forgotten there are mortals who want to destroy and take over Faerie? We need to stop them before we go on some pointless quest."

The words cut at her insides. He was right. As much as she wanted to find the dagger, her first priority had to be keeping Faerie safe. And how had she forgotten about her younger sister, Grace?

Now that Faerie was healed of iron poisoning, she could return home and the scurpus that had infected her younger sister should hopefully be gone completely. But her magic had only healed six courts, since she had only known of those courts at the time. This seventh court needed to be healed too, or at least protected so the mortals couldn't destroy it with iron like they had done with the other courts.

"You're right." Her voice caught on the words. "Since I know how to heal the land now, I believe I can do it in this court too, even without the ingredients I needed before. Come on. Let's go outside. I'll heal this court so the mortals can't destroy it."

His shoulders shifted along with his eyes. He glanced down at the fabric in his hands while the smallest hint of blush reddened his cheeks. He cleared his throat. "There is something else we should do first."

3

CHLOE STARED DOWN AT HER new red-and-gold dress, unable to tear her eyes away. Quintus had gallantly stayed in the library with his back turned while she changed into the new outfit inside the dead king's study. Quintus had crafted her a dress before, but this new one had magic she could scarcely explain.

She twirled around in the stunning dress, the dark red bodice adorned with intricate golden embroidery that glinted in the light. The waistline of the dress was accented by a graceful split in the skirt, revealing a layer that draped elegantly to the ground and a cascading layer on top. Form-fitting sleeves covered her upper arms. At the elbow, the sleeves flared out dramatically, creating a split that allowed her to move her lower arms with ease.

The fabric was sturdy and thick, giving her definition in all the right places. Somehow, it also managed to be lightweight and smooth as silk.

"Chloe." Quintus stayed completely still with his body still turned away. His voice came out gravelly though. Gravelly and hungry and so deep it made her insides tingle.

Heat rushed through her veins, and she stopped herself from twirling another time. "I'm done. You can turn around."

Almost involuntarily, the twirling began again. She didn't spin in a complete circle, but she did twist back and forth a few times so that the skirt flared out.

A half smile crept onto his face, which only deepened the heat in Chloe's cheeks.

They were doing it. They were staring at each other with the same ridiculous expressions Chloe had once rolled her eyes at when it had been her parents staring at each other. And then she had seen Elora and Brannick do the ridiculous staring too.

Somewhere during her teenage years, Chloe had stopped rolling her eyes at the looks and started longing for someone who might stare at her that way instead. Back then, her chest would fill with warmth and her heart would beat, and she could almost taste how wonderful it would be to have someone look at her in that way.

Experiencing it now felt so much different than she could have imagined. So much better.

Her chest still filled with warmth, and her heart still thudded against her rib cage. But flutters filled her stomach too, and her head swam, imagining all the different ways she could kiss him.

"It's perfect. I have never seen such a magnificent dress." Darting forward, she intended to simply wrap her arms around Quintus and maybe stare into his eyes a little.

He clearly had other ideas. Taking her in a strong embrace, he held her body flush against him. All those different ways she had imagined kissing had suddenly become a reality. He pressed his lips on hers and the warmth in her chest grew tenfold. She lifted herself onto her tiptoes, but he immediately dropped his head lower, making it easier to reach him.

Kissing him didn't just feel right. It felt *needed*. As needed as air.

His hand trailed up her back and slipped into her hair. He tried to stroke through it, but the knots and tangles stopped him. After one last extra embrace and kiss, he pulled away.

"I have a brush for your hair. I intended to help you fix it before I did anything else, but…" His hand lifted to her cheek, stroking it softly. "Sometimes you are too beautiful for me to think clearly."

Her insides jumped at that statement. They spun and fluttered, making her feel like she could fly. She would have kissed him more, except he had moved a step too far away. He reached into his magical pocket and pulled out a gorgeous brush made of black crystals and green emeralds. After gently turning her around, he began brushing through her knotted hair.

The soothing rhythm of the strokes reminded her of her favorite harp song. As a professional harpist, Chloe's mother had diligently taught the harp to all of her three daughters. Chloe had always enjoyed it, unlike her older sister, Elora. Even though neither of them possessed the natural talent of their youngest sister, Grace, Chloe had still always loved the harp.

The steady gentle strokes gliding through her hair now reminded her that it had been ages since she'd brought her fingers to the strings of a harp. Without a thought, she started humming as Quintus worked.

Losing herself in the moment, the soft sound filled the space around them with a peaceful and romantic melody. The delicate touch of Quintus's hands and the soft hum of her voice seemed to intertwine, deepening the bond between them. Just then, the tattoo of stars on her face started tingling.

No longer did the deepening bond seem purely metaphorical. She could feel it truly deepening now. The magic between them grew stronger. More intimate.

As he worked, she closed her eyes. She could feel how he expertly smoothed the tangles from her hair. The weight of her hair lifted as he tended to her tresses. A sigh of contentment fell from her lips.

He must have finished then because he dropped the brush back into his pocket and, from behind, reached his arms around her stomach. He buried his face in her hair and whispered against her neck, "Now, where were we?"

Shivers ran over her skin. She leaned into him basking in the moment. But just before he could turn her around and start kissing her again, she caught sight of the king's journal, which she had left on top of her magical book from Faerie.

Reluctantly, she turned to him, her brow lightly furrowed. "We should probably get outside and heal the court of iron poisoning before the mortals get here."

She felt his nod against her hair, but he didn't stop there. Pulling her closer, he left a soft kiss right below her ear. Only then did he release her.

At least he took her hand before attempting to leave the library. If she'd had to walk on her own, she probably would have melted into a puddle. Even as it was, they kept stealing glances at each other as she gathered her magical book and the king's journal into her leather bag.

Down the castle hallways, she counted at least three times she lost her balance. It would have been believable to blame it on her wooden foot, since even without pain, it still felt much different than the real foot she'd once had. Though truthfully, she knew the stumbles happened because she kept staring at him instead of watching where she was going.

Once outside and down the steps to reach the path, even the sight of golden trees and sparkling jewels couldn't hold her attention longer than him. It was only by thinking of the threat of mortals invading and poisoning the land that she managed to drop to her knees and focus on the task at hand.

Since her magic only worked while touching Quintus, he obligingly knelt at her side and held out one hand toward her.

As she closed her eyes and placed one hand in Quintus's, her other hand reached for the strands of tiny jade gems that made up the grass beneath them. When she healed the rest of Faerie, it had been deeply infected with iron. This process might be different since no iron infected this new court, but hopefully it would work anyway.

To start, she imagined pouring the special liquids onto the jade grass and black soil of Crystalfall. Black thorns steeped in vinegar went first, then fermented wheat cider from Noble Rose, and finally the sulfur waters from Mistmount.

When she had performed this magic before, magic had tingled at her fingertips, and she could almost feel the land beneath her hands responding. Now, she felt nothing. The land didn't react. Even her fingertips felt as ordinary as usual.

That wouldn't stop her from finishing her attempt, though. She visualized sprinkling Dustdune sand and Swiftsea salt on top of the liquids. After that, she pictured tiny speckles of dark orange appearing everywhere the sand touched. Finally, she imagined the sharp tangy scent of rust that the salt should have brought.

During those final steps, her fingertips felt even more empty of magic than before. She dared to peek out of one eyelid and glanced at the ground. It appeared no different from how it looked when she started.

Stopping herself from sighing, she completed the final step. In her mind, she cut open a Fairfrost acid fruit and then squeezed the liquid onto the salt and sand. She pictured the mixture fizzling and popping, creating white bubbles that turned into foamy mounds. Orange threads of rust stretched over the ground afterward.

But as soon as she opened her eyes, she was met with the same black soil and tiny jade gems as before. Just as she feared, the process hadn't worked.

Quintus frowned, knowing the truth even without her saying it.

"Don't worry," she said with fake confidence. "I have one other idea."

She dug into her bag and found a small item at the very bottom of it that she had been avoiding since she arrived in Faerie. Her finger and thumb clasped an iron needle that had accidentally been swept up with the ingredients she used to make poultices.

At the very bottom of her bag, the tiny iron needle had done no harm to Faerie, so she hadn't thought much about it. But it could be useful to her now.

Slipping the little needle into her fist, she then brought it close to the ground.

Quintus leaned forward, his head cocking to the side. "What is that you have in your hand?"

"Oh, it's nothing. Don't worry about it." She opened her fist the smallest amount, just enough to point the needle toward the soil.

Unfortunately, that was all Quintus's keen eye needed. "Is that iron? Are you trying to stick iron into the ground?" His voice rose in volume with each word.

She let out a long sigh. "That's just the way infections work. I can't heal an infection if there is no infection."

"So, you somehow believe the best option is to infect this untainted court with iron?"

She had to purse her lips together to keep from rolling her eyes. "Would you rather have the mortals infect the land with cauldrons full of molten iron? That didn't turn out very well last time they did it."

He grimaced, but he didn't answer.

Her hand lifted to show off the tiny needle in between her fingers. "Yes, I'm hoping that this amount of iron will be enough to infect the land in this court. But it's obviously only going to infect it a tiny bit. Look how small it is. Then I can heal the infection, and the land in this court will know how to heal itself of iron poisoning in case it ever gets infected again."

The snarl on his face did not look promising.

"Do you need me to explain it again?"

Her patronizing tone did the trick. He waved his hand through the air. "No, I understand. I just…"

"I know. You don't want to hurt the land after seeing all the destruction the other iron poisoning caused. I understand that. But this is just a teeny tiny bit of iron. It will infect the land just enough to create an actual infection for me to heal. Then the magic should work, and the land should be able to heal itself after that."

His face remained stoic as he said nothing.

"Don't you want this court to be safe from the mortals?" She opened her eyes wide and tried to make them as sweet as possible.

He had to look away before he could answer. "Fine. Just do it quickly. I want the infection healed as fast as possible."

"No problem." With the needle between her fingers, she went to stab it into the black soil between two blades of jade grass.

But just before the needle could reach the soil, her hand bounced backward, as if she had hit an invisible shield. Narrowing her eyes, she attempted to stick the needle into the soil again. Just as before, her hand bounced backward just before the needle could touch the soil.

"Interesting," she said, but she meant *frustrating*. How was she supposed to infect the land now?

Quintus's own eyes narrowed at the jade grass strands. His gaze jumped from the needle to the ground where she had tried to stick it. Still staring, he spoke in a hushed voice. "What was that word you used before? Hibernation?"

Her eyebrows jumped upward as she nodded. "Yes, hibernation. It seems like this court is asleep. Waiting. Like it's not really alive yet."

His eyes went alight at that explanation. "This court is still sleeping, yes. It cannot be infected with iron while it is in this state."

She wanted to sarcastically thank him for choosing to share that information *after* she attempted to stick iron in the ground instead of *before*. Instead, she just asked, "How do you know that?"

Pulling his gaze away from the ground, he stared directly into her eyes. Even with the direct look, he stared blankly. He said nothing. After several breaths, he finally shrugged. "I did not know. But when you tried to stick iron in the ground…"

He held one hand out like he was trying to grasp the right words with his fingers. Even that didn't seem to produce the result he wanted. At last, he sighed. "I just know. I cannot explain it beyond that."

Instead of being discouraged, Chloe tucked the iron needle back to its spot at the very bottom of her leather bag. "That's great. That means the mortals can't infect the land either."

"For now." He must have seen the scheming in her eyes because he lowered his eyebrows and pinched his mouth into a knot. "The court will be in danger again once it comes out of hibernation."

Donning an innocent smile, she raised her eyebrow. "But since the court is safe for now, can we go looking for that dagger? The one that used to be the Crystalfall crown?"

His expression soured as he got to his feet. He tugged his hand out of her grasp without ceremony and waved it in a circle. A swirling Faerie door opened before them. "We should return to Crystal Thorn Castle. Your sister will be wondering where you are."

He was right. She and Quintus had disappeared after the battle with the mortals, not bothering to explain to anyone where they were going. But now that they had explored some of the new and mysterious court of Crystalfall, it was probably a good time to return to the high court.

"Fine." Chloe got to her feet and stepped forward. Maybe she'd go with Quintus now, but that wouldn't stop her from trying to get him to search for the lost dagger. Deep down in her bones, she knew that's what they needed to do next.

4

BLACK SPIRES STRETCHED INTO THE air, high above Chloe's head. The castle's crystalline surface glinted in the darkening light. Night was starting to fall.

This same castle had lay in ruins day after day while the iron poisoning plagued Faerie. Elora and Brannick had done their very best to rebuild it, but their efforts seemed to get worse with each attempt.

But now that Faerie had been healed, they had clearly rebuilt the entire castle with ease. No one stood outside it now.

Quintus tilted his head toward the front doors. "They must be inside."

Chloe nodded and followed him into a hallway filled with lush vines and a gentle breeze. The air smelled like crisp rain and wet moss. After a few turns, they entered a large room with twelve trees growing straight out of the stone castle floor. A long table stood in front of the trees. Elora and her beloved, Brannick, stood near the trees with their backs turned away.

They might have been whispering, but they probably used their nearly-silent fae whispers, which were far too soft for Chloe to hear.

Mishti, the mortal young woman who had helped them fight against the other mortals, sat at the long wooden table. She stared at a dagger in her hands like she didn't know what to do with it. Ludo, the Fairfrost fae who had helped them find different items throughout Faerie, also sat at the table. His eyes were closed as he conjured plates of food.

Each plate held a slab of seasoned pork, a chunk of crusty bread that had a nutty scent, and a juicy ripe plum.

Mishti noticed Chloe and Quintus first. She started to smile and stand, but then didn't seem to know what to do with herself. A frown overtook her face as she sat back down.

The movement caught Ludo's eye, which then led his gaze to Chloe and Quintus. He immediately grumbled and looked down at the food he had just finished conjuring. Four plates, just enough for the four people in the room.

Rolling his eyes, he let out a huff. "I suppose you want me to conjure more food now that I have just finished and gotten comfortable?" He huffed again. "You will have to allow me to at least get a drink first."

With a wave of his hand, he conjured a wooden goblet filled with a dark purple liquid that looked delicious.

At the sound of his voice, Elora and Brannick turned and moved toward the table. Elora's eyes lit up after noticing her younger sister, but of course, her older sister instincts took over and worry etched across her face. She glanced between Chloe and Quintus as she sat down at the table. "Where have you been?"

Chloe took her own seat right across from Mishti. "Oh, just discovering a new court."

Dark purple liquid spewed from Ludo's mouth as he involuntarily spat what he had tried to swallow. He used his hand to mop off his dripping chin. "Discovering *what?*"

Everyone had food now, except for Chloe and Quintus, yet none of them ate. All of them just stared at Chloe with eyes open wide.

She had to hold back her grin as she shrugged. "Actually, it's not new. It's old, but it got destroyed by a mortal who touched the creation magic and then immediately used his powers for evil."

All trace of his earlier grumbling left Ludo's face entirely. His blue-and-red eyes glowed as bright as the expression of awe now filling his face. "I forgot an entire court. This…this explains everything. Once I see it, once I start gathering things…" He shook his head. "I can only imagine the memories that court holds."

He let out a chuckle of pure glee and started conjuring two more plates of food. Not a single complaint left his lips this time.

Chloe sat a little higher in her chair. "The new court is more beautiful than you can imagine. The trees are made of gold and the leaves are made of emeralds. It smells like vanilla and lilacs. Even the birds are made of gems. It's called Crystalfall, by the way."

Ludo passed the newly-conjured plates across the table to Chloe and Quintus. Quintus had the same food as the others. Chloe's plate was mostly the same. It still had seasoned pork, crusty bread with a nutty scent, and even a plum. But her plum had been cooked. Ludo must have been in a giddy mood if he remembered that her fruits and vegetables had to be cooked first before she could eat them.

At the head of the table, Brannick sat on a throne made of trees. His long black hair shifted across his shoulders as he leaned forward and repeated the name Chloe had just said. "Crystalfall?"

Quintus scoffed and turned toward the high king. "Tell her how ridiculous that name is. The new court cannot be named Crystalfall when this court we currently sit in is already named Crystal Thorn."

Elora swept a portion of her brown hair over one shoulder as she turned to her beloved. She raised one eyebrow and showed off a half smile. "We were just saying how we miss the name of Bitter Thorn and felt it fit this court better."

"Bitter…" Quintus shook his head faster only stopping when he slapped himself on the forehead. "Are you serious? This court was named Bitter Thorn as an insult. It was a curse to High King Brannick after his mother brought mortals and their emotions into Faerie."

That seemed like the perfect moment to start eating. Chloe decided to try the cooked plum first. The juices filled her mouth, delighting every tastebud. She had expected a cooked plum, but she hadn't expected the extra flavoring of balsamic vinegar. The acidity of it perfectly balanced the sweetness of the plum. It brought out the sweet flavor even more and made it just savory enough for an evening meal. She devoured another bite without even thinking. Somehow, the second bite tasted even more delicious than the first.

Brannick sat taller in his throne. He took on that high king look that he only used when he intended to say something grand and important. She had to think for a moment to remember who he was responding to.

Once he sat tall and heroic looking, Brannick finally spoke. "A curse is only a curse if you let it be. And sweet is not sweet without bitter. Perhaps we need to embrace our crystalline bitter thorns even more. We should not run from the word *bitter*. This court should be named Bitter Thorn once again."

Since Chloe was currently biting into a magnificently delicious plum flavored with tart balsamic vinegar, she had to agree with him. Bitterness did an excellent job of complementing sweetness. She had never gotten used to calling this court *Crystal Thorn* anyway. Bitter Thorn had always seemed more natural.

Quintus shook his head. "You would truly change the name of your court? Again? Just because a different court *once* had the name of Crystalfall? Why not give the new court a new name?"

Brannick stared at Quintus, but the high king didn't answer right away. His eyes narrowed as he leaned forward. After an extra-long beat, he finally spoke. "Why did you call it *my* court? Why did you not call it *our* court?"

Quintus blinked in response. He opened his mouth but said nothing. After staring a little too long, he finally sat back in his chair. Clearly, he had no idea how to answer. Instead, he stared down at his food, which he still hadn't touched.

Well, if he wouldn't answer, Chloe was happy to do it for him. She donned a smirk. "After I healed Faerie, Quintus was drawn to the new court just like you and Elora were drawn to this castle while it was broken and ruined. He was *drawn* to it."

On the tip of her tongue sat the explanation that Quintus must be the leader of the new court. In the end, she chose not to say those words out loud. The others would probably be more convinced if they came to that particular conclusion on their own.

Instead, she gestured toward Quintus's outfit. "Inside the castle, we even found those clothes all fresh and new just sitting around for him. It can't be a coincidence the clothes fit him perfectly, right?"

Mishti raised a single eyebrow, her expression stony. "What about your clothes? Did you find those in the castle too?"

"No." Chloe shook her head hard to make the point. "Quintus made this dress for me, but *his* clothes were just sitting in the castle, as if they were waiting for him."

Ludo waved a flippant hand. "Quintus's greatest magic is in crafting. He could take any clothes from anywhere and make them fit perfectly."

Those words perked up Quintus's features. He sat forward and gestured toward Ludo. "Yes, he is right. You see, the clothes mean nothing."

He ended the point by taking a huge bite from his chunk of crusty bread.

"*Mmhmm.*" Chloe folded her arms over her chest. "So, *did* you use magic to make the clothes fit perfectly?"

Instead of answering, he just chewed his bread and stared at his plate. The expectant eyes of the others did nothing to convince him to answer.

She asked again, a little more forcefully this time. "Did you?"

He glanced across the table, probably realizing he wouldn't be able to ignore the question. His gaze turned back toward his plate. When he finally answered, the word came out quiet. "No."

With a satisfied nod, Chloe sat back in her chair. It was hard to decipher how the others took this exchange, but all of them wore curiosity at the very least. Maybe they just needed a little *more* to be curious about.

After taking a bite from her own bread, she pulled the king's journal from her leather bag and held it high for all to see. "I also found this journal inside the castle. It belonged to the previous king of Crystalfall. He was worried people were trying to usurp him, so he broke his crown apart and turned it into a dagger and a few other items. If we find all the pieces, Quintus can craft them back together, and Crystalfall will have a crown once again."

At that, Quintus scoffed. "More ridiculous notions. The crown probably got destroyed when the court got destroyed. And we have to focus on the mortals while—"

"You must find this crown." High King Brannick sat forward on his tree throne, his voice as regal as his title. He stared down at Quintus, reaffirming the words with his expression.

Quintus swallowed, cowering ever so slightly. "What?"

Sitting even taller, Brannick gave a slight nod. "You must find the pieces and make the crown again." He placed a hand over his heart and squeezed it into a fist. The magic in the high king's eyes swirled and pulsed. Energy filled the room around them, making the little hairs on Chloe's arms stand on end. Brannick stared even harder at Quintus. "You must."

Quintus scowled, but he couldn't do much else. For all their faults, fae did follow rigid guidelines. And Quintus had always been especially loyal. If the High King of Faerie gave a direct command like that, only a fae wishing for death would defy it.

It only took a moment and then Quintus nodded. "Yes, my king."

Chloe clapped her hands and rubbed them together. "Excellent. We can leave for our quest in the morning. Ludo, we'll need your magic in finding things. We have a map, but I'm sure your magic will work faster. And Mishti." Chloe's voice faltered as she turned to look at the young woman across from her. "I suppose you don't have to come with us, but I'd rather not be the only girl. And I'm sure Elora and Brannick have a duty to stay here in their own court that, apparently, we're calling Bitter Thorn again."

Using the dagger to stab the morsel of pork on her plate, Mishti grinned. "I'll come with you. A quest sounds a lot more fun than a battle. At least this way, I shouldn't have to kill anyone."

Ironic that the one who had the least desire to kill was also the person who chose to use a dagger to eat her food.

Sitting back in her chair, Chloe nodded. "It's settled then."

Elora lifted her eyebrows high on her forehead. "You are forgetting one thing."

"What?" Chloe asked.

Now Elora donned a very big-sisterly expression. "Grace. You said she had scurpus when you left the mortal realm. But now that Faerie is healed, Grace's illness should be healed too."

"It is," Chloe responded, but her tone came out as non-committal as possible.

Ignoring the indecision, Elora took one last bite of food from her plate and stood. "We can go back to the mortal realm now, then."

Before her sister could do something drastic like open a door to the mortal realm, Chloe stood up too. "Wait." She rubbed a hand across her forehead, trying to remember all the recent events she had just experienced.

"I just healed Faerie today." Chloe's head cocked to the side. "Was it today? Or was it yesterday?"

Time didn't exist in Faerie, which made it very difficult to answer questions like this. She glanced at every person in the room, yet none of them had an answer for her. Not even

Mishti, the only other mortal, could say when exactly Faerie had been healed.

No matter. The healing of Faerie had happened recently, and that's all that really mattered. Chloe spoke more decisively this time. "We can go back to the mortal realm soon, but I think we need to wait at least another day or two. I want to make sure Faerie is fully healed before we return, otherwise Grace might still have scurpus when we get there."

Elora pouted, but she conceded too. "Fine. We will visit her once you find the dagger."

Chloe nodded, reality starting to set in. The new court of Crystalfall was safe from the mortals, for now. But she and Quintus and the others still had to find the pieces of the crown and put them together before the court came out of hibernation.

And if the mortals somehow found out about the dagger or the crown, the results could be disastrous.

5

THE KING'S JOURNAL LAY OPEN on Chloe's lap, its edges worn and frayed from use. Just as she did in the Crystalfall Castle library, she breathed long and deep onto the map she had discovered. A blue line appeared. The line started at the castle and ended with an X right on top of a cluster of trees.

"That's it." Chloe traced the line with one finger as she turned to look at the others. Quintus, Mishti, and Ludo all huddled around her. Mishti glared at the journal like it might try to stab her if she didn't keep it in its place. Ludo stared at it like it had already ruined his day, even though day had only just dawned.

Quintus looked mystified. He usually met every obstacle with confident heroics. But now that he had realized he might be the rightful leader of Crystalfall, he had suddenly withdrawn into himself. He looked to others to make decisions. He looked to Chloe to explain.

She didn't mind. He just had to find his confidence again. He just had to accept that the seventh court of Faerie was his to rule. If she had to help him do that, then so be it. Turning to him expectantly, she asked, "Can you open a door to that cluster of trees?"

His gaze turned to the journal, but then he took a step back. "I am not sure. It is possible to open a door to a place you have never been before, but you still must have a way to describe it in your mind. I fear if I open a door to *the cluster of trees in Crystalfall*, it will be too vague an instruction. There are probably dozens, maybe hundreds of other clusters of trees in Crystalfall."

It took her a moment to calm herself before she could respond. That was not at all the answer she wanted. This constant second guessing would make their quest a lot longer than it needed to be.

But he had been there for her through plenty of insecurities. She could be here for him through his if that's what he needed. Leaning closer to the map, she carefully examined it. There had to be a land feature of some sort near the cluster of trees that would make it easier to identify. After a moment, she found the perfect one.

"Look at this." She pointed to the map. "You see this small valley with that large tree growing in the very middle of it? What if you open your door to *the cluster of trees that is near the small valley with a large tree at the center?*"

Quintus winced. "I do not know if that will work either. I have never seen the valley. It may be very different from how it looks on the map. It is much easier to open doors to places I have been before. And even new places are easy, but only if it's a specific location. Nothing here is named."

"Will you just try it?" Her patience had worn thin. She snapped the journal shut, dropped it into her leather bag, and then motioned at the air ahead of them where she wanted a Faerie door to appear.

Begrudgingly, he waved his hand and a swirling door opened ahead of them. The black tunnel had golden sparkles inside it that twinkled alongside emerald sparkles. The emerald sparkles were new, though now was probably not the best time to mention it.

All four of them stepped through the door. When they got to the other side, they did walk straight into a cluster of trees in Crystalfall. But these trees were clearly not the trees from the map. Rather, they stood just past the black caves that separated Crystalfall from Bitter Thorn. They had landed only barely inside new the court of Crystalfall.

Chloe started to sigh, but Mishti's complete look of awe stopped her. The young woman's long black braid swung as she darted forward. "The trees really are made of gold. I thought you meant that metaphorically. Or maybe that you meant they were golden in color, but these are..."

She trailed off as she placed her palm against the nearest tree trunk. "It's even warm from the sunlight. And the leaves really are made of actual emeralds."

To see someone who usually glared at everything so in awe was truly inspiring. Still, it was nothing to how Ludo's face lit up.

His mouth had dropped open completely. Glowing filled his blue-and-red eyes as he stepped deeper into the court. He drew in a long inhale. "Vanilla, lilacs, parchment." After another deep inhale he spoke again. "An underlying metallic scent and some jasmine and gardenia too."

Even before he finished speaking, he drew a vial from his pocket and started collecting samples from the area around them. He first preserved an emerald leaf. Then he broke off a small piece of a golden branch. A strand of jade grass went into a vial next.

Their reactions brought a smile to Chloe's lips. She did want to find that dagger as soon as possible, but she couldn't fault Mishti and Ludo for needing a moment to take in the beauty of the court.

Turning to Quintus, Chloe found him on the verge of a chuckle. She nudged him with her elbow. "Do you think we were just as wide-eyed the first time we saw this court?"

"Yes." Now he *did* chuckle. "But it seems even more enchanting watching others discover it."

Before she could agree, Ludo bounded forward and took Quintus by the shoulders. "I have been here before."

Ludo immediately let go and danced around in a circle. "I have been here! I do not have any memories of it yet, but I am gaining vague recollections. I knew how that waterfall would look before I even saw it. My lost memories will assuredly return soon."

Mishti threw a sidelong glance toward him. "What are you talking about? What memories have you lost?"

Ludo swirled around to cast a dumbfounded expression at her. "If I knew, I would not be looking for the memories, would I?"

He rolled his eyes, but then he started down the nearest path. "Forget the door. We can walk to that cluster of trees. It may take longer, but I want to savor every single part of this landscape. There is no telling what could jog my memory."

Her eyebrows drew together, and her lips turned down to their usual glare, but Mishti followed without complaint.

Despite her expression, Chloe guessed the young woman probably wouldn't mind walking through the court either.

With the two of them leading the way, Chloe started after them. She had only gone a few steps before Quintus came to her side. His gaze flicked toward her for a brief moment, but it immediately flicked away again. He opened his mouth, as if to speak, though he closed it a moment later. Then he took her hand.

After their fingers interlocked, she squeezed gently to put him at ease. That did the trick.

When he opened his mouth again, he spoke in a low whisper. "Tell me you are going to come back to Faerie."

She turned toward him, pinching her eyebrows together in confusion.

He cleared his throat, which only served to make him appear even more nervous. "You and Queen Elora want to see Grace in the mortal realm. I understand that. I would never try to keep you from her. But…"

His voice broke over the final word. It squeezed at Chloe's heart, but it wasn't like she could set all his fears at ease. This problem between them had not been resolved. In fact, the more time they spent together, the worse the problem became.

She might as well tell him the truth. "I'm afraid to go back to the mortal realm for good. No one there would want me anymore."

His frown pulled downward as he glanced at her. "Anymore? What does that mean?"

Lifting her skirt, she kicked out her boot-covered wooden foot Quintus had made for her. She could almost walk without a limp now, but she still had limitations most mortal young women didn't have to worry about. She doubted any mortal young man would care to share a bed with a young woman who had to remove one foot before climbing into it.

Quintus stopped walking, pulling her to a stop too. His one hand firmly held hers, but with his other hand, he touched her cheek. "Of course other people would want you, but none of them matter. *I* want you. I want you to live here and only go to the mortal realm when you are visiting family. I want you to be with me."

His lips looked so tantalizingly soft, she had to rip her gaze away just to think. "That's what I want too, but you know it's not that simple."

Maybe she shouldn't have been so candid in expressing her love to him, but she couldn't very well deny it now. Not after everything they'd been through. "I know we can't change how we feel. I know it's too late to…"

He squeezed her hand reassuringly, just like she had done for him earlier.

She sniffed, desperate to keep back the sudden tears that pricked at her eyes. "It's still going to hurt you when I die someday. I still can't bear the thought of inflicting that kind of pain on you."

He shook his head. "Why worry about the future when life is happening right now? Just be with me now. Just promise you will come back to Faerie after you visit your sister. We can deal with the future when the future is here."

It sounded so nice when he said it like that, but she knew it wouldn't be that easy. It would never be that easy. She couldn't deny him either though. Not when he looked at her with those big brown eyes filled with glints of gold.

Her heart twisted in a tangle of nerves and fear and heartache just thinking about how their love would surely destroy at least one of them someday. But when he looked at her like that, the future wisped away. Her mind and body filled with the present moment. Maybe he was right. Maybe their problem would have a solution. Someday. Maybe she could enjoy their love without choking it with so much fear.

Her chest expanded as she took a long, deep breath. Even then, it took effort to speak. "I will come back."

He looked at her carefully. Waiting. Probably afraid of what she might say next. She could feel his gaze on her, heating her skin. Once a tingle spread through her, she knew she couldn't stand there any longer.

Jerking her body forward, she continued walking, trying to focus on the path. "I will come back to Faerie after I visit Grace. I will stay *here*. Live here. For now."

He probably would have pulled her in for a kiss that she'd be embarrassed for the others to see, but she tugged her hand out of his before he could. "I better catch up to the others." Mishti and Ludo had gotten far ahead now. Chloe hadn't realized how long she and Quintus had been stopped.

Reaching into her bag, she retrieved the king's journal. "Since I'm the one with the map, I should probably be at the front of the group."

Quintus let her go without a word, but he also donned a broad smile when she glanced back at him. It was the sort of expression she'd never forget. One that would warm her if she ever felt lonely. It was a smile that made her want to leap into his arms and do anything he asked.

This problem of theirs had just grown a lot bigger with her commitment, but for once, she didn't care in the slightest.

By the time night fell, they still hadn't reached the group of trees marked on the map. They were getting closer though. Much closer.

They made camp and settled in and slept for the night.

After a surprisingly restful sleep, the soft rays of dawn hit their sleeping mats. A bright light beckoned Chloe to open her eyes.

Dusky darkness still filled the air, though dawn ate away at it. Even more remarkable, two other lights hung in the air above Chloe. These glowing lights were not green like the light of sprites. These were bright white orbs that hovered in the air, almost like hummingbirds.

She climbed off her sleeping mat and took a step toward the lights. Both of them moved away slightly, as if leading her forward. When they moved, they gave off a sound like jingling bells.

She grinned. Perhaps today's travels would go faster than the day before. It seemed Faerie itself had sent some help to lead them on their way.

6

HARSH WHITE LUMINESCENCE FILLED THE space around Chloe and the others. Everyone had finally put away their sleeping things, but no one stepped up to the lights as eagerly as she did. When she beckoned the others forward, not one of them moved.

Ludo eyed the orbs with a twitching nose. "I do not trust anything that makes noises as pleasant as jingling bells."

Chloe rolled her eyes at him.

But Quintus merely nodded in agreement. "If something in Faerie seems nice, it probably is not. Why would these lights lead us anywhere? How would it benefit them?"

Mishti said nothing, but she did glare at the lights ominously. Then again, she glared at everything, so that didn't mean much.

Just then, the glowing orbs jingled and moved forward a little more. To Chloe's delight, they moved toward the same path she and the others needed to take anyway. She took that as a sign. "What if these lights were sent by Faerie itself? We already know Faerie itself wants us to find the crown. Doesn't it make sense that Faerie would send help if it knows we'll need it?"

That argument got the others moving. Finally. They still eyed the orbs warily, but since the lights kept flying in the same direction the map led anyway, the others continued to follow.

By midday, everyone had stopped complaining. Ludo even forgot to check the map every few steps, just to make sure the lights were still going in the right direction. Now, he only checked whenever the path changed.

As they reached the top of a hill, a group of trees at the bottom of the hill came into view. Chloe jumped a little at the sight of it. "There it is."

On the way there, part of the path ahead was obscured by a golden and emerald thicket, but she was certain that just a little farther past that, they had found the cluster of trees where the dagger would be hidden.

At the top of the hill, optimism warmed her chest, but that changed the moment they began their descent. All at once, a dark mist surrounded them. The strange mist stuck to their skin like honey, but even worse, it made it nearly impossible to see.

Without any words between them, Chloe and the others huddled close together. They stood shoulder to shoulder: Mishti, Chloe, Quintus, and then Ludo. As they pushed through the thick, sticky mist, unease wriggled in Chloe's gut. The mist seemed to cling to her skin, almost like a net, making it difficult to move forward.

Through it all, the white orbs acted like a beacon of hope, lighting the path just ahead so they could see where to walk. She chose not to mention it, but it seemed more certain than ever that she'd been right to insist on following the lights.

Despite the mist's thickness and darkness, the group moved forward with relative ease. Suspended in air, the orbs cast just enough light to shine on the path ahead. Maybe their jingling bell sound seemed more jangling and off-key inside the mist, but at least the lights never disappeared.

When the jangling noise grew louder and more stilted, the others faltered in their steps. Chloe hoped her confidence would convince them to keep moving. She stepped forward, ahead of the others.

"Come on, we can't stop now. The lights will show us where to—"

Her voice cut off sharply when one of her feet suddenly, frighteningly, no longer had ground beneath it. And then she was falling. She must have started falling instantaneously, but for one terrifying moment, she seemed frozen in the air as she realized she no longer stood on solid ground.

Now she could only wonder. Just how far would she fall?

Her screams echoed through the darkness. She reached out, desperately searching for something to grab onto. With the thick and dark mist hanging in the air, she couldn't see anything. Not even what she was falling into. She could only hope it was a small hole and not a giant chasm.

While her arms flailed, searching for a handhold, she heard Quintus yell out her name. His footsteps ran closer, but the mist must have obscured his vision, since he hadn't gotten to her yet. He had to rely solely on her voice to guide his movements.

She screamed again. Maybe it would help him find her. And maybe she just needed to scream. Her heart raced as she threw her arms out in front of herself. Finally, her hand connected with something solid. Latching onto it with all her strength, she managed to let out a little whimper. Maybe that sound would help Quintus find her among the mist.

Whatever she held onto was sticky and wet, but at least she had stopped falling. Her relief was short lived. Her belly churned as she realized the stickiness and wetness had nothing to do with the item she had grabbed and everything to do with her own hands. They were covered in blood.

Panic had coursed through her too deeply to notice earlier that the item she had grabbed onto was sharp as glass. She could feel it now, though, as she held on tighter. Would the sharp object cut through her bone if she kept holding it? She didn't have much of a choice.

Wincing in pain, she tried to find a ledge or something for her feet to stand on. Her good foot touched a crumbling, dirt wall. It found a few rocks jutting out but none big enough to hold her foot. When she did find one just big enough to fit her toes and the ball of her foot, it jutted out far enough away that she couldn't reach it with her good foot.

Tentatively reaching out with her wooden foot, she attempted to rest her weight on the rock. But of course, her wooden foot couldn't do what her real foot could. She couldn't curl in her toes and angle the wooden foot right. It wouldn't fit, so she couldn't use it to support her weight.

Quintus had gotten closer but not close enough to see. He called her name twice more. She tried to answer. Her mouth opened. And closed. Pain and fear tightened her throat, making it sore and rough. When her handhold sliced even deeper into her palm, she let out a whimper.

"Chloe!"

Finally, she mustered up enough energy to call out. "I'm here."

She heard slapping noises above her but couldn't feel anything except loose dirt falling onto her face. After spitting some of the dirt out of her mouth, she managed to speak again. "I think I fell too far for you to reach me with your arms."

For a moment, she heard nothing, and then she heard shifting and rustling fabric. The next thing she knew, a thick piece of fabric dangled across her face, dropping lower with each breath.

She let out a heavy exhale and immediately grabbed the fabric with both hands. The slices in her palms ached and stung, almost worse than when she'd been holding the sharp object. "I've got it."

Her voice came out as little more than a whisper, but for Quintus's fae hearing, that was enough. He immediately started pulling her up.

But just when an inkling of hope started swelling in her chest, her wooden foot hit hard against the sharp object her hands had been holding onto. She tried to rip her foot away from it, but somehow, that only got her foot even more caught than before.

Mishti and Ludo had caught up to them then. She couldn't see them—she couldn't even see Quintus—but she could hear their whispers and breaths.

"What are you holding onto?" Quintus asked. "You need to let go, or I cannot pull you up."

An unconscious grunt escaped her lips. "I'm not holding onto anything. My foot is caught."

In response, Quintus just pulled harder on the fabric carrying her. The action caused the fasten holding her foot to her leg to loosen.

"Stop!" Chloe shouted, barely able to catch her breath enough to inhale. "If you do that again, my foot will fall off."

Quintus immediately stopped.

"Your foot?" Mishti asked. "You mean your wooden foot? Just let it fall."

Quintus sucked in a sharp breath.

Chloe gasped. "I can't. The wood it's made from is special."

Mishti scoffed. "More special than your life?"

Luckily, Chloe didn't have to make that determination. She wriggled her leg and pushed her foot against the dirt wall. In doing so, she managed to get her leg snug inside the fastening once again. It also managed to free her foot from whatever had caught it.

"I got it free. You can pull me up again."

The fabric began moving tentatively, slowly pulling her up. "Any problems?" Quintus asked.

In relief, Chloe answered that everything was fine.

Right then, the pulling went from tentative to determined. In only another breath, Quintus had pulled her onto solid ground and held her tight in his arms. She leaned against him, scarcely able to catch her breath. Her heart felt like it would pound right out of her chest if she didn't calm it soon.

After another moment, the cut in her palms bit with pain. She pulled herself out of his arms just enough to bring her hands out in front of herself. The glowing white lights had vanished completely. Even with her hands directly in front of her face, she could only make out the basic outline of them.

She leaned into Quintus and pressed her back against his chest. "I don't suppose you have a lantern or a torch inside your magical pocket, do you?"

He squeezed her shoulders and then pulled away from her. "I can craft a lantern. I have just enough metal left over from…"

His voice trailed off, but she could hear him working behind her. Blood slid down her palms onto her forearms. It helped to keep her hands held above her heart, but blood still dripped from her wounds.

Suddenly, a small magical fire lit inside of a lantern. Quintus hoisted the lantern, holding it toward Chloe. He gasped when he caught sight of her bloody hands.

"It's fine," she said, not quite masking the strain in her voice. Just wrap your hand around my elbow. Once we're touching, I'll be able to heal the wounds with my magic."

She failed to tell him that the healing would be more difficult now that her breaths had gotten so short. But right after she healed Faerie, she had healed an arrow wound in her own throat. So certainly, she could heal this.

Closing her eyes, she immediately felt magic rise to her fingertips. She imagined the healing process for her wounds, from cleaning and dressing them to the wounds scabbing and scarring, and then eventually to the scars fading away completely. By the time she opened her eyes, only the blood remained from the injury.

Quintus handed the lantern to Ludo, then carefully wiped her blood away using the fabric in his hands.

Mishti stared ahead, examining something on the path, but Quintus blocked Chloe's sight of it.

Ludo, on the other hand, stepped right in front of Chloe with his hands on his hips and his eyebrows knotted together. "Do you have anything to say for yourself?"

"Do I…" Chloe shook her head. "What?"

Ludo huffed and gestured at the empty air. "The glowing lights. We told you things in Faerie that seem nice are usually not nice at all."

"Oh." She let out a sigh. "Yes, you were right. I was wrong after all. The glowing lights obviously intentionally led us to danger. I'm lucky I was the only one who followed them on those last few steps." Her voice lowered. "I'm lucky the rest of you were here to save me."

"Yes, you are." Ludo gave an exaggerated nod with his head. "You should have trusted us."

Chloe lowered her head, which apparently, Ludo accepted as a good enough apology.

"Look." Mishti pointed ahead now that the rest of them had finished talking. With the light from Quintus's lantern, they could finally see what Chloe had fallen into.

A deep ravine lay before them, one with no bridge anywhere in sight. She was lucky she had managed to grab onto something with her hands. The ravine walls looked mostly made of dirt and didn't have many handholds at all.

Ludo scoffed in disgust at the ravine. "Blasted pixies. They think it's so fun to disguise themselves as friendly balls of light and then to promptly lead people to their deaths."

"Pixies?" Quintus asked.

Now Chloe folded her arms over her chest. "You knew those were pixies? You knew those creatures intentionally lead people to their deaths, but you never explicitly said it? Maybe you're the fae creature who isn't as nice as he seems."

Such an accusation usually would have sent Ludo into a long-winded rant. He even said the first word in a shout. "I…" But once that first word left his lips, he immediately trailed off. He tapped his chin with one finger. "How *did* I know that? I did not know that when we first saw them. And why did I say *blasted*? Is that a thing I say?"

He glanced at the rest of them, genuinely anxious for an answer. *Did* he say *blasted*? She couldn't remember ever hearing it from him, but maybe she just hadn't paid close enough attention.

"I've never heard you say that." Mishti's calm voice cleared any remaining tension from the air.

Ludo's face relaxed more. "Those glowing lights *were* pixies. I am certain of it now, even though I did not know before. I cannot recall any memories with them. I just … I just know it somehow."

Chloe only partially listened to the conversation. She dug into her bag for the king's journal and opened it to the map. Quintus glanced at her questioningly.

"We'll have to worry about your memories later, Ludo, because I just found the cluster of trees from our map. It's right there." She gestured ahead with a scowl. "Across that ravine."

7

AT THE EDGE OF THE deep ravine, Chloe's veins thrummed as she surveyed the wide expanse before her. A thick mist obscured the bottom of it, making it impossible to tell how deep it went. At least the sticky mist that had darkened the air around them had finally started clearing out. Soon, they wouldn't even need the lantern Quintus had crafted. Even so, she couldn't shake a feeling of dread. They had to cross that ravine.

Luckily, she had an idea.

Turning to Quintus, she quirked up an eyebrow. "You can open a door there, right? It's a specific place. You can see it. You can do it this time, can't you?"

He stared thoughtfully at the trees just across the ravine. He didn't nod or give any acknowledgement that a door would work, but he did lift his hand. After waving it in a circle, nothing happened. No swirling tunnel appeared.

Ludo gulped loud enough for everyone to hear. "Is it iron poisoning again?" Their recent bout with iron poisoning that prevented Ludo and Quintus from opening doors must have been more traumatic for Ludo than he originally let on.

But Quintus answered quickly to assuage those fears. "No."

Tugging a dagger out from one of her arm bracers, Mishti raised both her eyebrows. "What is it then?"

Quintus turned and looked straight at Chloe. "Remember that island your brother, Vesper, kept going to in Swiftsea?"

She did remember, but she had to think back hard since that had happened during her first visit to Faerie. That had been before Vesper returned to the mortal realm. With the memory so vague in her mind, she couldn't figure out why Quintus would bring up that particular moment right now.

But then the memory sharpened, and the relevant information became clear. Her eyebrows raised. "There's magic over there that prevents you from opening a door to that spot, isn't there? Just like that island in Swiftsea."

"Exactly." Quintus nodded.

"Wonderful," Chloe said with a huff.

Ludo stared at her with one eye narrowed. "Wond... That is not wonderful at all."

She rolled her eyes at him. "I was being sarcastic. It's something fae are incapable of since you can't lie."

He responded with a look of confusion so pure that even his grumpy demeanor couldn't make it dark.

It almost made her chuckle. Before she could react though, Mishti used her dagger to point at a nearby tree. "Maybe we could chop down one of these golden trees and use it as a bridge."

Ludo wrinkled his nose. "I have a better idea. What if we give up and return to Bitter Thorn? Maybe this is Faerie's way of telling us the Crystalfall crown is best left where it is."

"Perhaps I can jump across." Quintus eyed the ravine. Then he stared at the path behind him. The mist had cleared out even more now, making the air almost completely pure. Perhaps the mist had been part of the pixies' trick.

With eyes narrowing, Quintus turned back to the ravine. "If I get a running start, I may be able to—"

"Never mind that." Chloe cut him off and took several steps to the side. "Look."

With the dark mist finally clearing away, a quick scan of the landscape had revealed a bridge built across the ravine. The old and rickety structure had weathered and splintered wooden planks. The ropes holding it in place had frayed so much, only a tenuous threads kept it together in a few spots.

But if the bridge had somehow managed to survive after the entire Court of Crystalfall had been destroyed, it had to be somewhat strong. And it wasn't like they had any other choice. There was no way she'd let Quintus attempt to jump across the ravine, not after she had only barely survived it.

Mishti's idea to build their own bridge would take several days at the least. It wasn't ideal, but the rickety crossing was all they had. They would have to make it work.

Unfortunately, the others didn't seem to share this optimism. Ludo scowled at the structure. She expected a snarky comment from him. Instead, Mishti spoke first.

"That looks like a sneeze could break it apart."

Ludo chuckled. "A sneeze from someone nearby maybe. If someone sneezed while on top of that thing, it might not just break apart. It might explode entirely."

The lightest hint of a smile flickered across Mishti's cheeks. The moment it appeared, Ludo's scowl melted away into a matching grin.

Chloe glared at both of them. "Do you see any other options?"

"My greatest magic is in crafting." Quintus rolled his shoulders back as he moved along the soil toward the rickety bridge. "I can craft and repair the bridge as we walk across it."

"Are you crazy?" Ludo spat out the words. "If we stay on that bridge any longer than it takes to cross it, we will fall straight into the ravine."

Mishti followed, but she eyed the bridge with a frown. "I still think we should make our own bridge. Even if we walk across as fast as possible, it might not be strong enough to hold our weight."

Chloe shrugged. "Then we can walk across it one at a time."

"No." Quintus and Ludo both said this at the same time.

Jabbing a thumb toward the structure, Ludo raised his eyebrows. "That thing is not going to last through multiple trips. Either we all go across or we are going to get separated."

Quintus nodded. "But we cannot go across it too fast either. That will put extra strain on the frayed ropes. Even if I do not repair the entire bridge as we walk across, I can make a few critical repairs. Then, at least, we can turn back if we need to."

Chloe was proud of their little group. Maybe they bickered and disagreed with each other, but at least they attempted a solution. And they attempted it together.

With trepidation buzzing in the air, the group set out across the bridge. Ludo first, Quintus and Chloe next, and Mishti at the back. Ludo started out slow and careful, testing each wooden plank with a sharp toe jab before he stepped onto it.

Quintus stood just behind Chloe as she stepped onto the rickety structure next. Magic sparkled at his fingertips, but as he promised, he only repaired a few fraying ropes every few steps.

Mishti stepped on last. Chloe didn't dare turn around to check, but Mishti's knees must have been knocking together because the bridge started gently bouncing as soon as she walked onto it.

Sucking in a gasp, Ludo immediately started moving forward faster. In only a breath, he had gone from a slow and careful walk to a near jog. The gentle bounce of the bridge turned to a jagged sway.

Quintus called out to Ludo, telling him to slow down. His voice echoed across the ravine. In a flash, the jagged sway turned to a violent shake.

Each one of them froze in fear, gripping the ropes tightly. Fear rose in Chloe's chest. The violent shake of the rickety bridge slowly, *slowly,* started to calm.

Only after the movement began to slow did Quintus take action. He reached out, emerald green magic emitting from his fingertips. The magic illuminated a frayed rope closest to him, one that looked ready to snap. In an instant, the threadbare rope filled out and the strands thickened. The once frayed edges had become like new again. Better than new, even.

With his eyes narrowed, he reached across Chloe and began repairing another rope near her. The heat from his arm seeped into her back. If they hadn't been on such a desperately dangerous structure, she would have inched closer to him. But with the bridge still lightly swaying, it would probably be best to stay as still as possible.

Mishti sucked in a sharp breath. She spoke in a stammering, quiet voice so unlike her usual one. "Should we turn back?"

"No," Quintus answered. "I think it is safe enough, as long as we move slowly."

"Are you sure?" The words burst from her lips even before Quintus had finished speaking.

Chloe dared a small glance backward.

Sweat sheened across the young woman's dark skin. Her knees knocked together. Her arms trembled so much she had a difficult time keeping hold of the rope.

"You can do this, Mishti." Chloe spoke as positively as she dared. It wouldn't help to speak too loudly. She turned and faced forward again. "We all can do this. Go ahead, Ludo. Nice and slow."

Ludo stepped forward again. He took three slow and easy steps. Only three. After that, his instincts must have kicked in because he started moving fast again. Too fast.

And then Mishti dropped to her knees as she let out a cry. The combination of the two movements was all it took.

A single rope on the bridge snapped.

Ludo gasped. Quintus lunged forward, eager to repair the snap before it led to more damage. But his lunge damaged the bridge even more. Two more ropes snapped. Then three. Four.

Mishti screamed as the bridge broke away from the edge of the ravine. But unlike they expected, it was the part of the bridge they had already crossed that broke first.

Perhaps Quintus has been right about needing to move slower so he had more time to repair the bridge.

The part of the bridge holding Mishti broke away from the ravine wall. Chloe threw her hand out to grab hold of Mishti's.

Mishti grabbed onto her hand just in time. But the force pulled Chloe away from the thin rope she held. Now Quintus had to throw a hand out and grab onto Chloe. Ludo rushed forward, grabbing onto Quintus's free hand to make sure he didn't fall.

That one last movement did even more damage than all the others. The rickety bridge was so decrepit, it really only needed one wrong snap to make it all fall apart.

Unfortunately, that one wrong snap had just happened.

Almost like it moved in slow motion, the bridge started falling. How lucky of Chloe that she got to plummet down this ravine twice instead of just once.

Her inner thoughts cut off short when she felt Quintus let go of her hand. She nearly gasped, but almost as fast, he reached that same arm tight around her stomach. It allowed him just enough movement that he could now wave his hand. He opened a door beneath them, which would have saved them. Should have saved them. But a sharp jerk in the rope bridge that Ludo still held onto moved their entire group away from the door at the last moment.

They had missed the door, and now, they might reach the bottom of the ravine before Quintus could open another door.

Grunting, Quintus sent a blast a magic from his fingertips. The magic exploded against the part of the rope bridge that fell down the ravine with them. Force from the magic pushed the bridge up against the dirt wall.

Shifting and wriggling his fingers now, Quintus performed more magic on the rope bridge. Somehow, even while falling, even while holding onto Chloe, who held onto Mishti, he managed to craft a repair in the bridge that held it tight against the dirt wall.

They had fallen far below the surface. The rope bridge held them against the dirt wall, but it didn't give them a way out. And due to how he had crafted the bridge, he now held Ludo in one hand, Chloe in the other arm, and Chloe still held onto Mishti.

Even a fae as strong as Quintus couldn't keep that up forever. And he probably wouldn't be able to perform more magic while he carried the weight of three extra people.

Closing her eyes, Chloe let a hard truth sink into her heart. This was her fault. She hadn't listened to Ludo when he made it clear he had every intention of walking across the bridge as fast as possible. She hadn't listened to Mishti when she suggested they build their own bridge. She hadn't even listened to Quintus, who could have repaired the bridge as they walked, so at least they could have turned back without plummeting down the ravine.

She had listened to all their ideas but still assumed her ideas were best. The ugly truth festered in her chest, scraping at her heart while she tried to steady her breaths. She had called herself the mastermind of this group once. But look where her master mind had led them now.

Quintus puffed loudly. He shifted his grip around her stomach, which probably didn't help him at all.

Gritting her teeth together, Chloe made a promise. She had gotten these people into this mess, and she would get them out of it. She had one last idea that was just crazy enough, it might work.

8

STRETCHING OUT HER FINGERS, CHLOE tried to use her free hand to grab onto a rope that had been magically attached to the dirt wall. Her voice strained as she tried to explain to Quintus. "I'm trying to grab onto the rope, so you don't have to carry the weight of all three of us."

With her back against his chest, she felt him nod. He said nothing though. Holding three people must have taken all his energy.

She did manage to grab onto a rope, but it didn't take enough weight off Quintus. It couldn't wait a single moment longer. She had to get them out of there as soon as possible.

With a deep breath, she closed her eyes and reached out with her mind. She hadn't seen her dragon since healing Faerie, but Shadow had to be somewhere. In the past, her dragon had always been able to come right away when Chloe asked.

Even with her mind reaching out, Chloe struggled to sense her dragon's presence. Perhaps it was because she was in

Crystalfall. Her dragon probably didn't know Crystalfall existed.

Sweat beaded on her forehead while she concentrated. Her fingers started slipping on the rope, which didn't help at all. Focusing all her energy, Chloe reached out just a little further.

At last, she felt a flicker of Shadow's presence. Latching onto it tighter, she issued her command.

Come.

Though their connection, she could sense hesitation from Shadow. The creature clearly wanted to come right away. She seemed to sense Chloe's distress and need. Despite that, the dragon's body didn't move.

Closing her eyes tighter, Chloe imagined the entrance to the black caves. She did her best to push that image into Shadow's mind. Then she pictured walking through the caves and into Crystalfall. Carefully, she imagined the path she and the others had taken to get to the ravine where they hung now.

At last, she could feel Shadow's wings beating. She was coming. She would be there soon.

It wouldn't be a moment too early either. Quintus huffed. His arm around Chloe's waist started shaking.

"Do not drop me!" Ludo shouted.

Apparently, Quintus's grip on Ludo was loosening too. His breaths came out even harder and slower than before.

"I…" Quintus released the word in a heavy puff. "Cannot…"

Chloe gripped onto the rope in front of her a little tighter. "Everyone, grab hold of the rope attached to the dirt wall. We cannot strain Quintus any longer."

The others acted immediately, but defeat had already overtaken their expressions.

"What now?" Ludo said through a grumble. "We hold on until our grips give out and then we fall to our deaths anyway?"

Chloe wanted to point out that, as fae, Quintus and Ludo had a fair chance at surviving, even if they did plummet to the ground. But since she and Mishti would certainly die if that happened, it would probably be best to not mention it.

Mishti shuddered hard enough to shake the rope they all held. "I would rather die by blade than by falling onto rock." Her eyes drifted to one of her arm bracers where her sharpest dagger belonged.

Quintus said nothing. Even though the others had grabbed onto the rope, he still strained to hold himself up. The strain must have made it impossible for him to speak.

Ludo shook his head. "I never thought I would die like this."

"Calm down." Chloe turned to Mishti now. "Both of you."

They both blinked back at her, hopefully startled enough to snap out of their desperation. She tilted her head backward. "Shadow is coming to save us. We only have to hold on a little longer."

"Shadow?" Mishti asked.

"Your dragon?" Ludo said with an eyebrow raised.

But just then, Quintus sucked in a gasp. The gasp turned into a grunt. In a breath, his grip on the wall failed.

Chloe hadn't realized it until that moment, but Quintus had been holding part of the rope bridge in place with a continual stream of magic. When his grip failed, the magic did too.

Not only did he fall away from the wall, all the rest of them did too.

Chloe's stomach flipped over on itself. How could she possibly survive a third plummet into this deep ravine?

But then her lips turned upward. The distinct sound of flapping dragon wings filled the air above. With an agile swoop, the dragon flew down and caught all four of them onto her back. They dropped against the golden scales with a heavy plop. Chloe spread her arms across the creature's golden back and buried her face against it.

"You saved us, Shadow," she whispered to the dragon. "You saved us just in time."

Shadow's sapphire wings sparkled in the light as the dragon flew in a wide circle above the ravine. At Chloe's side, Quintus breathed out his heaviest breath of all. After Chloe pushed an image of the cluster of trees into Shadow's mind, the dragon flew down and settled directly in front of the trees.

Mishti jumped off the dragon's back and landed on all fours onto the black soil of Crystalfall. Her cheek pressed against the soil as she let out a long, contented sigh. Ludo stumbled off the dragon's back. He then traipsed across the ground muttering about how he had forgotten what it felt like to have ground under his feet.

After the terror Mishti showed while on the bridge, her reaction made sense, but Ludo was just being dramatic. Then again, Ludo always acted that way.

With her arms still wrapped across the dragon's back, Chloe pushed her gratitude into the dragon's mind. It had seemed so strange at first to be connected to this dragon in any way. Now, the connection almost didn't seem like enough. Chloe wished she could hear Shadow's thoughts the way Shadow could hear hers.

Chloe turned now toward Quintus. He lay on his back with his chest heaving. His entire body—not just his limbs—trembled.

She placed a hand on his chest. He glanced toward her, but he didn't speak. And his position didn't change at all.

Leaning closer, she brushed a stray curl off his forehead. "I think I can heal your muscles. I don't know as much about muscle injuries when it's from strain instead of from a wound. But I know enough that I can at least attempt it."

His chin dipped in a short nod.

Her hand drifted off his chest and wrapped tight around his hand. Closing her eyes, she thought back on the studies she had done on muscles. Some of the books she had read on the subject she had read a year ago or more. But Quintus had just saved them from certain death. Surely she could remember a few passages she had read years ago.

Once certain she understood muscles enough, she then imagined the healing process in her mind. That didn't make it any easier to open her eyes. What if it didn't work?

"That is *much* better." Quintus released a heavy sigh and gently squeezed her hand.

Opening her eyes came easier now. She glanced down at him, reaching for that same stray curl she had brushed away earlier. Now she twirled it around her finger.

Quintus's eyed her like he wanted to grab her around the waist and pull her against him. Without any distraction, he probably would.

Before he could do anything, however, Ludo climbed onto the back of the dragon. "I just remembered the token."

Mishti clambered onto the dragon after him, her face had returned to its usual expression of stone. "What token?" she asked.

Still lying on his back, Quintus tucked both hands behind his neck to prop his head up. "The token from our bargain?"

Chloe's eyebrow raised. She had forgotten Quintus and Ludo had a bargain. As far as she remembered, Quintus had to help Ludo find something, though Quintus was allowed to wait until after Faerie was healed and the mortals defeated.

Her head tilted to the side. Perhaps he couldn't wait anymore though. Both of those things had already happened in the battle of Bitter Thorn Castle.

"Yes, *that* token. It is a scarf." Red colored Ludo's fair cheeks, not from a blush but from excitement.

"Do you have to help him find it right now?" Chloe asked Quintus.

Mishti raised an eyebrow, speaking in a cutting tone. "Why does Ludo need help finding anything? Isn't your greatest magic in finding things?"

Even that remark did nothing to hinder Ludo's excitement. "Yes, but I have been trying to find this particular item for as long as I can remember. My magic never did any good because I could never remember what the token was. But now we are in Crystalfall, and I finally remembered."

Quintus squished his mouth into a knot. "If I know what kind of scarf, I can try crafting one that looks like it. Perhaps after seeing a replica you will then remember enough to use your magic to find it."

"Yes, perfect." He clapped his hands together. "It is a blue scarf, a simple knitted one."

Staring at the sky above, Quintus squished his mouth up even more. He then pulled a sketchpad and pencil from his pocket and started drawing. He had left the realm with the others and entered a realm all his own where only his pencil and the paper in front of him existed.

Why did he have to look so ridiculously handsome when he sketched like that? The care and attention to detail he put into every stroke reminded Chloe of how carefully he sometimes held her. And kissed her.

Shaking that thought from her head, she turned to Ludo. "Do you remember when you lost your token?"

He wrinkled his nose at the question. "It is not *my* token. The scarf belongs to my brother."

Her head jolted backward as she blinked. "You have a brother?"

His eyes widened. After a hard swallow, he scrambled off the dragon's back and walked toward the cluster of trees. "Now that we are here, do we have any clues to help us find this mysterious Crystalfall dagger?"

Pressing her eyebrows together, she glanced toward Quintus. "Did you know he had a brother?"

"No," Quintus answered. But since his eyes never left the paper and his sketching never slowed, she wasn't entirely convinced he had even heard the question.

At least Mishti looked as surprised about the interaction as Chloe. Mishti used her head to point toward Ludo. "For someone who loves preserving memories, he certainly has a lot of secrets."

Chloe agreed with a nod. Now she shoved Quintus's shoulder. "Put your drawing away for now. We need to find that dagger."

His face turned comically offended when she shoved him. And he looked positively aghast when she tried to take the pencil from his hand. "I will, I will. There is no need to turn uncivilized."

She turned away from him long enough to roll her eyes without him seeing. Mishti chuckled at the reaction. Chloe and Mishti reached the ground at the same time. Quintus joined them a moment later.

Once on the soil, Quintus turned back to glance at the ravine. He shuddered at it. "That is not natural."

Narrowing her eyes, Chloe stepped toward him. "What's not? The ravine?"

He nodded, his gaze still fixed on the wide chasm. "The ravine, the rope bridge. The materials are not right. The ravine is…" After pausing for a moment, he shrugged. "It is not supposed to be here. It was not formed naturally. I cannot explain it."

She didn't know how to explain it either, but she knew what he was saying. Maybe she didn't *know* it, but she did feel it. In a way.

Ludo glanced around the cluster of trees, eyeing each one carefully. "Do we have any clues about where to find this dagger?"

Nodding, Chloe retrieved the king's journal from her leather bag. "We have two clues. Do you think your magic can find it with only two clues?"

He lifted one shoulder. "It depends on how vague the two clues are."

She opened to the journal's last entry with the map and pointed to the drawing of the dagger. "We know what it looks like." Her finger then trailed across the paper to the bottom of the page. "And we know this."

She traced under the words written there.

The dagger is hidden under a rock that is not a rock.

Glancing up at Ludo, his eyes had turned thoughtful. Hopefully his magic would be able to find the location of the dagger soon enough. Then again, something told her that retrieving the dagger would be more complicated than just finding it. After dealing with the ravine, she could only guess what obstacle they'd face next.

9

SCANNING THE CLUSTER OF TREES, Chloe searched for any sign of the elusive rock that held the key to their quest. Plenty of rocks and boulders scattered across the black soil. Some had a golden sheen as beautiful as the golden trees. Some of the rocks were made of amethyst or obsidian. Just like everything in Crystalfall, the rocks were beautiful, yet none of them matched the cryptic clue they had been given.

The dagger is hidden under a rock that is not a rock.

Frustration bubbled inside of her, but she wouldn't let it take over. They still had another option. She turned to Ludo. "Do you think your magic can find our mysterious rock?"

He nodded, determination taking over his face. Closing his eyes, he released his magic. The opalescent shower of sparks that left his fingertips immediately swirled and danced throughout the cluster of trees. At first, the beautiful sight filled the area with a lovely fluorescence. But the longer the magic swirled and danced, the longer it became apparent the magic might not be able to find their rock.

Quintus grabbed Chloe unexpectedly and tucked her behind the nearest tree. He didn't whisper, but he did speak in a low voice. "Tell your dragon to hide among trees with us."

"Hide?" She angled her head upward to cast a confused glance at him. In response, he jutted his chin out, pointing across the ravine they had just crossed.

Something moved at the top of the hill on the other side of the ravine. People? It certainly looked like people. But who else even knew this court existed?

And then she remembered. Julian, one of the leaders of the mortals, had written the note that helped her unlock the Court of Crystalfall. Somehow, he knew about the court. Both he and the other leader, Portia, had managed to escape during the battle at Bitter Thorn Castle. Had they already found Crystalfall and entered it?

Chloe immediately flicked her gaze toward her dragon. In her mind, she told the dragon to come hide among the trees with the others.

Shadow heard the command, but she didn't seem to understand the fear behind it. Rather than quietly walking over on just her feet, the dragon shook out her sapphire wings and stomped heavily toward the cluster of trees. Her wings hit several trees, causing sharp rings to sound. The action made an enormous amount of noise and movement.

If the people coming down the hill hadn't noticed Chloe and the others before, they certainly must have seen them now. Shadow made sure of that.

Chloe slapped herself on the forehead.

Quintus slanted one side of his mouth downward. "Maybe we should have just let her stay where she was."

Mishti came to Chloe's side, gazing across the ravine at the moving figures coming down the hill. "Don't fae have extra-powerful vision or something like that?"

Quintus glanced toward her for only a moment. "Yes, why?"

Gesturing forward, she asked, "Can you tell who those people are?"

Instead of answering, Quintus just sighed.

Chloe's heart sank at the sound of it. "It's Portia and Julian, isn't it?"

"Yes." Quintus frowned. "And a few other mortals too. Everyone that escaped the battle at Bitter Thorn Castle must have congregated together again."

Mishti nodded. "They probably had a rendezvous point in case anything went wrong during the battle. Then they could escape in all directions, making it difficult to catch them all, but then they could still easily find each other afterward. And now, somehow, they've also found us. Again."

Chloe scowled. "It must be because we walked here. We didn't use a door, so they must have followed our tracks like they've done before."

Quintus tilted his head to the side. "But Crystalfall is in hibernation. Can we even leave tracks when the court is asleep like it is?"

Mishti did her signature single eyebrow raise. "How else could they have found us?" She didn't stay for an answer. Instead, she ambled through the cluster of trees, kicking rocks and contorting her face in an expression of frustration.

The expression on Quintus's face was worse though. He looked very nearly in danger of giving up.

Wrapping an arm around his bicep, Chloe looked up into his eyes. "It's fine. The mortals will never be able to cross that ravine now that the bridge is gone. And Shadow can fly us away after we find the dagger. The mortals won't be able to follow us then."

He nodded but didn't look especially convinced. Even though the mortals couldn't cross the ravine, it would probably be better if Chloe and the others could find the dagger sooner rather than later.

Spinning around, Chloe looked at Ludo. "Any luck?"

His scowl answered the question without a word. Deep lines of frustration etched across his forehead. His opalescent magic continued to swirl around without any sort of aim or direction. It clearly hadn't found anything.

Mishti huffed, kicking another rock as she did. This one looked like a large ruby, but when her boot made contact, the rock let out a metallic clanging sound. Maybe it looked like a ruby rock, but only metal could make such a sound.

Her expression brightened as she raised one eyebrow. "I think I just found our rock."

Both Chloe and Ludo moved toward it eagerly. Quintus glanced back at the rock for a moment, but then he turned his gaze to the mortals on their way down the hill. "I will stay here and keep watch."

Chloe wanted to roll her eyes and remind him the mortals had no possible way of crossing the ravine without the rope bridge that was now destroyed. But ignoring what others said had just gotten them into serious trouble, so she decided to let him keep watch.

Dropping to her knees in front of the ruby, she started pushing to try and turn it over. When that didn't work, both Mishti and Ludo dropped to their knees at Chloe's side and added their strength to hers. It took a few heaves, but they managed to get it moving.

The rock looked convincing from a distance, but up close like this, it was easy to discern that a dark metal had simply been painted to look like a ruby.

Taking a deep breath, Chloe pushed with all her might. Mishti and Ludo did the same. After that one last push, they finally turned the fake ruby over. It revealed nothing but black soil under it, but perhaps there was more to it than that.

Using her hand, Chloe brushed away the top layer of soil. It took a few more brushes, but soon, she uncovered a stone box buried in the dirt. They'd have to dig it out. Since her hands were already dirty, she dug at the edges with her fingers.

Mishti joined, but she used the dagger from her left leg bracer to hack at the soil in the most difficult spots. Ludo retrieved a spoon from his magical pocket and used it to help with the digging.

While they worked, Quintus called out to them from his spot at the edge of the trees. "The mortals are still making their way down the hill toward the ravine." His voice lowered and a note of worry infected it. "There is no dark mist obscuring *their* view, though."

The last bits of dirt finally got cleared away from the stone box, but Chloe couldn't help feeling a sense of disappointment. The box had hinges and an obvious lid, but at the front of it, it also had yet another obstacle. A lock.

Ludo frowned. "Nothing is ever easy for us, is it?"

Mishti glared. "You want me to try and break the lock with my sword?"

Chloe took a deep breath, trying to push aside her disappointment. "Breaking it might work, but maybe we should try opening it with magic first."

She looked to Ludo expectantly.

Ludo immediately turned to Quintus. "He is the one who can craft keys just by looking at the lock. He needs to do it."

"What?" Quintus tore his gaze away from the mortals just long enough to glance at the stone box. He turned back to the mortals and let out a frustrated sigh. "Fine, but I am going to do it from here."

He reached into his pocket and produced a small bit of metal. Magic pooled from his fingertips. He glanced back and forth between the lock and the piece of metal several times. Once the key was finished, he tossed it back to the others with his gaze already fixed on the mortals.

Once again, Chloe had to bite her tongue. She snatched the key from the ground and tried to stuff it into the lock. It didn't work. It wasn't that the key was the wrong size or anything. In fact, the key probably fit perfectly. Instead, some sort of barrier prevented the key from even entering the lock.

Her nose wrinkled at the sight.

Ludo huffed. "It must have magic preventing any magical object from entering it."

Mishti raised an eyebrow. "Now can I try breaking it?"

Chloe nodded.

But that didn't work either. Mishti slammed the hilt of her sword against the lock, which didn't even make a dent in it. She then tried slicing it with the blade of her sword. That only served to dull the blade.

Chloe stood, refusing to be defeated. "Maybe Shadow can blow fire at it or break it with her claws or something." She lifted the box and brought it to her dragon. The creature did everything Chloe suggested, but none of it worked.

With a groan, Chloe slumped to the ground.

Quintus called back to them. "The mortals have nearly reached the ravine."

81

"Of course they have." Chloe groaned again.

Mishti stared at the stone box for a moment. She held her sword in one hand and picked at the leather covering the hilt with the other. "I...know how to pick locks."

Chloe sat up with a start. "Why didn't you say so before? Let's try that."

Mishti held her hands up, as if in surrender. "I mean, well, I probably shouldn't have said it like that. I have the knowledge of how to pick locks. I've studied the methods." Her face contorted into a grimace. "But I've never actually done it before."

With a shrug, Chloe pushed the box in front of Mishti. "It's the only chance we have. Just do your best."

Mishti nodded. "Okay. I can use one of my daggers, but I also need something small and thin and long."

Chloe's mouth lifted upward, remembering the iron needle at the bottom of her bag. "I have the perfect thing."

And it *was* perfect. Since Mishti had never picked a lock before, she certainly didn't pick this one with ease. But little by little, she worked at it. Sometimes her progress got ruined when she made a mistake, but soon she said it was almost there.

Mishti sat so close her nose practically touched the lock. She angled her dagger into the lock with one hand and poked the needle in with the other. Her tongue kept flicking out and licking the corner of her mouth while she worked. "Almost there," she said.

She had said the same thing as least four times now, but hopefully that just meant she was getting closer each time.

"Got it." A satisfying click sounded as Mishti grinned.

No one had any time to celebrate though. The moment the lock came undone, it immediately let out a crackling sound.

Mishti had just enough time to jerk her face away, but then the lock burst apart in an explosion.

Fire shot outward along with small bits of metal. Somehow, none of the bits lodged into any of them, though Chloe could have healed them with her magic if they had.

Ludo eyed the stone box with disgust. "Someone liked explosions a little too much."

But his grumpy attitude couldn't bring them down now. The lock may have exploded, but it also left the stone box unhindered from being opened. Sadly, Chloe's iron needle had been destroyed in the explosion. But since the court was in hibernation, she didn't need the iron needle anyway.

Holding her breath, she lifted the lid of the stone box.

Sitting right inside it was the most beautiful dagger she had ever seen. A masterpiece of craftsmanship, the dagger's golden color glinted in the light. Intricate emerald accents adorned the hilt, drawing the eye to the large, sparkling gemstone at the top of the pommel. The hilt itself was formed of glittering emeralds with a decorative gold leaf pattern gilded on top, creating a truly breathtaking sight.

The cross guard had more emeralds, these ones surrounded by sparkling white diamonds. They added even more elegance to this already magnificent weapon. The sheath was equally impressive, crafted from gleaming gold and adorned with decorative emeralds across its surface. A golden chain hung from the sheath, allowing the dagger to be attached to a belt and carried with style and grace.

Smiling, Chloe reached for the dagger. But just like with the lock, some sort of barrier stopped her before she could touch the weapon. She tried again, just in case, but it ended in the same result. She couldn't reach the dagger no matter how hard she tried.

Without a word, Mishti tried. She failed too.

Ludo let out a long grumble, not even offering to try and grab the dagger.

"What is taking so long?" Quintus stomped over, checking over his shoulder every few steps. "The mortals are nearly here, and they have bows and arrows. We need to get out of here before they attack."

He glanced down at the dagger inside of the stone box, then looked at each of them in turn. "It is right there. Someone grab it."

Chloe bit her bottom lip. "Well, you see—"

She got cut off when an arrow whizzed through the air just past her face.

Quintus sucked in a sharp breath. He reached down and plucked the dagger out of the stone box just as easily as he picked up anything else. With the dagger in one hand, he used it to point at Shadow. "Everyone get on the dragon. We need to leave."

Chloe's mouth dropped as she stared at the golden and emerald weapon in Quintus's hand. She glanced down into the box to make sure he had actually taken the dagger from it. The stone box did indeed sit empty.

He jabbed the weapon toward the dragon again and looked pointedly at all three of them. "Now."

Another arrow flew past, landing in a bush made of emeralds and jade. It didn't pose much danger, but it shook everyone out of their stupor at least.

Chloe, Mishti, and Ludo immediately stood and darted toward Shadow. As they moved, they all glanced at each other. Their looks confirmed one thing. Yes, it *was* strange that none of them had been able to touch the dagger, yet Quintus had done it without even trying.

Dozens of arrows came flying at them now. Chloe buried her face in the golden scales of Shadow's back. Being in the midst of a fight still filled her with more fear than she knew what to do with.

But even with her face covered, a loud crackling sound caught her attention. It sounded louder than the shouts from the nearby mortals. Braving a glance, she looked down at the cluster of trees Shadow flew them away from.

Sparkling magic erupted from the area they had just left.

Her eyes filled with wonder at the magic. Her gut curled too as she remembered the advice she had ignored once before.

If something in Faerie seems nice, it probably isn't.

10

CRACKLING SOUNDED FROM THE CENTER of the trees where Chloe and the others had just been standing. Suddenly, the ground beneath them began to shimmer and pulse with an ethereal energy.

Colorful lights rose from the ground like wisping flames, swirling and dancing in the air. The lights continued to rise until they filled the entire sky in a spectacular display of auroras. Hues of pink, purple, green, and blue blended together in a mesmerizing dance.

Chloe's hand rose to touch her lips as her mouth dropped in astonishment. This was unlike anything she had ever seen before. It didn't just match the beauty of Crystalfall, it enhanced it.

Auroras at night had their own beauty, but these auroras during the day stole her breath away. The colors shone brighter and more vivid than the trees, the display more grandiose. The entire sky had come alive and put on a show throughout the whole Court of Crystalfall.

As the auroras continued to dance above them, a sense of magic and wonder filled the air. The crackling sound turned to more of a light and airy ring, as if the air itself was filled with the sound of silver chimes.

Turning slightly, she caught sight of Quintus. His face was a picture of wonder and awe. Wide eyes took in the spectacle before them. He didn't focus as much on the sky as he did the ground below. With relaxed features, his gaze trailed over the grassy hills made of jade and the golden and emerald trees.

His eyes moved, but the rest of his body didn't. Perhaps he feared that any movement would break the spell and make the scene disappear.

A niggle of fear still edged into Chloe's gut, reminding her that pretty things didn't always have pretty intentions. But how could this go wrong? It was simply a beautiful, magical display that sent glowing energy throughout all of Crystalfall.

Quintus clearly felt the same. Nothing about his expression showed any worry at all. He threw his head back, closed his eyes, opened his arms wide, and basked in the energy all around them.

But then he whispered three simple words that changed everything. "It is alive."

She understood his meaning at once. Crystalfall Court had come out of hibernation. It continued to sparkle and glitter, but it also *lived*. She could feel it as soon as he said it. The emerald leaves started rustling and the golden branches swayed, as if a gentle breeze blew through them.

It should have been a purely joyful moment, especially for Quintus, since this court was his home.

But just as the auroras and the chiming started to die down, Quintus jolted up straight and his eyes flew open. "The court is in danger."

He jerked his head toward Chloe and grabbed her by the shoulders. "You must heal the land before the mortals can hurt it. Where is that iron needle?"

Suddenly, the little niggle in her gut made sense. This was why the spectacular display also brought danger. If the court had come out of hibernation, then it was now susceptible to iron poisoning.

She gulped. "I don't have the iron needle anymore. Mishti used it to open the lock on the stone box, and it got destroyed when the lock exploded."

His eyes opened wider the longer he stared at her.

It might have continued longer, but Mishti gestured toward the hill below. "Look at how many mortals there are."

Ludo scrambled to the edge of the dragon's back, being careful to avoid the sapphire wing. His nose immediately wrinkled. "There are hundreds of them."

Mishti nodded. "Portia and Julian must have found a way to free the mortals who got captured during our last battle."

"We do not know that for sure." Quintus glared at her suggestion.

But Mishti's expression didn't change. "I lived among those mortals for years. I am certain that at least some of the mortals who got captured during the battle are here now. With Portia and Julian."

Chloe's mouth suddenly went dry. She rubbed her palms on her skirt, trying to wipe away the sweat on them. Of course the mortals were back already. Of course they had found the new court. And soon they'd find a way to threaten it.

If Faerie was in danger again, then the mortal realm was in danger too. For now, all scurpus was fully and completely healed. But who knew how long that would last. The safety she had brought when she healed Faerie was already starting to drift away. They didn't have long before new threats would plague them.

Squirming in her seat, she made a decision. "I want to go home." She swallowed hard. "To the mortal realm."

Mishti raised an eyebrow at this announcement.

Chloe turned around, facing the same direction as her dragon. Her palm pressed against the creature's golden scales. "Shadow, take us back to Bitter Thorn Castle." She took in a small breath before she could speak again. "I'm getting Elora and then we're going back to the mortal realm to see Grace."

Ludo scoffed. "You want to do that right now?"

"Yes, right now." Chloe pushed the words out forcefully, speaking a little louder than necessary. Her fingers found the edge of the cascading layer of her skirt, which she immediately began to scratch and roll between her finger and thumb. "Faerie is healed right now. The mortals might poison it with iron again soon, but right now, it's completely healed."

With wide eyes and an open mouth, Quintus leaned away from her, almost as if he couldn't bear to look at her. His eyes kept blinking like he wanted to process her words but couldn't. He just whispered, "Now?"

Feeling her chin start to tremble, Chloe turned her gaze to the red fabric she kept rolling between her finger and thumb. "She's my baby sister." Chloe sniffed, hoping she'd be able to blink away the tears that started forming in her eyes. "I can't wait anymore. I need to see her well again. I need to know I saved her before the…"

As much as she hated her tears, they did do an incredible job at shifting Quintus's demeanor. Soon, he leaned toward her, angling his head to try and catch her gaze. His voice came out gentler now. "I understand you must go to the mortal realm, but you will return to Faerie afterward? You said you would return."

Her chin quivered as she nodded. Scooting closer, Quintus wrapped his arms around her and tucked her head under his chin. "We probably should not stay long, but we can go to the mortal realm."

Ludo pinched his eyebrows together. "What are Mishti and I supposed to do while you are gone?" He turned to Mishti. "Wait, you are not going to go with them, are you?"

Her eyebrow raised, though the rest of her expression remained stony. "If I return to the mortal realm, I will die."

His eyebrows ticked upward. "Oh, right. I forgot about that."

She glanced toward the green sheathed dagger, still in Quintus's hand. "Ludo and I can stay here and try to decipher the next clue while you two are gone."

Ludo scoffed. "The next clue? I never said I would help with that. I want to find the blue knit scarf. It should help me remember…" After a not-so-subtle pause, he cleared his throat. "Quintus is supposed to help me. I never said I would help him."

Mishti slowly pulled a dagger from her arm bracer. Angling it against a metal plate sewn into the long sleeve of her midnight blue tunic, she began sharpening the dagger. "You fae love bargains, don't you? Why don't you and I make a bargain?"

She drew the dagger even slower across the metal plate, making the scraping sound even more horrifying. "If you help,

I'll let you live. If not…" She raised her eyebrows and glanced down at her dagger, scraping across the sharpener.

Ludo shuddered, but then he shook his head. "I know you are lying. You hate killing people."

Her eyebrow raise could have frozen the sun itself. "Care to test that theory, do you?"

His eyes watched the dagger sliding slowly across the sharpener. When it made that same scraping sound, he shuddered again. "Fine. I do like having something to do, and I suppose I can look for the blue scarf as I help look for clues anyway."

Just then, they reached the entrance to the crystal caves. Chloe thought nothing of it until Shadow tried to fit through the entrance. Her enormous body must have cracked some of the cave in her rush to save Chloe and the others from the ravine.

Huge fissures spread through the cave walls. Hopefully, Faerie itself would be able to repair it. Flapping her wings slower, Shadow landed on the ground and began walking through the cave. She had to walk all the way through it, and even then, her body only barely fit.

For a dragon, the entrance was more than a little inconvenient. It was strange that there was only one small entrance to the court. The other courts had long expanses of land where they attached to another court. There were some natural barriers, but in general, it was much easier to get from one court to another. It seemed strange, but maybe that one small entrance could be used to their advantage in some way.

Eventually, Shadow finished walking through the cave and lifted herself into the air once again. Soon, she landed in the clearing just in front of Bitter Thorn Castle.

The others climbed off the dragon and headed straight for the castle doors. Chloe hung back for an extra moment. She placed her hand on the dragon's jaw and dropped her nose until it touched Shadow's.

She had no idea what would happen if she said *thank you* to a dragon. Maybe she'd owe her dragon a favor, maybe not. Regardless, it would probably be best to keep those words out of any conversation for as long as she stood in Faerie. But with the magical bond between her and her dragon, she didn't need words anyway.

Breathing in deeply, Chloe pushed her gratitude into the dragon's mind. She imagined how frightened she'd been when she started falling. Then she imagined the huge sense of relief she felt when Shadow had been there just in time to save them.

When she finished, the dragon puffed a happy snort from its nostrils. Then it released a deep growl that might have sounded like a purr if it had been any quieter.

Chloe used one hand to rub her dragon on the top of her nose. "I'm going to be leaving for a little while, but I'll be back soon."

A short whimper rumbled from Shadow's throat.

After a soft chuckle, Chloe rubbed the dragon's nose a little faster. "I'll be back soon. I just have to visit my sister."

Shadow pressed her nose up against Chloe's again, and then the creature bounded off into the forest. Her wings knocked down several branches and leaves as she merrily jaunted away. Shadow really needed to recognize she was much bigger than she realized.

Shaking her head with a smile, Chloe turned and finally entered the castle. Quintus stood at the doorway, waiting for her. The others had already gone inside.

Bitter Thorn Castle showed even more signs of life than it had since the last time she'd been there. Voices drifted through the hallways, making it clear several people had already moved back in. A little rabbit-sized brownie even scurried past Chloe and Quintus, muttering about how it needed to clean the sheets before anyone used the beds.

Quintus gestured onward. "I assume your sister and High King Brannick are in the council room. They usually prefer it to the throne room when there are things to arrange."

Chloe nodded without speaking. Considering the castle had only just been rebuilt and they had to notify all the people who had once been living inside the castle that it was finished and then help everyone get situated again, there was probably plenty of business to do.

As they walked through the halls, she found herself taking slower and slower steps. Quintus must have sensed her apprehension. He looked at her carefully and reached for her hand. But before he could ask any questions, a new figure entered the hallway with them.

Elora appeared, throwing a section of rich brown hair over one shoulder. Her eyes lit up as she clapped her hands together. The vines growing on the castle walls vibrated with the same energy as her. When she smiled, the air itself seemed to sweeten. "Are you ready to go see Grace?"

A noncommittal sound drifted from Chloe's lips. She'd planned to answer yes with as much excitement as Elora showed but had been unable to do it. With her free hand, Chloe's fingers found the edge of the upper skirt on the dress. Once again, she began rolling that skirt edge in between her finger and thumb.

Faerie was healed, so Grace should have been healed too. But maybe that wasn't what plagued Chloe with apprehension.

Maybe she was just nervous about returning to the mortal realm. Would she still be eager to return to Faerie once she walked in the mortal realm again? Or would she finally realize how silly it was to think she could make a life for herself in Faerie?

There was only one way to find out. It was time to return home.

11

ICY WIND CUT ACROSS CHLOE'S face and under her hood. She knew it would be winter in the mortal realm, since that was how she left it. But even wearing her blue fae-made cloak, the cold still caused her to gasp.

Elora stepped ahead without anything covering her shoulders, yet she didn't so much as shiver. Her fae nature must have kept her warm. She moved toward their brother Vesper's house as confidently as she did anything.

Quintus walked at Chloe's side. He said nothing. Even without words, Chloe got the sense that he feared she still might not return to Faerie with him, despite her promise.

She hated to admit it to herself, but he was right to worry. But she wouldn't think about that right now. Right now, the only thing that mattered was Grace.

Elora didn't knock when she got to Vesper's front door. Like she always did, she threw open the door and stepped inside as assuredly as if the house had belonged to her. Chloe and Quintus followed immediately after.

The walls of the house looked dim. Sconces with flickering candles hung on the wooden planks of the wall, but the flames seemed smaller than usual. Perhaps the iron poisoning still affected the mortal realm.

An even more terrifying thought sent a jolt through Chloe's gut. Maybe she'd just gotten so used to the way things looked in Faerie that the mortal realm now seemed bland.

They rounded a corner, and Elora threw open the door leading to Grace's bedroom.

Their youngest sister sat at her harp with her fingers carefully plucking the strings. Her red hair looked radiant. A light blush colored her fair cheeks, but it seemed like a healthy blush, not one from a fever.

Her mouth turned to a wide grin as she pushed back her stool and stood to face her sisters. Now she raised both her hands, which had absolutely none of the gray tinge associated with scurpus.

Flicking her gaze toward Chloe, Grace wriggled her fingers. "You fixed it. Just like you promised you would."

Air rushed from Chloe's lips as she placed a hand against her collarbone. "It worked? The scurpus is healed?"

Grace gave a delighted nod.

Before her head could bounce a second time, both Elora and Chloe had lunged forward and took their youngest sister into their arms. The three of them pulled each other close. They dropped to their knees, becoming a mess of tears and arms and so much love it almost hurt.

Relief poured in, lifting a weight Chloe didn't even realize she had felt on her shoulders.

After holding on long enough that her arms started to get sore, the three of them finally pulled away. They stayed right there on the floor, but they moved back just enough to see each other easily.

Chloe glanced toward the bedroom door, which still hung open. Quintus had disappeared. He must have realized the sisters needed this moment alone and went off to find Vesper.

Elora reached out and rearranged Grace's hair and then placed a hand on her cheek. "You are getting so grown up. I do not know if I am ready for you to look like a young woman."

Lifting a sassy eyebrow, Grace folded her arms over her dark green dress. "If you came to visit more often, I wouldn't grow up so fast."

Elora's nose wrinkled, but she didn't respond.

Chloe bit her bottom lip, almost afraid to ask all the questions in her heart. "So, what happened to the scurpus? Did it just disappear? How long has it been for you since I left?"

Tapping her chin, Grace narrowed her eyes for a moment. "It is early morning, and you left late last night."

Chloe nodded. "We thought it would be best to arrive a few hours later, just in case the scurpus needed time to heal. It sounds like Quintus opened his door to just the right time."

Grace looked down at her fingertips. "I got worse after you left, and it happened very quickly. Vesper had to carry me to bed since I collapsed in the hallway. But then everyone else got sick too. Cosette, the children. Even Vesper started showing the signs, though it was not as bad for him."

Elora swallowed hard, leaning forward with each of the words. "It is my fault. I let the mortals go, and then they poisoned the land, and—"

Rolling her eyes, Chloe waved a hand in front of Elora's face. "Never mind that. What happened next, Grace?"

97

Their youngest sister reached for a section of her red hair and held it with both hands. "Then...well, I felt something first. There was this sort of bubbling, fizzy feeling in my chest. It spread through my arms, my legs, my head. And then... Then everything just faded away. The red splotches, the gray tinge, it just shriveled up and disappeared."

Chloe's eyebrows bounced upward. "Did you feel well immediately after, or did it take some time?"

"It took time." Grace ran her fingers through her hair. "I could feel the illness leave, but my body was still weak. The children recovered the quickest, but even Cosette got better before me. Resting through the night helped immensely."

Reaching for her youngest sister's hand, Chloe pinched her eyebrows together. "But you are better now? You are certain the scurpus is completely gone?"

"Yes." Grace's simple answer had the wrong inflection to sound completely convincing.

Chloe pinched her eyebrows even tighter together, which made Grace squirm.

Grace turned her gaze downward and spoke in a lower voice. "We think everyone in town got it. Vesper already told a few people a fake explanation, but you know how he is. He convinces people with his confidence alone. I think everyone has stopped trying to make sense of anything he says. They just accept it."

It was clear that Grace was trying to soften a blow of some sort, which only made her words that much more of a punch to the gut. Letting out a sigh, Chloe braced herself. "What did he tell them?"

Grace bit her bottom lip. "Um, he said that your apothecary skills had grown so much, you probably figured out a way to put medicine in the air itself."

Elora raised her eyebrows, impressed. "Clever. Not technically a lie, but the words still created a deception."

On the other hand, Chloe was not impressed at all. She just rubbed her temples and let out a groan. "Why would he tell people I put medicine into the air? That makes me look as eccentric as he is."

Elora jerked her head toward Chloe while throwing a glare. "Who said eccentric was a bad thing?"

Instead of trying to defend herself, Chloe just responded with a noncommittal chuckle.

Luckily, Elora accepted the answer. She rose to her feet and started toward the door. "I am going to find Vesper and Cosette. And then I need to give a hug to all my little nieces and nephews."

The moment she shut the door, Chloe leaned closer to her youngest sister and spoke in a conspiratorial whisper. "*Everyone* says eccentric is a bad thing. At least all the mortals do." She shook her head. "Finding a husband is nearly impossible for an eccentric young woman. And they don't even know about my foot!"

Grace tilted her head to the side. "Your foot?"

Chloe sighed again. "It got chopped off." She stuck her wooden foot out from under her skirts. A leather boot mostly covered the wood, but a bit of it was still visible where the prosthetic attached to the end of her leg.

She ran a finger over the leather attachment. "Quintus crafted this wooden foot for me, which is wonderful. It really is." She sighed. "But it's not the same."

At the mention of Quintus, a micro-expression appeared on Grace's face. She glanced at the door, probably recalling how Quintus had been standing there too when Chloe and Elora first arrived.

Hoping to avoid *that* conversation, Chloe stood and trailed over to the harp in the middle of Grace's room. Her hand ran over the wooden base, admiring the carvings along it. Then her fingers slid across the strings. A few of them she gently plucked, just enough to give off a quiet noise.

From her spot on the ground, Grace's face suddenly looked wise beyond her years. She stared at Chloe's moving fingers and then glanced into her sister's eyes. "How long were you in Faerie?"

"I don't know." Chloe forced her hand away from the harp, smoothing her dress with it instead. "You know there's no time in Faerie. That makes it impossible to tell how long it's been. All the days run together and seem like one day or every day or… You know how it is."

Grace got to her feet and stared more pointedly. "If you had to guess, how long would you say?"

Chloe traced a finger over a swirl of golden embroidery in her bodice. "Maybe six months."

With a knowing nod, Grace gestured at the harp. "Play it. I'm sure you miss it after six months."

It didn't take any more prodding. Chloe dropped herself onto the stool and pulled the harp base against her shoulder. Her fingers trailed across the strings, comfort overcoming her at the feel of them. She started playing one of the few songs she still had memorized. Then again, it had always been her favorite. Hers and her mother's. The sweet melody lilted through the air, expanding in her chest and squeezing at her heart.

As she played, the room came to life. The warm glow of the candle flames danced across the wooden walls, casting flickering shadows that seemed to sway in time with the music. The harp's soft strums filled the space, creating a peaceful ambiance that had been missing since she'd traveled back to Faerie.

Chloe closed her eyes, letting herself get lost in the music. The weight of the harp against her shoulder along with the familiar sensation of strings beneath her fingers felt like the safety of a warm blanket. The melody flowed through her, transporting her to a different place, one where her mother sat nearby on her own stool, ready to give directions once the song was finished.

Their mother had taught the harp to all three of them, but each one had a different experience. Elora fought it the most. Grace learned the most. But Chloe. Chloe had loved it the most. She loved spending time with her mother. She loved getting better at it and having new accomplishments to be proud of. Most of all, she loved how it brought her to a place all her own. One where her worries could vanish and nothing but the music existed.

Tears pricked at her eyes, slipping down her cheeks. When had she started crying? And why? Even more tears fell, but now, she had finished the song.

When she opened her eyes, Grace stared with that same wise-beyond-her years look in her eyes. "You're not staying, are you?"

Chloe gulped, using the back of her hand to wipe away her tears. "I do have to return to Faerie for now. I promised I would return to help with…" She swallowed again. "There are these mortals who are trying to take over. They—"

"But you'll stay in Faerie, even after that, won't you? You're only going to come back here to visit, not to live." Grace said the words in a matter-of-fact tone, not allowing for argument.

Sniffing, Chloe shifted her gaze to the carvings on the harp base. "How can I leave the mortal realm for good? It's my home."

Grace shrugged. "Technically, we were born generations ahead of this time in the mortal realm, so this place isn't exactly your home either."

With a sigh, Chloe lifted the harp base away from her shoulder and set it upright again. "So I suppose I don't belong anywhere."

But Grace wouldn't accept that answer. She stepped forward and donned a serious expression. "Home is where you make it."

The words sounded nice, but Chloe still frowned. "I feel like I'm abandoning you."

Grace gestured to the room around them. "This is where I want to be. That might change someday, but this is where I belong right now. It's okay if you belong somewhere different."

Just like that, another rush of tears flowed into Chloe's eyes. She got to her feet and pulled her sister into a tight hug. Grace embraced her back, just as tight. It was the healing sort of hug only sisters could give.

When they pulled away, both of them had teary eyes. Grace blinked hers away and nudged her elbow toward the harp. "You should get Quintus to craft you a harp so you can play while you're in Faerie."

Chloe's heart expanded at the thought. "You think so?"

Now Grace wrinkled her nose. "Yes, you need lots of practice. *Lots.*"

Chloe snorted at that, playfully shoving her sister away.

Giggling, Grace walked over to her bookshelf and tapped her chin. "I'll loan you some exercise books. You definitely need to start practicing your scales again." She took a book off the shelf and held it in one arm while the other hand traced across the other books on her shelf. "Oh, and a book on plucking. And this one has some lovely songs that sound nice but aren't too difficult."

Soon, she had a large stack, which she dropped into Chloe's hands with a stern look. "You better practice while you're in Faerie. Mother would be horrified if all your talent went to waste just because you decided to move to a magical realm."

Chloe's chuckles grew with each word her sister spoke. "I don't know if I'll have time to practice. I've been busy saving the entire realm."

Grace mockingly waved a pointed finger at her. "That's no excuse. If you can make time to eat, you can make time to practice."

As she spoke, a figure appeared in the doorway. Quintus stood there, looking into the room with more than a little apprehension.

Chloe immediately turned to Grace. The two of them shared a knowing glance, acceptance and understanding flowing between them.

With a short nod, Chloe pulled the harp books close to her chest and took a step toward Quintus. "Let's go back to Faerie. We need to find those other pieces of the Crystalfall crown and then take care of those mortals."

Quintus stared at her for a beat and then he let out a sigh that lifted his shoulders. It seemed an enormous weight had been pressing down on him as well. But, for now at least, the two of them moved one step closer together. One step closer to being together and letting the problems between them be ignored.

It might not work forever. But it worked for now.

And right now, they had a crown to find.

12

BACK IN THE COURT OF Crystalfall, Chloe's heart pounded with a mix of adrenaline and fear. She stared hard at the iron needle in between her finger and thumb, so hard that her eyes began to water. How could such a tiny piece of metal feel so cold and heavy? She had thought to grab the small needle just before she, Elora, and Quintus had left the mortal realm.

Elora had returned to her own castle and duties. Chloe and Quintus, after meeting up with Mishti and Ludo, had then made their way back to Crystalfall. They didn't go inside the castle this time, however. Chloe tucked the precious music books from Grace inside her leather bag. Thanks to its fae magic, the bag still felt weightless on her shoulder.

In the clearing, Mishti eyed the castle, but she didn't seem eager to enter it.

Chloe sat on the jade grass at the edge of the clearing. Quintus, Ludo, and Mishti watched her expectantly.

A twinge of guilt twisted in Chloe's heart as she stared at the iron needle. Poisoning the court was somewhat drastic, and potentially dangerous, but what choice did she have? At least the needle only had a tiny amount of iron.

Taking a deep breath, she jabbed the needle into a bit of black soil amongst the strands of jade grass. Unlike before, the iron sank deep into the soil without any resistance at all. In a single breath, tiny white striations stretched out from the needle like bolts of lightning.

She swallowed. At least the iron had started poisoning the land already. Now she should be able to heal Crystalfall, just like she had healed the other courts.

As before, she imagined the healing process she had attempted earlier. But this time, when she poured the liquids of vinegar, wheat cider, and sulfur water, she directed them to fall right on top of those white striations coming out from the iron needle. The sand and salt went on next. She was careful to imagine the appearance of orange rust spots, as well as the sounds and smells.

Again, her focus stayed on the needle and healing that specific spot of ground in Crystalfall.

With her eyes still closed, she pictured the final part of the healing process with the sprinkling of acid fruit juice. This produced imaginary fizzles and pops that formed white bubbles and foamy mounds. She made sure to imagine such powerful bubbles that the little needle rusted all the way down to its core.

The sharp, tangy scent of rust filled her nose as she dared to peek through one eyelid. She held her breath as she glanced down at the ground.

Where the needle once rose above the soil, it had now turned to a sickly looking inch of rust.

Letting out a deep sigh, Chloe allowed herself to relax and let go of the tension inside her. It had worked. The tiny amount of iron had been enough to infect Faerie with iron poisoning but not enough to harm it.

Quintus flicked the rusted needle, which exploded into a shower of orange dust. "The court is safe from iron poisoning now?"

Chloe nodded. "It should be just as safe as the other courts. Now the land here knows how to heal itself from iron poisoning. It should be able to do it by itself if it ever gets infected with iron again."

Ludo scowled. "The mortals are smart though. They might find another way to get a stronghold, even without poisoning the land."

"He's right." Mishti stood, untucking the emerald dagger they had found earlier from her leather belt. "This court is especially in danger since it currently has no leader. You can be certain Portia will take advantage of that."

Without a word, Mishti held the sheathed dagger out to Quintus.

He drummed his fingers against his thighs and stared at her incredulously. "Why are you handing that to me? It is not mine."

She raised an eyebrow, clearly not accepting this statement. When he still wouldn't take the dagger, she pushed it against his chest and let go.

It slid down, falling immediately. He caught it in one hand just before it touched the ground.

Turning to Ludo, Mishti said, "Tell them about the poem."

Ludo tore his gaze away from the dagger and reached into his pocket. He retrieved a worn piece of parchment that was burned on one edge. "We found this inside the dagger's sheath.

It has to be the next clue. I do not know what kind of ruler the king of Crystalfall was, but I can safely say his poetry was not the most profound. It is easy enough to decipher at least."

All of them leaned in close to read the poem.

Where liquid cascades from a great height,
And the golden trees shine in a brilliant light.
Over the pebbled soil, and the valley of beryl,
And the sound of water is like a soothing lull.
Listen to the song of the rushing stream,
And you'll find what you seek, or so it would seem.
The true answer lies just behind,
That is where the key you'll find.

Chloe had to read through the poem twice, but then her eyes darted across the landscape before them. "It's hidden behind a waterfall?"

"That's what we guessed too," Mishti answered.

Since the map only had one waterfall with significant detail, and since that particular waterfall stood near a valley filled with teal beryl flowers, Chloe knew exactly in which area to start their search.

Quintus turned contemplative as he rubbed his thumb over the large emerald at the center of the dagger's cross guard. "Do you think the poem refers to a literal key? Or does it just mean an item and that item is the key?"

Shrugging, Chloe started marching down the white pebble-dotted path that led to the waterfall. "Who knows? But I'm sure the sooner we get to the waterfall, the sooner we'll find out."

Mishti ran up to her side, taking a quick glance back at the others. She lowered her voice and leaned closer to Chloe. "Did you tell Quintus what happened when you and I tried to grab the dagger?"

With lightning quick speed, Quintus had moved to Chloe's other side. His eyes narrowed. "Why? What happened when you tried to grab the dagger?"

Chloe had to suppress a chuckle. Mishti clearly hadn't learned how perfect fae hearing was. She turned now to Quintus. "We couldn't touch it. There was some sort of barrier that stopped our hands from getting close to the dagger." Her eyebrow raised significantly. "When *you* tried to grab it, though, you were able to touch it without even trying. It is almost as if you were destined to touch it."

His body froze for a moment as the words sank in. He swallowed hard and ran his fingers through the black curls on top of his head. "That means nothing." He gave a half-hearted attempt at laughing it off, which didn't sound convincing at all. "It probably only happened because…"

He trudged forward with his mouth agape, as if he wanted to say something, but the words eluded him. His footsteps fell heavier, perhaps because this new responsibility had started to weigh down on him more greatly.

Chloe gave Mishti an inconspicuous but knowing look. Conflict etched across Quintus's face whenever his fate came up, but that didn't change anything. He could continue to deny it as much as he wanted, but the truth became increasingly clear to everyone—Quintus was meant to be the next leader of Crystalfall.

Ludo slapped him on the back. "Cheer up, Quintus. If you do not want the crown, I am certain the mortals would be happy to take it off your hands."

Shoving Ludo away, Quintus burned him with a glare.

"Why does the crown matter anyway?" Mishti asked. "Why can't we just make a new crown?"

Ludo touched his heart and dropped his mouth open wide. "*Make* a crown? Like it is just some piece of jewelry or trinket?" He shook his head. "Not even Quintus, a master craftsman, could do that."

Since Ludo clearly had more interest in reacting in the most dramatic way possible rather than answering, Chloe gave an actual explanation. "No one can make a crown unless Faerie itself helps. The crowns the leaders all have now are the same crowns that were created when the courts were created. Each crown shifts when a new leader is named. The crown changes to match that person specifically, but at its core, it's still the same crown."

Quintus nodded. "Even more notably, crowns hold incredible power. The fae who wears the crown is given that power and uses it to take care of his or her court. But the fae can also use that power for other, less honorable things as well."

Mishti raised an eyebrow. "So, at any time, another fae could just steal the high king's crown and then that fae would suddenly be high king and have all that power?"

Ludo let out a loud belly laugh. Even Quintus and Chloe chuckled.

Wiping away her amusement, Chloe did her best to explain. "Another fae cannot simply take the crown and wear it. The crown can only belong to one person at a time. To take the power of the crown, the current leader must first be killed. Then, the next person who wears the crown will gain its power."

"But do not forget the incredible power a crown gives to the wearer." Quintus raised both his eyebrows to make the point. "That power belongs to the fae, even if the fae is not wearing the crown at that moment, though most Faerie rulers do wear their crowns every day. But no, no one can just go up to High King Brannick, kill him, and then wear the crown to become the next high ruler. High King Brannick is far too powerful. Killing fae is difficult enough, but killing a high ruler is nearly impossible."

Mishti's eyebrows raised higher with each of his words. "But what if the mortals did get the crown? What if they somehow found the pieces and Portia crowned herself queen? Would a mortal get that incredible power and then become nearly impossible to kill?"

"No." Both Quintus and Ludo answered at the same time. Ludo even shook his head hard enough that his blond hair shifted on his head.

Ludo said, "I only wanted to tease Quintus before. A mortal might wear a crown, but it would not have the same effect as it would on a fae. The mortal could not gain the power of the crown."

Chloe narrowed her eyes at him. "Is that something you know for certain? Or is it just something you *believe* to be true?"

He answered with a scoff, which wasn't a true answer anyway. But by now, they had arrived at the waterfall. With a new item to search for, this question would be tucked away and probably never brought up again.

It didn't matter anyway. Quintus already had the dagger, and he'd never let the mortals get their hands on it. Soon, they'd get the second piece of the crown hidden behind the waterfall. But even as she tried to ignore the question, Chloe did wonder. Could a mortal gain the power of a Faerie crown?

If so, they had to do everything in their power to make sure neither Portia nor Julian ever got that chance.

13

THE GLITTERING WATERFALL HAD LIQUID that appeared to be half water and half blue gems. Anticipation surged in Chloe's chest as she reached out to touch the fluid. It turned out, the sight of gems was only an illusion, and it was just water after all.

Even more disappointing, the waterfall had nothing behind it except a thick stone wall. Taking a step back to admire the cascading water, Chloe made a decision based on gut instinct. She urged Quintus, Mishti, and Ludo to search for an opening or a compartment of some sort where the key might be hidden inside the stone wall.

While the others scoured the area behind the waterfall, Chloe settled next to a golden tree and opened the king's journal. Her heart pounded as she turned back to the very first page.

She knew the king had feared for his life and that his crown would fall into the wrong hands. She knew an evil mortal man destroyed the king's court, probably killing them both in the process. But now she wanted to know the details, the events that led to that point. Questions like that could only be answered by starting at the beginning, so the beginning was where she started.

Opening the journal to the very first page, she began to read.

Everyone calls Crystalfall the court of misfits. I like to think of it as the court of those too big, too magnificent for where they were originally born. This court has no fae who were naturally born here, but everyone who chooses to live here feels more at home here than they did where they first lived.

Mortals and fae live harmoniously here. The mortals are treated like equals, which is very unlike how they are treated in nearly all the other Faerie courts. They feel they belong here just as much as the fae.

But it is the mortals who do not trust me.

I will let them stay as long as necessary, but if they try to turn against me, they will regret it. The power I have from the Crystalfall crown makes it easy to remind others who is in charge.

Even still, I must remember to keep my axe sharpened and carry it with me everywhere I go.

Chloe sucked in a breath and traced the last line until her finger landed under the word *axe*. Her mind swirled with possibilities, which she tried to brush away. It probably signified nothing. Still, she couldn't stop herself from remembering another significant person who had also carried an axe.

Quintus's father.

She shook her head, trying again to shake the thought from her mind so she could keep reading. But now that it had been planted, the idea only grew.

All Fairfrost fae used axes in their fights, so it probably just proved the king of Crystalfall had originally been born in Fairfrost. But what if it was more than that?

What if it was more than just a coincidence and even more than destiny that Quintus could grab the emerald dagger from that stone box when the rest of them could not?

What if Crystalfall's last king was also Quintus's father?

Despite the intriguing idea, it did not bring any comfort. Quintus's father had tried to murder Quintus when he was only a small child. He drove Quintus out of his home and away from his mother and forced him to survive on his own when he was barely old enough to start learning to read.

And later, Quintus's father found Quintus again, but he didn't try to make amends or get to know him. Of course not. His father destroyed Quintus's home, with him still in it, and forced him to live in uncertainty while he searched for a new place to belong.

Her heart squeezed as she scowled. Hopefully she was wrong. Hopefully Crystalfall's last king was better than *that*.

Turning the page, she started reading the next entry.

I started growing a mole, which I blame entirely on the magic from my crown. It cannot be a coincidence that it appeared only days after I was crowned. I did not mind the imperfection at first, but then I overhead a mortal young woman making fun of it.

How dare such a simple creature make fun of a powerful being like myself?

I will have to choose whether I want to kill her or just use a glamour to cover the mole. I will let my mood decide.

Chloe shook her head at the words. Even if this king wasn't Quintus's father, he clearly wasn't some virtuous fae either. Then again, almost all fae cared only for themselves. Their sense of right and wrong came from bargains and vows, not from consideration of others' lives or feelings.

Before she could read more, a loud, thunderous splash disturbed the water right in front of her. Gasping, she shoved the king's journal inside her leather bag. Thanks to Vesper's magic, anything inside the bag would stay dry, no matter how much water fell onto it.

Her outfit and hair were not as lucky. An entire bucket's worth of water slapped against her, nearly making her fall backward. She clutched her leather bag tight to her chest. Fury ignited in her belly as the water soaked into her gorgeous red dress.

Whoever did that was about to hear her shout and rage like never before. It was probably Ludo. He probably thought it was hilarious, but he'd change his mind once she tore into him.

Her teeth gritted together as she wiped a sheet of water off her face.

But when she opened her eyes, it wasn't Ludo's smirking face she found. She didn't see Quintus's curls or Mishti's signature eyebrow raise either.

The splash of water had come from a huge rock, thrown at her companions from the very top of the waterfall. Terror seized her as she realized they were no longer alone.

The mortals had found them again. The mortals had attempted to *kill* them again.

Another huge rock dropped from the top of the waterfall. Quintus held onto the stone wall directly next to the waterfall, gripping a handhold he had probably crafted himself. His eyes flashed as he caught her gaze. He shouted a single word: "Run!"

Keeping the leather bag tight against her chest with one hand, she used the other to bring the strap over her head and onto the opposite shoulder. Her knees shook as she tried to get to her feet. Her first few steps resulted in stumbles that sent her back to the ground.

Short, tight breaths escaped her mouth so fast, she could barely get enough air to her lungs. By the time she managed to get to her feet and take a step forward, two mortals jumped out from behind a glittering bush.

They tackled her to the ground, shoving her face into the dirt. Crumbles of soil got stuck in her eyes, stinging them. When she tried to blink the dirt away, it just caused more soil to get caught.

A pricking, burning sensation filled her eyes. But even her tears couldn't remove the dirt. The water just blurred her vision even more. When she tried to suck in a breath, she swallowed a mouthful of dirt.

From behind, she heard a sinister chuckle from the mortal who had a strong chance of becoming her least favorite mortal ever. Julian. "What was that you were reading?"

His voice tickled at her ear, sending ice down her spine that stung worse than her eyes. Never had she been more grateful to have fallen right on top of her leather bag holding the journal.

The mortals had certainly come to that spot to attack them. But if they got the journal, they could learn about the crown, which would be disastrous. No matter what Quintus and Ludo said, Chloe was not convinced the magic of a crown only worked for fae.

Shouts and clangs rang through the air.

Quintus, Mishti, and Ludo probably all had their weapons out—a spear, a sword and daggers, and an axe. And here was Chloe with her face shoved against the ground, as useless in a fight as she always was.

Right on cue, heat flushed at the back of her neck. Tingling pricked across her shoulders, rendering her arms immovable. She wanted to bang her head against something, but since it was already pressed up against the ground, she couldn't even do that.

She was supposed to be working through this, wasn't she? She was supposed to not be so afraid of a fight.

But then she remembered what had allowed her to enter her last two fights. Her dragon. Did she dare call the creature to her now when it might be injured?

The question got answered for her when a sharp metal blade prodded her just under her chin. Chloe couldn't see him, but she could feel Julian move closer. His breath felt like needles on her skin. "I *said*, what were you reading?"

Slamming her eyes shut, Chloe called Shadow to her. She pushed forward images of the fight, directing as much urgency as possible to her dragon.

When Chloe didn't answer, Julian pressed the tip of the blade into her skin until it sliced open. Now he let out a feral laugh. "Once you're dead, I guess I can find out for myself."

The blade moved deeper into her flesh. Quintus had always done everything in his power to protect her, but he didn't come to her aid now. His own life must have been in danger too. Shadow had yet to come rescue her. She was all alone with nothing but the dirt beneath her cheek for comfort.

If she stayed there doing nothing, she'd die. The thought did not improve her anxiety. Fear ran through her veins like a river of molten iron, sapping her strength and making it impossible to lift her arms. Every muscle in her body tensed as the blade pressed deeper into the delicate muscles under her jaw.

She could feel blood dripping from the wound. Life drained out of her, yet still no one had come to save her. Truth finally reared its ugly head inside her mind. Maybe this was one fight she would have to face on her own.

Her arms would shake. Her knees would knock together. She had to remember to account for that. But if she moved quickly enough maybe it would still work. Unable to stop the fear from controlling her limbs, she forced herself to take a deep breath.

The knife wound under her chin sliced even deeper when she shoved herself upward. Just as she knew they would, her knees knocked together horribly. Instead of trying to work against it, she allowed herself to move awkwardly and focused solely on backing up as quickly as possible.

For once, it had helped her that this enemy knew her. They knew she always cowered and never tried to get away. Just this once, she had somehow used that to her advantage. Julian and the others had been taken so off guard at her actual attempt to get away that she managed to just barely escape their grasps.

Tangled nerves made it hard to breathe. Dirt and tears still obscured her vision, but judging by the enormous golden and sapphire mass that had just appeared ahead, her dragon had finally come to rescue her.

Her feet stumbled over each other as she continued backing away. Someone lunged toward her, probably Julian. With all the soil in her eyes, she couldn't tell for sure.

An enormous golden arm swiped at the person, sending him flying. Chloe couldn't catch her breath. Even with Shadow there now, she couldn't possibly climb onto the safety of the dragon's back. The entire world closed in on her, turning into a blur of color and sound. Each breath was so short it could barely be called a gasp.

She clutched at her chest, trying to calm her racing heart. Her palms were slick with sweat, probably leaving a mark on her already wet dress. If only she could catch her breath.

Enormous claws wrapped around her middle, lifting her off the ground. Apparently, her dragon didn't want to wait around for her to jump onto its back.

Wind whipped through Chloe's hair as she rose higher into the sky. The grip around her waist tightened just enough to snap her out of her complete panic. For the first time since the mortals arrived, she managed to take in a regular breath.

A rumbling whimper escaped Shadow's mouth. The dragon flapped its wings, rising higher and higher into the sky. Shadow continued to hold Chloe tight around the waist, but also lifted her until Chloe's nose touched the golden scales of her own nose.

Chloe sucked in another deep breath, this one filling her lungs. Her vision had started to return too, which only improved as she worked to blink away the rest of the dirt in her eyes.

Shadow whimpered again, shaking an entire cloud that hung near them.

With quivering hands, Chloe reached out to rub the golden scales of her dragon's arm. The comforting gesture worked to undo the tension knotted inside her chest. Shadow brought her nose close to Chloe's, nuzzling against her.

The steady presence of her dragon brought the feeling of safety that only an enormous, dangerous creature could. It also helped her to focus her thoughts on something other than the fight below.

Each time Chloe stroked the creature's scales, her anxiety calmed a little more. She found her breathing slowing and her heart rate returning to normal. Little by little, her body relaxed. At last, she could breathe enough to speak.

After a hard swallow, she issued her first command. "Put me onto your back."

With a quick thrust, Shadow threw Chloe into the air, then swooped down and caught her perfectly onto her back. From that angle, Chloe would have a much better view of the fight. Tucking her body behind the shield of one of Shadow's wings, Chloe instructed her dragon to fly lower.

It only took her a moment to assess the situation. Quintus had killed a few of the mortals already. He roared and thrust his spear at anyone who tried to oppose him. Julian didn't seem to have any damage though, and Portia didn't seem to be part of the fight at all.

Mishti and Ludo stood in the stream, not directly under the waterfall but close to it. If Shadow moved quickly enough, she could fly close enough for the others to jump on her back and then they could all fly away to safety.

The biggest problem would be trying to convince everyone to get on the dragon without arguing first. At least, Chloe hoped that would be the biggest problem. But with an enemy as cunning as these mortals, she never knew exactly what they'd face.

14

DUCKING BEHIND HER DRAGON'S WING, Chloe wrapped both arms around her leather bag and held it tight against her stomach. After a deep breath, she told Shadow to swoop down close enough to Quintus that he could jump onto the dragon's back.

Chloe's head ducked lower as a volley of arrows shot through the air above her. At least Shadow's dragon scales were too thick to be injured by arrows. As the dragon lowered toward the ground, Quintus leapt far higher than a mortal ever could and landed on Shadow's back.

He scrambled forward until his legs settled on either side of Chloe's legs. His chest pressed against her back as he wrapped his arms around her stomach. He breathed heavily and spoke right into her hair. "I tried to get to you."

She found his hand and placed hers overtop it. "I'm fine now. Let's just get the others and get out of here."

But when Shadow swooped down toward the others, Mishti just jabbed her thumb at the waterfall. "We still have to get the key."

Ludo scrambled onto the dragon's back without hesitation, yanking on Mishti's arm until she was atop the dragon too. But then Ludo immediately grabbed Shadow's harp string reins and led her near the middle of the cascading waterfall. "I think I can get it. I saw a glimpse of something just before the mortals attacked."

Mishti used her hands to try and angle some of the waterfall away from Ludo's face so that he could better see the stone wall behind the waterfall. "Get over here, Quintus. We need you to pull the key out of its place."

Quintus grunted, tugging Chloe closer to himself. He had produced a cloth of some sort and used it now to wipe the blood away from her chin. She'd have to heal the wound once they got to safety, but she couldn't do it now. Not while her heart was racing this fast.

Even after a frightening glare from Mishti, Quintus still didn't move.

Two swords came slicing through the air, both hitting dangerously close to Mishti and Ludo. Mishti even crossed both arms in front of her face, ducking her head behind them.

When the blades struck Shadow's back, the dragon released a thunderous growl. Her entire body shook as she screamed. Then, opening her mouth wide, flame poured from her mouth in a steady stream.

The two mortals who had thrown the swords let out blood-curdling screams as the fire danced over their skin.

"This one is different," Ludo shouted. "I think any of us can touch it, but the angle is…"

As he trailed off, Mishti came closer. She must have seen exactly what he was trying to describe. Whipping out the dagger from her left leg bracer, she stuck the tip into the stone wall. Her tongue flicked out, wetting the corner of her mouth.

"Almost got it." She leaned even closer.

"Oh, Mishti." From above them, a sickly-sweet voice rang out.

Chloe looked up just in time to see Portia standing on the ground right next to the top of the waterfall. The woman had a crazed look in her eye. Her severely tight bun bounced as she jumped.

In an instant, Portia had jumped onto the back of the dragon with them. The woman didn't have any of the agility or skill that Mishti had, but apparently that wouldn't stop her. She produced an axe that sent a shiver down Chloe's spine.

She recognized the axe at once. How could she forget it? It was the very axe that had chopped Chloe's foot off forever. Her entire body went rigid with it so close by.

Despite her reaction, she could feel that just behind her, Quintus had gone rigid too. A low sound erupted from the back of his throat. It was very nearly a growl. In another instant, he had pulled away from Chloe and lunged toward the woman with his spear aimed at her heart.

But Portia must have had a plan. She didn't use the curved blade of her axe at all. She only jabbed the wooden end of the handle into Mishti's side.

In an instant, Mishti's eyes grew as big as the sun itself. All air seemed to escape her in a single rushing breath. Her body froze as she gripped her stomach and fell face forward onto Shadow's back.

An evil chuckle left Portia's lips as she calmly jumped off Shadow and into the stream below. She moved so unexpectedly that even Quintus's spear missed when he tried to kill her.

At least Ludo had kept working the whole time. He ripped a golden key from out of the stone wall. "Got it!"

As soon as he spoke, he immediately turned back to the stone wall. "Oh, there is something else here."

He pulled a small slip of paper from the wall. The moment he pulled it out, an enormous boulder crashed onto Shadow's back. Screeching, the dragon jerked its body hard. The boulder rolled off her back, but the small piece of paper in Ludo's hand also got jerked away.

His fingers clasped at the air, trying to grab the paper. But the little parchment kept fluttering farther and farther away.

"What is that?" Quintus growled, slipping his legs around Chloe and pulling her close again.

"The clue." Ludo slapped his hands against his cheeks. "We need that. Tell your dragon to fly us down so we can get it."

But the little piece of parchment had already reached the ground. It landed on the black soil right at Julian's feet. With his blue eyes lighting in a wild frenzy, he lifted the paper from the ground and read the words on it.

Chloe's stomach sank. The clue. Julian had read the clue. Maybe he didn't know what it led to, but if he happened to find part of the crown, any part of the crown, that could stop Quintus from being able to craft it back together. They needed all four pieces to properly restore it.

But just as she started telling her dragon to fly down so they could get the clue, Julian gave a truly frightening grin. He then popped the piece of paper into his mouth. His jaw worked up and down as he chewed. And then he swallowed.

123

Chloe sucked in a gasp.

The clue was gone.

"Shadow, get us out of here," Quintus shouted, pulling Chloe even closer than before.

"But the clue," she said weakly. "We need—"

He held her tighter around the waist, and she realized how much she leaned on him. "Your skin is losing color. We need to get to safety so you can heal your wound."

Even as he said it, the wound Julian had inflicted under her chin stung. Why had Quintus reminded her of it? Now she could feel it twice as great as before. She probably should have protested more, but her body had grown too weak for it.

She could barely even see the landscape as Shadow flew them closer to the Crystalfall castle. When black spots started to appear in her vision, it seemed the time to heal herself had come.

Clenching her jaw, she let out a low groan and she reached for Quintus's hand. He offered it instantly, his strong grip wrapping around hers. Just as it always did, his presence offered a sense of comfort and support. Having grown accustomed to healing wounds with magic, it almost became second nature to her to heal this one.

Still, this injury under her chin was deep and painful. Agony coursed through her even stronger now that she paid more attention to the pain. Focusing her mind, she carefully imagined the healing process. Each step felt like a battle, but she pushed through the pain. Each wince and each tremble was worth it as she reached the part where the wound started to scab over. Finally, she could breathe like normal again.

When her eyes fluttered open, she found Quintus only an inch away from her face. He examined the wound, his nose wrinkling at it. All at once, he realized she had opened her eyes.

In a breath, he released her hand and used both arms to pull her tight against him. His chest expanded, pressing against her and warming the clothes that had gotten splashed with water.

He whispered into her hair. "I wish I had been there, but I am grateful Shadow answered your call. I might have to give her an extra rub on her belly for it."

Chloe chuckled, snuggling her cheek against the soft green vest on Quintus's chest.

"Um." Ludo cleared his throat. Normally in a situation like this, he probably would have made some comment about how disgusting Chloe and Quintus were acting, but something was different this time. His voice stretched with a smidgeon of fear. "I think Mishti is broken."

If the fear in Ludo's voice hadn't been so palpable, Chloe would have laughed about how he chose to phrase that. Instead, she glanced over her shoulder to where Ludo and Mishti sat.

Except Mishti didn't sit. Her body was splayed out across Shadow's back. She held both hands in tight fists, which squeezed tighter every few moments. At the same time, her face would also wince.

Sucking in a breath, Chloe immediately pulled away from Quintus and crawled across Shadow's back to where Mishti lay.

The young woman's dark skin had turned sallow. Dark circles had appeared under her eyes.

Chloe swallowed hard as she did a quick visual examination over the young woman's body. "Did a sword cut you? I can heal the injury if—"

"You can't." Mishti pushed the words out through her gritted teeth. Her jaw clenched even tighter after that. She probably would have squeezed her eyes shut tighter too, except they were already as tight as possible.

This conversation was getting nowhere. Since Chloe could see no injuries, she tucked a hand under Mishti's shoulder and tried to turn her over.

In response, Mishti jerked her shoulder away and pressed her face even closer to the dragon's scales. "Don't."

Chloe wanted to throw her hands into the air. "But I can heal it. You just have to tell me where it…"

She trailed off as a memory hit her like a bucket of ice poured over the head. Mishti had told Chloe about how all the mortals who had once lived in Ansel's house each got their own enchanted injury. Ansel would use the injuries to keep the mortals compliant if they ever tried to escape or act out in any other way.

The mortals all kept the location of their injuries secret from each other. To Chloe's knowledge, only one other mortal knew the specific location of Mishti's enchanted injury. And of course, that very same mortal had landed on Shadow's back before jumping into the water below.

Chloe wanted to scream. Instead, she gently placed a hand on Mishti shoulder. "Portia did this, didn't she? She hurt you right in the spot where you have the enchanted injury from Ansel."

Mishti's entire body winced as her chin dipped in a nod. Her mouth parted like she intended to say more, but the pain must have been too great. Her fists just clenched even tighter, and her eyes clamped shut once again.

Glancing up, Chloe tilted her head to indicate that Quintus should come closer. He did, but his gaze stayed fixed on the landscape below them. She took his hand. At the very least, she could try to use her magic to give Mishti some pain relief.

She closed her eyes and imagined administering valecea in both a tonic and a poultice that she spread onto Mishti's chest.

But even after she finished, Mishti's wincing hadn't eased at all. Apparently, an enchanted injury was not affected by pain herbs.

Unless Chloe saw the injury with her own eyes, she wouldn't be able to heal it. Her heart sank at the thought, but she did understand why Mishti continued to keep it secret even now. They had grown close in their time together, but not close enough.

Mishti had once trusted Portia enough with the location of the injury and that clearly hadn't ended well. Still, Mishti would hopefully trust Chloe enough someday to show her the injury. Chloe would just have to wait until then to heal it.

With his eyes still on the landscape, Quintus shook his head. "Look at how the mortals have desecrated that waterfall. They threw boulders from the top and smashed them down where they didn't belong. The stream is damming up now. Even if we go back later and put the rocks back where they should belong, the damage might be too much to fix completely."

Ludo huffed. "Blasted mortals."

Nodding once, Quintus folded his arms over his chest. "All they bring is destruction. Mortals do not belong in Faerie."

She could understand his anger, but Chloe still shot him her most lethal glare. They hadn't argued about this in so long, but now the argument felt as fresh as it had ever been. How could he complain so much about mortals when *she* was mortal? He couldn't condemn them all.

It took him several breaths for him to even realize she stared at him. When he caught sight of her glare, he clearly didn't understand it. But then understanding dawned on his features and yet, he remained silent.

He'd regret that silence. Her hands landed on her hips. "Mortals don't belong here, huh? I guess I should just go back home then."

Letting out a puff of air, he gestured vaguely at the ground below the dragon. "*Those* mortals. Those mortals do not belong in Faerie."

Her hand stayed on her hips as she narrowed her eyes. "Not all of them are evil."

His mouth pinched into a snarl. "You keep saying that. I know they all suffered greatly at the hands of Ansel, but are you so certain their hearts are pure? None of them came to your defense when Julian had that blade at your throat."

She let out an accusatory laugh. "That's probably because they're afraid of him."

Quintus raised an eyebrow. "What have *any* of them done to prove they are different from their leaders?"

Her hands dropped to her sides, the fight leaving her when she had the sudden realization that maybe Quintus didn't want to understand. She turned away from him. "We have to give them a chance. They've never even had a chance to make their own choices. We can't judge them until then."

Ludo rolled his eyes. "Do you two ever stop bickering? We need to figure out what to do next." His eyebrow raised as he stared at them. "Or have you forgotten? The mortals have our next clue."

Groaning, Chloe looked away. "Technically, no one has the clue. Not anymore."

"What." Mishti forced the word out between heavy breaths. "Happened?"

"Julian ate it," Quintus replied.

Ludo whirled his head around. "What do you mean he *ate* it?"

Chloe pantomimed as she spoke. "He picked up the parchment, stuck it in his mouth, then ate it. That clue is gone now."

Ludo's eyes bugged out. "He actually *ate* it?"

"He's crazy," Chloe said with a shrug. "Is there sense to anything he does?"

Quintus spoke gravely. "Julian read the paper before he ate it. The mortals might not know what we are looking for, but they do know where to go next. At least Julian does."

Swallowing hard, Chloe's stomach sank. What were they going to do now? If the mortals got any piece of the crown, it could cause problems too devastating to fix.

15

WITH BOTH ARMS WRAPPED AROUND her stomach, Chloe knelt on her dragon's back as it hovered in the air. She stroked its golden scales, hoping an idea might come to her that way. Shadow rumbled a purring sort of noise from the back of her throat. As nice as it was, it didn't help to come up with any ideas.

Now, Chloe turned to Quintus. She didn't even know why. He wasn't the one who usually came up with ideas. And he was especially unlikely to now. He'd been resisting this quest from the start, still afraid to admit that he might be the next leader of Crystalfall.

But something in his eyes sparked differently than before. Determination? Perhaps it was just because he remembered how High King Brannick had given him a direct order to find the crown. Or maybe it was because he was finally starting to accept his responsibility.

He stood a little taller and glanced down at the jeweled landscape beneath them. Speaking in a definitive voice, he said, "We need to wait for the mortals."

Ludo snarled. "Wait for the mortals to do what? Destroy more of this court?"

Unaffected by the harsh words, Quintus gestured down at the ground. "They have been following us, but now they are the ones with the next clue. We need to wait for them to act and then we will follow them."

Chloe froze mid-stroke across her dragon's golden scales and sat up straight. "That's brilliant. We'll follow them, watch them, and when they find the next piece of the crown, we'll just steal it from them, along with the next clue."

Quintus raised an eyebrow. "I hoped we might jump in before they get their hands on the crown piece, but yes, that is the general idea."

From the middle of the dragon's back, Mishti gasped. Her hands clenched into tighter fists, her eyes squeezing shut even tighter than ever.

Ludo's eyes pinched together in an odd expression stuck somewhere between annoyance and concern. His head tilted to the side. "How long is Mishti going to be broken?"

The words sent pain to Chloe's chest. She longed to heal the injury for her friend, but if Mishti wouldn't volunteer to let her see the injury, then Chloe could do nothing. All they could do now was wait for Mishti to recover from the incident.

Still standing, Quintus took Shadow's harp string reins into his hands and began directing the dragon to the ground. His eyes stayed focused as he worked. "We will have to sleep in Crystalfall, near the mortals' camp. I can see the land they have desecrated with their tents and fires. We will stay far enough away to not arouse their notice, but we will still be close enough that I will hear when they are leaving the camp."

For that small moment, Chloe had to calm her breathing. Quintus had been so unsure of himself lately, she had very nearly forgotten how difficult it was to resist him when he knew exactly what to do.

By the time they laid out their sleeping mats and blankets, she had entirely forgotten their earlier argument about how mortals didn't belong in Faerie. She kept sneaking glances at him through the side of her eye, her stomach flipping each time.

Except, this last time, he caught her gaze and held it so steadily she couldn't even dream of looking away. Electricity sparked in her veins, tingling across her skin.

He stepped toward her with that same surety in his demeanor that made her stomach flop even more. By the time he caught her in his arms, she was ready to give him everything.

Before Quintus could kiss her or stroke her hair or do anything really, Ludo made a gagging sound. He exaggerated it even more when Chloe glanced back at him. His entire face had contorted. "You two are disgusting. First the bickering, then the adoring looks. I can't decide which one is worse."

Apparently, Quintus took that as a challenge. He tucked one hand tight around Chloe's lower back, dipped her backward, and then kissed her with the most passionate kiss possible in such a short time.

After a breath, they were standing back up again, and she felt desperately in need of a fan to cool the heat from her cheeks.

Ludo rolled his eyes. "The bickering. The bickering is definitely better."

From atop her sleeping mat, Mishti let out a whimper. Some of the color had returned to her cheeks, but she laid on her back with her fingers clenched into fists at her side. When they had landed on the ground, she hadn't even been able to get off Shadow's back by herself. Ludo had had to carry her.

He stared at her now with that same mixed expression of annoyance and concern, except this time, it leaned heavily toward the concern side. Shaking his head, he attempted to wipe the expression from his face.

With a heavy plop, he dropped onto the ground and turned his gaze to Quintus. "We have a bargain, remember. You said you would attempt to create a replica of the token to hopefully help me regain my lost memories."

At the sound of those words, Quintus wrapped his arms a little tighter around Chloe. He even looked into her eyes, causing her stomach to flutter.

Ludo cleared his throat. Loudly. "I do not care how much love or affection or whatever emotion you feel right now. We have a bargain, Quintus. You cannot keep avoiding it."

When it came to bargains, no one, not even mortals, could defy them. The magic of Faerie forced everyone to do what they promised.

Cold air swept across Chloe's back when Quintus pulled his arms away from her, but she knew he had no choice. Soon, he sat on the ground with his legs crossed under him. He pulled out a lumpy ball of blue yarn from his pocket.

He held it toward Ludo with a question in his eyes.

Ludo nodded. "The color is almost right, but it needs to be a little lighter."

Nodding, Quintus released sparkling magic from his fingertips which then enveloped the ball of yarn.

After the magic dissipated—and even before Quintus could hold it up again—Ludo shook his head. "No, that is still too dark. A little lighter."

Chloe settled down next to Quintus and across from Ludo. She sat close to Mishti too, but hopefully not too close to bother her. While Quintus worked, this was probably a good moment to read more of the king's journal.

But when she grabbed the journal, it suddenly occurred to her that some of the answers might be closer than she first thought. She turned her gaze upward. "Ludo, who was the king of Crystalfall?"

He shrugged in response, his eyes carefully watching the lumpy ball of yarn in Quintus's hand.

If he only paid her half attention, then maybe now was the time for a wild guess. It might get him to look at her at least. "Was it your brother?"

Just as she hoped, Ludo's eyes flicked upward, immediately looking straight at her. Instead of denying the question like she expected, he just stared. And then he stopped staring at her, instead staring off into the distance. His jaw flexed as his eyes narrowed to smaller and smaller slits. Maybe her wild guess had been closer to the truth than she expected.

But finally, he tore his gaze away from the distance and went back to staring at the ball of yarn. His only response was to shrug again.

For a moment, she'd really thought he remembered something. But maybe he just remembered something that *he* wanted to remember. Or maybe the memory flitted at the corner of his mind, just out of reach.

With a little more prodding, who knew what she might learn. She'd start by asking more about the scarf, and hopefully, that would lead her to even greater answers.

16

SITTING IN A CIRCLE ATOP their sleeping mats, Chloe and the others would soon go to sleep for the night. She had to make sure she got answers before that happened. With Quintus attempting to re-create a scarf for Ludo, at least she had time to get Ludo talking.

"How is this?" Quintus held up the yarn.

Ludo nodded, more serious than she had possibly ever seen him. "Yes. That is the exact color."

Hoping to steal his attention, she asked, "Where did the scarf come from anyway?"

"I stole it off a dead mortal's body in Fairfrost."

Her shoulders shuddered at the thought. It wasn't just the idea of stealing something off a dead body. It was the utter lack of remorse in his statement. Like any fae, he had merely seen something he wanted and taken it. If the mortal had been alive or dead, it probably wouldn't have mattered to him.

Almost involuntarily, Chloe glanced back at Mishti. The young women still had every muscle in her face scrunched up, but she managed to share a look with Chloe too. She rolled her eyes and mouthed the word *fae*.

Chloe nodded and rolled her eyes too. It wasn't just that the fae were so lacking in emotion. It was that they were so unaware of it. Clearly, it didn't even occur to Ludo that he should feel at least a little strange about stealing a scarf like that.

"No, no, no. That is the wrong stitch." Ludo leaned forward, frowning at the scarf beginning to take shape in Quintus's hands.

Quintus glared. "This is how to knit. I learned it from a mortal, so I know it is not wrong."

Ludo pinched his eyebrows together. "But that is too smooth. It should have bumps, but the bumps are small and uniform and look like they are supposed to be there. And it should not look different in the back and the front. It should look the same on both sides."

Unraveling the yarn, Quintus clenched his jaw tight. When he started the knitting again, he looked even less pleasant than before.

Chloe turned to Ludo, still hoping for more answers. "Do you remember your brother?"

Ludo's eyes never left the scarf, but he answered in a vaguely nostalgic voice. "I remember him well. He often took me fishing in Fairfrost, at Lake Iridescence, which was near a dozen dragon coves. While fishing, we would always watch the dragons flying in the distance. If they ever flew too close, we would have to hide. They are ferocious when not trained. They could eat us up in a single gulp."

Despite her need for answers, Chloe's lips still turned up at the idea of Ludo fishing. It seemed too boring an activity for someone as prone to grumbling as him.

Quintus held up the scarf, which now only had a few rows, but this time in a different stitch.

Ludo narrowed his eyes at it and then approved with a nod.

Chloe smiled. "How nice that you got to go fishing so often with your brother."

Wrinkling his nose, Ludo slumped. "We did until King Pavel called my brother to be a soldier for him."

Chloe's eyebrow raised. "King Pavel?"

Quintus answered. "That is King Severin and the late Queen Alessandra's father."

She nodded. "What happened to your brother once King Pavel called him to be a soldier?"

Ludo's face became increasingly annoyed. "My brother left, and he hardly ever got to come back home. The king said he would call me too once I became an adult, but I did not want to go. I saw how my brother's life seemed to be sucked out of him. He had to be gone more and more. Then we suddenly were not allowed to fish anymore, though the king never explained why. Then we were told we could not leave the Court of Fairfrost without permission. My brother wanted to leave. He had heard of Crystalfall and said the court would welcome us. He said some soldiers had found a way to escape, but they needed a token first."

"What is a token?" Mishti's voice came out gaspy and harsh, but she had strung four whole words together, which was progress. Her entire body flinched once she finished speaking, so clearly pain still had a strong hold on her.

Chloe turned back with a smile. "A token is an object imbued with emotion, usually from a specific, highly emotional moment. They are also sometimes called trophies. The harp string reins on Shadow are a token." As the words came out, Chloe suddenly turned back to Ludo with a sneer on her face. "Is that why you stole the scarf off a mortal? Because you knew you didn't have enough emotion to find your own token?"

"No." Ludo hardly even recognized the accusation in her tone. "I stole the scarf because I liked it. It wasn't a token at that point. But I was growing older. I was very nearly an adult and would soon join the king's soldiers, which I did not want at all."

"Does this same pattern continue for the entire scarf?" Quintus had crafted a decent portion of the scarf and held it up high.

Ludo tapped his chin, staring carefully at the scarf. "I believe it had a twisty pattern in the middle." He gestured just above the portion of the scarf that was already completed.

With a nod, Quintus began crafting again. He seemed to understand Ludo exactly.

Staring off into the distance, Ludo continued with his story as if he had never stopped. "One day, my brother came to tell me that he was going on an assignment for the king and probably would not come back. He would not tell me where he was going, but I have always wondered if he was going to Crystalfall and intended to stay there for good, leaving me behind. We had one last day together. We decided to defy the king and went fishing just like we had done when we were younger. A dragon—this one trained by the king—attacked us, probably because we were defying the king's orders about fishing. We hid, avoiding the dragon at exactly the right moment, but we moved too quickly. The ice on the lake cracked, and my brother, Revyn, fell in."

Chloe wanted to take a moment and let the name Revyn sink in, but she couldn't. Instead, her body tensed as she remembered how she too had once fallen into a lake of ice. Her lungs squeezed. Even though she sat safe in the Court of Crystalfall, cold still flooded her limbs. Involuntarily, she shuddered.

Ludo went on, unaware of how his words had affected her. "Fae can survive much, but he got caught under the ice and could not get out by himself. If he had stayed under water, eventually, he would have died. In that moment, I realized I did not want him to die."

Mishti scoffed, which sounded like a grunt of pain as well. "You only realized it in that moment?"

"Yes." Ludo shrugged. "Faerie has changed greatly. Back then, emotions were much rarer. Fae only care about preserving our own lives, finding our own joy. We only help others if it will help ourselves."

Chloe bit her bottom lip. "But helping Revyn wouldn't have helped you because he was leaving anyway."

At the sound of his brother's name, Ludo's eyes twitched. Something sparked in them, almost like a memory. "Yes."

Quintus had stopped crafting the scarf. He leaned forward. "What happened?"

An entirely new look overcame Ludo, one unlike any face he had ever made before. His lips turned upward, and his eyes sparkled. "I saved him. I used the blue scarf and helped pull Revyn back onto shore. I got him home and found him dry clothes. I even gave him the scarf since it seemed to bring him comfort. I said he could keep it. I did not know or understand why I did any of it. I just know I felt better. I was glad that he was alive."

Chloe couldn't help but smile too. How miraculous that an emotion-less fae had somehow reached a tiny bit of emotion. And without the help of a mortal even. Perhaps she'd underestimated Ludo. And now she was thinking that maybe her wild guess that Ludo's brother was the previous king of Crystalfall hadn't been so outlandish as she had first assumed. He probably would have made a good king.

"Then what?" Mishti asked.

Ludo sat a little taller. "My brother thanked me. He asked me what favor I wanted him to grant me. I told him I wanted him to find a way for both of us to escape Fairfrost. And he did." Now he pointed his finger at the unfinished scarf in Quintus's hand. "Finish that up, will you?"

Quintus blinked hard and turned his gaze downward. He went back to crafting immediately.

Chloe brushed a finger over the golden embroidery in her bodice as she thought. "Is that when the scarf became a token? When you used it to save your brother's life?"

Ludo stared at the scarf, which was nearly finished now. "Yes, although it became an even stronger token on a visit my brother took to the mortal realm. The scarf got damaged and then repaired. Apparently, the emotion in those interactions was stronger than anything my brother or I had ever experienced in Faerie. He even brought back a mortal girl with him. She and my brother inexplicably fell in love, and I did not mind. I liked them together very much."

Chloe had to blink several times before she could get her brain working again. Ludo's brother had fallen in love with a mortal girl? She whipped open the king's journal, intending to skim through the last entry she had just read. Instead, she found herself reading a new entry, which was even more telling.

None of the women like me. I have so much power, but I suppose it is too much for them. They do not know what they are missing.

If Ludo's brother had fallen in love with a mortal girl, surely he would not have cared about whether the women in Crystalfall liked him. This king of Crystalfall couldn't be Revyn then. It was someone who had never been in love. Someone who maybe even pretended to detest it, but that disgust was probably just a way to disguise his jealousy.

"Finally." Ludo jumped up and grabbed the finished scarf from Quintus's hands.

Quintus stood too, pointing to the center of the scarf. "I did a few simple cables in the middle, but I do not know if the pattern is exactly the same as your brother's scarf. I tried to keep it simple, since the original was mortal made, but—"

"This is good enough." Ludo waved him off and ignored everyone else as he climbed onto his sleeping mat. He wrapped the scarf around his neck and closed his eyes.

Apparently, Ludo was done talking about his brother. He had memories to uncover, after all. Closing the king's journal, Chloe glanced at Mishti once more. Her breathing seemed a little steadier than it had been. She just needed rest now.

Now Chloe climbed under her own blanket. They had a busy day ahead of them. But as long as the mortals tried to follow the next clue, Chloe and the others should be able to find the next piece of the crown.

All they could do now was wait for the mortals to travel somewhere.

17

THE SCENT OF BLOOD DRIFTED into Chloe's nostrils. Hoping it was left over from her dream, she popped open one eyelid. A dead animal sat directly in front of her, its mangled remains touching part of her blanket.

With a gasp, she sat up and backed away. But then another animal came into her view. Shadow sat behind the dead carcass, her sapphire eyes glittering as she stared unblinking at Chloe.

"What is it?" Mishti held one hand against her side as she came closer from her sleeping mat.

Chloe swallowed before answering. "It looks like some kind of deer."

With the animal now in her sight, Mishti's eyes went wide. "Oh." And then understanding dawned once she caught sight of Shadow sitting there proud as could be.

"It's…" Chloe couldn't bring herself to finish the sentence. She didn't want to think about the poor dead creature, or how her dragon had—what seemed like gleefully—presented it to her.

"It's like I said before," Mishti said, gesturing toward the dead animal. "Your dragon is bringing you a present just like cats do in the mortal realm."

Trying to ignore the way her stomach churned, Chloe glanced around their camp. "Where are Quintus and Ludo?"

Mishti knelt down, polishing her sword with a gray cream and a stained rag. "They said they were going to go scout out the mortals' camp. For all their talk about their incredible fae hearing skills, I guess they still trust their eyes more. I'm sure they'll be back once the mortals start going somewhere."

Chloe grinned at that. Sometimes the fae did talk bigger than they acted. But she hoped Mishti was right. Quintus and Ludo had better come back so they could all four go after the mortals together. She didn't want to dream of what might happen if the two of them tried to face hundreds of mortals, without even Shadow to help.

Just then, the sound of rustling gems filled the air. A moment later, Quintus and Ludo emerged from a swirling black door with golden sparkles.

Quintus threw Chloe a grin as he eyed her entire form. Ludo rolled his eyes at the action.

Chloe stepped forward, her cheeks warming at how Quintus still stared at her. "Are the mortals moving already?"

At that, both Quintus and Ludo frowned.

"No," Quintus answered, but he gave no further explanation.

Ludo wrinkled his nose. "They are not leaving. They are waiting for *us* to move before they act."

"For us?" Chloe bit her bottom lip, staring off to the side. "I wonder if Julian didn't tell them about the clue. Maybe he's planning to go after the crown piece by himself."

Quintus shrugged and leaned against the nearest golden tree trunk. "Maybe, but he is with the mortals now. He does not seem to have any intention of going anywhere. We might be stuck here unless we force them to act."

Chloe would have grumbled, except right then, she felt a warm presence nudge against her leg. She glanced back to see Shadow's bright sapphire eyes. The dragon's chest puffed out with pride.

Despite the situation at hand, Chloe found herself smiling. The dead deer had been more than a little disturbing, but her dragon had clearly meant to do something nice for her. She would find a way to be grateful for it.

Reaching up to rub her knuckles over the dragon's nose, she nodded. "It's a lovely present. Well, a thoughtful present anyway. I'm proud of you."

Shadow chirped happily and nuzzled against Chloe's hand. Her heart warmed, which helped to clear her head. Now she stood tall. "If they're waiting for us, and we're waiting for them, I guess there's only one thing we can do. We need to sneak into the mortals' camp."

At that, both Quintus and Ludo straightened up. Mishti, still polishing her sword, also paused to look over.

"You want to sneak into their camp?" Mishti asked. "And then what? March up to Julian and ask what was written on that paper he ate? I'm sure that will go well."

Chloe felt her stomach lurch. Taking a deep breath, she attempted to steady her nerves. "Well, we don't have to be so blunt about it, but I was hoping we could try and talk to him.

At the very least, we can find out if any of the other mortals even know about the note. Maybe Julian didn't tell anyone."

Quintus raised an eyebrow. "You want to go in using glamours, I assume?"

Chloe drew in a slow inhale and forced a smile on her face, even though her insides quivered. Deep down, she knew this plan could go horribly wrong, just like so many of their other plans had. But that wouldn't stop her from hoping. "Yes. Let's glamour ourselves to look like ordinary mortals, and then let's leave some sort of glamours here as well, so it looks like we never left."

In a few hand waves, their faces and clothes all changed to that of ordinary mortals. Around their camp, bushes and trees got glamoured to look like them.

Before long, they traipsed right into the mortals' camp, which looked completely different than the camp they'd had back in Bitter Thorn. They still had tents with long stakes driven into the black soil, but there were no pens for animals. There were no cooking pots or cutting knives. Apparently, these mortals had the same problem that bothered Chloe when she very first stepped foot into Crystalfall.

Food. How was anyone supposed to get food? For her group, they had Ludo's food conjuring magic to help, but these mortals obviously didn't have that. Considering the hollow, sunken eyes before them, food was clearly a problem.

Even stranger, a long golden table with simple gold plates covering it sat at the very center of camp. Portia stood at the head of it with Julian nearby, but her expression was even more displeased than usual.

The other mortals milled about, sometimes glancing at the empty table with the empty plates, but they must have known better than to get too close to their leaders without being asked.

145

Chloe had no such reservations, especially since they were here to get information. She walked right up to a nearby tent and began fiddling with the rich silk fabric in one corner of it. Portia and Julian didn't pay her any attention.

While standing there, she heard Portia whisper to Julian. "Are you sure this is going to work? If it doesn't, we'll have to leave this court to get more food."

The wild look in Julian's eye flashed as he sported a slanted grin. "It will work. I told you, I saw the pixies using this table last night. Why do you think I woke up so many mortals and had them carry it back here?"

Portia's nose wrinkled. "How do you even know it's the table that's magic? Maybe it's the plates."

A strange noise left Julian's throat that didn't quite sound like a chuckle. He reached for one of the plates.

All at once, Chloe's body tensed. She glanced back at the others. It took her a moment to realize Quintus, Mishti, and Ludo all stood nearby, since right now, they looked like ordinary mortals. They looked the same as her, with eyes widening as they leaned forward and peered intently at Julian. What did he mean he saw the pixies *using* the table?

Holding the golden plate carefully in his hands, Julian spoke firmly and clearly. "Apple Egg Pancakes."

Suddenly, a delicious smell filled the air that certainly must have tugged at everyone's hungry bellies. Even more remarkable, right there on Julian's plate was a scrumptious-looking pancake with apple slices baked inside it.

The other mortals stared in awe. Chloe stared in awe.

So this was how people ate in Crystalfall. They didn't get food from the trees or bushes or animals. They got it from magic alone. Her mind whirred with possibilities as another thought struck her hard. Julian—a mortal—had just conjured food. Somehow, this magic table worked even for mortals.

Scrambling over each other, mortals started grabbing plates off the table. Chloe held her breath, fearing that maybe she was wrong about the magic working for any mortal.

But each time a mortal said the name of a dish, that dish suddenly appeared on a plate, hot and steaming and ready to eat.

An array of different dishes appeared—pancakes, bacon, strawberries. Some plates had dishes that clearly came from very different places in the mortal realm—rice, crepes, steamed buns, wrapped meat.

Many of the mortals gasped when the food appeared, even though it had happened several times now. Amazement etched firmly onto their faces.

Considering the snarl on Portia's face, she didn't seem especially excited that Julian's trick had worked. But hunger must have plagued her too because she eventually snatched her own plate and conjured a bundle of plump grapes and a wedge of hard cheese.

Chloe turned to the mortal nearest her, which she was pretty sure was Quintus. In her quietest voice, she whispered, "Crystalfall seems like it was made for mortals. This magic works even for them. They don't even have to ruin the landscape to get food."

For some reason, she naïvely thought that would excite Quintus. Or maybe it would make him thoughtful. She didn't expect the face in front of her to distort into a fierce glower.

He leaned in close, his jaw clenching tight. "Faerie was made for the fae. Mortals do not belong here, even if this magic works for them."

She threw him her nastiest glare and then marched straight up to Julian. If all Quintus was going to do was argue about ridiculous things, then she'd leave him behind and get her own answers. It was time to find out about that clue.

She didn't know how she'd do it, but with someone as unhinged and wild as Julian, she'd be able to sneak it out of him somehow.

18

HOLDING HER BREATH, CHLOE GRABBED Julian's arm and pulled him out of earshot of Portia and the other mortals. Hopefully from this far away, their conversation would remain private.

She could only hope Julian would be so surprised by the action that he didn't notice the person following close behind them. Though the man appeared to be mortal, it was truly Quintus under a glamour.

So far, Julian didn't seem surprised by Chloe's actions. He didn't even seem interested. He just picked at a thread in his coat that suddenly held his complete attention. Maybe she'd been silly to worry, but she knew this next part of the conversation would take delicacy.

Her gaze turned upward as she batted her eyelashes exactly twice. When she clasped her hands behind her back, he appeared as unaffected as ever. But hopefully, a saccharine tone of voice would win him over. "I saw how you fought those fae yesterday. You're always so brave."

She clasped her hands tighter, waiting for his response. He continued to pick at the thread in his coat, not bothering to make eye contact with her. "I don't remember seeing you there."

Her stomach knotted as she forced down a lump in her throat. "I was with the group at the top of the waterfall."

He nodded without speaking.

Apparently, there was no use trying to use her charm against him. He didn't notice it anyway. It would probably be best just to get right to it. "I saw you eat that parchment."

That got his eyebrows to rise. For once, he finally pulled his gaze away from the thread and looked at her.

She turned her expression as innocent as possible. "What was written on that paper? Do you know what those fae and those two mortals are after?"

Tension bubbled in the air between them. Her heart skittered, waiting for his response. She had caught his attention now, but even that didn't seem to ensure she'd get what she wanted.

He said nothing. He didn't even offer a cryptic response or a smidgeon of change in body language. Instead, he simply narrowed his eyes, studying her face as if trying to read her mind. His lips drew into a tight line while the rest of him stayed completely still.

This was going nowhere. She tried again, from a different angle this time. "If you tell me what was on that paper, I can help you. I want to help you."

Was Julian the sort to even be taken by a young woman? After being abused by the fae Ansel for so long, maybe Julian and the other mortals were too empty to care about being noticed.

Julian's demeanor finally changed. The crazed look in his eyes dimmed until he almost looked normal. Slowly, he turned his gaze downward. "I only told one person what was written on that piece of paper."

It lasted for just a flicker of a moment, but he turned and glanced at a young woman eating strawberries and crepes from a golden plate. When he pulled his gaze away from her, he sucked in a sharp breath. Then his gaze turned to Chloe. Was he checking to see if she had noticed his look toward that girl?

Not wanting to let on that she had noticed anything, Chloe widened her eyes. "Who was it? Who did you tell? All three of us can work together if you want."

He glanced back, apparently unable to take his eyes off that same girl. His fingers fidgeted with his shirt. He no longer played with the same loose thread, instead pinching and tugging at different parts of the cloth, though it never truly captured his attention. Pulling his gaze away from her a second time, his throat bobbed with a hard swallow.

With his nerves so blatantly on display, this had to be the time to act. If she could ever get the information out of him, it was now. She just had to put a little bit more pressure on him. But how?

Her body leaned forward, shifting her weight onto the balls of her feet. She parted her lips, hoping the words might come forward once her mouth had opened.

But suddenly, words didn't matter anymore. Maybe they never did.

Flashing his teeth, Julian struck out a fist and pounded it into the stomach of the mortal man standing nearest to him.

In horror, Chloe watched as the man doubled over. Julian's cruelty at punching an unsuspecting mortal was more sinister than she first realized. The mortal wasn't a mortal at all. It was Quintus.

Julian's brute force broke through Quintus's glamour, exposing his true identity. She sucked in a breath, glancing down at her own body. It had only been for a flash, but her own clothes had changed too.

Maybe not all the mortals had seen, but several of them must have. A tilted grin stretched across Julian's face. Too many of his teeth showed as he stepped toward Chloe. "I could smell you the moment you entered our camp."

Gasping, Chloe threw her hands up. From behind her arms, she could still see Julian. His eyes danced with maniacal delight. Even worse, Portia moved closer each moment. Chloe's heart rammed against her chest. "Don't hurt me."

The words sounded pathetic, even to her.

Portia's mouth curled into a cruel smirk. She let out a dark chuckle. Lifting one leg, she drove a heeled shoe straight into the tender flesh of Chloe's chest.

The point of the heel drove into Chloe's skin, drawing blood on impact. Breath rushed out of her lungs. Her feet stumbled. Her body fell backward.

Quintus responded with a low, threatening growl. His shoulders tensed as he lifted his arms to fight.

Nearby, Ludo stepped away from the gathering crowd. His skin had gone pale with fear.

That's when the weapons started to appear. Axes were drawn from belts, bows and arrows pulled from backs. But even the threat of hundreds of mortals couldn't stop Quintus now.

He lunged forward, knocking Portia off her feet. His fists raised to punch her, but a mace with nails coming out of it sliced him across the neck. It only served to slow him, and soon he landed his first blow across Portia's jaw.

Fear tightened Chloe's limbs, her chest. Everything. She glanced back to see Ludo backing away farther. Even Mishti stood at the edge of the crowd. One hand clutched her side as she eyed Portia. Her breaths turned short at the sight of the woman.

None of them were thinking. Chloe couldn't move when fear gripped her tight like this, but at least her mind could spin. Sucking in a short breath, she shot a glare back at Ludo. "Open a door."

If Ludo heard the words, it didn't matter, because a flying dagger soon landed straight in his chest. A heavy breath puffed from his lips as he fell to his knees.

Mishti's eyes went wide. Her hand still held her side as she rushed to Ludo.

Taking a deep breath, Chloe knew she'd now have to convince the most preoccupied one of their group. Her gazed fixed onto Quintus. She spoke with as much determination as she could muster. "There are too many of them. Just open a door and get us out of here."

If an arrow hadn't lodged straight in Quintus's shoulder at that exact moment, it probably would have been impossible to convince him. But the injury had done the trick. He jumped up straight, rammed a heavy kick into Portia's side and then ran toward Chloe.

Two more arrows landed in his skin, one in his back, the other in the back of his leg. Both caused him to gasp, but they didn't slow him down.

Soon, he had reached Chloe and scooped her into his arms. Only then did he wave one hand and open a door. The moment the door opened, Julian seemed to think it was time he joined the fight.

He ripped a spear right out of the hands of a nearby mortal and threw it with near perfect precision. The spear tip landed in Quintus's neck when he was a single step away from the door. A howl tore from Quintus's throat, one that shook the emeralds in the nearby trees.

"Keep going," Chloe urged. "I can heal you once we're safe."

Her heart skipped as she checked over Quintus's shoulders for the others. Relief flooded her veins when she saw both Ludo and Mishti were only a step behind.

Soon, all four of them stepped through the door. In another flash, Quintus closed the door before any of the mortals could step through.

Chloe closed her eyes, only barely registering that Quintus had brought them inside of a room instead of back to their camp on a hill in Crystalfall. Her cheek pressed against his chest, trying to let the heat sink into her. He pulled her closer, though he also winced when he took a step forward.

"Where are we?" Mishti asked. Her voice came out shakier than Chloe had ever heard it.

Instead of answering, Quintus adjusted his grip on Chloe, pulling her even tighter still.

"Is this the Crystalfall Castle?" Ludo asked. "I know you mentioned coming here earlier, but I never thought to ask, how did you get *in* here?"

Chloe could feel when Quintus turned his head. His low voice rumbled in his chest. "What do you mean how did I get in here? Why would you assume there would be difficulty in entering the castle?"

This intrigued Chloe enough to open her eyes.

She caught sight of Ludo blinking with his mouth hung open slightly. "The court was asleep. I thought the castle..." His head tilted as he stared off at a corner of the room they stood inside. "I suppose we watched the court wake up when you found that dagger. The castle must be open to anyone now."

As Chloe narrowed her eyes, she glanced up at Quintus to see if he shared an expression of confusion like her. His expression did seem confused, but pain marred it too much to be certain.

She pressed against his grip, reaching her toes toward the ground. "Set me down. I can heal you now."

He obeyed and immediately slumped into a nearby chair.

Once on her feet, Chloe could see that the four of them stood in the secret study connecting the library to the king's personal quarters. A cold draft in the room sent goosebumps across her skin. The bookshelf against one wall was stuffed with old, musty books and scrolls. Stray books and papers scattered the desk and the floor, mostly due to her earlier search, which had eventually led her to find the king's journal.

Reaching for Quintus's hand, she started healing his injuries. The wound in her chest from Portia's heel still smarted, but considering Quintus and Ludo both had wounds from blades and arrowheads, she'd make sure to heal them before worrying about her own injury. She dealt with Quintus and Ludo and finally went to Mishti, but the young woman still shook her head at the mention of healing.

Giving up on healing Mishti, Chloe sat on the floor and let out a heavy sigh.

The moment she moved away from him, Quintus stood tall, his frame filling the small room. "This is where we will rest."

Though she couldn't explain why, tension slipped under Chloe's skin. Slowly, she lifted her gaze up to him, her brows furrowing as she did. He had a strange look in his eye, one that made her stomach knot with apprehension.

Avoiding her gaze, he stood even taller. "Julian will not tell us what was written on that parchment. He is too dangerous to deal with when so many mortals answer to him, but luckily for us, he told one other mortal about the clue." Quintus turned, bringing his face even farther out of Chloe's sight. "We will capture that mortal and force her to tell us what she knows."

The comfort Chloe had felt at being safe in Quintus's arms got smashed to bits in that single declaration. She jumped to her feet, jabbing a pointer finger in his face. "You want to torture an innocent mortal girl? Is that what you're proposing?"

His face turned stoic as he lifted his chin into the air. "I am prepared to do whatever it takes to find all the pieces of the Crystalfall crown. We all know the dagger and key are not enough."

Her entire body trembled as she tried to force words to her lips. "How could you possibly…" She had to clench her teeth together just to keep herself from spewing out words she'd regret. "If you want to capture and torture someone, capture Julian, not that mortal girl."

"I just said Julian is too difficult to deal with right now." Quintus jerked his head toward her, flashing his teeth as he did. "Do not forget, this court is my home."

The words rang out, filling the entire room and drowning out every other sound.

He hadn't claimed he was the rightful leader of Crystalfall, but that statement was the closest he'd ever gotten to it. He turned away, his jaw flexing as he did. "I will do whatever it takes to protect my home, including capturing a mortal."

"Enough." Mishti dragged her feet across the worn rug covering the floor until she stood between the two of them. "You two are no longer allowed to speak until after all of us have gotten some rest."

Dropping her head into one hand, Mishti gestured vaguely toward the floor. "Rest."

Even though she hadn't been addressing him directly, Ludo happily dropped to the ground and conjured a thin blanket to cover himself.

Chloe threw a sharp glare at Quintus, though she kept her mouth shut.

He returned the glare with one of his own, but he also reached into his magical pocket and pulled out a sleeping mat and blanket for her.

Mishti had already collapsed into a corner, breathing heavily. As long as it stayed quiet, sleep would overtake her soon.

Anger had a firm grip on Chloe's chest, but maybe some sleep would do her good. And even if it didn't do that, it would at least give her time to think of more scathing arguments to fling at Quintus.

They still had to figure out the next clue, but whatever happened, Chloe would absolutely not let them touch that mortal girl.

19

SLEEP ENVELOPED CHLOE'S MIND, CLINGING tight even as someone shook her shoulders. She moaned, trying to push away the arms on her. That only turned the arms more insistent. It took great effort to crawl out of her sluggish state and force open one eyelid.

Quintus leaned over her, his hands still tight on her shoulders. Relief entered his features, but another expression took over until the relief had vanished entirely. Was he afraid that she had awoken? That didn't make any sense, since he had been the one to shake her out of her slumber. But his eyes certainly seemed to quiver with fear.

"We need your help." He gulped and took her hand, pulling her upright. "Come with me."

Her body toppled over as soon as he tried to take a step forward. Sleep still hung heavy in her eyes as she glanced back. "I need…" Her sentence stopped short in a long yawn.

"Come on." He tugged her forward again, which forced her to hop and stumble. His head tilted to the side. "What…"

"My foot." She gestured at her wooden foot sitting neatly inside her laced boot.

Instead of taking the few steps back to her bed and letting her attach the foot, he lifted her into his arms. "That will take too long. We must hurry."

He rushed out the door of the study and into the library. Chloe could just make out Mishti lifting her head from her own sleeping mat. The young woman shook her head, glancing around the study and then at Quintus carrying Chloe. Mishti raised an eyebrow questioningly, but Chloe couldn't respond with a shrug or explanation or anything. Right at that moment, Quintus turned a corner, putting Mishti out of sight.

Stinging itched in the center of Chloe's chest. She bounced in Quintus's arms as he ran through the castle hallways, which tugged and stretched at the pain. Her vision blurred as she tried to blink the last of the sleep from her eyes. Why did her chest feel sore?

Shifting in Quintus's arms, sharp memories from the night before edged into her mind. How could she forget? Portia had driven a heeled shoe into Chloe's chest, breaking the skin on contact. And then, in Chloe's frantic haste to heal everyone else, she had forgotten to take care of her own injury.

A groan drifted from her mouth.

Quintus's gaze stayed fixated on the hallway ahead. "I will go back and get your foot later. We have to hurry now, or it will be too late."

Her nose wrinkled at his lack of concern for her. That served as the perfect reminder. She was still angry with Quintus. Did she dare attempt to touch his skin now in order to heal herself?

159

And on that note, how could he so brazenly force her to help with some unexplained thing before they had resolved their fight?

Fury churned in her belly, clenching her fingers into fists. The tattoos under her right eye tingled just then, which only tensed her fists even more.

It wasn't fair that she needed Quintus to use her magic. She understood why Faerie itself placed a block on her magic, considering the first mortal to have magic used it to destroy the entire Court of Crystalfall. Chloe had never been perfect. She respected that the block kept her from going wild with magic the way that mortal had.

But *why* did her magic have to rely on Quintus? Why couldn't she have grabbed a simple rock like she had intended when she very first did the ritual to get her magic? It seemed like a morbid trick from Faerie itself that she had bonded with the fae she loved and sometimes hated more than anyone else in all the realms.

Life in Faerie would have been much simpler if she and Quintus had never been bonded at all. Why hadn't he let her fasten on her wooden foot first anyway? Although… This bouncing in his muscular arms and being close to his pounding heart made it difficult to stay angry.

In fact, she couldn't even remember why she had gotten angry with him in the first place.

But then it hit her like a boulder. Dread rushed through her so fast, her body went rigid. The mortal girl. Quintus had wanted to capture and torture that mortal girl to find out the next clue.

And now he had just awoken her from a very deep slumber, said they didn't even have time to put on her foot, and rushed her quickly through the castle. Too quickly.

Her eyes flew open, sleep no longer claiming any part of her consciousness. She sat up straight—as much as she could while in Quintus's arms—and looked him dead in the eye. "What did you do?"

His gaze jumped to hers for a fraction of a second. After that, he trained his gaze forward, avoiding eye contact at all costs.

At least they had reached the doors of the castle now. He pushed through them, entering the crisp early morning air of Crystalfall. The sky had turned light gray along the horizon, proving day had not quite dawned.

Chloe's jaw clenched tight. She needed to scan the surrounding area, but the dread in her gut told her not to.

Despite the dread, she forced herself to glance around. Her gaze found Ludo first. He stood wringing his hands in front of himself, his eyes twitching and his head shaking. No matter how he moved his head, he took great pains to avoid looking at a certain spot on the ground.

Naturally, that spot was exactly where Chloe's gaze leapt next.

The mortal young woman lay still on the ground. Her chest was completely still, not rising or falling from any breaths. The sight felt like a knife in Chloe's heart.

Letting out a scream, she shoved herself free from Quintus's arms. It only took one step to realize she had forgotten her foot once again. After tripping over herself, she collapsed into a heap on the black soil.

Quintus reached out, attempting to help her up. She clenched her jaw and hissed at him through her teeth. He wisely took a step back.

Gathering her skirts into one hand, she then crawled on her elbows and knees over to the mortal girl. Through every

161

shaky movement, one question left her mouth and pierced the air. "What have you done?"

She'd never forgive him for this. How could she?

Her knees dragged across the soil. Tears pricked at her eyes. By the time she reached the young girl, Chloe's chin trembled.

The girl appeared calm, peaceful. Like she was simply resting. Such a face did not bode well for the two fae who had brought her here.

Chloe whipped her head toward Ludo, knowing he'd be the first to speak without thinking.

"I forgot." The words erupted from Ludo's mouth in a rush. He immediately clamped his mouth shut and gulped twice. When he opened his mouth again, he spoke in a quavering voice. "I forgot how fragile mortals are."

Rage burned at the back of her throat, fed by the tears welling in her eyes. "*You* did this?"

Ludo's entire frame shook as the pointed a finger at Quintus. "He helped me capture her."

With nostrils flaring and heat creeping up her neck, Chloe lifted a weapon from the ground. She tightened her fingers around the handle until her knuckles had turned white. "This is *your* axe."

He stepped back, wincing hard. "But Quintus did not stop me. We both made this mistake."

The rage at the back of her throat sparked into a fire that burned through her insides. Slowly, carefully, her gaze turned to Quintus.

His body tilted like he couldn't decide whether to stand, to sit, or to collapse into a heap. His face winced. His fingers twitched. He must have known. He must have known she'd never forgive him for this.

After a hard swallow, his shaking hand gestured toward the girl. "You can heal her, right? You can heal anyone."

Letting out a dark chuckle, Chloe lifted her leg that ended just above what should have been her ankle. "I couldn't regrow my foot though, could I? Mortals can only endure so much."

His knees knocked together as he took a step forward. He gestured toward the girl more insistently. "You can heal her. We brought her to the castle so you would be nearby. So you could fix any damage we did."

The first tear slipped down Chloe's burning cheek. Her abdomen tightened when she forced herself to look at the girl again. The peaceful look on the girl's face was marred only by the blood surrounding her body.

Just then, Mishti came rushing out from the castle doors. She held up Chloe's booted wooden foot and her other boot. She opened her mouth and spoke in a voice that was half a yawn. "I brought your…"

The yawn stopped abruptly, probably because she had sensed the energy in the air. Her gaze trailed over the scene ahead and then her face hardened like ice. She glanced down at the mortal girl. Clenching her teeth together, she glared at Ludo. "*You.*"

His body language had given him away. Or maybe she just assumed his lack of emotions made him the only one capable of this atrocity. Either way, Ludo flinched at the accusation. "It was not supposed to be like this. We just wanted to get the information we needed." He took a step back and waved a hand at Chloe. "She is going to heal the girl. Go on. What are you waiting for?"

But of course, Chloe still hadn't bothered reaching out for Quintus's hand. It didn't take much of an examination to see what had happened.

The axe had done the damage. Ludo had sliced into a single vein, probably hoping to extract more information the deeper he sliced. But he had indeed forgotten how fragile mortals were compared to fae. Unknowingly, he had sliced right into a vein that had caused death within only a few seconds.

Closing her eyes, Chloe reached for the mortal girl's hand. Checking the pulse in her wrist, she confirmed what she already knew. The girl was dead. Beyond healing. She had died long before Chloe had ever made it outside the castle.

It didn't mean much now, but it brought her some comfort to know the girl had not suffered, at least. There would have been some pain, but death had closed in only a few moments later.

Icy tears slid down Chloe's scorching cheeks. Her jaw ached from clenching it so tight. Hand shaking, she placed it onto the girl's shoulder. Maybe the girl was already dead, but Chloe made a promise to her anyway. A vow.

This would not go unpunished.

In a flash, the rage boiling and burning in her belly turned to something steady and sure. The heat of it still itched at her skin, squeezed at her heart, but it also shifted into a strange calm.

It became all too clear what she must do. After a few simple lies, this wrong would be righted. And Quintus and Ludo would pay.

20

CALM FUELED BY FURY DIRECTED Chloe as she fastened on her wooden foot and then put on her other boot. She ordered Quintus to open a door to the black caves.

He did open a door, but when they stepped through it, she found they still had a bit of a walk before they'd reach their destination. Perhaps Quintus thought the added distance would serve to pacify her before they reached the caves. He thought wrong.

Her feet trailed across pearlescent pebbles and black soil. Her heart beat steadily, giving her even breaths and relaxed steps. The strange, rage-induced calm still overtook her, but the energy in the air had turned far more sour. It pricked at her skin, turning every face around her into a worried mess.

Quintus, Mishti, and Ludo followed her, but none seemed to know what to do with themselves.

Quintus stumbled after Chloe, never quite catching up to her completely. His hands fumbled for his pockets and then through his hair. He kept trying to catch her eye, but she wouldn't look at his face. That only sped up the movement of his fidgeting fingers. "Chloe."

She ignored him and kept walking, restraint still resonating through every part of her.

"Where are we going?" Ludo's voice came out timid.

She kept walking.

Daring to reach out, Quintus touched her shoulder. His hand drew back at once, as if he had touched something sharp. Still, he tried to catch her eye. "Say something, Chloe. Say anything."

With her entire body as calm as a leaf in a gentle wind, a lie came easily to her lips. "We are going to get an ingredient."

From behind, Mishti increased her speed until she had nearly reached Chloe's other side. The young woman's dark eyes opened wide. "But…she's dead. Isn't she dead?"

Chloe locked eyes with Mishti for a split second. Neither of them spoke. No explanation was given. In that short moment, Mishti seemed to understand. She didn't know where they were going or why, but she seemed to understand this was not the time for questions.

Lifting her chin high, Chloe spoke to the air in front of her. "The ingredient is near the crystal caves."

Quintus let out a sigh of relief that relaxed his shoulders. "I knew you could heal her." He ran one hand through his hair, messing up the curls so they stuck out haphazardly. He didn't seem to notice. Instead, he just sighed again. "I got you as soon as we realized it had gone too far. We knew you would be able to heal her."

The words stung Chloe's skin. They pricked at it, prodded, and then dug down and burrowed themselves into her bones. In that position, they writhed and wormed through her. How could he pretend to be innocent? He must know this mistake was too much. The calm that had held her so easily was starting to crack. She took in a slow and steady breath just to keep herself walking.

They had nearly reached the crystal caves. She only had to hold on for a little longer.

Quintus must have sensed the change in her. His head whipped toward her. She could feel his gaze boring into her skin, aching for her to look his way.

She did not. If she said anything now, she'd fall apart before they ever got to the caves. Just a little farther.

Still staring, he reached one hand toward her, but he wisely stopped it before it could touch her arm. When he parted his lips, she got the urge to smack him upside the head before he could say anything.

But then he spoke in a whisper so quiet, not even Mishti would be able to hear it. These words were for Chloe and her alone. He spoke slowly, arduously, and achingly. "I am sor—"

And then he stopped. He stopped himself before he could truly apologize. Even if he hadn't spoken the words, she could tell he had wanted to say *sorry*. She could feel it through their bond. But this moment only proved that he was fae through and through.

Even after killing an innocent mortal girl, even after making a mistake he must have known Chloe wouldn't forgive him for, even then, he still couldn't say it. He couldn't say the words that would make him owe Chloe a favor.

A part of her wanted to chuckle. To sweep away the hurt that came from knowing he didn't trust her enough to even apologize. To trust her enough to be indebted to her. But it was good. It would just make this next part even easier.

They rounded a corner, and the crystal caves came into sight. Their black walls twinkled with golden glints and pearlescent pebbles. Golden and emerald trees stretched high just outside the cave entrance. The gentle roar of the nearby sparkling waterfall filled the air. Here at the entrance to the crystal caves, the scent of vanilla and lilacs wasn't as prominent, but it still danced on the gentle breeze.

This court had beauty like none of the other Faerie courts. It had magic that worked for mortals as well as fae. This court was special, and she would do everything in her power to take advantage of its special nature.

When they were only a few steps away from the caves, Quintus stared at her harder than ever. "Chloe." He said it slow, methodical, wanting.

She'd held it together so far, but the crack in her calm demeanor shattered with that one word. Her jaw clenched tight as she slammed her hands onto her hips.

She whirled around, finally staring Quintus right in the eyes.

At first, delight overtook his features, probably just happy she had finally acknowledged his presence. But then he glanced over her, noting her hands on her hips and the tightness of her jaw. Now he gulped.

Her eyebrows raised. "If you had bothered talking to me *before* you left this morning, you would have realized one very important thing."

He took a small step back, toward the black caves. He tugged at the open collar of his emerald-green vest. "What?"

Dried tears itched on her cheeks, making it easy to sharpen her gaze. "That girl knew nothing."

Quintus's eyes grew wide, not just surprised, not just fearful: horrified. The words darkened his gaze and turned his face slack. But then he shook his head, harder with each word. "No. I saw Julian when he spoke to you. He said he told only one other person what was on that note, and then he looked at that girl. I saw him look at her twice, and he did it subtly, like he did not want us to notice."

Chloe trembled as rage thrummed through her body, slowly overtaking every inch of it. Emotions boiled in her gut, a seething cauldron of pure fury that threatened to explode out of her at any second. Never before had she experienced such an all-consuming anger.

Clenching her jaw tighter, she stabbed him with a pointed glare. "Yes, and what happened immediately after Julian looked at that girl?"

The sight of her anger must have kept Quintus from thinking clearly. He kept staring at her face, then tugging at his collar. He even pulled out his golden and emerald dagger, running his finger over the hilt while he tried to form words. "After Julian looked at that girl, he…" Quintus shook his head. "He…"

Chloe stepped toward him, her face filling with livid heat. "He punched you in the gut so unexpectedly that you lost control of your glamour."

Quintus's mouth fell open. Truth hadn't sunk all the way in yet, but it would come soon. And it would hurt.

Chloe dropped her hands to her sides, leaning forward. "Julian knew who we were from the moment I walked up to him. He wasn't looking at that girl subtly, hoping we wouldn't notice. He was distracting us, so his punch would be unexpected enough to force you to lose control of your glamour."

"But…" The word left Quintus's lips lonely and aching for more words to join. None did.

Scoffing, she turned away. "Julian tricked you. That girl knew nothing."

Quintus swallowed hard. "No. He must have… Part of it had to be true. Part of…"

For confirmation, Chloe glanced back at Mishti and raised her eyebrows questioningly.

Mishti caught the gaze and then looked down at her booted feet. "Chloe's right. Julian doesn't tell his secrets to anyone. Even Portia only knows some of them. But if there's one thing he *is* good at, it's a misdirect."

Dragging both hands down the sides of his face, Quintus groaned. He shook his head, probably trying to shake the words from his mind. He spoke in a tight whisper. "What have we done?"

All at once he sucked in a sharp breath and turned to Chloe. "But you can heal her, right? You said we needed an ingredient, which must be so you could heal her."

Silence met his question, an answer all on its own. It roared even louder than the rushing waves of the nearby waterfall. Mounting pressure told her the moment had come for her to act. It would hurt, but it had to be done.

Repeating those words in her head provided little comfort. Instead, she drew courage from the image of that mortal girl on the ground. The dead mortal girl. While Quintus tried to catch her eye, she kept her gazed trained on the pretty blades of jade grass just outside the entrance to the black caves.

Tingling pricked at Chloe's fingertips. She had to do this for the mortal girl. She had to do it for Mishti and the other mortals who were simply innocent victims in all of this. They needed this.

She swallowed hard and took a step forward. One quick glance made her aware of every person. At some point, Ludo had retrieved his new blue scarf from his pocket. He had the scarf wrapped around his neck and kept fiddling with the pattern in the center of it.

Quintus stood near Ludo, only a few steps away from the crystal caves.

And just where she needed to be, Mishti stood a few steps behind Chloe.

Taking another step forward, Chloe gestured toward the caves. "The ingredient I need is on the other side of the caves back in Bitter Thorn."

No one moved.

She gestured more insistently, staring at both Quintus and Ludo before speaking again. "Just through there. Go on."

Still picking at the pattern in his scarf, Ludo stepped into the caves. A deep frown etched across Quintus's features. He kept trying to catch Chloe's eye. His fingers stretched out, as if he wanted to touch her but didn't know how she'd react.

Chloe stepped forward. But then Mishti started moving, even faster than Chloe did. Chloe had to grab the young woman by the wrist to keep her from advancing any further.

Quintus had already entered the cave, but the moment Chloe blocked Mishti, his eyes widened with alarm. At the same moment, the star tattoos on Chloe's face itched, as if they were alive. Their bond had grown stronger again, even stronger than it had been when she awoke that morning. But with that bond came an undesired consequence. Quintus could sense that something was wrong. He could feel it.

If she ever needed a distraction, she needed it now. Wincing, she touched the wound in her chest. It stung, but her mind whirred too much to care right now. Still, she flooded her voice with the slightest whine. "I never did heal the wound Portia left in my chest. I got too distracted last night with so many other injuries to heal."

Quintus threw his hand toward her, holding it out for her to take. The confusion in his eyes erased, replaced with concern, duty. For the first time that morning, he seemed grateful to do something right.

She took his hand willingly, once more checking the position of every person. Ludo and Quintus stood just inside the cave. Chloe and Mishti stood just outside it in Crystalfall. Briefly closing her eyes, Chloe confirmed that Shadow also rested within Crystalfall.

Nodding to herself, Chloe squeezed Quintus's hand. Magic burst from her fingertips, coming forth when she called it. Golden magic swirled out, filling the space between them.

Her timing had to be just right. She needed to touch Quintus in order to use her magic, but if she formed it while touching him, it should still last even after she let go.

His eyes narrowed, head tilting to the side. He must have realized this magic looked nothing like her usual healing magic. He must have realized something entirely different was happening.

But if he did realize exactly what she was doing, he realized it too late.

Magic continued to swirl until a golden barrier formed right across the cave entrance. She kept her hand against his until the last possible moment, and then she pulled away. And just like she had intended, a magical barrier shined between them.

When she touched it, the magic turned a brighter gold, preventing her from moving her hand any deeper into the cave.

She had done it, then. She had locked the Court of Crystalfall once again.

Quintus stared, understanding not quite dawning. But it would soon enough, and she could only imagine how he would react once he realized he had just been locked out of the very court he had only just discovered.

21

CHLOE WAS MORE CERTAIN THAN ever that she had done the right thing. But waiting for the realization to hit Quintus stung at her insides. She swallowed, afraid to see how his face would change but also afraid to walk away.

Realization slowly crept over his features. He reached out one hand, cautiously touching the barrier. Golden light glowed around his fingertip, which then spread until the entire barrier glowed. As soon as he took his hand away, the golden light disappeared.

Even though they couldn't see the barrier anymore, it was still there.

Quintus threw his hand out faster, ramming it against the barrier. Despite the speed and strength of that blow, the barrier stopped him just as completely as it had before. Once again, the golden light glowed at the spot he touched.

Confusion crinkled his forehead. He glanced between her and the barrier and then back to her again. His brow furrowed deeper, and his jaw flexed. Confusion melted away to anger, but he managed to hold it back.

Tipping up an eyebrow, he looked straight at her. "I understand why…" He trailed off and gestured toward the cave entrance. "But I have learned my lesson. Now, unlock the barrier and let me back in."

Her arms folded in front of her chest. "I can't unlock it without magic."

His nose twitched as the words settled in. He closed his eyes for an extra-long moment. He shook his head and then he shook it again. "Touch me then. Touch me so you can use your magic to unlock the barrier."

Pressing his palm against the barrier, he opened his eyes expectantly. She let out a sigh and pressed her own palm against the barrier across from his. The two hands had less than a fingernail's width of space between them, but it was enough.

He huffed and tried to push harder against the barrier. The magic was too strong. It kept him back, no matter how he shoved and tried to angle his hand. Now he realized what Chloe already knew. The barrier would not allow them to touch. And if they couldn't touch, she couldn't use magic.

Heat rose into his neck in splotches. He stepped back from the barrier, clenching both his hands into fists. "What have you done?"

She held her chin higher, refusing to meet his eye. "I did what I had to do to protect the mortals."

"No!" He banged both fists against the barrier, his hair whipping back from the effort. "This is my home." His voice broke as he lowered his hands. "I finally found the place where I belong. You cannot lock me out."

A lump lodged in her throat, so thick it made it difficult to breathe. She had to turn away just so she wouldn't have to look at the glassy tears he tried to blink from his eyes.

Attempting to swallow the lump in her throat. She tried a second time anyway. And then she folded her arms back over her chest. "This court belongs to the mortals now. The barrier will let mortals inside, but it will not let them out. And fae cannot pass through the barrier in either direction."

Ludo had stepped forward now. A truly horrified expression etched across his features as he tried to reach through the barrier. When the magic stopped him, he sucked in a breath. "But my answers are in Crystalfall. The token is probably there."

Quintus had dropped his head into his hands. He kept shaking his head back and forth and digging his fingers deeper into his hair. But then, in a flash, he looked up. His mouth dropped open as a puff of air escaped his mouth, like he had just thought of an idea.

He had dark circles under his eyes, which made him look a little crazy as he lifted one hand. "Why am I so worried about a barrier? A barrier will not stop me now that I know the court exists."

His hand whirled in a circle and opened a door. He chuckled at its appearance, but it was a crazed sort of chuckle.

Chloe reached for her dress, pinching an edge of it between her fingers and thumb. She held her breath as she watched. Waited. She had thought of this. She had imbued magic into the barrier to prevent this. But what if she had done it wrong?

Throwing his head back, Quintus stepped into the door with a gait that looked half swagger, half stumble. He certainly wanted to believe he could open a door into Crystalfall.

But as soon as he disappeared through the door, he stepped right back out of it in exactly the same place he had started. Chloe's magic had stopped him from even opening a door into the court.

His eyes opened wide as he took in his surroundings. He gulped hard, realizing all too soon that even a door couldn't help him. Whirling around, he crashed both forearms against the barrier. A guttural scream erupted from the back of his throat.

"You cannot do this. You cannot lock me out of my own court."

She had to turn away from the barrier completely, unable to bear the sight of Quintus. Closing her eyes, she let out a sigh. "Since mortals are such a scourge to Faerie, we finally have a safe place where we cannot bother you fae. And more importantly, you cannot bother us."

Her feet stepped forward then, away from the barrier, away from the caves. Away from Quintus.

He let out another feral scream. Ludo joined, switching between shouting curses and begging for mercy.

But it was too late now. Even if she wanted to, there was nothing she could do. The barrier prevented her from touching Quintus, and if she couldn't touch Quintus, she couldn't do the magic necessary to unlock the barrier.

She had done it that way on purpose to be certain she wouldn't change her mind after seeing aches and tears and panic in Quintus's eyes. Now it was too late to do anything.

For the first time since Faerie began, the mortals and fae were finally separated. Her footsteps fell heavy on the black soil. Mishti followed her, not saying a word.

It occurred to Chloe that it might take them all day to get back to the castle now. They couldn't use doors anymore. And the stinging wound in her chest couldn't be healed with magic either. Her nose wrinkled at the thought of it. She should have healed herself before she locked Quintus out.

Shaking that thought away, Chloe focused on the castle again. She was an apothecary, wasn't she? Just because she couldn't use magic to heal didn't mean she couldn't heal. She'd just have to go back to doing it the slow way instead of the fast way.

At her side, Mishti stomped in silence. Chloe hadn't been expecting the young woman to praise her or anything, but she hadn't been expecting this silence either.

Mishti's face hardened even deeper as she marched ahead. "You will never be able to see your sister again. You'll never be able to see either of them."

The words cut into Chloe, driving a deeper crevice into her already breaking heart. "I know." She brushed a finger under her eye, catching a tear before it could slide down her cheek. She swallowed. "Sometimes doing the right thing requires sacrifice."

A noise left Mishti's mouth that sounded like disapproval. The young woman kept her mouth shut, though. She kept walking with a hardened expression and hands stiff at her sides.

Since Chloe had just locked out their only other companions, it wouldn't do to start this new life in a silent argument with her other companion. Her only companion. For now, her only friend in the world. Letting out a slow breath, Chloe turned and looked more pointedly at the young woman. "Out with it. I know you're thinking something. Just say it."

Mishti needed no more provocation. "Maybe Faerie would be better if mortals and fae found a way to live in harmony instead of being separated forever."

Chloe let out a scoff so disbelieving that it almost sounded like a snort. "I'm sure it would be better. And I'm sure I'd fight better if fear didn't immobilize my body whenever I was near a battle. I'm certain I'd run better if I still had both my feet. But none of that matters. Just because something would be better doesn't mean it's possible."

Mishti narrowed her eyes, letting the words sink in. After a moment, she nodded. She didn't agree with Chloe's actions. It was just a guess, but a pretty informed guess based on the clear body language Mishti showed. But even if Mishti didn't agree, she must have realized it was too late to change anything.

What was done was done. Their only choice was to move forward.

Stopping on the path, she tilted her head toward the landscape around them. "There's no point in going after the rest of the crown pieces now."

Chloe nodded, biting her bottom lip. "Yes, I know. I made sure Quintus still had the dagger before I locked him out. I'm pretty sure he has the key too. And since the last two pieces of the crown are hidden here in Crystalfall somewhere, I don't think the crown will ever be restored."

Mishti raised an eyebrow. "You wanted it that way?"

Running a hand over her skirt to smooth a wrinkle, Chloe exhaled. "I don't care what Quintus and Ludo said. I'm afraid that a mortal might gain power if he or she wears a crown. I don't know if any mortal is honorable enough for that responsibility."

Mishti seemed to understand. But her head tilted even more to the side. Something in her expression sent tension into the air. "If we aren't going to go after the crown pieces, then what are we supposed to do now?"

What indeed. Chloe wrapped her arms around her stomach, hugging them tight against herself. Searching for clues and a broken crown had been an exciting quest, to be sure. But now, an even greater one was about to begin.

PRESSING HER LIPS TOGETHER, CHLOE tried to find some courage from deep inside her. The consequences of locking out the fae had already started to weigh on her, but she did her best to think positively.

"We need to join the other mortals, band with them to defeat Portia and Julian, and then we can..." She bit her bottom lip. "Then we can just live. The mortals will finally have peace."

Mishti raised a single eyebrow. "You're assuming all the other mortals want Portia and Julian defeated."

"You think they don't?" Fear wriggled into Chloe's belly.

Shrugging, Mishti dug her toe in the dirt. "I have no idea what the others want. We never had much chance to befriend each other while living with Ansel. And after we were freed, everyone feared me because of how Portia used me. I was an enforcer, not a friend. The only person I ever really connected with was…" She gulped and looked down at her walking feet. "Mila."

An ache stung through Chloe's throat. Mila had been killed by Portia not so long ago. Mishti had Chloe now, but maybe she feared getting to close to someone since the last person she got close to died.

Swallowing hard, Chloe hooked her arm around Mishti's. She attempted a smile, but recent events made it impossible. "We'll figure this out. I know it's going to be hard, but freedom is so close. Without any fae to worry about, we only have to focus on one thing. Getting rid of Portia and Julian. For now, let's go back to the castle and gather our things. Then we can start making a plan."

Only a few steps down the path, a new problem bloomed. Chloe's stomach growled with hunger. It hadn't been too loud, but Mishti walked close enough to hear it. The young woman glanced at Chloe's stomach and then she looked up at Chloe's face.

The same thought must have occurred to her that also occurred to Chloe. How were they supposed to get food? Ludo had been conjuring all their meals, but they obviously didn't have that option anymore.

Crystalfall's food magic worked as well for mortals as it did for fae, but it still required that they have one of those tables. But Chloe and Mishti couldn't enter the mortals' camp without glamours. And no magic meant no glamours.

The wound in her chest itched at that exact moment. Her leather bag filled with apothecary supplies still sat back at the castle. She gritted her teeth against the pain, doing her best to ignore it. Traveling would take much longer now that they couldn't use doors. And what if she didn't have enough supplies in her bag anyway? She hadn't been paying attention to supply levels since she'd been using magic to heal everything. But now she had no magic.

Her gaze swept across the landscape ahead of them. The glittering jewels looked as lovely and sparkling as they always did. They were also completely useless. Jade grass strands couldn't fight infection. Rose quartz berries couldn't help to form a poultice. If she ran out of supplies, how was she supposed to get more?

The growling in Chloe's stomach didn't improve as they marched on. At least Mishti was kind enough to ignore it. The loud grumbles rang through the air, making Chloe grimace each time. Whatever they did, they really needed to get rid of Portia and Julian as soon as possible or Chloe might starve first.

Starting up a hill of jade grass and amethyst flowers, a familiar sound tainted the air. Jingling bells. Chloe's stomach twisted as memories of the glowing lights that tried to lead her to her death filled her mind.

Mishti's hand immediately wrapped around the hilt of her sword. She continued but at a slower pace than before. With each step, her eyes scanned the area. When they neared the top of the hill, she directed Chloe to hide behind a bush where she joined a moment later.

Through the emerald leaves and obsidian branches of the bush, they looked down the hill into a meadow. Dozens of tiny, winged creatures flitted about. They looked just like the high fae with pointed ears and stunning features, except these creatures stood no taller than the length of a forearm. Just like the high fae, their skin colors ranged from dark to light, with hair and facial features as varied as in the mortal realm.

They wore clothing made of the same glittering gems that filled the landscape. Dresses of diamonds, coats of sapphire, tunics of ruby, and many other stunning outfits covered the little creatures. Their golden wings gave off the sound of jingling bells each time they flew. Laughter joined the bell chimes.

Despite their laughter and twinkling appearance, Chloe gulped. These creatures may have seemed tiny and innocent, but they had already tried to kill her and her friends. These were not friendly helpful creatures, but mischievous tricksters.

Showing off this mischievous nature, many of the pixies snatched jeweled berries from the bushes and threw them at each other. Magic must have helped to propel the gems because each time a pixie got hit, it would jolt and lose control of its wings and nearly crash into the ground. The creatures always gained control again just before they touched the ground, but the closer a pixie got to the ground, the more the others cheered for the one who had thrown the berry. That must have been the game. To see who could throw hard enough to get a fellow pixie closest to the ground.

Chloe wrinkled her nose. "How barbaric."

Mishti opened her mouth to respond, but she never got the chance. Chloe had forgotten about the hearing ability of fae creatures.

A flurry of pixies swarmed in around Chloe and Mishti. Their wings chimed as they pinched and poked at the two young women.

"Mortals, mortals, we found two mortals," the pixies sang. Tugging on Chloe's blonde hair, they pulled her into the meadow. Other pixies tugged Mishti's braid and clothing until she stood in the meadow too.

Chloe tried to bat the little faeries away, though she failed miserably. The creatures just flew over or under her hands, pinching her skin in retaliation. "Leave us be. We weren't bothering you, now just let us go."

Tiny pixie laughs rang through the air, their antics growing wilder by the moment. Even Mishti got frustrated. She drew a dagger and tried to use the flat side of it to swat the creatures away, but they all flew too fast.

One of the pixies flew up to Chloe's nose and blew a cloud of glittering dust into her face, causing her to sneeze and blink in surprise. The creature laughed and threw more dust into the air above until it drifted down on everyone like a waterfall of glitter.

"What is this?" A pixie wearing a dress made of amethysts flew into the meadow. Her little face scrunched at Chloe and Mishti, thought it wasn't clear if it was because of their presence or their mistreatment.

The other pixies froze in place and then immediately swarmed around the pixie in the amethyst dress. "Plumia," they called out in delight.

Their bell-like wings seemed a lot more enchanting now they had stopped bothering Chloe and Mishti. Chloe cast a subtle glance toward the hill they had come down to get here. Could they sneak away while the creatures were preoccupied with this new pixie?

"Why are you tormenting these mortals?" Plumia said in a surprisingly stern voice for such a tiny creature.

The other pixies covered their shocked open mouths, flitting away from her. "But mortals are awful creatures," a pixie with dark skin and moss-like hair said.

While nodding, another pixie—this one wearing pearls in her black hair—flew forward. "Remember how mortals stole our golden table?"

Plumia shot a hand upward, holding the palm out and rigid. The other pixies went silent at once, most of them hovering a little lower too. Shaking her head, Plumia continued. "Not all mortals are awful. Some have honor."

Chloe had just started sliding to the side, hoping to get to the hill without the pixies noticing. But hearing Plumia's words, Chloe's head immediately jerked back toward the amethyst-wearing pixie. For a fae to describe honor in such a way, it didn't feel natural.

Her head tilted at the tiny creature. "Have you met a mortal who had honor?"

Plumia shifted her gaze toward Chloe, and even flew a little closer to her too. And then the pixie stared off into nothing, her eyes narrowing to smaller and smaller slits. All around her, the dozens of other pixies in the air did exactly the same thing.

The look immediately reminded her of Ludo, who had often worn the expression while trying to remember something. After a few moments, the pixie shook her head, as if giving up. Instead of answering, she flew closer and pinched her mouth into a knot. "Who are you? Are you not one of the mortals we tried to trick into the ravine?"

Chloe blinked at that, taking a step back. Had Plumia been one of the bright lights that tried to kill her? She already knew the lights were pixies, but she hadn't expected this creature talking about honor to be one of them.

If the pixie wanted to answer a question with a question, then Chloe would do the same. Her eyebrows lifted. "Were you here before this court got destroyed? Do you know who the king of Crystalfall was?"

Plumia's head tilted to the side. All around her, the other pixies did the same. After a moment, the creatures started turning to each other with questioning gazes.

Turning toward the nearest pixie, Plumia raised an eyebrow. "Before. Was there a before?"

The pixies fluttered their jingling wings and flitted around in erratic jumps and curlicues. It seemed to come out of nowhere, but maybe this was a pixie's way of pacing while thinking.

"I do not remember a before," one pixie said.

"It feels like there was a before. Can you feel it?" another pixie asked his friend.

"I feel it. I feel the before."

"But why can we not remember it?"

Plumia pressed her eyebrows together, her expression turning more confused the more the other pixies spoke. When she lifted her hand, once again, they immediately went silent. She grew even more serious as her gaze shifted yet again. She didn't turn to Chloe. This time, she looked straight at Mishti. "Do you know what happened to our memories?"

A look of discomfort contorted across Mishti's features. She tucked one foot behind her ankle and rubbed it up and down the back of her leg. The stone-like hardness that usually covered her face had turned soft. More open. "I don't know what happened to them." She swallowed. "But I know you're not the only ones with lost memories."

Nodding once, Plumia flew back. The pixies around her wore the same grave face, likely contemplating how much those lost memories might contain.

Mishti loosened her grip on her sword, letting her braid swing freely as she glanced around the meadow. "How do you eat without your table? Do pixies have some other magic that allows you to conjure food?"

Two pixies covered their mouths and erupted in a fit of giggles. A third pixie wearing a jeweled robe flitted down until she hovered just in front of Chloe and Mishti. "Oh, we do not mind. We just fly in whenever we please and conjure food for ourselves."

A fourth pixie flew down wearing a mischievous grin. "And if the mortals try to stop us…" The pixie flashed his teeth. "We bite them."

The third and fourth pixies chuckled, then took each other by the hands and flew away, circling around each other like a dance.

Chloe arranged her mouth into a smirk, raising both her eyebrows. "It must be frustrating to have it moved, though. Don't you want to get revenge on the one who ordered the mortals to steal your table?"

Plumia herself flew down closer to Chloe's nose. "You know which mortal ordered the others to steal our table?"

Letting her smirk grow, Chloe nodded. "I'll tell you exactly what the two leaders of the mortals look like." She lifted one shoulder in a shrug. "And then you can use that knowledge however you like."

Each pixie flew a little closer, their eyes growing greedy at the prospect of tormenting a mortal they already had a grudge against.

After carefully describing both Portia and Julian and exactly where to find them, the pixies let Chloe and Mishti go back to the path.

They waited until they had moved far away from the pixies, and hopefully out of earshot, before either of them spoke again.

Mishti opened her mouth first. "You don't think those creatures will be able to harm Portia and Julian, do you? Portia and Julian are not naïve enough to be led off to a ravine the way you were."

But Chloe's scheming was only just beginning. She glanced over with a grin. "You're probably right, but I'm sure the pixies can keep them occupied for at least a little while."

Knowingly, Mishti raised an eyebrow. "And what are we going to do during that time?"

Chloe rolled her shoulders back. "First, I'm going to get some food." Her stomach grumbled, as if on cue. Now she lifted one corner of her mouth. "And then, I'm going to convince those mortals to leave Portia and Julian behind and join us instead."

23

HEADING FOR THE MORTALS' CAMP with Mishti at her side, Chloe feared what lay ahead. No matter what, she had to convince the mortals to leave the tyranny of Portia and Julian. Her gut swam with fear at the prospect. Yes, she knew Portia and Julian cared only for themselves and merely used the other mortals as weapons and pawns, but could she convince the other mortals of the same thing?

Mishti led them forward, hiding behind trees and bushes when needed to make sure none of the mortals caught sight of them early. Soon, the mortals' camp came into view.

"Do you see Portia?" Chloe whispered.

She leaned around the tree they hid behind, narrowing her eyes and craning her neck, hoping for a better glance. Plenty of mortals roamed through the camp, but the leaders were nowhere in sight.

"Stay back." Mishti grabbed hold of Chloe's collar and pulled her back until the trunk hid her completely. Then, Mishti leaned the tiniest amount around the tree, watching the camp with only one eye.

"I don't see either of them. Do you think the pixies got them?"

Just then, the sound of chimes and bells drifted out of one of the largest tents in camp. Muffled shouts escaped from the tent too. They heard a distinct "Why, you!" in Julian's voice, which got cut short almost at once.

Chloe grinned. "It sounds like the pixies are doing their job."

She was ready to charge into camp right then, but Mishti held back. Her eyes narrowed at the tents, probably trying to decide the best position or time to enter the area.

Waiting less than patiently, Chloe's stomach growled with hunger. Her arms immediately covered her stomach, as if that could erase the noise. She shook her head, loose blonde curls shuffling over her shoulders. Her stomach growled again, making her wince in embarrassment. If they didn't get into camp and get some food soon, her stomach was sure to betray their presence anyway.

Mishti must have realized that because she took a step to the side and gestured forward. "We'll go in quietly. Keep your head down and try not to look too conspicuous. We'll get some food first and then we can try talking to the others."

Nodding, Chloe stepped out from behind the tree. She went to step forward, but Mishti pushed her back. Shaking her head, Mishti said, "Stay behind me."

The young woman didn't seem to know how to traipse or amble. She only seemed to know how to march.

Would it look strange if Chloe walked behind her with a casual gait instead of a soldierly one? Hopefully not because

191

Chloe wasn't sure her body could be forced to do anything in a soldierly way, no matter how hard she tried.

None of the mortals paid them any attention as Chloe and Mishti walked into camp. Instead, they kept their eyes focused on their individual tasks. One woman was mending a pair of trousers with such force that it almost looked like she'd create an even bigger hole than the one she was repairing.

The only time any of the mortals did look up was when muffled shouts or shaking disturbed the large tent near the center of camp. They'd look up and stare with worry or confusion, but then they'd immediately glance down at their work once again.

Chloe's mind traveled back to the party the mortals had back when they still had control of Bitter Thorn Castle. It had been different then. The mortals laughed, spoke openly. There had even been a group of young women giggling over a young man who'd been flexing and showing off for them.

It was hard to believe these were the same mortals. As much as it hurt to see how trampled down they'd become, it also proved now was the perfect time to try and get them on Chloe's side. The little freedom they'd gained after Ansel had now been eaten up by Portia's greed and plans of her own.

Swallowing hard, Chloe went up to the golden table littered with simple golden plates. Mishti gazed across the camp with one hand tight over the hilt of her sword. Chloe reached for a plate.

Her mouth had already started watering, even before any food appeared. Whispering, she said the name of her favorite dish that the family cook had made—back when her parents were still alive and her father won enough tournaments to provide the richest foods.

In an instant, a steaming bowl of beef stew appeared on her plate. In a single sniff, she could tell the broth of red wine and spices would taste just as delicious as the one from her family's cook. The cooked vegetables and succulent beef chunks floated through the broth, causing Chloe's mouth to water even more.

Smelling the food was worse than just simple hunger, though. A loud grumble rang out from her stomach.

Several mortals across the camp dared a glance upward at the strange sound. All of them reacted upon seeing her. Their eyes widened and several of them turned toward the tent where Portia and Julian must have been.

With so many gazes on her, Chloe took a step back. Part of her soup splashed over the rim, landing in the soil with a slop.

She had to eat. If she didn't eat, things would only get worse. Yes, she needed to talk to them, but she knew her body. Food came first.

Using one trembling hand, she reached into the soup bowl and grabbed the largest chunk of beef she could find. But somewhere on its way to her mouth, the beef chunk slipped from her shaking fingers.

She gulped at almost the same moment the meat dropped onto the ground. The mortals were making eye contact with each other now. With her eyes on them, Chloe tried to pinch out another morsel of beef or even a cooked vegetable. But every time, her fingers grasped nothing but broth.

And now the mortals had seemed to make a decision with only their looks.

One man stood from a chair where he'd been sharpening a dagger. "Get them!" he shouted. His pointer finger jabbed toward Chloe and Mishti.

Chloe's plate and her mouth-watering stew fell to the ground in a splash. She sucked in a breath, unable to step back fast enough to avoid getting the hem of her gown covered in broth.

The mortals all started standing, moving closer.

Mishti grabbed Chloe by the upper arm and tried to force her to run. Chloe's feet stayed planted on the soil. For once, this was a choice, not a result of fear immobilizing her.

Mishti pulled more insistently, forcing Chloe back a few steps. The young woman was strong, but not as strong as Quintus.

Regaining her balance, Chloe shook her arm out of Mishti's grasp. Chloe whirled around, her eyebrows raising high. "We have to talk to them now. The pixies won't keep Portia and Julian busy forever."

The look of utter repulsion on Mishti's face made it clear that she thought staying wasn't just a bad idea. She thought it a deadly one.

Just in case, Chloe closed her eyes and reached out for Shadow. Hopefully they wouldn't need the dragon, but it wouldn't hurt to have her there waiting.

A wriggle jolted through Chloe's gut. Shadow heard the call, yet something was…strange. Was she coming?

With more mortals closing in by the second, Chloe shook the thought away. She didn't have time to worry about that right now. She could only worry about the mortals. She just had to trust Shadow would be there right when Chloe needed her.

Gathering her skirts into one hand, Chloe climbed onto the golden table. The mortals continued closing in around, but their weapons all faltered slightly after seeing Chloe go toward them instead of away.

Clearing her throat, Chloe fiddled with the edge of her cascading skirt. Her hand immediately dropped to her side in the next breath. Mother had always taught her presentation and confidence were just as important as words.

Rolling her shoulders back, she stared down at the mortals. "I offer you freedom." Her voice came out a little shakier than she would have liked, but hopefully another quick swallow would add more conviction to her tone. "Portia has used you exactly how Ansel used you. She gets you to do what *she* wants and doesn't care what *you* want. Your actions are defined by her choices instead of your own."

Confidence and conviction had finally emerged about halfway through her words. Many of the mortals stared at her in disbelief. They didn't seem to trust her, but they didn't reject the words immediately either.

Well, most of them didn't.

From the back of the crowd of mortals, a young man stood taller. "Portia doesn't control my actions."

Chloe raised an eyebrow. "Really? How many times has Portia injured your enchanted wound to force you into compliance?"

The young man's shoulder slumped forward so fast, it almost looked like he might fall over. A dozen other mortals in the crowd did the same, many of them reaching for their stomachs or sides.

But her words hit harder than she expected. Many of the faces that had been indifferent now turned cold. Seeing how their faces changed sent chills through Chloe. Soon, the little hairs on the back of her neck stood on end.

Would she regret bringing up the enchanted wounds?

24

FROSTY EYES STARED AT CHLOE while her insides tumbled. If anything could convince these mortals to join her, certainly it had to be the fact that Portia used their enchanted wounds to force compliance. But with them staring so intensely, she wondered if she should have kept quiet about it.

Near the table, a young woman with pretty black eyes shivered. "Who told you about our wounds?"

In almost the same moment, the young woman's gaze trailed over to Mishti. Many of the other mortals in the crowd turned to glance at Mishti too. Their feeling of betrayal was palpable.

Chloe gulped. She wanted to connect with the mortals on a personal level. She didn't want them feeling betrayed by someone who used to walk among them. This would take some work to fix.

Lifting both hands into the air with the palms facing out like surrender, Chloe hoped to steal everyone's attention again.

"I know about the wounds, but I don't know the location of them. I don't know the location of any of your wounds."

It wasn't until that moment that she realized she'd never be able to heal Mishti's wound now. Without magic of her own, Chloe couldn't heal the wound, even if she did know the location of it. Her lips dove to a deep frown.

Shaking her head, she continued. "I know about the wounds, but I would never ask the location of those injuries. Because I would never use violence or pain to force compliance."

The tiniest light of hope shined in the eyes around her. It was a subtle change. Hopefully just enough.

Someone from the back of the crowd started pushing forward to the front. "What injuries? And who is Ansel anyway?" The woman threw her head back, revealing a smattering of tattoos covering her neck. "Portia has done nothing but give us food and the most incredible place to live. Once we claim this land for her, she will return us back to our homes with our pockets filled with more gold and jewels than we ever could have dreamed of."

Chloe's eyes widened at this declaration. By the end, a feeling of dread settled into her belly as a dark realization came over her. She had forgotten not all these mortals had lived with Ansel. Many of them had been recruited much more recently. And these new mortals clearly didn't know the truth about the tablets Portia had given them once they first entered Faerie.

As she spoke, many other mortals in the crowd shouted in agreement. They reached for their weapons, already eyeing Chloe.

But some of the mortals, those whose eyes had seen too much in life, looked down. They stared at their feet and shifted as they swallowed. The mortals who had been in Ansel's house, they knew. They knew what the other mortals did not.

Chloe looked out into the crowd. Near her, a young woman wore a forlorn expression, except she also looked like she was about to be sick.

Pointing to the woman, Chloe said, "You tell her." She then tilted her head toward the tattooed woman who had claimed Portia wasn't using them. "She won't believe it if I say it."

The young woman bent over and opened her mouth, as if to vomit, though nothing came out. She shook her head and then shook it harder.

Would it help to give her a more pleading stare?

The pleading stare did nothing since the young woman wouldn't look up. It seemed no one wanted to say the horrible truth.

But then a young man on the other side of the table raised his hand into the air. "I will tell them." He took a deep breath before speaking again. "You can't return home. None of us can. That was a lie told just to get you here. If any of us return to the mortal realm, we will die within minutes."

The woman with the tattoos snarled at the words. "Why should I believe you?"

But then another mortal from the crowd spoke just loud enough to be heard. "It's true."

A few other mortals nodded. One young woman even wiped away a tear as she nodded. "Your life was taken the moment you swallowed those white tablets Portia gave you. Now you're stuck in Faerie."

Chloe's heart squeezed. She was overcome with the desire to jump down and give each of those mortals a warm hug. It had clearly been too long since they'd ever gotten one. But now that the truth was out, these mortals were primed for her true purpose.

She stood a little taller. But just then, the tent across from her started shaking. The muffled shouts turned to true shouts. Fear gripped her veins. Portia and Julian were getting away from the pixies.

Swallowing, she tried to raise her voice and increase her conviction. "We don't have much time. I think you all know— at least those of you who lived with Ansel—that Portia and Julian are not your friends. When they come out of that tent, we can defeat them together. You do not have to fight on their side anymore. And once they are beaten, we can all live in freedom together."

All her days of reading epic poems came back to her now. How many times had she read about great heroes offering rousing speeches that turned every soldier and citizen to their sides? Her heart beat strong and steady. Battles had never been her forte, but maybe she had finally found her place in life as someone who could speak to the masses.

Flickers of hope lit the eyes around her. Not everyone was convinced, but at least many of the mortals who looked older, wearier, seemed to want what Chloe offered. Maybe they didn't believe she could give it to them, but wanting it was a good first step.

But then Portia stormed out of the tent with four pixies yanking tiny fists of hair out of her head. Her clothes had been stained with some sort of liquid. Red marks around her mouth and hands proved the pixies had captured her and bound her in some way. But she was free now. And despite the pixies still pulling her hair and pinching her skin, she ignored them completely.

Her gaze turned directly to Chloe. Through clenched teeth, she said, "Kill her. Kill them both."

The mortals moved slowly. Some looked at Portia, others looked at their weapons. Fear trickled like a bucket of ice down Chloe's spine. This was the moment of truth. If the mortals chose her side, she'd be safe. But if they chose Portia's side, Chloe was stuck on that table, now surrounded by mortals, with no way out of camp.

She could have gulped. She could have let her trembling hands hang at her sides for all to see. Instead, she clasped her hands behind her back and donned her a daring glare.

Julian exited the tent next. His face had contorted into a rage that made even his eyes seem red. With teeth bared, he grabbed an axe from the nearest mortal and swung it straight into the mortal's chest. A sickening crunch accompanied the blood that sprayed out.

Now he turned to the other mortals. "Kill her or we'll kill you."

He didn't wait to see if they'd comply. With a practiced flick of his wrist, he sent the axe flying toward Chloe.

If she'd been alone, the axe would have hit her and killed her instantly. Fear had already seized every muscle in her body. But she wasn't alone.

Mishti grabbed onto her arm and yanked her down from the table just as the axe flew across it. The young woman pulled harder, forcing Chloe to move when her feet wouldn't. Weapons immediately started falling down on the two of them.

In desperation, Mishti grabbed a golden plate off the table and used it to shield her head from a volley of arrows. At the same time, she managed to force Chloe and herself forward even more.

Chloe's body had turned completely useless, like it always did at a time like this. Somehow, she still managed to close her eyes and call out with her mind. She spoke to Shadow, commanding her dragon to come as quickly as possible.

It had been less clear before, but it was more obvious now. Something was wrong. Shadow wasn't coming. Chloe didn't understand why, and now clearly wasn't the time to fix it, but her chest still ached.

Mortals lunged forward. Weapons clashed against the golden plate in Mishti's hand. She kept pulling on Chloe's arm and running, but it wasn't fast enough. Without intervention, they'd soon be caught and killed.

25

CHLOE TRIED TO CATCH HER breath, tried to get her feet to move forward. The mortals were coming closer than ever. Mishti held on tight to Chloe's arm and dutifully pulled her, even though Chloe's legs hardly worked at all.

Mishti had dedication and determination, but with hundreds of mortals after them, those wouldn't be enough.

If they'd been alone, it would have been over right then. The mortals would have captured them. Julian would have killed Chloe—*gleefully*, considering how aggressively he'd tried to kill her the last few times she'd seen him. They would have been dead before night fell.

But it seemed they had made some allies in Crystalfall. Well, maybe not allies, but they shared a common enemy for now. The pixies must have hated Portia and Julian even more after tormenting them inside that tent.

Whatever the reason, one of the pixies, one wearing orange crystals and a hat made of an orange peel, released a dark fog.

The sticky darkness erupted just behind Chloe and Mishti, enveloping the mortals and their entire camp.

After a quick glance over her shoulder, Mishti tugged Chloe harder and continued ahead. Arrows, spears, and daggers still shot through the dark fog, but now that the mortals couldn't see Chloe and Mishti, the weapons didn't come as close to their targets.

They were still in danger, though. If one of the mortals got lucky, the weapon could still hit. And Chloe didn't have access to her magic anymore to heal their injuries.

They had moved quite a distance before Mishti finally released Chloe's arm. The young woman breathed heavily, even more than running a great distance usually caused for her. Considering she'd had to drag Chloe during that run and that she had to do it while hungry, it made sense.

Running on her own now, Chloe wrapped her arms around her stomach and groaned. "We need food."

"Not yet." Mishti had to speak through heavy pants, but she managed to keep moving. She gestured toward a hill covered in sparkling trees. "If we can get down that hill without any the mortals finding us, then we can rest."

Chloe nodded, but her legs weakened with each push forward. A bit of terror clenched her gut as well. She glanced back toward the mortals' camp. The sticky fog still enveloped the entire area, growing toward them, probably as mortals tried to escape it.

With her mouth curling to a frown, Chloe glanced to the side. "Why do you think the pixies helped us?"

Mishti shrugged, her gaze never leaving the hill they needed to climb down. "Maybe because they hate Portia and Julian more than they let on. I noticed they were crueler with them than they were with us."

The look of apprehension on Chloe's face must have given her feelings away because Mishti turned toward her and raised an eyebrow. "Why are you worried about it?"

Chloe swallowed hard. "I just wonder if the pixies will expect a favor from us." She raised both her eyebrows significantly. "One we can't give."

After a distinct lip curl, Mishti shrugged and increased her pace. "We can't worry about that right now. We need to get back to the castle and far away from these mortals before they catch up and kill us. Can you call your dragon?"

Panic writhed in her limbs, weakening them with each breath. "No," Chloe answered.

Mishti closed her eyes for an extra-long moment, pausing her feet too. But then she stomped forward again, resigned. "Shadow is on the other side of the barrier, isn't she?"

"No." Chloe shook her head, glancing around the area around them, as if that might help. "No, she is in Crystalfall, but something is wrong. I'm not sure what it is."

A dagger slicing through the air right between them served as the perfect reminder that they weren't safe yet. Increasing their speed, they ran faster toward the hill. But when they reached the bottom of that hill, Mishti insisted it still wasn't safe.

They kept running, but the dark fog stayed in sight behind them. Mishti then decided they needed to take a more erratic route instead of simply following the path ahead. That helped significantly to miss the weapons flying toward them, but it still took an entire day before Mishti determined they were safe enough to stop.

Chloe dropped to the ground in a heap and started crying the moment she got off her feet. Her leg was sore, but she didn't have any pain herbs or even water to help. The wound in her chest stung and burned, which probably signified it had gotten infected, but she was too afraid to check. A pit filled her stomach, growling and grinding and begging for food.

Mishti walked around the area three times before she finally sat down across from Chloe. Even then, the young woman kept glancing over her shoulder. When Chloe let out a small whimper, Mishti turned her gaze forward and held out the golden plate she had taken from the mortals' camp.

A golden plate. *Wonderful.* In a court filled with gold and gems, that was the last thing they needed. But then Chloe's eyes opened wide as she sucked in a breath. "You think the plate has the magic to get food?" Even as she said it, her shoulders slumped forward. "But Julian said the magic was in the table, not in the plate."

Pushing the plate forward more insistently, Mishti lifted a shoulder. "Maybe Julian was wrong. It won't hurt to try."

That was true. Daring to hope, Chloe took the plate in both hands and closed her eyes. She said the name of her favorite beef stew and then imagined the scent and taste of the spiced broth.

It remained purely imaginary, though. When she opened her eyes, the plate sat as empty as before. Letting out another whimper, Chloe laid down on her side and curled herself into a ball.

The sun had begun descending down the horizon, which brought a cold breeze rustling through her hair. She shivered at the feel of it. The weather in Crystalfall was a pleasant mild temperature during the day, but night would be difficult without a blanket or cloak of any kind.

Knots filled her chest as she remembered her blue, fur-lined cloak wasn't even waiting for her at the castle. Quintus had it in his pocket along with the other sleeping mats they usually used. Her fingers reached up, scratching at the wound in her chest. The burning was getting worse.

"Why do you keep scratching that spot?" Mishti kept her face hardened, but the tiniest hint of concern glinted in her eyes.

Chloe huffed and pulled her knees closer to her chest. "Because Portia kicked me with her heel during our last fight with them, and I forgot to heal it before I locked Quintus out. If I had my herbs and honey, I could heal it, but those are in my bag back at the castle."

After staring ahead, clearly unable to think of what to say, Mishti stood and walked around the area twice more. She followed her evening ritual of sharpening her weapons. In the morning, she'd polish them. But her work kept getting interrupted because even *her* stomach had started growling now.

In the morning, they'd have to travel to the castle on even emptier stomachs. Their paces would be difficult to maintain in such weakened conditions.

Eventually, Mishti settled on a flat piece of ground with a tree at her side and her weapons under her stomach. She even held one dagger in her hand when she closed her eyes.

Shivering limbs told Chloe she probably wouldn't sleep much no matter how hard she tried. Instead of trying, she bit her bottom lip and opened her mouth. "Mishti, have you lost memories?"

Mishti opened one eye, sending a piercing gaze toward Chloe.

Chloe turned onto her back and looked up at the dusky sky. "When you said to Plumia that she was not the only one who had lost memories, I thought you meant Ludo. But I've been thinking about it more, and I wondered if you weren't only thinking of him."

Without her gaze upward, Chloe couldn't see her friend's face, but she could still feel the piercing gaze. It only lasted a few moments.

Mishti let out a heavy sigh and then she spoke slowly. "There are some moments—many moments—from Ansel's house that I do not remember. I know he did awful things to all of us, but when I try to remember them…"

She trailed off leaving a thick silence in the air. It probably wouldn't help to prod. Mishti always wore a hardened face and a rough exterior. If she was ever going to open up at all, it would only happen on her own terms.

Waiting, Chloe stared at the sky above, noting the lack of stars and moon. The only stars and moon in Faerie had been tattooed onto Chloe's and Quintus's faces by Faerie itself. But that connection was now severed thanks to the barrier Chloe had put up. Her fingers twitched just thinking about it. Her hunger and infection and cold all made it very difficult to keep from doubting her actions.

At least Mishti started talking again, turning those doubts to the side for a little while. "I guess it shouldn't bother me that I can't remember all the things Ansel did. Regaining the memories would probably hurt worse than it does now, but it is unsettling to know things happened and to have no memory of them at all."

Chloe perched herself up on her elbow and looked across the clearing. "You don't remember anything?"

With her gaze toward the sky, Mishti answered. "I remember many things, especially the things Ansel did to others. But I only remember very few instances of things he did to me. He stole from our essence in order to make powerfully magic gemstones, so maybe that process just took our memories with it."

That didn't seem right. Elora had gotten her essence stolen and made into gemstones by Ansel, and she remembered all of it. Chloe sat up with a start, vaguely remembering something she had read years ago in an obscure book. Her eyes narrowed as she tried to capture the words. When she did speak, she did it slowly, trying to remember even as the words came out. "I read about blocked memories once. Sometimes people can hide memories from themselves when those memories are too much for their minds to handle."

"Mila said that too." Mishti let out a sound that was soft and hurt, but almost seemed like a chuckle. "I think Mila came from a place in the mortal realm that was far more advanced than where I came from."

Biting her bottom lip for a moment, Chloe finally whispered a question she'd been afraid to ask. "Did you...love Mila?"

"Yes." Mishti sighed. "Like a sister." Now she rubbed her forehead. "She's the only one who blamed Ansel for the orders I carried out instead of blaming me."

Chloe sat up even more. "He made you hurt people? The other mortals?"

While Chloe moved to a more open position, Mishti turned inward. Her eyes lowered and her chin dropped to her chest. Even her voice came out tighter and quieter than before. "I hurt mortals, tortured them." She swallowed hard, speaking quieter still. "Killed them. I'm good at those kinds of things. I trained as a soldier in the mortal realm, but even then, I have a natural talent for it."

A scoff drifted from Chloe's lips as she shook her head. "I'm sure that natural talent got taken advantage of both by Ansel and Portia."

Pressing the heels of her palms against her forehead, Mishti let out a pained sigh. "I have lost parts of my soul I don't think I can ever gain back."

Chloe sat up completely now. She pinched her eyebrows together and set her face as seriously as she could. "It's not your fault for following orders. Did you ever *want* to hurt any of those people? Or did you only ever do it because of orders?"

After dropping her hands to her sides, Mishti raised one eyebrow. The corners of her mouth lowered to a frown that held as much grief as her darkened eyes. "You don't know what it's like. Even if the order came from someone else, even if I only did things because they threatened to kill me otherwise, I still committed horrible atrocities. You can only shift the burden to someone else so many times before you start to carry it yourself."

"But—" Chloe intended to say more, but one murderous glare from Mishti shut her mouth tight.

Gulping, Chloe sank back to the ground and settled into as comfortable a position as she could find. When she did speak again, the question came out timid and soft. "How did you get to Faerie? Did Ansel get you himself? Were you taken forcibly, did you get tricked into a bargain, or did the fae somehow make you believe you chose to come willingly?"

A somber chuckle escaped Mishti's lips. "Somehow make me believe I came willingly? You'd know all about that, wouldn't you? Quintus brought you here while you were unconscious, and yet you still claim you came willingly."

Chloe wrinkled her nose at the thought. "True." Now she folded her arms over her chest. "This is why we're better off without the fae."

Mishti raised an eyebrow. "Having a fae that could conjure us food would be nice. There are no edible animals or vegetation in this court. We can't even cut down trees for shelter or fire. It seems like survival in Crystalfall might require magic, magic mortals like us don't have."

Huffing, she laid back down and turned on her side away from her friend. After permanently locking the fae out of the court, she had no desire to hear about how mortals might need them. "This land is ours now. We'll find a way."

Her stomach growled right then, which only served to punctuate Mishti's point. It didn't matter. Chloe was more determined than ever. They would find a way to survive because if they didn't, they'd die.

Somehow, they'd find a way. She'd make sure of it.

26

A NEW IDEA STRUCK CHLOE'S mind the next morning, waking her from a fitful slumber. She sat up with a start. Her head whirled around until her gaze landed on her friend. Hunger gnawed at her stomach, echoing in the air between them. Ignoring it, she whispered loudly.

"Mishti." Chloe jammed her wooden foot onto her leg and reached for her other boot. "Mishti, wake up."

With a groan, the young woman covered her face with her hands. "Didn't we just fall asleep?"

Now that she had her foot and her boot on securely, Chloe reached across the clearing and pulled one of Mishti's hands away from her face. "The sun is up, which means day has dawned, so no, we didn't just fall asleep. And anyway, I have an idea."

Yanking her hand out of Chloe's grip, Mishti groaned again. At least she sat up this time. Judging by the dark circles under her eyes, she must have slept as fitfully as Chloe. A chorus of grumbles erupted from her stomach, proving hunger had claimed them both.

Rather than be dejected by that, Chloe just smirked. "I bet the castle has one of those golden tables."

Mishti had one hand on a boot, but she immediately released it and flicked her gaze over to Chloe.

Chloe's smirk just grew. "The castle still has curtains and clothes and books. People obviously lived there at one point. And I know the castle probably had brownies and other fae who could conjure food, but the pixies had a table, and they can probably conjure food too, yet they don't. I bet everyone in Crystalfall used those tables for food, which means—"

"The castle probably has a table." Mishti finished.

Chloe nodded, but it didn't seem to be necessary. Mishti donned her boots and gathered her other things in a matter of moments.

They made it to the path soon enough, but walking took more effort than usual. Chloe's stomach felt like it was eating itself from the inside out. Loud rumbles erupted from her belly every few steps.

Maybe a little conversation would help. Chloe raised her eyebrows. "See, I told you we didn't need the fae. Once we get back to the castle, we'll have a way to eat."

Hunger curved Mishti's worn face into a prickly expression. Truthfully, it didn't look that much different from her usual face. Her voice did have a bit more edge to it, though. "What about building a fire? I don't know about you, but I got cold last night. How are we supposed to do anything about that when all the usually flammable things in this court, like wood, are made of gold and jewels?"

Chloe wanted to hold her chin high, but the words cut into her more than she liked. "We don't need the fae."

Raising a single eyebrow, Mishti turned her head. "What if we do?"

The question wriggled into Chloe's gut, aching even more than her hunger pains. Despite her best efforts to stay positive, a lump formed in her throat. "We don't because…" She squished her mouth to the side, desperate for an explanation that made any sort of sense. "Because the fae don't need us. It's not right that we should need them."

Mishti stomped forward expressionless, only responding after several steps. "The fae need us to know emotion."

Chloe felt her lip curl at the truth in those words. Long ago, High King Brannick's mother, who had been high queen at the time, opened a connection between Faerie and the mortal realm. Through that connection, mortal emotions slowly seeped into Faerie.

Some fae—like Ludo—seemed to naturally understand how to incorporate these strange new emotions into their lives, but many of them seemed as confused about emotions as Mishti seemed about smiling. As far as Chloe knew, the fae who had learned the most about emotions had learned it from mortals.

Letting out a huff, Chloe lifted her chin. "They don't need to know emotion. They were doing just fine on their own."

"Just fine?" Mishti narrowed her eyes. "Didn't they curse High King Brannick while *on their own*? And didn't another evil fae queen try to take over with Ansel at her side? And wasn't your sister, a *mortal*, crucial to saving Faerie?"

That same curl turned Chloe's lip up again. "Elora was fae when she defeated Ansel and Queen Alessandra."

Mishti folded her arms over her chest. "But Elora wasn't fae when she first got here. Her mortal nature took everyone down a path they never would have gone if not for her."

With a huff, Chloe waved a flippant hand through the air. "That's not important. Maybe they needed Elora, but that doesn't mean they need mortals."

Her arms were still folded over her chest, but Mishti spoke a little gentler. "You saved Faerie too. You did what the fae could not do, despite their power and magic."

Chloe scowled as Mishti spoke. Her words had truth Chloe had no desire to acknowledge. It would be so much better if the mortals could thrive without the help of the fae. They needed to be independent in this magical land or else they wouldn't survive.

"Well, I can't unlock the barrier now," Chloe said, throwing her hands into the air. "It's too late for that. We'll just have to do what mortals do best and innovate. Be creative. If anyone can figure out how to survive in a court with no herbs, no firewood, and no food, it's us."

Despite her determination, Chloe couldn't shake the hopelessness winding itself around her like a rope. It would be difficult learning to live in this court, far more difficult than she realized when she created the barrier enchantment. But what other choice did they have?

Her hand reached up as her fingers tenderly touched the wound in her chest. Even with the fabric of her dress covering it, the scab still stung at the touch. She could feel heat around it too, confirming an infection really had started.

If she'd thought to heal herself before creating that enchantment, the wound would have been gone already. Now, she'd have to get honey and herbs from the golden table that the castle hopefully had. And even with them applied properly, it could take weeks for the injury to heal. Her misery intensified, squeezing even tighter when her stomach growled.

At least the ruby spires of the castle had come into view. She couldn't increase her pace, no matter how desperate she was to find a golden table. Hunger had overcome her limbs too much. But slow steps would still get her there. She just had to keep going.

When they finally reached the clearing in front of the castle, an even more discouraging sight met her eyes. Her heart thundered in her chest while the lump in her throat turned hard and aching. Chloe's dragon, her loyal companion and protector, sat outside the castle walls looking weak and distressed. Shadow moaned softly, a sound so mournful it could have been turned into a hauntingly beautiful melody.

Guilt panged inside Chloe's empty stomach as she realized why her dragon never came to help her during the fight the day before. Hunger gripped her dragon's belly just as it gripped her own.

The court didn't have berries or nuts or fruits or vegetables, and it also didn't have animals, at least not ones filled with meat. The only animals in Crystalfall were ones made of glittering gems.

Shadow had once been able to fly to the other courts to hunt and feed on animals there. But now? The barrier designed to protect the mortals from the dangers of the other courts was now hurting one of the creatures she loved most.

Tears welled in Chloe's eyes as she approached her dragon. Her fingers rubbed the golden scales along her dragon's nose. "I'm so sorry, my friend." The words came out in a choked whisper. "I never thought this would hurt you too."

Mishti stood silently at Chloe's side. She could have gloated or pointed out how this proved yet another reason they needed the fae, but she didn't. Seeing such a large and ferocious creature reduced to this groaning pile of dull golden scales had sobered them both.

Chloe touched her nose against her dragon's and took in a deep breath. "I'm going inside the castle to look for food. If I find it, I'll bring some out to you as quickly as I can."

She didn't have to say anything else. When she turned and marched toward the castle, Mishti came too. They didn't say anything. Their gazes were pinned on the castle door, never wavering as they walked those last steps. Once inside, they began searching through the rooms and hallways, but their focus stayed as sharp as ever.

Most of the doors led to bedrooms, studies, and parlors. After opening one door, Chloe stepped back with a gasp.

A frightening creature stood in the corner of the room. Its thin and bony frame almost blended into the shadows. Despite its delicate build, it had an intimidating presence that caused a shiver to run down Chloe's spine.

She stepped back, but it immediately became clear that it was too late. This creature had heard them, and it wouldn't let them get away without a little conversation first.

27

FEAR TENSED CHLOE'S NERVES AS she stared at the thin and bony frame of the creature that blended into the shadows. She wanted to force herself to swallow, but even that seemed a little too difficult with this new presence before her.

No taller than an eleven-year-old child, the creature's lithe and slender body looked as if a gust of wind could knock it over. It had dark skin, but its skin was so thin it almost appeared translucent. It was an eerie sight, like looking at a living shadow.

She had caught the creature licking dust off the surface of a desk. Its disturbingly long tongue reaching out to gather up the particles. With every lick, its body shimmered and pulsed, as if it were feeding off the energy of the dust it consumed.

At Chloe's side, Mishti visibly shivered. Chloe donned her most polite smile and grabbed the doorknob to pull the door shut. "Excuse us."

But when she tried to shut the door, the creature lunged forward and slipped its bony fingers through to stop it. She was struck with the urge to gag at the sight of fingers twice as long as any mortal's but just managed to stop herself.

"You want something?" It spoke in a wispy voice, as light as the air itself.

"Yes." Chloe dropped her hands to her side and took a step backward. "We are looking for one of those golden tables that can conjure food."

The creature lifted its eyebrows, which showed off its blood orange eyes.

Tipping her nose into the air, Chloe turned. "But we don't need help from you."

Its face glinted with mischief. "You do not know what I am."

She cocked her head to the side and shot him a gaze that she hoped looked more confident than she felt. "On the contrary, I know exactly what you are. You're a wraith. You live in the shadows, feed off dust, *and*..." She tipped up one eyebrow. "You grant wishes."

Mishti's eyebrows flew up her forehead as she took a step back. "How did you know that?"

Turning to look at her through the side of her eye, Chloe sighed. "One of these days I'll convince you to read. It has to happen eventually."

The conversation only served to draw a smile to the wraith's mouth. He grinned at them, showing off sparkling white teeth that were all sharpened to deadly points. "Yessss." Its voice danced and wisped around them. "I do grant wishes."

Mishti shivered and reached for her sword. "Should I kill it?"

"It?" The wraith touched a hand to its chest. "I am not an *it*. I am a *he*."

Mishti started pulling her sword from its sheath.

"Don't bother," Chloe said, gesturing at the sword. "Wraiths can't be killed. They are not immortal like the high fae. They are undead."

The wraith placed its elongated fingers on its waist that was no thicker than a teapot, intertwining his fingers in the front. "I am not just a *he* either. My name is Chandril, and it was very rude of you not to ask."

His head stood no higher than Chloe's shoulder, but he still filled the space with his terrifying presence. His movements were slow and graceful, like that of a predator. It seemed almost hypnotic, drawing Chloe's gaze, despite the fear rising in her gut. This wraith was surely as dangerous as he was mysterious, a reminder that gloom lurked in the shadows.

She donned another polite smile and patted him on the head, exactly the way her nephew Gideon hated. "We will have to visit another time, Chandril, though it was a pleasure to meet you."

After a quick look at Mishti, the two of them scurried away.

Chandril scoffed. "*Time*." His voice chased after them like a rush of wind. "There is no time in Faerie."

Luckily, the wraith did not follow them, and their search continued. Perhaps the creature had been a good luck charm because they soon stumbled upon a large room with a long golden table standing in the center. Dust scattered its surface, and it was dauntingly empty of any dishes.

Not daring to breathe for a moment, Chloe whirled around. "Do you still have that plate from the other table?"

Mishti had already started pulling it out from under her tunic before the sentence was finished. Chloe let out a heavy sigh of relief at its appearance.

Without another word, Mishti held the dish over the table and beckoned a plate full of food. It had a doughy wheat roll dipped in butter, herbed lentils, and a healthy portion of chicken. She used one hand to scoop up some lentils and then held the plate out to Chloe.

Gratefully, Chloe grabbed the roll and took the largest bite she could manage. Through the roll she asked, "Do you think we could set the food onto the table and conjure another plate?"

Mishti raised an eyebrow, her own mouth full of a second bite of lentils. "You don't like this?"

Chloe shook her head and glanced back toward the doorway they had entered.

Understanding dawned as Mishti touched a hand to her forehead. "For Shadow. Of course."

After brushing away the dust on that corner of the table, she plopped the food onto its surface.

Chloe immediately took the plate and closed her eyes. "Deer."

She imagined a living deer, hoping the animal could dart through the halls and leave the castle itself where Shadow could get to it.

But apparently, the table could only conjure food and not living creatures because nothing appeared on her plate. Shaking her head, she tried again. "Deer."

This time, she imagined a raw, bloody hunk of deer meat that still had some of the fur attached. Such meat appeared on her plate exactly as she pictured. It filled her with excitement and nausea at the same time.

Mishti stuffed a huge bite of chicken into her mouth as she glanced down at the mangled carcass. "What if Shadow is the sort of creature who needs to hunt? You don't think she'll lose her will or purpose or anything if she's just given dead deer meat, do you?"

Tightness wound around Chloe's heart, clutching it tight. "This has to be better than nothing." Guilt twinged at her insides, making her stomach feel emptier, even as she ate.

"I suppose." Mishti ripped a huge chunk out of the roll Chloe had eaten from earlier.

After they both finished off the rest of the food, they hurried outside.

Shadow snapped up and swallowed the bloody meat in one bite, nearly eating the golden plate along with it.

"I'll get you more." Chloe snatched the plate off the ground and dashed inside the castle once again. The stinging in her chest reminded her, it would be prudent to conjure herself some herbs and honey to take care of her wound before she conjured more raw meat.

The herbs came out crushed and ready to sprinkle on food, but they would work. The honey came in a drizzle instead of a pot, but she could make do. Slathering the honey and herbs over her heated and tender skin, she closed her eyes and hoped it would heal quickly.

Then she conjured more food for her dragon.

It took six trips back and forth to get her, Mishti, and Shadow all full. By then, Chloe could do nothing but lie on her back right next to her dragon. Every once in a while, she'd reach out and rub Shadow's belly, which always produced a fiery and contented sigh from the dragon's mouth.

Even Mishti sighed. She also lay on her back with her hands clasped over her stomach. "I don't know if it's just because we were so hungry, but that was some of the best food I've ever tasted."

Chloe licked her lips, savoring the taste that still lingered there. "I agree."

In a perfect world, their simple contentment could have lasted forever. But this was no perfect world. This was Faerie.

A heavy breath escaped Mishti's lips. Then she sat up and crossed her legs underneath her. "What do we do now? Let the mortals live their own lives while we live here at the castle?"

"No." Chloe sat up and removed her wooden foot so she could massage the end of her leg. "Portia and Julian would never let us be. Also, we need to rescue the other mortals from them. Those other mortals deserve peace and freedom as much as we do."

Mishti raised her eyebrows skeptically. "The mortals will never join us unless we can prove we have just as much power as Portia and Julian."

Chloe's gaze drifted toward the castle. A subtle smile played at her lips as she thought of a shadowy, dusty room. "That's not a problem. If we wish for power, I know exactly how to get it."

28

GETTING HELP FROM A FAE always came with unintended consequences, but at least books had taught Chloe what to expect. She readjusted the leather strap on her shoulder. After going without her trusty bag for more than a day, it felt nice to have it back again. She checked inside it for the hundredth time.

Her magical Faerie book was tucked right against the journal written by the previous king of Crystalfall. In the extra pockets, she had stuffed as many herbs and honey as would fit. Now that she couldn't heal things with magic, she didn't ever want to get stuck in a position where she ran out of healing herbs.

"Are you sure this is a good idea?" Mishti marched next to Chloe, but she was far from at her side. Her presence felt more like an unwilling participant than a companion.

"Yes." Chloe kept her response to one word. Hopefully that would minimize how obvious her terror was.

It did nothing though because Mishti just huffed. "You were not so eager for that creature's help yesterday."

"That's because wraiths are tricky. You never want to make any sort of bargain with a fae creature if you can avoid it."

Tilting her head, Mishti gave a patronizing look. "Can't we avoid this?"

Chloe pursed her lips. "Did you have an idea for proving to the mortals that we have enough power to stand up to Portia and Julian? I thought about bringing Shadow, but they've already attacked us with Shadow there, and we still had to retreat. I'm pretty sure that's not enough."

"Maybe we could…" Mishti trailed off, her gaze darting around, probably as wildly as her thoughts. If she *could* think of an idea, it would certainly be better than what they were about to do. Judging by her silence and the slowing rate of her darting gaze, she came up with nothing.

"It's okay." Chloe checked her bag once again, looking pointedly at the king's journal. "I know what it wants, and I know how to trick it. We aren't the ones who will have to pay."

Mishti raised an eyebrow, showing off her disbelief. She didn't have time to comment since they had just arrived at the room where they had found the wraith the day before.

Taking in a sharp breath, Chloe pushed open the door. Just like before, the wraith's thin frame took up residence in a dark corner of the room. The creature held a golden plate in his hands, licking the dust off it.

Unlike before, he was no longer alone. A female wraith with pale skin and yellow eyes stood next to him, hovering over the plate, as if waiting for her turn. She wore a lilac dress that fluttered with each of her movements. She was as tall as the male wraith, Chandril, but her thin arms and legs, somehow, looked longer than his.

Upon their entrance, Chandril shot his gaze upward. His dark skin had the same translucent quality as before, stretching over his bones tight and thin.

"Back again?" His mouth bent into a smile, showing off his sharp white teeth. "I knew you would be."

The female at his side grinned, showing off a set of teeth sharpened to the same points as Chandril, except her teeth were black. Together, they took graceful and predatory steps toward Chloe and Mishti.

A shiver shook through Chloe, which she tried and failed to suppress. How could creatures no taller than children be so frightening? If she'd known about wraiths as a child, she would have been certain these were the creatures who hid in the scary shadows in her room at night.

She gulped and reached for the handle of her leather bag. Maybe that would ground her. "I'd like to make a wish."

"Of course you would." Chandril used his disturbingly long pointer finger to stroke his jaw. "Mortals can never resist a wish."

Letting out a chuckle as breathy as the air itself, the female wraith clapped her hands together. At the same moment, her yellow eyes seemed to glow.

Chloe gulped again. "I want a shield of protection. I want the shape of it to change into any shape I imagine in my head. I want it to grow and shrink at my command, and I want it capable of growing large enough to protect an army."

The wraith rolled his eyes and placed his bony hands on his hips, clasping the fingers in front. "You have to *wish* for what you want."

"I know that," Chloe snapped. She gripped her leather handle tighter. "But I want to hear from your lips that you can give me what I want before I make the wish official. You may be undead, but I know wraiths are incapable of lying just like all other fae creatures. So, tell me, Chandril, can you do it?"

The wispy eyebrows on Chandril's forehead twitched. Did she dare to believe he looked impressed? He certainly didn't look as smug as he had earlier.

He went back to stroking his chin. "Hmmm, a shield of protection that can change size and shape at your mental command."

"It needs to block bodies, weapons, and even magic." She only added the part about magic in case the wraith decided to follow her and Mishti into battle. Then again, the pixies had magic too. Even though she shared a common enemy with them, she didn't trust their mischievous nature to always take her side.

"Interesting."

Chloe narrowed her eyes at the creature before her. "Can you do it?"

The frail wraith's grin grew wider, causing her to take an involuntary step back. His bony fingers reached out toward them. Mishti had her sword drawn in a single breath, blocking him from reaching out anymore.

Chandril chuckled, the sound like slivers in the skin. "Yes, I can do it."

Despite the predatory nature of the wraiths before her, Chloe let out a sigh of relief. Her grip on the handle of her leather bag relaxed.

Mishti remained tense, eyeing the wraith warily. "How long will the shield last? I assume it won't last indefinitely." Her voice came out sharp.

"Such inquisitive mortals," the female wraith said, her voice laced with amusement.

"Indeed, they are, Charlona," the male wraith responded with a nod.

Chloe stepped forward, setting her jaw firmly. "Answer the question. How long will the shield of protection last?"

Grin fading, Chandril steepled his bony fingers in front of himself. "I can make it last until night falls."

Tightness squeezed at Chloe's chest. They had just woken up and done nothing but eat and feed Shadow, so they still had the whole rest of the day. But it had taken them more than a day to return to the castle on foot. Without the protection of the shield or the protection of the castle walls, how safe would the mortals truly be?

Her dejection soon got whisked away by a spark of excitement. She glanced to the young woman at her side. "If Shadow flies us there, we should have plenty of time."

The mortal army had hundreds of people, but her dragon was large enough to carry two to three dozen people at a time. She could use her shield of protection to keep everyone safe as Shadow carried them in shifts back to the castle.

Anticipation skittered in her veins as she took a deep breath. "Okay." She had to steel herself before speaking again. "I wish for a shield of protection that can change size and shape at my mental command. It must last until night falls, and it must protect us against bodies, weapons, and magic."

Chandril narrowed his blood orange eyes, studying her intently. "So thorough." He continued to stare, his eyes flicking to the side every few moments. He was probably looking for a loophole to exploit. Judging by the disappointment in his features, she had done an excellent job at filling all those possible loopholes.

He sighed heavily before speaking. "I will grant your wish, and in return, you will give me one day from your life."

"One day?" Mishti's eyes widened, her body shrinking away from the wraiths. "You'll take one day off her life, and she'll die one day earlier? A whole day."

"Hush, mortal." Chandril's voice came out like the high-pitched sound of wind trying to fit through too small a crack. "You are not part of this bargain."

Chloe desperately wanted to roll her eyes. How contradictory of the wraith to accuse them of not asking his name, when he clearly had no intention of learning theirs.

Standing tall, Chloe spoke in a steady voice. "I will not give you a day from my life."

Chandril jerked his gaze toward her. "Excuse me?"

She shrugged. "I prefer to keep all my memories."

The wraith's eyes narrowed, suspicion clear in his gaze. "I never said anything about taking memories."

"Yes, but remember, I've read about wraiths," she responded calmly. "I already know all about your magic and about…your memory elixirs."

Mishti's eyes opened wider than ever. She had tucked her sword back into its sheath, probably remembering the wraiths were undead and couldn't be killed anyway. But now her eyes shimmered with realization. The coincidence of them running into a fae creature that could alter memories right when both her and Ludo's lost memories had recently been discussed was not lost on her.

When Chloe stood a little taller, both the male and female wraiths before her flashed their pointed teeth. It took great effort to keep herself from shivering. She looked Chandril right in the eyes. "You grant a wish and ask for a day in return, but you always fail to mention the *day* you take is a day from the past. In return for a wish, a person loses all memory of a single day, usually the very best day of their life."

Puffs of air burst from Chandril's nose. His nostrils flared as he gritted his teeth together. "You asked for a wish. I will not grant it without payment."

"You can have a day of life, just like you desire." She raised one eyebrow significantly. "But it won't be mine."

The confusion on his face quickly turned to greed as he watched her tug the king's journal from her leather bag. By the time she held it out for him to see, longing shimmered in his eyes. His lips parted, almost as if the journal had caused his mouth to water.

"This journal once belonged to the king of Crystalfall." She flipped through the pages.

Chandril leaned closer, his breaths growing heavier and his mouth dropping wider.

She stopped flipping the pages, letting the book open somewhere around the middle. "You can have one page from this journal in payment for my wish."

Sparks lit in his blood orange eyes as he reached for the journal.

Just before he could touch it, she pulled it back and snapped it shut. "Grant my wish first. I'll give you your day, but only after I've used my wish. Only after I prove it works exactly as you promised."

He pouted, gaze still stuck on the closed journal.

With him watching, she carefully tucked it into her leather bag.

Only after it was out of sight did Chandril respond. "Fine. Your terms are acceptable."

A sudden rush of power filled the space around Chloe. Airy and ethereal magic swirled around and through her in a blustery way. Despite the emptiness she felt within it, she couldn't help being awed as it worked its way through her body.

This was nothing like the magic she had once possessed when she was still connected to Quintus. That magic had been strong and focused, full of purpose and intention. The wraith's magic felt airy and unstructured but still powerful in its own way.

Though it would help her, it served as a painful reminder of what she had lost when she created that barrier. Her gut curled into tight knots at the thought.

Hesitantly, Chloe reached one hand out. She held her breath, which sent a tingle up her arm and down her legs. Vibration shook inside her as she mentally commanded a shield of protection to appear between her and the wraiths.

Instantly, a shield materialized exactly where she had pictured it. A shimmery silver shield as transparent as a bubble filled the space.

It looked pretty enough, but now she needed to know if it would work. Tilting her head toward it, she said to Mishti, "Try throwing a dagger through it."

In a single breath, Mishti drew a dagger and sent it whirling toward the shield. The moment the blade touched the shield, it immediately bounced off it and clattered to the ground.

Chloe grinned. "Perfect."

They finally had exactly what they needed to get the mortals on their side. For the first time ever, the mortals would finally have a choice. They would finally be given the chance to decide their own fate.

With true protection, the mortals could finally choose whose side they were really on. In her mind, Chloe commanded the shield to disappear, which it did at once. She then turned on her heel and started for the castle exit.

Now, she just needed to recruit some mortals.

29

CHLOE AND MISHTI CREPT UP to the mortals' camp, the sound of their footsteps muffled by the soft black soil beneath their feet. Chloe's heart thundered in her chest, even when she willed it to settle. She had to stay calm and focused. No matter how tightly dread held her, she had to keep going.

It helped to constantly remind herself she had the shield of protection from the wraith in place, but it didn't ease her fear completely. Her steps had turned uneven, leaning into her good foot like she always did when nervous. Heat trickled at the back of her neck, spreading like spiderwebs across her shoulders and down her back.

The shield would protect them. Chandril had promised, and a fae like him couldn't lie. The shield would protect them. Each of Chloe's breaths came out uneven and clipped, but at least she hadn't stopped yet.

At her side, Mishti's hands shook. She tapped her sword hilt with one hand and a metal plate sewn into her tunic with the other.

With the shield of protection, they had nothing to worry about, but it seemed they could do nothing except worry.

They had reached the edge of camp now. Tents stood tall, covering most of the ground. Mortals wandered through the area with their gazes pinned to their shoes. The golden table that sat at the middle of camp was near, but Chloe chose not to stand on top of it this time.

It would probably be easier to keep Shadow protected with the shield if Chloe stayed closer to the edge of camp.

Since the mortals all kept their heads down, no one noticed when Chloe found a wooden crate and stood on top of it. The silvery shield shimmered, covering her, Mishti, and Shadow with its protection. For a brief moment, Chloe's shaking limbs stilled as a glimmer of hope flickered within her.

This was it. They could finally give these mortals what they had never been offered before. A choice.

For a moment, the camp stood silent, even the footsteps seemed muffled. No one had noticed Chloe yet. But then the silence was broken by two mortals whispering. They rounded a corner and came face to face with Chloe. She gulped and then cleared her throat.

Immediately, every gaze in camp turned and fixed onto her. Her hands unconsciously smoothed her red skirts embroidered with gold. She donned a confident and charming smirk that even her mother would have admired.

And then she called out in a clear voice that everyone in camp would hear. "Join us."

It took no more than a single breath before Julian appeared through a tent opening. He thrust a spear with a sharpened stone tip right at Chloe's heart.

She gasped hard, which sent a pang through her chest. But just as the wraith promised, the shield kept her safe. The spear bounced off the magical surface, dropping to the pebbled black soil.

It took Chloe several beats before she remembered to breathe.

Julian tilted his head to the side, shuffling his blond hair. The mole on his chin stretched with the movement. His gaze focused as he narrowed one of his eyes.

At first, she assumed he stared at the silvery shield that had protected her. But...was he looking at her ring?

Her hand curled into a fist as her thumb slid over the golden band. Emeralds decorated the top of the ring, which Quintus had given her after she saved Faerie. The ring had once belonged to his mother, and he had entrusted it to Chloe.

And then she locked him out of his own court.

Her stomach writhed at the thought. She couldn't let guilt consume her now. The deed was already done, and she still believed it had been the right thing. If fae and mortals couldn't get along, the only logical solution was to separate them.

Straightening her back, she cleared her throat a second time even as Julian commanded the other mortals to attack. In an instant, a barrage of weapons got thrown toward her. The shield of protection blocked every one.

The heat at the back of her neck melted away as she raised both her eyebrows. "I say again, join us. Live in Faerie in peace and freedom. Get away from Portia and Julian forever."

Portia had left the tent by now. She threw weapon after weapon at both Chloe and Mishti. All of them bounced off the shield and dropped to the ground.

Chloe raised her voice to be heard over the sounds of weapons hitting the shield. "As you can see, we are protected from these leaders who have controlled you for too long. If you join us, you will be protected too. No weapons will harm you when you join our side."

The mortals slowly stopped their attacks, their weapons now strewn across the ground. They finally realized the shield couldn't be penetrated. Despite this, they didn't seem particularly enthused about Chloe's proposition.

A man stepped forward, his eyebrows pinched together. "But Portia said she might be able to find a way past that barrier in the caves so that we can get back into the other courts again."

Chloe's gut wrenched with a sharp twist. She couldn't decide what was worse. The fact that the mortals had already discovered her barrier, or that they wanted a way past it.

Her heart squeezed as she shook her head. "The other courts? But we're safe here in Crystalfall. Why would you want to get back into the other courts? Is it because of food? Firewood?"

A nearby woman scoffed. "We don't care about firewood."

"What then?" Chloe asked.

Grim expressions settled onto the mortals' faces. Hundreds of mortals had gathered, all standing in different areas of camp. Even the ones farthest away had gloomy features. They glanced around at each other, perhaps waiting for someone who would be brave enough to speak their thoughts out loud.

Finally, a woman spoke up. "We want to get back into the other courts so we can destroy the fae."

Destroy the fae.

Chloe mouthed the words to herself hoping the others would protest. They did not. In fact, many of the other mortals nodded. Chloe's shoulders slumped as the words sank in. It felt like the air around her had been sucked away as a cold dread crept into her pores.

Maybe these mortals weren't as pure-hearted as she had always believed. She had locked Quintus out of his own court because he refused to give a chance to these mortals. She had defended them. Given up her magic and her beloved for them. And they wanted to destroy the fae, just like Quintus had claimed.

Through the shield, Julian threw her a smug grin.

Tears prickled at her eyes. It took a hard swallow to chase them away. "Surely." Her voice broke over the word, and she had to swallow again. "Surely, there must be some among you who want peace. Aren't there any of you who wish to be free of Portia and Julian?"

Silence rang loud in Chloe's ears. She had given up so much, and for this? Everyone deserved a choice, but what was she supposed to do if they all chose evil?

Chloe's heart stung and her stomach churned, but she wouldn't give up now. She refused to believe Mishti was the only mortal from this group who wanted freedom from Portia and Julian. Standing taller than ever, Chloe called out her last, desperate plea. "Anyone? My shield can keep you safe. You do not have to stay just because the other mortals choose to stay. You do not have to kill or destroy; you can just live and be happy."

Finally, the first flicker of movement appeared at the center of the crowd. A woman with short hair and wrinkles around her eyes stepped forward. The mortals around her immediately drew weapons, shoving them toward her. With a thundering heartbeat, Chloe frantically called out to the shield, directing it to protect the mortal. The shield covered her just as a sword nearly gutted the woman. She was safe. The shield moved with her as she dashed across the soil closer to Chloe and Mishti.

Before Chloe could catch her breath, another person stepped forward, this time a man with brown pants and a thinning crop of black hair. Her mind sent the shield to him, but Julian managed to strike the man with an axe before it got there. Julian's second strike failed now that the shield was in place around the man.

Her training as an apothecary kicked in as she quickly assessed the injury. Relief washed over her, noting that it was nothing more than a superficial scratch. Now that she had healing supplies, she could fix him up once they got back to the castle.

More and more mortals began to step forward. Chloe had to concentrate hard to shield them before any weapons found them. A few others got injured, one a little more seriously on the arm, but most of them got to the edge of camp with no problem.

Despite the danger, Chloe stood tall and held her ground, determined to protect those who sought refuge with her.

Weapons flew and clashed again. Nearly every mortal tried to break through the shield, slamming against it with increased brutality. Even with the shield to protect them from people and weapons, it did nothing to block the palpable tension thickening in the air.

Julian called out, his eyes wild and ferocious. "Destroy the fae. Take Faerie for ourselves." He said it again, even louder.

On the third repetition, other mortals joined in. They chanted the phrase louder and louder, filling the air with hateful energy.

"Destroy the fae. Take Faerie for ourselves."

Chloe had to scream to be heard over the chanting. "This is your last chance. If you want peace and freedom, come with me now. Otherwise, we'll be forced to fight against you."

Two last mortals lunged forward, her shield protecting them just in time. She waited another few beats, but every single mortal outside the shield was now chanting Julian's phrase. If the shield hadn't been there, they probably would have torn Chloe apart limb from limb using nothing but their bare hands.

It was time to go.

Beckoning Mishti, they jumped onto her dragon's back, along with the mortals who had chosen to join them. She chose not to think about how the small group of mortals all fit on Shadow's back, making it unnecessary to take multiple trips.

Her heart skittered, but she shoved the thought away. Instead, she focused on keeping the shield in place and asking Shadow to return them to the castle. Even as Shadow's enormous sapphire wings started beating and lifting them into the air, the mortals below continued to chant and throw every weapon imaginable at the flying creature.

Unease curled into Chloe's belly. Would the mortals come after them? Would they follow them and attack the castle and try to kill them all? Portia, Julian, and the other mortals didn't know it, but the shield of protection would only last until night fell.

Her hand clasped over her heart as she forced herself to take a few deep breaths. Even at a fast march, it would take more than a day for the mortals to get to the castle. Chloe,

Mishti, and the few mortals who had joined them were safe for now.

Shadow flew faster, soon carrying them far enough away that the mortals' camp could no longer be seen nor heard. Finally, Chloe dared allow herself to count the mortals behind her.

Twenty-three. Twenty-three mortals, and that included her and Mishti. She recognized nearly all of them as mortals who had once lived in Ansel's house. Still, there had been hundreds of mortals in that camp. Chloe had always tried to believe they were kind-hearted and just needed a chance, yet only two dozen had taken it. The others were just as bloodthirsty as Portia and Julian.

No words, no poem, no song could describe the depth of her devastation. She now had just less than two dozen people on her side. She had promised them protection from the others, but how was she supposed to deliver it when her shield would soon be gone and their enemies so numerous?

An even more disturbing thought wriggled into her mind when the castle came into view. She had used her shield now. It had worked exactly as needed, but now the time had come to pay for her wish.

Something told her it wouldn't be as easy as she hoped.

30

IN THE CLEARING IN FRONT of Crystalfall Castle, Shadow roared as Chloe and the other mortals jumped off her back. The new mortals gasped and ran for the castle doors. Chloe tried to calm her dragon friend, but the creature just roared again and threw herself against the shield keeping her near the castle.

Chloe immediately rearranged the shield so that Shadow stood outside it. That calmed the dragon slightly, but her wings were still shaky as they carried her into the air. The dragon had rescued the mortals and been there when Chloe needed her, but she didn't seem to like the shield.

Or maybe this had nothing to do with the shield. Maybe Shadow just wanted to hunt, like Mishti had suggested, except Crystalfall still had no animals for her.

Biting her bottom lip, Chloe tried to ignore that thought and darted inside the castle. She'd figure out what was going on with Shadow later. Right now, she had wounds to tend to.

A few of the mortals stared at her skeptically as she slathered honey over scratches. It wasn't until Mishti explained how Chloe had been an apothecary in the mortal realm that they finally allowed her to work without interruption.

After wrapping a piece of spare fabric around the last wound, Chloe made a note to herself that she needed fresh fabric. And then she remembered she now lived in a court where the only fabric that existed was from the clothing everyone wore along with some old, fraying, and definitely-not-clean fabric left over from before Crystalfall had been destroyed.

She sighed, her chest tightening in pain. One more thing to add to the list. Crystalfall had no firewood, no animals, and it also had no way to make new fabric.

At least they had food.

As if Faerie itself was mocking her, a mortal chose that exact moment to taste a bite of food he had just conjured using the golden table in front of him. He scowled at it. "This tastes terrible."

Another mortal stepped forward, using one finger to scoop up a bite of the smooth sweet potatoes. She recoiled once the food touched her lips. "It's sour."

Another mortal pushed forward, grabbing the plate and knocking the food off it. "That's probably just because you imagined it wrong. You have to imagine excellent taste as you imagine the food you want."

But when the woman conjured a pastry and took a bite out of it, her nose wrinkled in disgust. "Sour. Something is wrong with this table."

From the corner of the room, a mortal man shook his head. "It's not this table. You never had a breakfast shift this morning, so you wouldn't know, but the same thing happened

240

with Julian's table. He said something is wrong with the magic here."

Chloe's stomach dropped. Her fingers found the cascading edge of her skirt and started rolling it between her finger and thumb. With her jaw tightening, she turned to Mishti.

The young woman's face appeared as unreadable as always, except for the slightly sickly look in her eyes.

They couldn't afford to have any issues with the table. That was their only source of food in all of Crystalfall. Maybe the pixies would know what to do.

She might have left to find the pixies right then, except Chandril appeared in the doorway. His long fingers steepled under his chin as he glanced at her expectantly.

A few of the mortals gasped at the lanky creature.

"Don't worry," Chloe said a little too fast. "He's only a wraith. Just don't let him or any of the other wraiths grant you a wish, and you'll be fine."

She spoke those last words over her shoulder. Once she reached Chandril, she pulled him into the hallway where she could pay him for his wish without any of the mortals seeing that she had failed to follow her own advice.

Mishti joined them in the hallway, throwing a cold stare at the wraith.

Chloe was grateful for her presence. She took the king's journal from her leather bag, but an inexplicable terror filled her when she held it out to the shadowy creature.

A greedy smile filled his face as he reached for the journal. Just before he could touch it, Chloe pulled it out his reach. She threw him a pointed look. "Choose carefully. You only get to keep *one* page."

He nodded, but the longing in his blood orange eyes only grew. Tension knotted through her as he took the journal and

241

started flipping through the pages. Or maybe she was just nervous about the table.

Either way, she simply couldn't stand here while he skimmed page after page without making a decision. She might as well keep herself busy while he made his choice.

She pulled out her magical book from Faerie, flicking her gaze over to Mishti for a moment. The young woman glanced back, a question in her eyes. But after glancing at the wraith for a split second, Mishti seemed to realize now wasn't a good time to ask what Chloe was looking for.

It didn't matter. Chloe would explain later anyway. For now, she filled her mind with the question she needed Faerie to answer.

How do we fix the table so we can have food again?

Her fingers flipped through the pages of her Faerie book, scanning each one quickly. No magical answers came. She just found page after page of information she had already read several times.

"Hmmm." Chandril tapped a page of the king's journal while one corner of his mouth lifted. "This one."

Since Chloe was already in the process of turning a page, she decided to finish before closing her book. Perhaps that page would have the information she needed to fix the golden table.

A magical message did appear in scrawling handwriting before her very eyes, but it said nothing of the table. Instead, it contained words that chilled her to the bone.

Do not give him the page he wants.

Her insides jolted. She glanced over at Mishti. Judging by how her own eyes had widened, she had read the words from Faerie too.

Before Chandril could get curious, Chloe snapped her Faerie book shut and stuffed it into her leather bag. Ice settled inside her, leaving the feeling of frost along her skin.

Chandril pointed to the same page again. "I want this one." His long fingers then positioned the page, ready to tear it free.

"No." Chloe violently yanked the book from his hand, settling her finger between the pages to keep her place. Her heart hammered in her chest as she tucked the journal behind her back. "I changed my mind."

The fae's pointed teeth were on full display as he sneered at her. "You cannot change your mind," he warned. "The magic of Faerie will not allow you to break a promise."

"I promised you a day of life." Her breaths came in shallow and quick. "But you can't have it from the king."

He raised an eyebrow, glancing over her form. "From you, then?"

Her throat ached at the very thought. Memories flooded her mind, memories of happier days when her parents were still alive, and troubles seemed as distant and mythical as fairy tales.

She then remembered when her sister, Elora, had inexplicably survived the process that turned her fae, and the three sisters had found happiness together again. Chloe thought of Grace, Vesper, Cosette, and her nieces and nephews and of all the wondrous days they had shared together.

But most of all, she remembered Quintus.

Every tender touch. Every gentle whisper. Danger had gripped so many of their moments together, yet they had still created wonderful magical memories she didn't dare give up.

He had kissed her in the crystal caves, held her lovingly when she cried. He had given her a foot made from the last remnants of his destroyed home. He had given her a ring and begged her to stay with him in Faerie.

Tears filled her eyes, slipping past her eyelashes before she could even attempt to stop them. She had locked him out of Crystalfall, knowing it would be forever. She had already lost all future memories with him, and now she was being asked to give up a past memory. Just one, but that didn't matter.

She wanted all of them. Needed them. When she'd never see him again, how could she bear to lose one precious moment of the one she loved?

Her body shook as she cried out. "Why do you take memories anyway? What do you get from them?"

Chandril stared back at her with a mixture of disbelief and annoyance. "I get the memory. I get to live it as if it were my own."

Her nose wrinkled as she scoffed. "Why live someone else's life when you can live yours?"

He raised an eyebrow, a smirk spreading across his face. "Of all people, I thought an avid reader like yourself would understand," he said, pausing for a moment. "I live my own life and enjoy it, but nothing can beat the pure thrill of escaping into another's world for a little while."

It only took that simple explanation, and now it hurt how much she *did* understand. That didn't make her any more willing to give him what he wanted. The thought of losing any of Quintus made her stomach feel even emptier than if she'd never eaten a single morsel of food in all her life. The emptiness was a physical ache that gripped her from the insides out.

Mishti stepped forward, her hand hovering over the hilt of her sword. Her voice came out as firm as her expression. "If escape is all you want, then you can take one of my days."

The wraith shrugged. "Fine. I will take any day. I do not care whose it is."

Mishti leaned forward, her eyes blazing with a fierce determination. No one had mastered intimidation like she had, not even a wraith as shadowy and gaunt as gloom itself. She raised an eyebrow. "But you won't take my best day. You will take my worst one."

Chandril took a step back in disgust. "I do not want your worst day."

A small twitch played at the corners of Mishti's mouth. "Every story has high points and low ones. Experiencing low points just makes the high points even more powerful."

Skepticism laced the wraith's voice. "I doubt it."

The twitch on Mishti's mouth turned to a tight smile. "You doubt it, but you don't know for sure. You don't know because you've never taken a bad day from anyone. So, now is your chance. Take my worst day, and you'll see."

Disgust still curled his lips, but the look in his eyes had turned to curiosity.

Without another word, the wraith's hand reached out and waved in a circle. A moment later, he had conjured a memory elixir inside a small corked emerald vial.

Mishti reached out, ready to take it.

Sucking in a sharp breath, Chloe shot her hand out to block Mishti's reach. "No. I can't let you do this for me. I'm the one who made the wish. I'm the one who should have to pay."

Before Chloe could grab the vial herself, Mishti's eyes widened, and her gaze turned toward the great hall with the other mortals.

Chloe swallowed hard, glancing back to see what had startled her friend.

Too late, she realized nothing had startled Mishti at all. It had been a ruse meant to distract.

In a flash, Mishti had snatched the elixir and took a swig, downing its contents before Chloe could stop her.

Chloe wrung her hands in front of herself, watching her friend swallow.

As she did, the wraith was momentarily overtaken by the magic of Mishti's memory. His body glowed as he absorbed it into himself. His frail and translucent frame became as opaque as a high fae.

With a final unreadable expression, the wraith disappeared, leaving Chloe and Mishti alone.

Pain etched into Chloe's heart. Her voice wavered when she spoke. "You shouldn't have done that. I…" She had stopped herself, so used to the rules of Faerie. But she realized now that she spoke to a mortal, not a fae, and no rules dictated this conversation. She swallowed. "Thank you. I don't know what memory you lost, but I'm sure you feel emptier now."

"It's nothing." Mishti's icy tone betrayed only a hint of sadness. "But don't bother asking me again how I got to Faerie, because now, I don't remember."

An ache curled in Chloe's gut, feeling sick at the thought of what had just been lost. She hated that she had put her friend in this position. If she hadn't been so attached to Quintus, a fae she'd never even see again, she could have given the required memory herself.

Mishti's voice turned a little less icy. "Did you happen to catch a glimpse of the page the wraith wanted to take from the king's journal?"

Smirking, Chloe nodded. Soon, they'd discover what had been so important about that page that had cost one of Mishti's memories.

31

CHLOE'S HAND EMERGED FROM BEHIND her back, revealing the page that was still marked with her finger. She smirked as she brought the king's journal out in front of herself and Mishti. "Let's take a look, and hopefully we'll find out why Faerie didn't want him to have this page."

Mishti leaned in, her gaze training on the open journal. "Or maybe Faerie just wanted to make sure *we* saw this page."

Chloe nodded absently as she began to read.

Memories have energy. I learned this from a wraith who seemed to regret revealing so much. The wraiths use this energy by reliving the memories of others as often as they like.

But I wonder, could the energy from a memory be transferred? Could memory energy be used to give a different sort of life? I am determined to experiment on this, even if I have to experiment on myself.

Furrowing her brow, Chloe read the words a second time. Mishti had given up a memory for this? What did this have to do with anything? It only proved the previous king of

Crystalfall was cunning and ambitious and perhaps a little too eager to experiment.

She wouldn't dream of giving up any precious memories, not even to extract energy from them.

Mishti seemed more intrigued and gestured that they should turn the page and read the back. That wasn't a bad idea. Maybe the back page would make more sense. The instructions and information from her Faerie book had never steered Chloe wrong before. She had to believe there was a good reason they kept this page instead of giving it to the wraith.

I made a wish just so I could get a memory elixir. I promised the wraith I would drink it, but I told her I needed an extra day first.

This is the perfect opportunity to use my vault, which I just finished building. No one, not even my lover, Dyani, knows about the vault. I will not be disturbed as I run my tests.

First, I will study the composition of the elixir. With any luck, I will be able to re-create it. I won't have time for more than that before I have to drink it and lose a day of my life, but that doesn't matter.

If I manage to re-create the elixir, I will be able to do even more experiments on it. I'll find out soon enough if the energy from a memory can be transferred into something more.

At some point, Chloe's eyebrows had raised high on her forehead. She knew she should have been intrigued by this information about memories, but her thoughts snagged on the king's mention of his lover.

Earlier in the journal, he had disdained romance, though it seemed more like he longed for it. And now he suddenly had a lover? And yet, somehow, he managed to write about her in a sterile, impersonal way. Apparently, he still had no idea what love truly entailed.

"Try blowing on the page."

Chloe shook her head, giving her most confused stare to Mishti.

Mishti just gestured toward the journal. "That's how you made the clue show up on the map, isn't it? Your magic book made sure we saw this page, the king mentions a secret place that no one knows about, and we still never found out the clue that leads to the third crown piece."

She gestured more insistently at the page. "I bet there's something there. Something Faerie wants us to find."

All thoughts of Dyani, the king's lover, left Chloe's mind as she brought the journal to her lips. Opening her mouth wide, she breathed out slow, hot breaths. Immediately, strange blue lines appeared on the page.

Mishti slumped only a moment later. "The lines all converge on this one spot, but what does it mean? There isn't even a word in that spot."

Chloe frowned, just as frustrated. But then she sucked in a breath. Holding that page with one finger, she flipped to the end of the journal with the map that had led them to the dagger. Now she turned back to the page on memories.

She had to breathe on the page once more and then flip back and forth quickly a few times, but soon she could see it. If she imagined the blue lines being drawn over the map instead of over that page on memories, they all converged over a mushroom patch next to a grove of trees, both of which had much more detail than most other places on the map.

A light glinted in Mishti's eyes. She pointed right at the mushroom patch. "That's it. That's where his vault is, and I'd bet anything that's also where the third piece of the Crystalfall crown is hidden."

Closing the journal, Chloe tucked it into her leather bag. Her gaze trailed back toward the room with all the mortals.

"We can't worry about that right now. Julian read the clue we lost, but even if he finds the crown piece, he can't do anything with it. He wouldn't even know what it is, and anyway, Quintus still has the dagger and the key. Without all four pieces of the crown, Julian would never be able to re-create it."

Mishti frowned. "And not even *we* know where the fourth crown piece is yet."

Nodding, Chloe reached for the ring from Quintus and turned it around her finger. She glanced at it, noting how it had the same emerald and gold as the other crown pieces. Pushing that thought away, she shrugged. "I doubt Julian even cares about that clue anyway. He probably just wants us dead."

"True." Mishti started eyeing the castle hallway. "We need to build fortifications. Once the shield is gone, we'll be vulnerable. Portia won't let the other mortals rest until she's dead or we are."

Chloe swallowed. "Exactly. So much work needs to be done. We also need to figure out what is going on with the table. I thought maybe the pixies would know."

Mishti reached for her sword, clearly ready to get started. "You take Shadow and see what you can find out from the pixies. I'll stay here with the others and fortify the castle for attack."

They separated, and Chloe started toward the castle doors. She had survived another encounter with a fae creature unscathed, but it came at the cost of one of Mishti's memories. At least this time she'd face the mischievous pixies alone.

But every fae creature was tricky. Would the pixies choose to help her like they had before? Or would they decide to hurt her instead?

32

SITTING ON HER DRAGON'S BACK, Chloe used her knees to grip the golden scales. Usually, doing such a thing was unnecessary, but Shadow flew strangely today. The creature jerked side to side and dropped in the air suddenly, only to rise again with her back nearly perpendicular to the ground.

Chloe had gotten the dragon plenty of food, but something was wrong. Instead of warm, Shadow's scales felt cold and slippery.

Whatever was wrong, Chloe would figure it out, but she'd have to wait until after she got help from the pixies. Portia, Julian, and their bloodthirsty mortals were on the way to Crystalfall Castle right now. Even with Mishti's soldier experience, they needed all the help they could get against their enemy.

At least Shadow could fly much faster than mortals could walk. In only a few minutes, the dragon flew her to the spot the pixies had been the last time Chloe saw them. When she found that spot empty, she hopped onto Shadow's back and commanded the dragon to find the pixies.

She hoped the creature would have some sort of magic that could sense the pixies, and luckily, she must have. Soon, Chloe scrambled off her dragon's back again.

She stood in a large valley with an enormous golden tree at the center of it. The tree glowed and pulsed, but something about it seemed off. The pulsing didn't seem magical. It seemed more like the flickering of a candle about to be put out by a gust of wind.

"Hello?" Chloe swallowed hard, glancing around for pixies.

A few pixies stood on branches, their wings that sounded like windchimes still and quiet. Plumia, the pixie in a dress made of amethysts, came flying down from a branch at the very top of the tree.

Her flower crown and curled hair glinted in the light as wondrous as ever, but her face looked sallow. Was it because of the tables? Had she gone without eating because all the food tasted sour?

Plumia's nose wrinkled after noticing Chloe. "What are you doing here?"

"Um." Chloe bit her bottom lip, noticing how all the other pixies had gaunt faces and slumped bodies. "I came to see if you might help me."

"Help you?" Plumia scoffed. Right then, her body suddenly dropped, as if her wings forgot how to fly. Halfway to the ground, she reached out for the tree beside her. Her hand made contact, but she kept falling. Just before her feet touched the soil, the tree pulsed with a golden glow. Right then, her wings started flapping again.

The pixie flew until she hovered at Chloe's eye level once again, but she looked even weaker than ever. Even her voice came out strained. "This tree gives us life, and it is dying. We cannot help you. We are too busy helping ourselves."

Chloe pursed her lips as the words settled in. This was a new problem. The golden tables were conjuring sour food, Shadow was behaving strangely, and now the pixies' tree was dying? Her fingers trembled at the thought. She had to curl them into a fist just to keep them still.

Her gaze drifted to the leather bag hanging on her shoulder. "I have a book that might know what's going on."

The sound of windchimes from Plumia's wings sounded more like clangs as she flew herself onto the nearest tree branch. "I think you mean a book that can *explain* what is going on. Books do not *know* things."

Instead of responding, Chloe just pulled out her magical Faerie book and crossed the valley until she found a boulder large enough to sit on. Her book most certainly *did* know things, but arguing about it would only waste time. If she found a way to help the pixies, she could make a bargain with them, getting their help in return for hers.

Now, she needed answers.

Opening the book to a page in the middle, she then brought the open spine close to her lips. Since the book hid her face from the pixies, they wouldn't see her whispering.

"What is wrong with the pixies' tree?"

After whispering the question, she settled the book onto her lap and started turning the pages. She came across a few recipes for poisons and their antidotes, but then finally the book spoke to her.

A blank page sat before her, but soon scrawling handwriting filled the parchment.

Faerie and fae have a bond. If that bond is severed, magic is lost. The pixies' tree will die without magic.

Slivers of ice pricked at Chloe's heart. She stared at the words, hating how they cut into her. But then she shook her head and brought the book closer to her face again so she could whisper into its pages.

"Do you mean the barrier I created? Because that's just an enchantment. There was a barrier in that same spot before and nothing in Crystalfall was dying."

With the book still close to her face, her gaze flicked to the page. Already, new words were forming.

Crystalfall is out of hibernation now, which means it needs more magic than it did then.

Chloe's heart squeezed, but the words kept appearing.

More important, the last barrier was created by Faerie itself. That barrier blocked fae but still let magic through. Your barrier blocks out both.

Heat rose in Chloe's cheeks as she gripped the book tighter. "My barrier does no such thing. I only wanted to block out the fae. What about the pixies and the wraiths? What about Shadow? They have magic, don't they? I wasn't trying to block out all magic, just the fae."

Slowly, the words before her started to disappear. Each word vanished one by one, leaving her breath hitched as she waited…and waited for new words to appear.

The page remained blank for several seconds. Only when she loosened her grip and opened her mind did something new appear.

Your bond with Quintus has been severed. It may never be repaired again.

The last breath inside her rushed out, as if she'd been punched in the gut. Holding the book with one hand, her other hand trailed up until her fingers brushed against the star tattoos under her right eye.

When she created the barrier, the tattoos had tingled and stung. Now they felt as dull as the rest of her skin. But that could never compare to the aching hole in her heart. It had been there since she locked him out. It had grown during her deal with the wraith, when she thought she might have to give up one of her memories of him.

And now the hole gnawed at her heart, threatening to break it apart. Her fingers had started trembling hard enough to make the pages before her flutter. Forcing herself to take a shaky breath, she whispered to the book again.

"Of course our bond is severed. He's on the other side of the barrier where he can't hurt any mortals and the mortals can't hurt the fae. That was the whole point. Now how do I fix Crystalfall so those of us who are stuck here can live?"

She stared at the page, but those same words as before stared back at her.

Your bond with Quintus has been severed. It may never be repaired again.

Her jaw clenched while she stared, waiting for the words to change. She must have stared at the page for a full minute, yet nothing ever changed. She even tried turning the pages, but those were all blank.

With a huff, she slammed the book shut. "I did the right thing." The harsh whisper through her teeth sent mist spraying from her mouth. "Did you want Portia, Julian, and their bloodthirsty mortals to destroy all the fae in Faerie? Because that's what they'd be attempting to do if not for my barrier."

The closed book sat in her lap, but she could feel when its magic withdrew from her. One moment, energy buzzed at her fingertips where they touched the leather cover, and the next moment, the energy vanished.

She huffed again and stuffed the magical book into her leather bag. Quintus and Ludo had killed an innocent mortal woman attempting to get information from her. They deserved what they got.

But then she remembered how she'd finally given all the mortals a chance and only two dozen of them had wanted peace and freedom. Even if Chloe, Mishti, and their new mortal followers managed to defeat the enemy mortals, they'd only have two dozen people left over. Two dozen people in all of Crystalfall.

Was that enough people to be the start of a new civilization? What if nobody in their group liked each other enough to have children? What if they all died out and Crystalfall was left empty because of her barrier?

Shaking her head, she searched for any morsel of hope within herself. They just had to get rid of Portia and Julian. They had to keep the barrier shut. Once Portia and Julian were gone, the other mortals would want to join their side. Then they'd have hundreds of people, which would certainly be enough to start a new civilization.

They needed a way to defeat those bloodthirsty leaders. If her Faerie book refused to help, she'd just turn to another one. The king of Crystalfall had liked experiments. Maybe he had some ideas.

The journal soon sat open on her lap. She found the page where the king first mentioned memories and his deal with the wraith, and then she turned several pages ahead. When she stopped, she was only a handful of pages until the end of the king's writings.

It took three more memory elixirs and three more lost memories, but I finally re-created a memory elixir of my own.

For a while, I thought I might never figure it out, so I attempted to extract energy from other Faerie items. The balance shards that can turn mortals into fae had the most power, but their instability and destruction caused me to give up on them almost as soon as I started.

I also tried extracting energy from trophies, which are also called tokens, but mine were never powerful enough. I even tried getting energy from stories the way the Swiftsea fae do, but that failed miserably.

Memories are the only viable option. My experiments will continue this evening.

Her eyes narrowed, reading the words carefully. Already, this was far more intriguing than any of the useless information her Faerie book had given her. She did wonder though, why did the king of Crystalfall need extra energy anyway? Maybe the answer would be on the next page.

My enemies are closing in. They want me dead. They want me off the throne. I cannot trust anyone. I have already killed two of my advisors after they started acting suspicious. I cannot be close to anyone.

I need to get rid of Dyani.

Then again, my lover mentioned several times how she misses her home in the high court. Now that I am thinking of it, I haven't seen her in several days. Maybe she left already and returned to her home there.

That is good. I cannot afford to have a lover right now. Fae do not have children often, but if she did happen to give birth, my child would only be a threat to my crown and my throne.

I will experiment with the memories and give myself life energy that will make me unbeatable.

From this day forward, I trust no one.

Once again, the mention of the king's lover interested Chloe more than anything else on the page. He clearly intended to kill her, but also seemed grateful she might have left him already so he wouldn't have to. Maybe it wasn't much, but at least he cared about her more than the two advisors he killed, simply because they started acting suspicious. No matter what she knew about this king, one thing was clear. He was paranoid. Whether that paranoia was founded or not probably couldn't be learned from his personal journal, but he did seem to worry more than necessary.

She read the words again, her gaze catching on a seemingly insignificant piece of information. *She misses her home in the high court.* Back when Crystalfall existed the first time, the high court hadn't been given a name yet. But it would get its name later when the other leaders cursed it. Bitter Thorn. So, this king of Crystalfall used an axe, and his lover was from Bitter Thorn. He also saw his own children—whether they existed or not—as threats to his throne.

Did that mean this king might attempt to kill his own son if he ever learned he had one?

Before her theories could get too tangled, the sound of clanging wind chimes filled the air. Two pixies dropped from their tree and crashed against the ground. The little creatures in clothing made of gems each groaned and got to their feet, proving they still had life in them.

It served as a reminder that the conflict with Portia and Julian would only get worse until Chloe found a way to defeat them. The pixies couldn't help. Shadow's strange behavior demonstrated she probably couldn't help either. Chloe's magical book refused to share any useful information, but it didn't matter, because it had inadvertently given her an idea.

Perhaps they didn't need more soldiers or more weapons. They just needed the right weapons. And then they could add a little something that would make them more effective.

Poison.

Chloe stuffed the king's journal into her leather bag and marched toward her dragon. Her magical book had showed her a page on poisons earlier, but she didn't need it. She was still a little mad at it anyway. Luckily, an apothecary like her knew enough about poisons without the book's help.

She'd get back to the castle, and then she'd make sure every arrowhead, dagger, and spear they had would all be laced with the deadliest of poisons.

Her lips tipped up in a smile. Maybe she couldn't use weapons, but she could still help her side win.

33

THE GOLDEN TABLE INSIDE THE castle continued to produce sour foods, but the belladonna it conjured would be as poisonous as ever. With any luck, it would be even more poisonous. Chloe dipped an arrowhead into a small cup of alcohol infused with a fatal amount of belladonna. The healing plant quickly turned to poison when too much of it was used.

After dipping the arrowhead, she brought it to her mouth and blew lightly until the alcohol dried to the metal. Now this arrow wouldn't have to hit a vital organ to kill. It would only have to break the skin.

She placed it carefully onto the pile of finished arrows and reached for one off the pile of non-poisoned arrows. Only a few more remained.

Mishti walked into the great hall holding two daggers in each hand. "Every exit has been sealed using the heaviest furniture we could find. And I found a few more weapons that still need poison."

She dropped the daggers onto the ground next to the pile of non-poisoned arrows. She then proceeded to pull from her belt two swords that Chloe hadn't noticed before. Then she lifted the midnight blue fabric of her pant leg and revealed a small mace and two more daggers stuffed into her hidden leg bracer. The bracer on her left leg had another sword and a few arrows.

Somehow, those weren't the last of the weapons. Mishti pulled a carrier off her back, which contained several arrows, two axes, and a scythe-like knife.

Finally, one last dagger came out from her arm bracer.

Chloe glanced at the weapons and then at her friend. She let out a small chuckle before dipping a fresh arrowhead into her belladonna concoction. "If I ever need help hiding a weapon, I know who to ask for help."

"I'm glad you finally asked."

Since Chloe hadn't actually asked at all, Mishti had clearly been waiting for a moment like this.

"You *should* start carrying a weapon," Mishti said. "A bracer on your leg would be completely hidden by your skirts, and on your right leg, it wouldn't interfere with your wooden foot." She ended the statement by pulling a leather leg bracer out from under her tunic.

Chloe's eyes went wide, making it difficult to blow the arrowhead in her hand dry. "You know I'm not any good with a weapon."

Mishti shrugged and lifted one of the small daggers that had already been poisoned. "With one of these, you don't have to be good with a weapon. You just have to barely slice the skin."

Even though Chloe shuddered at the thought, Mishti would not be deterred. She gestured at Chloe's leg insistently until Chloe frowned and pushed her leg out from under her skirts.

"Finally." Mishti attached the leg bracer and slipped the dagger inside it, taking care to keep the poisoned blade against leather, so none of it touched the skin. "I thought I'd never convince you to carry a weapon."

It still didn't seem like a great idea. Chloe froze with terror in the middle of fights. She'd never be able to use a weapon. It probably wouldn't help, but it probably wouldn't hurt either, and with a battle at the castle on the horizon, she could use all the extra help she could get.

Just as Chloe dipped another arrowhead into the belladonna concoction, a mortal with green eyes and a faded purple coat rushed into the room. He spoke in a near shout. "Portia's army is here."

Only a few people stood in the room with Chloe and Mishti, but all of them jumped at those words. They gathered weapons from the piles Chloe had already poisoned and dashed out of the room. When Chloe had first returned to the castle after visiting the pixies, Mishti had explained all sorts of strategies Chloe hadn't understood at all.

One thing she did know, though: the other mortals knew exactly what they were supposed to do now that their enemies were here. Mishti had taught and trained them as much as she could in their single day.

Chloe wouldn't do any good attempting to fight Portia and Julian, but she could make sure the rest of the weapons got poisoned. Her mind focused as she worked to coat each blade and arrow with belladonna.

Once they had all been covered, she gathered a pile of arrows into her skirts and carried them toward the front of the castle.

It seemed too quiet for the midst of a battle. No one shouted. No one even seemed to be throwing weapons. Was it too dark for Portia and her soldiers to see? The castle had gotten much darker than when she first arrived, proving that night had likely fallen.

Finally, Chloe found the turret where Mishti and three other soldiers stood. The young woman's long black braid swung as she glanced over to see Chloe enter the room. Her gaze only stayed on Chloe for a moment before she turned back to the small slit window in front of her.

"They're making camp for the night. They've been marching all day, so it makes sense they want to rest and not begin fighting until morning."

Chloe started arranging the poisoned weapons in a corner of the room. "You don't sound so sure of that. Do you think they are only pretending to make camp so that they can do a surprise attack once we let our guard down?"

Mishti's grip on her sword tightened. "It doesn't matter because we aren't going to let our guard down. We have four people in each position throughout the castle. We'll all rest in shifts, so everyone can sleep, but we'll also have at least one person in each position awake and watching throughout the night."

Nodding, Chloe stood from where she had finished arranging the pile of arrows. Mishti probably hated being in a position where she'd have to kill people again, but clearly, she knew what she was doing.

Mishti turned to the other three people in the room. "You three stay here, and I'll explain the plan to everyone in the other positions. Hester, you have first watch."

A woman near the window nodded, while the other two men stepped away and found places in the room to sleep.

When Mishti left the room, Chloe followed her. "Um." She drummed the side of her thigh with her fingers. "Now that all the weapons are poisoned, what do you want me to do?"

"Find somewhere to sleep." Mishti answered without hesitation. "I want you somewhere deep inside the castle and away from any windows. Then I won't have to worry about you in case the battle begins before dawn."

Chloe nodded, already retracing in her mind the steps she'd have to take to get to the library.

"Everyone knows to aim for Portia and Julian. I went over it several times during our training. We want to kill as few people as possible, preferably eliminating Portia and Julian soon after the fight begins."

It took a hard swallow before Chloe could speak again. "Do you think I'm right that the other mortals will stop fighting once Portia and Julian are dead?"

Mishti didn't answer. Her face turned even more hardened than usual as she went to turn down a new hallway. "Get some rest. We can worry about everything else in the morning."

Of course they both knew there was a chance the other mortals would continue to fight even after their leaders were killed. They had already talked it over a few times. But what choice did they have? Either the others would stop fighting once Portia and Julian were killed, or they'd keep fighting and the battle would continue.

They wouldn't know until it happened, and Mishti was right, it wouldn't do any good to worry about it right now. For now, all Chloe could do was sleep.

She found a cushy garnet-colored velvet chair in a corner of the library and settled her head against the arm cushion. As sleep overtook her, Chloe was grateful Mishti had blocked every exit. No one could get inside the castle now without being

264

vulnerable to the soldiers inside the castle who were all armed with poisoned weapons.

Then again, Bitter Thorn Castle had a few secret entrances that only Brannick, Elora, and their very most trusted advisors knew about.

For a moment, Chloe's eyes flew open. She forced them closed almost immediately and settled herself deeper into her chair. What did that matter? It wasn't like the king of Crystalfall himself was there. He had clearly been paranoid enough to kill anyone who had information like that. She had to believe the knowledge of any secret entrances must have died with him.

34

Darkness shrouded the library when something yanked
Chloe from a deep sleep. Someone was holding her hand. Was
it a dream? She had felt like she got awoken, but perhaps she
simply fell into a new dream.

Her mind drifted off to another time she had woken with
someone holding her hand. Back then, she had thought she fell
asleep holding a rock, but it was actually Quintus's hand. And
with that fateful mistake, she had bonded herself to him
forever.

The world seemed to drop out from under her at the
thought.

Not forever. That bond had now been severed, and
according to Faerie, it may never be repaired again.

Sleep left her completely when the hand against hers
moved more insistently. This hand was wrinkly and cold,
nothing like Quintus's had been. Even worse…

She gasped as she finally recognized the movement. Someone was trying to steal her golden and emerald ring.

Yanking her hand back, she also curled it into a tight fist. "Who is that?"

She whisper-shouted the words and scrambled off the chair. The person in front of her wore a cloak with a hood blocking the face.

Fine by her. If the person didn't want to be revealed, she didn't care. She just wanted to get away. She tried backing up, but her legs had cramped. At least she'd left her wooden foot attached to her leg through the night. It hit the ground hard on every other step as she attempted to steady herself.

The hooded figure lunged toward her, somehow gripping her fist. Whoever it was, this person really wanted her ring.

Stepping to the side, she also managed to use her free hand to pull the hood back.

Julian stared back at her with a wicked smile and fire in his eyes.

She gasped, losing her balance completely as she ran into a golden bookshelf. "How did you get in here?" she asked breathlessly.

His grin showed off teeth that looked yellow even in the darkness. "I found a secret entrance. The other castles have them. I assumed this one did too."

When he lunged for her hand again, she turned on her heel and started limping for the library doors. He tackled her to the ground, using his fingernails to try and unclasp her fist.

"I...need...that...ring." He spoke through his teeth, fighting against her as he pushed the words out.

"Get away from me." She shoved him off and managed to step just outside the library doors.

The moment she made it outside them, he tackled her down again, this time, pressing both knees against her stomach.

She gagged, trying to breathe while also trying to keep him from uncurling her fist.

He laughed at her efforts, the frenzied sound filling the hallway. His eyes lit up at the sight of the golden and emerald ring around her finger. "I need this, along with a few other items." His gaze turned more sinister as he turned to face her. "The only reason I haven't killed you yet is because I'm pretty sure you know where those other items are."

For a moment, her fist relaxed. Terror seized her gut as the meaning of his words sank in. The crown. Was he talking about the pieces of the Crystalfall crown? He saw the clue that would lead him to the third piece, but he never read the journal. How could he possibly know what the piece was for?

She gulped, clenching her hand into a fist again. "What other items? I have no idea what you're talking about."

His nostrils flared as he grabbed her shoulders. With a sharp jerk, he lifted her shoulders and shoved them against the ground. The movement snapped her head back until it crashed against the ground too.

Stars exploded in her eyes as pain rushed into her skull.

He laughed, reaching for her hand, which had lost some of its grip. "You think you're the only one who knows how to find out information? Do you have any idea how long I've been in Faerie?"

She only vaguely noticed how he had finally gotten her hand unclenched. Ringing filled her ears, pain stabbed her skull, and all she could think was how old he looked in this light. Of course, Mishti had mentioned before that he was the oldest of all Ansel's mortals. He had been there longer than any of the rest of them.

Still, his wrinkles seemed deeper up close, his skin more saggy.

With a sharp inhale she realized he had Quintus's ring more than halfway off her finger. Fear gripped her tight, but something else gripped her tighter. She wasn't about to lose the one thing she had left from Quintus. Thrusting her foot upward, she caught Julian right in between the legs.

He let out a high-pitched grunt and fell onto his side.

That was deeply satisfying. Gathering her skirts, she got to her feet and pushed the ring back onto her finger. Mishti was only a few hallways away. Chloe just had to run and hope Julian would come after her. Then, once she got close enough to shout, Mishti would come and kill him and then they'd only have Portia left to deal with.

The plan would have worked perfectly if Julian hadn't tackled her to the ground the moment she stood. He shoved her down the hallway in the opposite direction she needed to go and even pushed her down a flight of stairs that seemed to come from nowhere.

She banged against the golden steps, each one bruising her as she tumbled down. But even worse than the pain, a new sensation took over.

Her heart hammered in her chest. Ice stung at the back of her neck, immobilizing what little control she had left of her arms. Anxiety overtook her completely. She was useless now. Then again, maybe she couldn't fight him, but even frozen, she could still talk.

"Are you going to tell me what was on that piece of parchment you ate?"

Julian traipsed down the stairs casually. She could hear his snarl that must have curled his lips at the sound of her question, as if he had just remembered chewing and swallowing the clue so that she and the others would never see it. She managed to glance over her shoulder to see his slanted grin quickly devolve into a wild laughter. "It's amazing what you can get away with when you're the crazy one."

Once Julian reached the bottom of the stairs, Chloe had to admit the truth of what had happened. Her body was frozen, completely immobilized. Every muscle in her body contracted tight, shaking like leaves in a storm. Tears stung in her eyes. Soon they'd slip through her eyelashes, no matter what she tried.

She hated losing control of her body like this, but at least she still had control of her mind. At least she still had control of her tongue. Staring him right in the eye, she spoke through her teeth. "I'm not telling you anything."

"Fine." All expression left his face as he pulled a sharp blade with no handle out from under his coat. In a flash of movement, he sliced the knife into her side so deep, even the top of it got swallowed by her skin.

Air left her in a rush. The pain in her skull dulled as this new slicing injury overtook it. Blood started pooling at the wound. She didn't think. She could barely even feel.

Instinct took over as she grabbed her side with one hand, pressing it against the wound. The action was truly a double-edged sword, because although it kept blood inside her, it also pushed the blade a little deeper.

A dark chuckle left Julian's mouth as he pushed open a door that looked nearly identical to the wall. He grabbed her free arm and dragged her across the ground. Her spine smarted as it went over the edge of the doorway. Soon, her back met black soil and the dusky light of a Faerie night hung above her.

Julian kept dragging her, his breaths growing shorter and shallower. But any time she tried to get away, he just kicked her in the side where that blade was lodged.

Only when he stopped to catch his breath did a sudden and urgent thought break through the pain clawing at Chloe's mind.

Shadow. Her eyes squeezed shut as she tried to call out to her dragon. *Come.*

She thought it with all the energy she could muster, but considering she'd been tackled, thrown down a flight of stairs, and stabbed with a blade, she didn't have much energy left.

Even worse, something was wrong with Shadow. Maybe it was because the creature needed to hunt like Mishti had suggested. Or maybe it was because her barrier that was supposed to save everyone had ruined everything instead.

All she knew was that she called to Shadow, and it didn't feel right. She could sense the creature, she could feel the bond between them, but it didn't seem as strong as it had once been.

But what else could Chloe do now? If Shadow didn't come, then Julian wouldn't give up until he got the information he wanted from Chloe...or until she was dead.

35

Faerie and fae had a bond.

Pain screamed through every muscle and limb in Chloe's body, yet those words rang in her mind as clearly as if she currently read them straight from her magical book. If the bond got severed, magic would be lost. Faerie and fae.

One could not survive without the other.

Her hand held her side tight, keeping every drip of blood between her palm and her skin. The fabric of her dress grew warmer and stickier, but at least no blood spurted. If she could just keep from bleeding too much, she could stay alive. Get away. Clean and dress the wound.

But even with her hand pressed tight enough to drive the small blade deeper into her body, her head still got woozy when she tried to sit up.

Julian rested his hands on his knees, trying to catch his breath after dragging her through a castle hall and out across the soil. Noticing her attempt at standing up, he immediately kicked her hand, driving the blade even deeper.

She gasped. Air entered her body, but it didn't stay. It was like it came in through her mouth and out the back of her neck, which didn't make any sense at all, but that's how it felt.

Leaning closer to her with a vicious expression, Julian spoke in a raspy voice. "Tell me where the other pieces are. I know you already found some of them."

She glared at him. Glared hard enough to make him think she wanted to be defiant. Or angry. Anything really. All she truly did was call out to Shadow again. Their connection had weakened, just like everything magic in Crystalfall had, but that connection had not been severed completely.

Her dragon friend came closer, close enough that she only had to hang on another moment.

Julian lifted his foot, already staring at her side.

"No." She gasped the word out, curling into a ball. It didn't help the blade situation. If only she'd had better control of her limbs. If fear hadn't clenched her so tight, she could have reached for the poisoned dagger that still sat in the leg bracer Mishti had given her.

But even curling into a ball had taken nearly all the breath out of her. How was she supposed to breathe when pain burned every inch of her body?

Just when she nearly gave up hope, her dragon appeared in a curtain of dull gold and flat sapphire. Her body had none of the sparkling brilliance it should have, but at least she was there. Chloe used her free arm to drag her body closer to the dragon.

When Julian went to stop her, Shadow reached out with her claws and lifted him off the ground.

"Good," Chloe said through her teeth. "Keep him. And help me onto your back."

The dragon used her other arm to grab Chloe and throw her onto her back. The creature let out a growl as she flapped her wings and flew away from the castle. If pain hadn't frayed every nerve in Chloe's body, she might have worried that such commotion would wake the still-sleeping mortals outside Crystalfall Castle.

When Shadow flew father away from the castle, Chloe didn't stop her. She could barely even breathe at this point. Now that her life didn't stand in danger, she could at least force herself to take deeper breaths. It cleared her thinking, but she'd need to take care of her wound soon.

Shifting as small amount as possible, she glanced over her dragon's shoulder and down at her arm. Shadow still had Julian in her claws.

Chloe's eyes dropped as she took in a deep breath. And then she issued a command that felt like ice in her throat.

"Kill him."

The words were cold, but maybe she should have felt guiltier than she did. Truthfully, she didn't feel guilty at all. It was hard to when his blade was lodged into her side. Even as an apothecary, she might not be able to heal from such a wound.

Not without magic.

A hard breath escaped Julian's mouth, proving Shadow was following her command. The dragon squeezed her claws, cutting off his air and perhaps breaking a few ribs as well. But then Shadow let out a shriek that shook the emerald leaves beneath them.

Julian had stabbed the dragon with an axe. The dragon immediately released her grip, dropping him to the ground far below them.

With any luck, the fall would kill him. Chloe glanced out over the landscape, judging the distance to Crystalfall Castle.

It didn't matter. Even if he survived the fall, the castle would take him at least half a day to reach. He certainly wouldn't be there before day dawned.

Did the other mortals know about the secret entrance Julian had used? Maybe they did, but Mishti always said he kept secrets to himself. If none of the other mortals knew about the entrance, then Mishti and the others would be able to hold them off for at least a day or two.

By then…

Chloe held her side tight and spread out on her back against Shadow's golden scales. By then *what?* What was she supposed to do now? Go back to the castle and try and clean and dress her wound with a table that conjured sour food? Would the herbs she conjured be sour too?

Her mind drifted back to the words from her Faerie book. *If the bond between Faerie and fae got severed, magic would be lost.*

She kept thinking of it so rigidly, she hardly noticed when Shadow flew right up to the crystal caves that led to the rest of Faerie. She must have led her dragon there without realizing it.

Something deep within must have given her strength, because somehow, she climbed off her dragon's back and dragged herself to the barrier she created. Her side split with pain, but still, she used her free hand to touch the magic.

The other mortals had gotten past barrier enchantments before. They managed it by using iron. Would poisoned iron be even more effective at destroying the enchantment? Probably.

All this time, she had told herself there was no way back. No chance to change what she had done. And yet, all this time, she had known deep down that it wasn't true at all. Even Portia claimed to know how to break through this enchantment.

It had never been impossible. It had only been unwanted.

But could Chloe do it now? Should she?

At every turn, it seemed Crystalfall was falling once again. It seemed to need the magic of Faerie, and this barrier blocked it.

Her heart squeezed—and not just because of the pain. She gripped her side tighter, ignoring the tears that pricked at her eyes. She could destroy the barrier, but what then?

The answer dawned clear in her mind as painful as the blade in her side.

Then she'd have to go back to Quintus. She'd have to face him.

He'd never forgive her. How could he after what she did to him? She claimed over and over that this was his court, his home. And then she took it all away from him with no chance for him to get it back.

How could she face him now? Even with Crystalfall at stake, even with her side dripping with blood and in need of a magical remedy, she still stared at the barrier without moving.

Heat burned at the back of her neck. Her skull throbbed from having been thrown against a golden floor. The bruised muscles in her body tensed and shuddered.

Still, she stood without moving.

His eyes. She could see the look he'd had in his eyes when he realized she had locked him out. Betrayal had gutted him, not from an enemy, not from a friend. From her.

His beloved.

How could she look into those eyes and ask for forgiveness?

Her stomach turned over on itself. Blood warmed her palm, still seeping through the open wound in her side. Her chin trembled as she reached out to touch the shimmering golden enchantment with her free hand. When her fingers made contact, the barrier pulsed with a brighter glow.

This wasn't about her anymore. The mortals inside the castle needed her. Shadow and the pixies needed her. She knew what she had to do. The time for skulking had ended.

Using her free hand, she ripped the poisoned dagger with an iron blade from her leg bracer. Holding the hilt in her fist, she jammed the point against the golden magic.

At first, it merely glowed brighter and pulsed faster. But she wasn't about to give up now. She pressed with all her might, shoving the blade deeper into the magic. Little by little, it sank in. After a few moments, the pulsing magic turned to flickers. And then the flickers turned to sparks.

A crackling sound like shattering glass filled the air. It grew until it exploded in a loud crack. With a flash of light, the barrier vanished. Wind rushed past her, blowing her blonde hair out behind her.

Strength in purpose filled her then. She stepped more decisively as she clambered onto Shadow's back. Pain became nothing more than a throbbing reminder at the back of her head. But now she could think well enough to command her dragon.

Fly to Ludo's house.

She pictured the house and where it sat in Bitter Thorn Forest. After crawling through the black cave, Shadow lifted into the air and beat her wings more powerfully than she had in days. Already, the gold in her scales seemed brighter, more magnificent.

The mortals inside the castle needed help, and it was time to get it from the only ones who could help. The ones who should have been there all along.

The fae.

Chloe gulped, already preparing herself for shouts and accusations. When Ludo's house came into view, pain gnawed at the wound in her side. For a split second, she hoped that maybe Ludo was there, but Quintus was not. Maybe she could put off that confrontation for just a little longer.

But as she slipped off her dragon's back and hobbled to the front door, she knew that hope was fruitless. Quintus was inside. She didn't know how she knew. She just knew.

And now she'd have to face him.

36

NERVES LIT INSIDE CHLOE, FILLING her with burning ice and freezing fire. Standing in front of the door to Ludo's house, she stared, afraid to knock. Afraid to speak. Afraid.

Gripping her side firmly, she glanced over her shoulder. Shadow's scales had turned brighter, but the dragon still fidgeted and squirmed. Her wings kept popping out like she couldn't keep them still.

She stayed near Chloe like she'd been asked to do, but her body clearly wanted to take her away. Using her free hand, Chloe waved off toward the forest. "Go on. Fly wherever you need to go."

She hadn't even finished speaking before Shadow released her wings—knocking several leaves and branches off the nearby trees—and lifted herself into the air.

But now Chloe had no one at her back. Shadow couldn't very well enter the house with her, considering the creature was at least three times the size of the house, but it had helped to know she was there.

Holding her breath, Chloe knocked on the door. Her hand ached at her side, still pressing hard against her wound to keep the blood inside. Tension stretched through it. The pain from the blade should have been too powerful to even notice the slight pain in her hand, but instead, she could feel both as achingly clear as the other.

And still, fear held her tighter than any of the pain.

Her lungs squeezed, screaming at her to take a breath, but she wouldn't. Couldn't.

The door in front of her opened a crack. It swung open slowly while every muscle inside her stretched and trembled. And then, at last, a figure appeared before her.

Quintus.

Just like that, she could breathe again. He stood tall, steady. Just as she remembered him. Well, almost. The curls on his head had been cut so only short black hair remained. His dark brown eyes had lost the glints of gold inside them. But his skin looked as beautiful and dark and coppery as ever before.

Air filled her chest, seeming to start her heart along with it. After just one look, the world had righted itself once again.

But as she looked, he looked too. While her world seemed to right itself, his must have slanted worse than ever before.

His face twisted into a snarl. "*You.*"

He spat the word out with such disdain, her chin trembled at the sound of it.

She swallowed hard and had to remind herself why she had come. Good people were trapped inside Crystalfall Castle, and the enemy mortals were about to attack. Not to mention, she had a blade embedded deep in her side.

She swallowed again, which did nothing. Her chin still trembled as she looked up at him through her eyelashes. "I need your help."

The snarl on his face changed to disbelief. He released a cold laugh, which then turned back into a snarl. "If you think I would ever help..."

He trailed off, scoffing and shaking his head. "How could I forgive you after..."

His nostrils flared as he clenched his jaw. At his sides, both of his fists clenched too. He stared at her, the glare in his eyes growing more heated by the moment. "Why would you think I would ever want to see you again? Why would you think I would ever want to speak to you again?"

The air that had filled her lungs only moments ago turned to dust now. Her throat went dry even as tears stung in her eyes. If she had any sort of dignity at all, she'd be able to control the trembling of her chin, but she couldn't.

She had known he would react this way. Of course she had known it. That was the only reason, buried deep inside her she now realized, that she waited so long to destroy the barrier enchantment.

But knowing it and experiencing were two different things. Seeing him look at her like this felt worse than having only two dozen mortals join her. Worse than being stabbed.

Her lip really started quivering now, and she had to catch it between her teeth to stop it.

He looked right at her lips and then he looked away. A piece of her heart tore away along with his gaze. His jaw flexed. "I think you should leave."

A lump filled her throat with pain that shouldn't have been noticeable with the blade in her side, yet it was all she could feel. That and the tears and the squeezing of her heart. She didn't attempt to catch his eye.

Somehow, she knew he'd never look.

Maybe she should have fought harder, but what could she say? Those mortals in Crystalfall Castle depended on her, but Quintus had depended on her too. She had failed both of them. What could possibly change his mind?

With an unsteady nod, she turned toward Bitter Thorn Forest.

Where was she supposed to go now? Maybe Elora would take pity on her. Then again, Chloe had locked her own sister out with that enchantment. Maybe Elora would never forgive her either.

Chloe pressed her hand closer to her side, ready to wander the forest until her strength failed her completely. Maybe death would claim her and then she wouldn't have to bear the weight of all this guilt.

But just before she could turn away completely, Quintus shot a hand out and grabbed her by the wrist. The warmth of his hand sank into her skin, breathing back life into her broken heart. If he had grabbed a little lower, he would have felt the warm blood soaking the palm of her hand, but on her wrist, he'd feel nothing but the pulse in her veins.

Perhaps it was a foolish hope, but she glanced back into his eyes.

He stared, his glare as heavy as ever. Except now heated breaths escaped his nose that coincided with the clenching of his jaw. He stared right into her eyes, not searching, not hoping. He just stared. He *hated* her. She could see it in his features. And yet, something kept his hand holding tight to her wrist. Something.

And then, with the slightest turn of his arm, he pulled her hand away from her side. His gaze flicked down, landing right on her bloody palm, which he had just exposed.

At the sight of the blood, he let out a puff of air, as if he'd been punched in the gut. His gaze jumped from her hand to the blood on her dress to the mangled skin underneath it. Another heavy exhale came out as he lightly squeezed her wrist. Gently. Carefully.

Turning away, he dropped her wrist. He refused to look her in the eye once more. Closing his eyes, he stepped toward her and lifted her off the ground and into his arms. His gaze continued to avoid her at all costs, but he carried her inside the house. He carried her so easily, not at all how Julian had dragged her huffing and puffing and having to stop to catch his breath. Quintus carried her like she weighed nothing more than a blanket.

Passing the tree growing in the center of the house, he turned into Ludo's parlor, which still held stacks of books and piles of random items. He set her carefully on the blue velvet couch and then took several steps away, his back to her.

Ludo sat on the high-backed wooden chair across from her, reading a book, which he had propped open on his lap. He glanced up only when he turned the page. At once, his eyes opened wider than his fists. Lip curling, he glared at her and said exactly the same thing Quintus had said. "*You.*"

His fair skin immediately started turning red. He had a right to be angry. Crystalfall had answers about his brother that he'd been desperate to find. She'd taken those away from him when she locked them both out. He bared his teeth and shook his finger at her. "How could you—"

"She is injured." Quintus's voice was still cold, but it wasn't completely unfeeling anymore. It only wavered slightly when he spoke, but she could hear it.

Ludo sat back in his chair and shrugged. "Good. Maybe she will die from the injury."

Quintus kept his back to her, but his shoulders shook. It wasn't a large, jerky movement, but more of a small quiver. After his shoulders, the rest of him started shaking too. He turned just enough to get a glance at her wound. Blood came out of it even faster now.

After seeing it, his body shook even harder. His eyes clamped shut, and he took a step forward. He dropped to his knees at the edge of the couch and held his hand out toward her.

Chloe's breathing had turned short and stilted long ago, but now it hitched until she lost her air completely. Did he want to hold her hand? Did he think that would help?

His hand moved toward her more insistently, though his eyes remained closed. And then it hit her. It hadn't even been long without him, but apparently their bond had been severed more than she wanted to admit since it took her so long to realize his intention.

She still hadn't touched him, and now he finally spoke. "Heal yourself." He held his hand toward her, keeping his eyes shut as tight as ever.

Her Faerie book had said their connection was severed. That it may never be repaired. Could she even use her magic anymore?

She might as well try.

Swallowing, she reached out to him. The smooth warmth of his skin against hers filled the gaps in her heart that his eyes had gouged out. She held him as tenderly as she could.

Closing her eyes, she called to the magic within herself. Right away, she could tell Faerie was right. Their bond had broken. The magic she'd once had was no longer hers to claim with only a simple touch.

Still, she went through the process of healing inside her mind, just in case. But pain continued to surge through her. When she opened her eyes and glanced down at her wound, the mangled skin still oozed with blood.

Quintus peeked through one eyelid.

The moment he saw her injury, he let out a groan very akin to a whimper. His body trembled even harder than before. He ripped his hand away from her, stood, and turned his back to her again. He couldn't even bear to look at her.

Clearing his throat, he spoke in a husky, strained tone. "You lost your magic too, then, it appears."

Too? Her eyebrow raised, trying to make sense of his words. She lost her magic when she put up that barrier enchantment because it severed the connection between them, but that only affected her. No one else had lost their magic. At least no one that she knew of.

And then truth sliced deep into her heart, cutting away the little threads trying to hold it all together. She gasped, throwing both hands over her mouth. It couldn't be possible. She glanced at him again, at his body language, how he'd acted from the moment he'd seen her.

Had he lost *his* magic? When she severed the connection between them, had it taken away his magic along with her own?

Her head shook side to side, her own body trembling now. No. That couldn't be. It couldn't be.

She looked at Ludo, anxious for any explanation that might prove her wrong.

But the expression on his face only confirmed her worst fears. He tilted his head toward Quintus. "Besides that door he opened immediately after you put up the barrier, he hasn't been able to do any magic. You took his magic and broke his heart all in a single enchantment."

"No." Tears spilled from her eyes, trailing down her cheeks like little needles. "No."

A sob wracked through her, which sent the blade inside her even deeper than before. A cry tore from her lips. "If I had known…"

She never would have done it if she had known this would be the consequence.

But now it was too late.

The injury meant nothing. Now, she might never breathe again.

37

CHLOE WANTED TO CURL HER knees to her chest and cry into them until every drop of water had drained from her body. She had taken Quintus's magic. It didn't matter that she had done it unintentionally. His magic was gone, and it was all her fault.

Her body shook on the couch, sending her hand to press against the wound in her side. The pain didn't bother her so much now. She deserved it. She deserved worse than it. If only she could figure out how to breathe through the pain.

"Ludo." Quintus said the name insistently, still standing up with his back to her. Since she couldn't see his face, she couldn't tell for sure what he wanted.

Ludo halfway stood up from his chair and glanced down at it. "Do you need to sit down?"

With his back still turned, Quintus threw a hand back, gesturing at Chloe. "Do something."

Sighing, Ludo settled even deeper into his chair than before. "Should I send a message to Bitter Thorn Castle? Their dryad friend has impressive healing skills, does she not?"

His gaze turned now to Chloe while a cruel smirk curled his mouth. "Your sister has been preparing a scathing lecture for you, and I, for one, would love to be here when she delivers it."

Chloe's breaths came out in stuttering bursts as she pressed her hand into her wound to keep blood from gushing out.

Quintus stepped toward his friend, his jaw clenching tighter. "Ludo, now."

Ludo huffed before answering. "Fine." He stood slowly and wandered across the floor as if attending to nothing more urgent than dusting his shelves. "I have a potion that should help. I guess I should ask. What sort of injury is it, anyway?"

"Blade." Chloe forced the word out, sucking in a deep breath before she could speak again. "Julian stabbed me with a blade that had no handle. It's deep inside me now. I can probably yank it out, but the blood will make it a little slippery. I might need some help."

Quintus whirled around, his eyes meeting hers in a gaze more horrified than she had ever seen him wear. His shoulders shook as he turned back around, refusing to meet her gaze once again. He only stood for a moment before he started pacing back and forth at the edge of the room.

Holding a stack of clean fabric, jars filled with strange liquids, and other various items, Ludo dropped to his knees at the couch's side. He closed one eye and stared with the other at Chloe's wound.

After a short nod, he lifted a pair of forceps from his pile. "This should do it."

Not gently at all, he jammed the forceps into her wound and harshly fished around for the blade.

She gasped when the metal touched her skin. And when he yanked the blade out, she screamed.

Quintus immediately stopped pacing and whirled around to shoot Ludo a lethal glare.

"Calm down." Ludo waved at him, indicating that he should turn back around. "That was good pain. It means the blade is out now."

She could barely breathe, but she managed to grab a cloth from his pile and used it to catch the blood pouring from her wound. Some had already stained his couch, but at least she could prevent it from getting any worse. "Stitches."

The word came out in a gasp.

Ludo wrinkled his nose at the suggestion. He poured a potion on her wound, causing her to gasp even harder, which he deliberately ignored. "Mortals are so fragile. It seems barbaric to have to string thread through skin just to heal it."

"To *what?*" Quintus's voice was equal parts gravelly and shaky. He stared at Ludo, then at Chloe. Maybe he expected one of them to explain that stitches weren't nearly as barbaric as they sounded. Since they were exactly that barbaric, neither Chloe nor Ludo said anything.

Maybe a clarification would help calm him. With her voice still breathless and gasping she forced out an explanation. "Stitches will stop the bleeding, and they will keep the skin in place so that it can heal."

"But it is..." He swallowed hard. "You have to put thread in the skin? With a needle?"

She nodded, clutching her side just as Ludo poured another burning potion onto her wound.

Quintus's jaw flexed. In only a few steps, he crossed the room and lifted her off the couch. In one swift movement, he sat down and pulled her onto his lap with his arms around her. His eyes narrowed at Ludo. "Go get her some pain herbs."

Ludo responded with a curled lip. "She does not deserve them."

"Now!" Quintus shouted in a voice so deep it could almost be called a growl.

Ludo rolled his eyes, but he stood up and wandered across the room to a shelf full of herbs.

Chloe's hand shook as she held the fabric against her side. Now that the blade was out of her body, blood had already soaked more than half the fabric. She knew she shouldn't do what she was about to do.

Quintus had every right to hate her. But it didn't matter if she shouldn't. She couldn't stop herself when she buried her head against his shoulder and let out the sob stuck in her throat.

His arms pulled her closer, holding her around the shoulders and far away from the wound.

Ludo appeared a moment later, holding out a bundle of herbs. "Hurry up and take them. I am ready to do the stitches."

She plucked several leaves off the stem and chewed them as quickly as she could manage with the shaking of her body.

While she chewed, Ludo retrieved a needle and a spool of clear thread. He looked almost gleeful as he started stabbing the needle into her.

She sank into Quintus, burying her head into his shoulder once again. Even once Ludo finished with the stitches, she couldn't stop shaking.

Her body trembled, tensing each muscle no matter how she tried to relax. The pain herbs had even taken the edge off most of her pain, but it did nothing for the shaking.

Now all that was left was for Ludo to wipe away the excess blood, which he did not do gently. Once finished, he touched a finger to the golden and emerald ring on her finger. His eyes narrowed at it while something sparked in his eyes. Did he recognize it?

"Where did you get that?" he asked.

She pulled her hand away from him, the memory of Julian trying to steal the ring still a little too fresh in her mind. "Quintus gave it to me."

The words came out before she could think, but now a thought entered her mind that rang crystal clear. Attempting to match her previous tone, she said something that might change everything. "It used to belong to his mother, Dyani."

She felt Quintus huff, the breath warming her cheek. "I regret giving it to you now. I never—"

His words cut off short as he narrowed both eyes. Suddenly, he was staring at her, as if trying to see straight into her soul. "How did you know my mother's name is Dyani?"

Her eyes opened wide. It had been a guess, an educated guess, but still a guess. She stared at him now with her jaw dropping by the second. "I didn't know for sure, I just thought maybe…" Her head shook side to side as disbelief overtook her. "Oh, Quintus."

Ludo looked up from his pile of supplies with one eyebrow raised. "Why does it matter what his mother's name is?"

Instead of answering, she just looked at Quintus.

He seemed to just barely realize in that moment that he had her in his arms and on his lap. His throat bulged with a swallow and then he pushed her away. He set her down on the couch as far from him as he could get her.

All the while, he threw her looks of the utmost disgust, but he also touched her gently and never once touched her anywhere near her wound.

Staring at him with a focused gaze she admitted what she had only just discovered. "Quintus, your father was the king of Crystalfall."

She swallowed and looked down at her hands. "I know why he tried to kill you the first time he ever saw you. He thought you threatened his place as king. He was paranoid. He thought everyone was after him."

Shrugging, she reached for the ring and spun it around her finger. It no longer seemed a coincidence that it had the same golden and emerald design as the other crown pieces. "I guess in a way he was right. Because now he's gone, and that means you are the heir. Now you really will take his place. You are the prince of Crystalfall."

Quintus stared without blinking, without breathing. Even Ludo had nothing to say. Quintus sat in silence, no expression on his face. When an expression finally did stretch onto his features, they only tightened his muscles. He looked down at his hands, wrinkling his nose at them. "How am I supposed to rule anything when I cannot even do magic?"

After staring at his hands for another moment, he then shoved them away from himself and turned away to look at the rest of the room. Anything but her.

She hated herself. Seeing his reaction hurt so much more than any blade. He was destined for this, and she had taken it from him. Her stomach might never settle again. For the rest of her life, knots would seize her chest, making it impossible to eat. Impossible to breathe.

Only once her thoughts had turned their darkest did the tiniest glint of hope appear. Her eyes opened wide as she whispered, "The crown."

His gaze flicked to hers for a brief moment before he looked away as dejected as ever. "What are you talking about?"

She sat up higher, ignoring how it stretched her new stitches. "Faerie crowns have power, don't they? If we put all the pieces together and remake the crown..." She held her hand out, giving him room to finish the sentence. He didn't, but it didn't matter. She could finish the sentence on her own. "The power of the crown will bring your magic back, won't it?"

A spark lit in his eyes as he dared to believe her words. It vanished a moment later in a disbelieving scowl, but it had been there for a moment.

She turned now to the fae who loved knowledge almost as much as her. Her eyebrows raised expectantly at Ludo.

He didn't answer, but he certainly seemed as intrigued as her. Rising from the ground, he crossed the room to a bookcase filled with haphazard stacks of books. After skimming a few of a particular book's pages, the blue in his blue-and-red eyes glowed. "I think she is right. If the crown is restored, and if you are the first to wear it, it will bring your magic back."

Chloe stood up, which sent her head spinning. Immediately sitting back down again, she placed two fingers against her temples. "Mishti and I think we know where the third crown piece is hidden."

Her gaze turned to her hand, to the golden and emerald ring so similar to the trees in Crystalfall. She bit her lip. "I could be wrong, but I think this ring might be the fourth piece. And the third crown piece is hidden in a secret vault where the king did experiments, so that room probably has all the items you'd need to re-create the crown."

Forgetting he was supposed to avoid looking at her, Quintus turned and stared at the jewelry piece. His eyes stayed focused, but they held no emotion.

She took in a little breath before speaking again. "There's something else."

His gaze flicked up to hers before he turned his back to her again.

Now she wrapped one arm around her stomach, hovering her hand over the blood in her dress that hadn't dried. "Crystalfall Castle is under attack."

Ludo raised both his eyebrows and then shook his head. "Great, so now we have to choose. Save the castle or get the crown?"

Chloe sat up straighter, ignoring how her head swam and pounded. "Not *we*." Her head turned away from Ludo, staring at the back standing before her. "Quintus has to choose."

38

AN OCEAN SEEMED TO FILL Chloe's head, whooshing each time she made the smallest movement. Even after taking pain herbs, her side still throbbed. She had nearly forgotten pain was only one of many issues that came along with an injury. They had so much to do, and now even walking would be difficult for her.

With her fingers pressed against her temples, she glanced up at Quintus. He wore the jade green shirt and emerald-green vest they had found inside the castle. The golden rivets along the bottom hem seemed a little brighter than when she had first seen him.

He stood completely still with his hands clasped behind his back. His gaze darted across the room, not looking at anything in particular. Clearly, this choice he had to make did not have an easy answer.

Save his castle or get his crown.

If he chose correctly, he could probably have both. But if he made a wrong choice, he might end up with neither.

His toe tapped against the earthy floor of Ludo's house. At once, his head shifted toward Chloe, but only just enough to glance at her from the side of his eye. "What about the barrier enchantment?"

"It's gone now. I broke it using a poisoned iron dagger." She must have left that dagger at the entrance to the crystal caves. Pain had ruled her too greatly to think of carrying it with her when she climbed back onto Shadow.

The whooshing in her head made it difficult to recognize how Quintus's expression had changed. Heat filled his face, sending fire into his eyes. "You said you could not break it without magic." His jaw clenched tighter. "You lied."

"No." She shook her head quickly and immediately had to grab it with both hands just to get the ringing in her ears to stop. "I truly believed the barrier could only be broken with magic. But I found out Portia planned to try breaking it. Mishti said they'd use iron, since that was how they've broken enchantments before. Their first attempts failed, apparently, but the iron I used had poison covering it too."

Her voice lowered to a near whisper. "I think that helped."

Ludo huffed, turning his back on Chloe and tipping his nose into the air as he spoke to Quintus. "I think you should go get the crown. Once your magic returns, and you get the added power of the crown, you will be able to destroy the attacking mortals with a single enchantment."

Quintus still had his body angled mostly away from Chloe, but she saw how he raised an eyebrow. "Those same mortals took over Bitter Thorn Castle, if you recall. Even High King Brannick and Queen Elora could not defeat them, and they have the strongest magic in Faerie. I doubt one enchantment would destroy them."

Holding her head with both hands, Chloe spoke in a timid, shaking voice. "It is a little different now. After the magic I did, the mortals can't use iron to poison the land anymore. Wasn't iron poisoning a big reason Elora and Brannick got defeated in the first place?"

Quintus turned just enough to glance at her. "You agree with Ludo, then? You think I should go after the crown?"

"No, I think you should save the castle." If only she could use both her hands to hold her head and wrap two arms around her stomach at the same time. Nausea rocked her gut while an ocean rocked her mind.

She had to close her eyes and take a few breaths before she could speak again. "For one thing, there are innocent people inside the castle who need your help. For another thing, if the enemy mortals do take control of the castle, it will be much more difficult to steal it back than it would be to defeat them now. We can easily go get the missing crown piece from the vault *after* the castle is secured and the enemy mortals beaten."

"What about Julian?" Quintus asked. "He saw the third clue."

Cringing, she held out her hand. "He also tried to steal this ring, which is part of why I believe it's one of the crown pieces."

"What?" The word shot from Ludo's mouth like a slap to the face. Quintus's face looked like he had been the one to receive that slap.

If her head hadn't been pounding, she would have nodded, sharing in their surprise. "I don't know how or what he learned, but he knows a lot more than what was written on that clue. Maybe he knows the pieces can be re-formed to make a crown or maybe he just knows the pieces are valuable. Either way, he definitely wants all four pieces."

Quintus touched a hand to his forehead. "Then we *should* find the crown piece first. Julian might be going after it right now."

"Well…" Chloe dragged out the word until both Quintus and Ludo looked at her. "Julian might be dead."

That caused one of Quintus's eyebrows to raise. "*Might* be?"

Ludo scoffed. "Knowing our luck, that is not likely."

Chloe cringed at the thought. Ludo was probably right, but she didn't want to dwell on that. She still thought they needed to save the castle first. "In his journal, the king emphasized how secret the location of the third crown piece is. It's inside a vault and probably filled to the brim with all sorts of useful items. I have a feeling it's going to take more work than just finding the location. And if there's more to it, Julian probably won't be able to get inside without help."

Quintus frowned. "But he has hundreds of mortals on his side. He could easily get help."

Chloe raised both her eyebrows. "Which do you think is more likely? That Julian will share a secret and ask for help or that Portia will use her army to gain control of Crystalfall Castle?"

It only took Quintus two breaths to consider her question. After that, he turned toward Ludo with a sharp expression. "Open a door to Crystalfall Castle."

He had taken her side. Maybe he still wouldn't look at her, but at least he had listened.

Ludo's door brought them directly inside the castle's main entrance. Before he had even finished closing his Faerie door, the golden doors before them shook from the force of some monstrously heavy object ramming against them. Clearly, the mortals were trying to break inside.

Sucking in a breath, Quintus pressed his palms against the golden doors and stared hard at them. Nothing happened.

Ludo sighed and spoke under his breath. "Did you want me to create a barrier enchantment for you?"

After a beat, Quintus stared at his hands, shook his head, and then stepped away from the door. His gaze dropped to his boots. Now he spoke under his breath. "No, I need you to seal the door completely. Melt the gold in the doors and the gold in the doorway until they are melded together completely and this is just a wall."

No other words were spoken as Ludo lifted his hands to perform the magic.

Even with the throbbing in her head, Chloe couldn't miss how Quintus dropped his chin to his chest. Every few moments, he'd glance at his hands and then shake his head again.

After sealing the main doors, whatever object had rammed against them before rammed again, but this time it didn't shake the door frame. As Quintus had requested, the doors had now been turned into a solid wall.

"Come on." Chloe beckoned them down a hallway. "Julian used a secret entrance to get into the castle last night. You should seal that one too, and then we can find Mishti, and she can tell us where the other entrances are."

"What am I supposed to do?" Quintus spoke with as much bite as a wolf.

Chloe wanted to roll her eyes, but that would probably just make things worse. She gestured at his hands. "You still know how to throw a spear, don't you? Once we find Mishti, she'll know where you'll be most useful."

He huffed as they continued walking down the hall, but at least he had stopped glaring at his hands.

After sealing the secret entrance, she led them toward the turret Mishti had been in the night before. Shouts rang out, getting louder the closer they came to the turret.

Through the castle walls, they could hear screams from the outside. They could also hear foreign objects slamming against the golden castle walls.

The battle raged, and walking through the halls wouldn't do any good. They needed to find Mishti, and they needed to find her soon.

39

HALLWAYS WHIRLED PAST AS CHLOE, Quintus, and Ludo rushed through them. Chloe's heart rate increased each time a shout rang out or a wall clanged from the impact of a weapon. Since those things kept happening every few seconds, her heart was positively hammering now.

They needed to find Mishti.

Just when Chloe lifted her foot onto the first step leading to the top of a turret, Mishti came rushing down around a spiral corner.

Catching sight of Chloe, Mishti let out a short breath of relief. "*There* you are. We already have two injured soldiers waiting for you in the great hall. What took you…"

Right then, her gaze trailed away from Chloe and onto the two fae standing next to her. Mishti looked from Ludo to Quintus and then back to Chloe again. A question lit in her eyes just as her mouth parted.

But then she shook her head and gestured ahead. "Let's get to the great hall. I need more arrows anyway, and you need to tend to the injuries."

Apparently, the news that fae were back in Crystalfall was not nearly as pressing as the battle at hand. This was why Mishti did so well in fights. She could filter out any non-urgent information at any given time, no matter how shocking it might be.

But when they had nearly reached the great hall, Mishti's gaze fell on Chloe's side. Her eyes narrowed, taking in the drying blood, the sliced fabric, and the stitched-up skin underneath.

Mishti's voice lowered. "You're..." Her voice trailed off as she gave a pointed look in Quintus's direction. Then she turned back to look at Chloe again. "Injured. Why didn't you heal yourself? And why didn't he repair your clothes?"

Quintus shrank at the sound of her words, immediately going back to glaring at his hands.

"That reminds me." Chloe tried to speak in her brightest voice. "Quintus needs a job with weapons. No magic. Ludo can seal the doors in the castle so they become walls instead of doors, but he needs to know where all the exits are."

Both of Mishti's eyebrows raised, but her surprise vanished as quickly as it had before. "Perfect. All our shooters in position three are down. Quintus." She gestured ahead. "Go down that hallway to the right and then head up the staircase. Ludo, come with me. Once I deliver the weapons to my position, I can take you through the castle and show you the other exits."

That was that.

In only a few words, each person had a job perfectly suited to their wildly varying talents. And Mishti had acted without hesitation. No wonder she'd been taken advantage of by her leaders. She really did thrive in this sort of environment.

Chloe hobbled into the great hall. Mishti ran inside just long enough to gather an armful of arrows. Ludo followed her, grabbing his own armful of arrows at her request. Quintus had already left for the turret that needed him.

Digging into her leather bag, Chloe pulled out her healing herbs and arranged them as neatly as possible. Then she crawled over to the first person with an injury. A man with gray eyes held his hand against his cheek. When she pulled it away, there sat a deep gash with blood dripping down it.

Nodding, she turned to her piles of supplies.

Her attention focused the way only apothecary work could attune it. She cleaned the wound then double-checked a recipe in her magical book before applying healing herbs. She had to use the table to conjure a few herbs she hadn't thought to conjure before. Luckily, the herbs looked as potent and fresh as the first time she had used the table.

Magic must have entered Crystalfall again because the table worked without incident. Her head bent, deep in her work again as she finished dressing the first injury and moved on to the second.

She stayed so focused, she hardly noticed when people ran in and out of the great hall to gather more weapons. As soon as she finished working on an injury, she almost always had a new person waiting to have some scratch or gash or stab dealt with.

At this point, she must have dressed at least one wound on nearly every mortal inside the castle. But more still came.

Perhaps she'd been wrong. This battle clearly wouldn't be as easy to win as they'd all hoped. Maybe they should have gone after the crown instead.

Her insides convulsed, but at least the whooshing in her head had calmed. She finished tying off a bandage and sent a mortal on her way. For the first time in a while, she had no one else to attend to.

Now she finally had a chance to clean up some of the mess she'd made with her herbs and bandages. She scooted across the floor, which would normally be highly inefficient. But with the wound in her side, scooting prevented her from stretching and twisting her injury while attempting to stand.

Besides, no one else was in the great hall with her anyway.

But even as she had that thought, she noticed movement out of the corner of her eye. At first, she assumed the wraiths were back to beg her for another wish. But a different presence filled the shadows now. A solid presence that made her heart flutter.

Quintus stepped out of the corner of the room and used his chin to point at an empty spot on the ground. "We have no more weapons left."

Chloe's stomach flopped over on itself. "Oh."

What a brilliant thing to say. *Oh.* Why couldn't she ask about the battle or if he needed anything or if he'd maybe consider forgiving her if she could somehow prove how much she cared for him and how wrong she had been?

These thoughts were getting her nowhere. Why did the sight of him have to turn her mind to mush anyway?

He stood several paces away from her, keeping his gaze on the ground instead of on her. "You have helped many people. You helped them, even without magic."

"Don't do that." She tilted her head to the side and pressed her lips together. "You're going to get your magic back. You don't need to be morose and try to convince yourself you still matter even without magic. You do matter, but you're going to get your magic back anyway, so no moping."

He might have responded or he might have stared off into the distance forever. She'd never know because just then, running footsteps sounded in the hallway near them.

At the sound of them, Quintus retreated to the shadows, moving even farther away from Chloe.

Mishti ran into the room with Ludo on her tail. She took one look at the floor and let out a heavy sigh. "Great."

Excitement glinted in Ludo's eyes as he stepped out from behind Mishti. "Great? So there *are* still weapons left?"

She rolled her eyes at him. "No, *great*, as in the weapons are gone."

His face slanted in confusion. "I know Faerie can translate language, but the way you mortals speak is still strange."

"It's just sarcasm, remember? It's not that strange." Mishti kept her face hardened and serious, but a tiny twitch at the very top of her lips revealed that maybe she enjoyed this banter. Maybe she had missed it when Ludo was gone.

Turning away from them, Chloe looked into the shadows. "What do we do now?"

Mishti started once she caught sight of Quintus. She clearly hadn't noticed him until Chloe addressed him. Ludo lifted his eyebrows too, though he didn't seem as surprised that Quintus had somehow wound up in the same room as Chloe.

Stepping toward them, Quintus stared at the ground with a somber expression. "We cannot win this battle without more weapons."

He said it as a statement, but he still glanced at Mishti for confirmation.

Her nose wrinkled as she frowned. "Probably not."

Nodding, he brought his hand to his chin. He stroked it before finally speaking again. "All the doors are sealed, correct?"

"Yes," Ludo answered.

Quintus's eyes narrowed as he stroked his chin again. At once, he relaxed his narrowed eyes and stood a little taller. "If the doors are sealed, no one should be able to break into the castle. But just in case, gather the other mortals and have them hide in the library. Ludo, I want you to create a glamour that makes the library appear smaller than it truly is. The mortals on our side will hide behind that glamour. If any of Portia's mortals manage to get inside the castle, at least those on our side will be hidden."

"What about us?" Chloe asked in her tiniest voice, almost afraid of the answer.

He turned away from her and lifted his chin higher. "The four of us are going to find that third crown piece."

Ludo's mouth dropped open wide. Then he pointed right at Chloe's face. "You want *her* to come?"

Quintus turned to him with his jaw flexed. "I am not going to lose my crown because of pride. If we meet any unexpected obstacles, it will be better that all four of us are there to figure them out."

A scowl broke across Ludo's face, which he directed at Chloe. But then he huffed, and said, "Fine."

Shifting his shoulders toward the doors and away from Chloe, Quintus spoke to the room. "Where is it? Where is the vault?"

She pulled out the king's journal. While she turned the pages, Mishti and Ludo went off to gather and hide the mortals in the library.

Chloe hadn't expected Quintus to suddenly talk to her more than ever, but she hadn't expected him to remain completely silent either. Through all her explanations—as she showed him the map and then showed him the page with the hidden blue lines—he just nodded and stared at anything and everything except for her.

At least he had made a decision without second guessing himself.

Now Ludo opened a door to an area somewhat near the vault that they all knew well. None of them discussed how they had failed to defeat the mortals, but dread probably bubbled in Quintus's and Ludo's guts just like it did in Chloe's.

Had they made the wrong choice?

Maybe they never should have come to the castle at all. Maybe they should have gone for the crown first. They'd know soon enough.

They were headed for the vault, ready to find that third crown piece.

40

THE KING'S JOURNAL SAT OPEN on Chloe's palms while she compared it to her current surroundings. Ludo had opened a door taking her, Quintus, and Mishti to the mushroom patch where the vault should have been hidden, but nothing except golden trees and various jeweled vegetation surrounded them.

Her gaze flicked to the map again. This had to be the spot. She had checked between the map and those blue lines on the page where the king first mentioned the vault. She had even insisted Ludo open a door to a place in Crystalfall that they had already been before. They walked the rest of the distance to the mushroom patch, which should have made it impossible to get the location wrong.

Except here they stood with no sign of a vault. Ludo let out an exaggerated sigh and lifted his hands. "Let me guess. You need me to do my magic in finding things. I suppose I have to save the day like I always do."

He wore a deep frown as he lifted his hands and whirled them around.

The action did little to calm Chloe's fears though. His magic hadn't found the box containing the emerald and gold dagger. It hadn't found the key behind the waterfall either. Both times, they'd had to be clever instead.

Mishti clasped her hands in front of herself and stepped up to Chloe's side. She spoke in a low voice, intended only for Chloe, but fae senses meant Ludo and Quintus would hear regardless. "Are you sure this is the right place?"

"It is," Quintus answered. He stood with his fingers twitching at his sides. His eyes twitched too while he stared at the space around them. His gaze never focused on any specific area, instead jumping from tree to mushroom to bush and onward, as if searching beyond what he could see. "I can feel it."

A light breeze drifted around them. It rustled through his hair that he had cut back to the short length Chloe remembered from her first visit to Faerie. Her stomach tumbled a little at his presence. She found herself longing for his black curls to grow back because then the breeze would rush through them, causing a few stray locks to tumble onto his forehead.

She had to shake her head to force the thought away. This was no time to be enamored by a fae who might never forgive her. She had to focus.

No matter how she scolded herself, her gaze trailed back to Quintus again. Except this time, she noticed his gaze had stopped wandering. Now it focused on a single spot. A large golden boulder sat ahead. At the base of the boulder grew sparkling green plants with sharp, and possibly painful, leaves. Two trees stood on either side of the boulder, their golden branches poking out at odd angles. Each branch was sharpened to a menacing point.

Now that was a spot she'd want to avoid. How had so much of the land spontaneously turned deadly in that one area when most of Crystalfall was just glittering and beautiful and a little impractical, but not deadly?

Her eyes opened wide at the thought and then she grinned. Unless it wasn't spontaneous at all. In fact, maybe the spot only appeared dangerous to prevent someone from walking near it.

With that thought, she marched forward. The wound in her side still smarted with each step, but that didn't stop her. She held one hand out, ready to push away the sharpened golden branches before she touched them.

In the end, that had been unnecessary because all of it— the plants with the blade-like leaves, the sharpened spear-like golden branches—were nothing more than a glamour. She walked straight through the image and found herself face to face with an enormous golden door.

The others followed and joined her in front of what could only be the entrance to the vault. Levers and golden rods covered the round door. It had been built into a sloping hill of jade and malachite. The scent of lilacs and vanilla that usually filled the Crystalfall air had been replaced with the vaguest smell of smoke.

On one side of the round door, hinges connected it to the hill. On the other side, a tall rectangle with a series of nine locks secured it. On a whim, she attempted to open the door, just in case the locks were for show.

It didn't budge.

Quintus reached out, trailing his hand along one of the levers. It connected to a golden rod, which then connected to one of the locks. Tilting his head, he narrowed his eyes. "Is it a puzzle? We just have to arrange these levers and rods and then the locks will open?"

"I think you're right," Chloe responded. But then Quintus went to move one of the rods and she grabbed his wrist to stop him.

Tingling filled her hand now that it touched Quintus's skin. She planned to pull away, but her hand wrapped a little closer to him instead. Heat rose into her cheeks as she used her other hand to point at the top of the door. "Do you see that box? It has a fuse coming out of it, which is also connected to these levers and rods."

Ludo stepped closer, eyeing the item she had pointed out. He snarled at it. "That box holding the dagger had an explosive too. The Crystalfall king definitely liked explosions a little too much."

Quintus remained completely still except for his gaze, which he dropped onto Chloe's hand, which was still wrapped around his wrist.

The moment he looked, she peeled her hand back, heat prickling even hotter in her cheeks.

Now his hand dropped to his side. "If we do the puzzle wrong, it will set off an explosion?"

Chloe nodded.

"Great," Mishti said in a huff.

Ludo turned to her with his head tilted. "As in, *not* great?"

"Exactly." Mishti frowned at the door.

Ludo glared at it.

Quintus sighed with the weight of someone who carried the fate of an entire court on his shoulders. He rubbed a hand across his forehead. "What do we do now?"

Turning her face as hard as stone, Mishti tilted her chin toward the door. "I think we should do the puzzle wrong on

311

purpose, jump out of the way, and hope the explosion destroys the door so we can get inside the vault."

"The mortals are probably going to get here soon anyway," Ludo said through a grumble. "Why even bother with the door? We should just give up."

Quintus narrowed his eyes, stepping forward and lifting both his arms. "Perhaps I can force the vault door open without completing the puzzle. My strength might be enough."

He didn't do it on purpose, but the movement tightened the sleeves over his arms. Through the stretched emerald fabric, his muscles flexed, emphasizing every curve and chisel.

Chloe blinked at least twice before she realized how intensely she stared at him. She had to swallow and jerk her gaze away just to be able to think again.

Everyone's suggestions now flickered through her mind. Already, they were back to the way they'd always been. Mishti offered a frightening idea, Ludo a grumpy idea, and Quintus a heroic idea that legitimately stole rational thought from Chloe's mind for at least a few moments.

Memories of the rope bridge and their epic failure in crossing it flitted in with everything else. She had ignored their suggestions then, which nearly cost them their lives. That wouldn't happen again.

This time, she thought through each suggestion, looking past the obvious for any deeper meaning that might be hidden.

Mishti was willing to risk setting off the explosion in hopes it would open the vault. That probably just indicated she wanted to hurry. She probably knew they didn't have much time.

Clearly, Ludo feared the mortals would show up and possibly attack them or even get the crown.

And Quintus, well, he just wanted to get his crown piece no matter what it took.

Drumming her fingers on the strap of her leather bag, Chloe tried to put the pieces together. She couldn't ignore their concerns. She had to find a way to work with them instead.

Turning, she pointed to a spot ahead. "Ludo, you stand watch over there. You'll be hidden behind the glamour covering this vault so no one who comes near will be able to see you. But you'll still be able to alert us the moment anyone shows up."

He folded his arms over his chest, showing off a classic Ludo frown. "And what are we supposed to do if mortals do show up?"

"We will attack them before they can attack us. Or we'll open a door and get away if we have to. If you're keeping watch, at least we'll know if anyone is coming." She gestured toward the spot again.

He grumbled under his breath, but he still moved into position. When he got there, his face grew serious and focused. Maybe he acted like she had bad ideas, but he clearly cared more about this job than he wanted to let on.

With a nod, Chloe turned to the others. "Mishti, I want you to think of a way to set off the explosion without any of us getting hurt. I want to try opening the vault with the puzzle first, but we'll need a backup plan in case that doesn't work."

"Got it." Mishti set her jaw and stepped a little closer to the vault. She eyed the box with the fuse and gently moved her lips as if talking to herself. After a moment, she went to grab her sword. It was gone now, lost along with all the other weapons used in the battle at Crystalfall Castle. After a quick nose wrinkle, she reached for a stick on the ground instead.

Taking a short inhale, Chloe now turned to Quintus. "Have you ever seen a puzzle like this before?"

He stared at the door, his lips turned down ever so slightly. "You do not think I can force the door open?"

He held up one arm, flexing the muscles even harder than before. Or maybe it just felt that way because seeing the tight fabric over his bulging muscles sent her heart into a flutter. She reached out, touching a hand over his bicep, which did nothing to improve her increasing heart rate. "You might be strong enough."

Her voice came out a little too breathless to be taken seriously.

Taking a step back, he pulled his arm away from her and dropped it back to his side. "We should probably try the puzzle first. Just in case forcing open the door causes an explosion too."

Mishti seemed completely oblivious to the tension between them. She used her stick to point to the edge of the door. "If we can direct the explosion on the hinges here, I think we'd be able to open the door on this side instead of on the side with the locks." Bringing the golden stick toward her, she then tapped it against her chin. "Although, it depends on how deep the locks are stuck inside the door. We might not be able to move it even with the hinges removed."

None of that made sense to Chloe, but it did get her mind whirling again. She glanced at the door when a new idea sprang forward. "Wait a minute."

She snatched the king's journal from her leather bag and quickly found the page where he first mentioned the vault. Blowing a slow and heated breath onto the page, the hidden blue lines appeared.

All those lines converged in a single spot, which had shown them the location of the vault, but what if there was more to it than that?

Quintus stepped closer to her, the heat from his chest warming her shoulder. He stared at the journal and then seemed to have the same thought she had.

Reaching out, he grabbed the rod at the very top of the door and moved it into the same position as the very top line on the page. He then moved to a lever and turned it until it matched a second line on the page. With the movement of those two pieces, an unlocking *click* sounded out. The first of the nine locks had just come undone.

Chloe grinned. "Excellent."

Quintus moved faster, using two hands to work with while Chloe had to use one to hold the book. Little by little, the lock on the second came undone.

"Excuse me." Mishti squeezed between them as they worked. She held a golden stick and a small rock, which she maneuvered against the box at the top of the vault door until it came away from the wall.

Still keeping watch, Ludo asked, "Is that the explosive?"

"Yes." Mishti stepped away, poking and grinning at the box she had just removed from the door. "I thought it would be easier to manipulate it once I unhooked it from the door."

Ludo let out a soft chuckle. "Good. Now if any mortals come, you can simply set off the explosion and throw it at them."

Chloe glanced his way just long enough to see him shiver before turning to keep watch once again.

Quintus moved a rod into place, unlocking the seventh of nine locks. They were almost done.

Ludo jumped back, moving into Chloe's sight once again. "I heard something," he whispered.

After a gulp, Chloe turned to Quintus. He stared at her with eyes wide. Without a word, they turned back to the vault door and moved the pieces even faster than before.

Soon, they had the eighth lock undone.

At their side, Mishti fiddled with the explosive, her face growing more frustrated by the moment.

Chloe glanced over her shoulder and noticed Ludo's wide blue-and-red eyes fixed on the forest ahead. His hands formed tight fists, and his feet shifted nervously in the dirt. Fear etched across all his features.

Luckily, Quintus put the last piece into place. A loud and satisfying click filled the air, which opened the ninth lock. When he went to open the door, it swung inward easily.

They had done it. They had actually worked together and used their separate talents without bickering or competing with each other.

Chloe might have celebrated the victory more, except Ludo scrambled backward until he reached the rest of them. Using both hands he shoved the four of them through the open door. His voice came out hurried and anxious. "They are coming."

Darkness filled the vault, but Chloe could still see outside it easily. Just as they all clambered inside, dozens of mortals came into view with Julian at the front.

"Shut the door!" Ludo shouted.

If he'd been silent, the glamour might have kept them safe.

But now the mortals knew where they were. They'd know to charge past the dangerous-looking branches and plants, since Ludo's voice had come from there.

Scolding him wouldn't help. Instead, she used her shoulder and heaved against the weight of the vault door. Once Quintus started helping, the door began closing easily.

They had nearly gotten it shut, but then it came to an abrupt halt just before closing completely. Her gaze dropped to see that a solid ball of iron had been rolled across the ground and now stopped the door from closing completely.

Just as she gasped, her gaze flicked up and she made eye contact with Julian. *Julian.*

His mouth curled into a vicious grin.

41

THE SIGHT OF JULIAN SMILING sent nausea crashing through Chloe's belly. She gasped, involuntarily reaching for her side where he had stabbed her earlier that day. Of course he survived Shadow's squeezing claws and a fall that should have killed him. It had been stupid to think he might have died.

Her throat had an aching bulge inside it, which she did her best to ignore. The golden vault door would close and separate her from the mortal who had tried to kill her. She just had to get the ball of iron that blocked it out of the way.

Lifting her wooden foot off the ground, she prepared to kick away the ball of iron. But just as she started swinging, she pulled her foot back and whirled around instead. "Mishti, do you still have—"

Mishti pushed her out of the way, the golden box in her hands.

She'd had the same idea as Chloe already. The young woman clenched her jaw and held her hands to the side. "Ludo, I need fire."

Shouts from outside the door shook the air around them. Dozens of mortals let out war cries as they lifted weapons.

Ludo held out his palm. A flicker of fire started to appear, but then he ducked and gasped at the commotion outside. His fire disappeared in a flash.

Just after he ducked, a spinning dagger flew through the tiny opening in the door. A moment later, it smashed into something inside the room made of glass.

"Hurry." Mishti held the box toward him again, her jaw clenched even tighter than before.

Ludo eyed the doorway warily.

An arrow flew through it, but this time, Quintus caught the weapon in his fist before it could hit anyone or anything in the room. His lightning-quick reflexes had protected them. Now he snapped the arrow in half and dropped to the ground. "Ludo, fire."

Nodding, Ludo opened his hand again. He stood still until a small fire roared to life above his palm. Now he directed the fire to light the fuse Mishti pointed to.

Quintus caught two more weapons with his bare hands, dropping them to the ground before they could cause damage.

But now the fuse was lit, and Mishti stared at the box without moving.

Chloe cleared her throat. "Uh, Mishti?"

"What?" Mishti didn't move.

Every hair on Chloe's arm stood on end as she gestured toward the fuse, which was already halfway burned. "Get rid of that thing."

Mishti continued to hold it without moving, her face as hardened as ever. "We don't want them to have time to throw it back as us, do we?"

Chloe's voice raised half an octave as she took a step back. "But now there's only a tiny—"

Before she could finish the sentence, Mishti chucked the golden box out through the door at the mortals who were running toward it.

Sucking in a breath, Chloe pushed her out of the way and kicked the ball of iron so it no longer kept the door open. In the next breath, Quintus slammed the door shut.

At exactly the moment the door closed, an explosion erupted just on the other side of it. A boom shook the ground under their feet, which was followed by screams. A few of the screams got cut off short. Those voices didn't call out again.

Even in the darkened room, Chloe still noticed how Mishti cringed at the sound of the shouts.

"Yes!" Ludo punched the air, still holding a small fire in his other hand. "Do you think we killed any of them?"

A vein in Mishti's jaw pulsed as she clenched her teeth tighter together. Her shoulders shuddered as she turned away. "Yes."

That caused Ludo to punch the air again, which only made Mishti slump even more.

Chloe touched her friend's arm. Her eyebrows pinched together as she tried to catch Mishti's eyes.

Mishti had probably killed people back at the castle too, but Chloe hadn't been there to watch it. Now, Chloe was forced to remind herself that she had pushed her friend to do the unthinkable. She had pushed her friend to kill when she only wanted peace.

Shouts continued outside, but they were quieter than before. There were fewer voices than before too. Quintus fiddled with some knobs on the back of the door. Soon, they could hear the clicking of the nine locks, locking up the vault door once again.

When a particularly loud wail rang out from the other side of the door, Mishti squared her shoulders and stepped into the room. Her face turned expressionless as she masked every emotion inside herself. It probably wasn't good for her to push her feelings down like that, but it wasn't exactly a great time for a mental breakdown either.

She glanced around the darkened room, probably looking for something to distract herself.

Chloe followed the action, quickly noticing sconces with candlesticks hanging on the wall. "Ludo, use that fire and light these, will you?"

Victory kept his features bright as he moved from sconce to sconce until all the candles were lit. The flickering light gave them a much better view of the vault.

A musty smell with the scent of various herbs and spices filled Chloe's nostrils. Shelves lined with jars and vials of different shapes and sizes occupied one wall from floor to ceiling, each containing a concoction of a different color and viscosity. Some potions glowed, others emitted a faint smoke or a hissing sound, a few had tiny creatures or foods suspended in them.

A large wooden table dominated the center of the room. Glass beakers, metal bowls, and various utensils cluttered its surface. A thick cauldron sat on top a stove, and Chloe could easily imagine waves of thick smoke pouring out of it and engulfing the room. The dented and scuffed surface of the cauldron proved it had gotten plenty of use.

Standing in the corner, a heavy bookcase was filled with dusty books and scrolls with faded words. On the walls, intricate diagrams and magical symbols had been etched in chalk and ink. Some depicted complex formulas while others showed fae creatures and their anatomy.

The vault gave off the impression of both chaos and order. Piles of ingredients, tools, and equipment were scattered around, but each seemingly sat in its proper place. One thing was certain. This place had housed heavy magical experimentation, where the boundaries of what was possible were pushed to their limits.

Mishti didn't seem impressed. Her face stayed even as she narrowed her eyes at the sconces. "Why would the king have candles in here? Why didn't he use magic to light the room?"

"Not every magic is easy for every fae," Ludo answered.

Chloe nodded. "And even if he could light the room with magic, the king probably needed that magic for his experiments. Maybe he couldn't afford to spare any energy on lighting the room."

Ludo and Mishti continued to glance around the room, but Quintus stood in the center of it completely still. His face had fallen, perhaps overwhelmed by how many hiding places this vault held. He spoke in a tight voice. "We do not even know what the crown piece looks like. It could be a bracelet, a cup, a rock. We do not know."

Chloe shrugged. "I'm sure we'll know it when we see it."

Lifting a few books off the shelf, Ludo blew a sheet of dust off them. "Where are we supposed to look? The crown piece could be hidden anywhere."

Quintus sighed hard, dropping his head into his hand.

Weapons clanged against the vault door, causing Mishti to jump. But the clanging did not lead to greater danger. The locks on the door kept them safe. For now.

Stepping closer to Quintus, Chloe adopted a gentle tone. "Where do you think the crown piece is hidden?"

He started turning toward her, but immediately looked away. "How should I know?"

She took another step closer, and she could see how his breath hitched at the movement. Her tone needed to be even gentler now. "Outside you said you could feel it that we were close. Maybe if you open your mind, you'll be able to find the crown piece."

One single golden glint appeared in his deep brown eyes. It lit just like the golden lights inside the black caves. But then he squeezed his eyes shut and kept them closed for a few breaths. When he opened them again, the golden glint had disappeared.

Stepping forward, he picked through a pile of items on the corner of the wooden table. That produced nothing of value. Next, he went to a shelf and pushed around vials and jars, but he didn't find anything there either. He huffed as he stepped away.

Chloe moved toward him again. "Trust yourself. I'm certain you can—"

"Stop." He spun on his heel just to shoot her a glare. "Do not try to encourage me."

Deliberately turning away from her, he moved to a different corner of the room, as far from her as he could get. As he walked, he flicked his hands, as if trying to get liquid off them. On the other side of the room, he kept his back to her.

She dropped her gaze to the ground as a heavy weight pressed into her chest.

Mishti came to her side and tilted her head toward Quintus. "He's still mad about the barrier, isn't he?"

From the other side of the room, Ludo scoffed loudly. "He is not the only one who is mad."

He probably would have continued in a long rant, except another clang rang out from the vault door. They were safe, but they probably didn't have forever.

Mishti cringed at the sound. She had to shake her shoulders and head before she could speak again. "You never told us, Ludo. How did you escape Fairfrost? You needed your brother's blue scarf, but for what?"

She was trying to distract herself, which was obvious to Chloe, but apparently not to Ludo. He had taken the question as a challenge.

Folding his arms over his chest, he lifted his chin. "How do you know I escaped Fairfrost at all?"

Mishti raised an eyebrow. "Because you don't live there anymore."

Before Ludo could respond, Quintus marched toward the wooden table. If he had been listening to the conversation around him, he gave no indication of it. Once at the table, he pulled from his pocket the golden and emerald dagger. Then, he pulled out the key they had found at the waterfall.

His gaze stayed fixed on the table, but he held one hand out with the palm up. "Give me the ring."

A spark of hope burned in Chloe's chest. She removed the ring and dropped it into his hand, watching him expectantly.

He set the ring on the table with the other items, his eyes narrowing at them. He kept narrowing his eyes tighter and tighter until they closed completely. With his eyelids dropped, he breathed in deep enough to make his chest rise. Then he let out a slow breath that never seemed to end. When it finally did, he reached out and hovered his hand over the three crown pieces.

Chloe chewed on her lip, watching his movements carefully. Her fingers pinched the fabric of her red dress, scrunching it absently. Mishti and Ludo stared with just as much interest as her.

After another deep breath, Quintus's eyes flew open. He turned and stared at a shelf on the side of the room. A marble box embedded with emeralds sat in the middle of it, which Chloe had not noticed before. He pointed, his expression and voice confident. "There."

Her lips turned up to a grin. He'd have his magic back in no time.

Another clang rang throughout the room. She glanced back at the vault door. As long as the mortals didn't break in before he could finish crafting the crown.

42

Chloe held her breath as Quintus crossed the room and lifted the marble box off the shelf. Her hand trailed up until it clasped over her heart. They'd been searching so long, she could hardly believe they'd now found the last piece of the crown.

She feared another obstacle like the many they'd already encountered, but it appeared this box had no lock or explosive or any other difficulties. Quintus reached for the lid. But just before he could lift it, a terrifying sound rang through the room.

A click.

With eyes opening wide, Chloe turned slowly to look at the vault door. The very top knob had turned, indicating the mortals had unlocked the first of the nine locks. Her stomach dropped down to her toes as she sucked in a gasp.

Her body moved before her brain even told it to. She rushed toward the door, anxious to lock the top lock once again.

Ludo got there first. His fingers pinched around the knob and then he attempted to turn it. Except the knob didn't budge. Ludo twisted and yanked and pulled, but no matter how he tried, the knob would not turn to lock again.

In a huff of frustration, he backed away. Chloe tried next. Considering she didn't have the fae strength Ludo had, she wasn't surprised when the knob wouldn't turn for her either. Mishti and Quintus tried too but also failed.

After gulping, Chloe frowned at the door. "They must have jammed rocks against the rods and levers to hold them in place."

As she spoke, they could hear the metal against metal as a rod and lever moved. They held their breaths until the pieces stopped. When they did, the next lock stayed as secure as ever. The mortals had failed to unlock it.

Seeing it, all four of them in the vault let out a breath of relief.

It didn't last long before Mishti shook her head. "I removed the explosive. Now they can move pieces and make mistakes without consequence. They can keep trying multiple positions until they find the right combination."

That thought sent needles across the back of Chloe's neck. She turned to Quintus, who held her gaze for a split second.

After that, he crossed the room and went back to the marble box. Clearly, they didn't have unlimited time. Quintus needed to get that crown back together as soon as possible.

He lifted the lid of the box and pulled out an amulet. The small, intricately crafted jewelry hung from a heavy golden chain. Thick and weighty, each link was polished to a high shine, despite the dust and grime that coated the rest of the vault.

At the end of the chain a gleaming gold setting with filigrees and diamonds held a large emerald gemstone. Its faceted cut created a mesmerizing pattern across the wall for each time it caught the light.

Quintus set it on the table next to the other three pieces and then set the empty marble box to the side. His fingers lifted each object one by one, carefully eyeing them and rubbing his thumb across many of the surfaces. After examining each piece, he then glanced at the cauldron.

Mishti used that moment to clear her throat. "Since no one else is going to say it, I guess it's up to me."

Everyone turned to look at her. She glanced at Ludo with a pointed stare, but he didn't seem to understand its meaning. She looked at Chloe and did the same thing, but Chloe was just as confused as Ludo.

With a sigh, Mishti opened her mouth again. "Quintus can't do magic anymore, right? Chloe never said that explicitly, but I've noticed…" She waved a hand through the air. "It doesn't matter what I've noticed. But I'm right, aren't I?"

Quintus's eyes went wide at this set of questions. Then he hunched forward, as if trying to shrink away. Using both hands, he covered his face.

Chloe put her hands on her hips, speaking a little more harshly than necessary. "That's true, but he'll get his magic back once he wears the crown."

"Great." Mishti probably intended for that to sound less sarcastic than it did. She gestured toward the table at the four items sitting on top. "But how is he supposed to turn all of that into a crown when he doesn't have any magic?"

Chloe's mouth dropped open as she blinked. A moment later, her hands fell to her side, and she laughed. It wasn't cynical or delighted, instead it was full of surprise. "Quintus doesn't need magic to craft things. He can melt the gold in that cauldron and use…" Her gaze darted around the room and then she gestured at a nearby shelf. "He can use those metal trays as molds or something or… okay, so obviously I have no idea how to craft a crown, but it doesn't matter because Quintus can craft anything, with or without magic."

Mishti raised an eyebrow, showing off her skepticism.

But now Quintus must have remembered the truth in Chloe's words. He still hunched forward, but at least he had dropped his hands away from his face. "Ludo, light a fire under the cauldron and make it as hot as you can."

Nodding, Ludo scrambled forward and lit a fire so hot it burned blue.

A glint of gold appeared in Quintus's eyes at the sight of it. He nodded and plucked the key from the table, dropping it into the cauldron a moment later.

After picking up the amulet, he reached for a strange tool sitting on top of the table. He used it to bend the metal pieces holding the emerald gemstone in place. Soon, the emerald dropped onto the table while the rest of the amulet still sat in Quintus's hand. He started removing the diamonds next.

Mishti raised her eyebrows, clearly realizing Quintus didn't need magic to craft. A mild expression of contentment had just started gracing her features when another click sounded through the room.

Sucking in a breath, Chloe rushed toward the vault door and tried to re-lock the second lock before the mortals could jam it in place. She got there too late. Just like the first lock, this one held no matter how she tried to turn the knob.

Palpable tension hung in the air. Mishti looked ready to glare the door to death. Ludo looked ready to be sick.

Soon, Mishti opened her mouth and turned to Quintus. Her mouth hung open for a moment before she shut it again and shook her head. If she had been about to tell Quintus to hurry, it was good she decided against it. He didn't need any added pressure.

Opening her mouth again, she turned to Ludo. "Tell us about your daring escape from Fairfrost."

Sporting a frown that was the physical equivalent to his usual grumbles, he asked, "Why?"

She glared back at him and then pointed at the vault door just as another lock came undone. "To distract us." She said nothing else, but her head tilted toward Quintus, implying that he needed the distraction more than anyone.

Understanding sent Ludo's eyes open wide. He nodded, but just as quickly, his face turned to a scowl. "You want to know about my daring escape from Fairfrost? Fine. It started on a pleasant evening after we finally had everything ready to go."

Ludo slumped against the nearest wall and stuffed a hand into his pocket. "Revyn had packed a bag with supplies. Clara—that was Revyn's beloved—added straps to the bag so one of us could wear it. She even made us harnesses in case we needed to strap ourselves in."

Mishti narrowed her eyes. "Strap yourselves in to what?"

With one hand still in his pocket. Ludo held his other hand out, as if the answer sat on his palm. "That is why we needed Revyn's blue scarf. You already know that a token can be used to train a dragon. We had those dragon coves near our home. All we had to do was get close enough to a dragon to wrap the scarf over its head."

Chloe turned her gaze away from to door long enough to catch Ludo's eye. "But weren't there soldiers near the dragon caves?"

Ludo nodded, the snarl on his face growing. "Yes, there were, and they did not like Revyn because of some lie Clara had told the Fairfrost king. She basically said Revyn was incompetent, which helped him get moved back to the town where I lived, but it also meant the soldiers looked down on him and were eager to prove themselves better than him."

That seemed like a recipe for disaster.

With a sad sigh, Ludo dropped his hand back to his side. "But I did not worry about any of that. I was so certain everything would go perfectly. We decided to wait until day dawned."

The blue in his eyes glowed, showing a hope he'd never displayed before. "I believed with every fiber of my being that we would wake up, sneak past the guards easily, claim a dragon, and then fly away to freedom without another care for all the rest of our lives."

After the last words left his lips, he stared off at nothing in particular, staying silent for several beats. But then his eyes fell closed and he leaned harder against the wall behind him. His shoulders slumped as he stuffed his hand deeper into his pocket.

The room had grown so quiet, Chloe jumped when Quintus dropped the golden dagger and sheath into the cauldron. The removed gems from all the crown pieces sat in a little pile on top of the wooden table.

Even once Quintus began to stir the items inside the cauldron, Ludo still said nothing.

Mishti stepped toward him. "So, what actually happened?"

Ludo scoffed. He wrapped both arms around his stomach, glaring at the ground. "What happened indeed?"

"Did your brother get hurt?" Chloe asked. "Did something happen to his beloved?"

"You wish to know?" Ludo raised his eyebrows, his gaze jumping between Chloe and Mishti.

Both of them nodded with somber intensity.

He scoffed again. "So do I." He swallowed hard. "That is knowledge I wish to find more than anything else in this entire realm. In all the realms."

His chin dropped to his chest. "I do not remember what happened. I remember nothing after that night."

He stuffed his hand back into his pocket as his eyes shimmered with a sadness that threatened to slice open Chloe's heart.

Mishti swallowed, which proved she'd been affected too. She stepped closer to him, her expression turning somewhat reassuring, which was a lot coming from her. "But you obviously did escape. You don't live in Fairfrost. You don't have soldiers after you or anything. You must have gotten away, right?"

When Ludo looked up, his eyes had darkened to a gloom even a wraith couldn't match. He pointed to himself. "I got away." With a heavy chuckle, his hand dropped away. "But Revyn? Clara? I have no idea what happened to them."

And then he did something Chloe wasn't even sure he was capable of. He teared up. Glassy moisture filled his eyes as he stared at the ground. His hand dropped into his pocket one last time, but it came out soon after. Now he held his blue knit scarf Quintus had crafted. When a tear dropped from his eye, Ludo caught it with the knit fabric.

He had searched and searched, but the fate of his brother remained as much a mystery as ever. No wonder he made a bargain with Quintus to help him find his brother's missing scarf. Ludo clearly still cared for his brother as much as he always had. He clearly ached for a reunion with him.

And he didn't even know if his brother was alive or dead.

Chloe's chest had gotten almost as tight as her throat. She would have thrown her arms around Ludo if she thought it might help.

But then the dread inside her grew. Another *click* sounded in the air.

She reached for the next knob, trying to lock it back into place. But then she noticed it wasn't that lock that had just come undone. That lock and the one beneath it, and the one beneath were already unlocked.

Now, only two locks still held in place.

Even from across the room, Mishti had just seen what Chloe did. The young woman's eyes widened as she turned to Quintus. "How close are you to being finished?"

"It depends on how quickly the gold cools." He had an ache in his voice, which may or may not have had something to do with Ludo's story. Regardless, his answer made it clear that they needed more time.

Chloe glanced at the others. "We need a better way to keep the mortals out, otherwise they'll break through before the crown is finished."

43

THE METALLIC SCRAPE OF A golden rod sang through the closed vault door. A shiver slipped down Chloe's spine at the sound of it. The mortals hadn't unlocked the last two locks, but they'd clearly figured out how to unlock the others. The last two would follow soon enough.

They needed a plan.

Mishti glanced around the room. "In the castle, we put heavy furniture in front of the doors to seal them. Maybe that will work here."

Chloe started to nod, but then the mention Crystalfall Castle gave her another idea. "Ludo, why don't you melt the door shut the way you did at the castle?"

Using the side of his fist, he hit the granite doorway, which held the golden vault door. She hadn't noticed until he called attention to it that the doorway was made of a different material than the door.

Now he grumbled. "I would have done that already if it were possible. I cannot melt the door and doorway together when they are made of two different substances."

Just then, the second to last lock came undone with a click.

Chloe's heart jumped into her throat. She tried to lock it again but failed just as she had done all the other times. Her breaths left her at too quick an interval. She turned to Ludo, using her head to point at the lock. "You have fae strength, right? What if you just hold the lock in place with your hands to stop them from unlocking it?"

His hand shot forward, holding onto the knob tightly.

Mishti pursed her lips and glanced at Chloe. "Those levers and rods on the outside of the door have better leverage. The mortals won't need as much strength to move them into place as Ludo would need to hold the knob."

"Fine," Chloe said through a hard puff of air. "We'll come up with another plan too then. Ludo, keep holding that knob as long as you can."

Crossing the room to the large bookcase, Mishti set her hands on one side of it. "This might be heavy enough to keep the door closed. At least for a little longer."

Chloe responded by darting across the room and grabbing the bookcase on the opposite side. It would have been much faster if either of the two fae in the room could move the furniture, but since they were both busy with more important tasks, it came down to the two mortals.

They scooted the bookcase forward little by little, huffing every few steps. Chloe tried at least three times to lift it off the ground. It took too much time to slowly drag and scrape it across the floor. But while Mishti had been able to lift the bookcase for a few moments on her side, Chloe had no strength to do so herself.

After moving it only a few feet across the ground, Quintus ran toward them. "Wait." He scoured the shelves, finally reaching for a pair of metal tongs with a strange stamping mark at the end of it. "I need these."

He whirled around, heading back for the table again. Halfway there, he turned back and rushed to the bookcase once again. "Oh, and I need this. And these."

A few moments later, he had several small tools and trays gathered in his hands. He muttered to himself as he finally made it back to the table.

Part of the gold had been poured into a makeshift mold, though most of it still seemed to be melting in the cauldron.

Mishti grabbed her side of the bookcase again. Just as she started inching it forward, she threw a pointed stare at Chloe. Then she whispered so quietly, Chloe only barely heard the words. "Will it matter if the crown he crafts doesn't look exactly the same as the original crown?"

"No." Ludo answered, still standing in front of the vault door. It hadn't mattered that Mishti whispered, the fae could always hear. It did seem like Ludo enjoyed calling that out every time Mishti whispered, though.

His knuckles had turned white as he pressed his fingers against the knob to hold it in place. "As long as all the pieces are there and they are shaped like a crown, it should work. Crowns usually change shape with each new leader anyway."

He had started the sentence speaking normally, but by the end, he huffed and strained. Red colored his neck, which had veins popping out of it. "I…"

His body angled, attempting to give himself more leverage on the knob. Now heat rose into his face. "Cannot…"

He held on for a few more moments, but then the knob turned, unlocking the last lock keeping them safe. His eyes bulged at once.

"Forget that." Mishti gestured toward the bookcase. "Come help us with this."

Quintus looked over his shoulder, his hands pouring a small portion of gold into a makeshift tray.

Ludo huffed and immediately ran for the bookcase. He lifted it off the ground, which sent his arms into a shaking mess. Apparently, even his fae strength could not carry the bookcase without effort. But even though it was difficult for him, he still moved it much faster than Mishti and Chloe had done.

Soon, he had it shoved up against the door. By then, the mortals had managed to slip another ball of iron between the cracked doorway, keeping it from being closed completely.

Chloe tried kicking the ball out of place, but they had set the bookcase in just the right spot that her foot couldn't reach the ball. At least the heavy furniture would keep the mortals from pushing open the door anymore.

Checking over his shoulder, Quintus sucked in a breath at the open door. "I am not ready yet."

"Don't worry about us." Chloe tried to keep her tone light as she shoved her own body up against the bookcase. A little extra weight against the door couldn't hurt. "Just focus on the crown."

Following Chloe's lead, Mishti and Ludo pressed themselves up against the bookcase too.

It was pointless to whisper since everyone in the room would hear regardless, but Chloe wished she could speak without Quintus hearing. Something like this might distract him. Still, it was probably better for them to be prepared.

She glanced at Ludo. "Maybe you should open a door for us to escape."

Quintus looked over his shoulder with harried eyes.

"Just in case," Chloe quickly added. "Just as a precaution."

"No." Quintus glared at her before turning back to the items on the table. He dropped a metal tool only to reach for another. "I have to stay here to finish the crown. I need the tools and the cauldron, and…"

He trailed off, not realizing for several moments that he had stopped talking. After finishing some detail on the crown, he spoke again. "We cannot leave until the crown is complete."

If he had looked back, she would have nodded at him with an understanding sort of look. Luckily, he didn't look back, which didn't require that sort of deception from her. Instead, she turned to Ludo and gave him a little nod.

Would he understand her meaning, even if she didn't say anything? Perhaps it wouldn't matter anyway. Once Ludo opened a door, Quintus would hear the sound of it materializing. But he might be less argumentative once it was already open.

Ludo did lift his hand, waving it in a circle. He had understood her message then. Ignore Quintus and open a door anyway. Just in case.

But after Ludo's hand wave, no swirling tunnel appeared before them.

Chloe jerked her head toward him; her eyes opened wide.

His nose twitched and he waved his hand around in a circle once again. Still, no door appeared.

Mishti shook her head with a huff, her back still pressed against the bookcase. "Let me guess. This room has magic that prevents you from opening a door."

Ludo nodded with a scowl.

338

It shouldn't have come as a surprise, especially considering how paranoid the king was during his final journal entries. The setback still felt like a knife to the heart.

As if to mock their hope, the bookcase at their back shifted slightly.

Chloe gasped and pushed all her weight against it. Ludo and Mishti were already leaning on it, but they started shoving harder against it too.

Soon, they moved it back where it had been before, yet that tiny ball of iron still kept the vault door open a crack.

The bookcase wouldn't work for much longer. It was brute force against brute force. They had the strength of a single fae, but the mortals had dozens of them on the other side of the door. Maybe some had been killed by the explosion, but it clearly hadn't hampered their numbers too much. And if Julian had managed to survive, then the mortals had unfiltered wildness on their side too.

"A barrier enchantment!" Chloe shouted the words too loud, especially considering the mortals might be able to hear through the small crack. No matter how she attempted to calm herself, nothing could contain her intensity as she turned to Ludo. "I know you can't open a door, but you can still create a barrier enchantment, right? Make one here that will hold the mortals out and keep the bookcase in place."

His lip curled up at the suggestion, staring at her a little too viciously. "Mortals can break through barrier enchantments with iron." His eyes narrowed. "You should know that better than anyone."

She rolled her eyes. This was no time for an argument, especially when her idea would work. "The iron won't break through it right away. Just make a barrier enchantment. It will give us time for Quintus to finish the crown."

He threw her a burning glare before turning and lifting both hands out in front of him. With a burst, sparkling blue magic shot from his fingertips until a shield shimmered between them and the doorway.

When the mortals shoved against the door again, the bookcase shook, but it didn't move forward. Ludo's enchantment held it and the door in place.

Chloe let out a breath of relief that would probably be ripped away in a few moments. But at least now she could appreciate the small victory.

"Ludo," Quintus called out from over his shoulder. "Come help me cool the gold. If I cool it too fast by myself, it can cause problems. But if cooled with magic, it should be fine."

Nodding, Ludo rushed to the table to perform the magic Quintus needed.

Fighting the urge to rush to the table herself, Chloe stared at the rattling bookcase and the shaking golden door. Mishti stood nearby, her hands out and ready, as if to catch anything that might fall. Truthfully, neither of them could do anything without any magic, but at least by watching, they'd know if and when something needed to be done.

The time for that came only a few moments later. A burning stick made of wood instead of gold got pushed through the crack in the doorway. Such a tiny fire shouldn't have been hot enough or big enough to light the enormous bookcase so quickly, but it did.

Chloe took a step back as the fire engulfed the entire bottom half of the wooden shelves. Crackling filled the air as the wood turned from an old, rotting brown to black. At least Ludo's barrier enchantment kept the smoke out of the vault.

Clearing her throat, Chloe did her best attempt at a calm voice. "Are you almost finished with the crown?"

The words trembled out of her, which probably made her attempt at a calm voice sound even more worried than ever. Though the barrier enchantment still held, the mortals managed to open the door a little wider, smashing the blackened wood of the bookcase in the process.

Ludo huffed. "Is their iron breaking through the—" He stopped short and then let out a little yelp.

He must have just turned and saw the fire and smoke.

"What is it?" Quintus asked, though his gaze stayed focused on the items in front of him.

"Fire," Ludo said through a small whimper.

Mishti flexed her jaw. "The fire is not a problem. But now the mortals have the door open enough that they can reach through."

She turned and threw Ludo a look. "They are jamming iron weapons into the barrier, which *will* break it eventually."

Fear gripped Chloe around the throat, suffocating her like the billows of smoke behind the enchantment. Her stomach had wound so tight, she had almost forgotten about the wound in her side.

They didn't have much time. The barrier enchantment would hold for a little longer, but not forever.

Just when her heart threatened to pound right out of her chest, Quintus whirled around with a golden glint in his eye. "It is done."

Her hand flew to her chest, pressing against it as if that might hold her heart inside. She breathed in relief while both she and Mishti crossed the room.

A sound like scraping filled the air, causing all four of them to glance back. Even with the bookcase destroyed, the mortals had only managed to open the door to a slightly wider crack. Two daggers, which were surely made of iron, were being pressed against the barrier enchantment. Whoever held them was hidden behind the mostly closed door.

But no matter how the daggers pushed and prodded, they didn't seem to have any effect on the barrier enchantment beyond a few pops and fizzles. It appeared they had more time than Chloe had first assumed.

Finally, she could turn her gaze to the crown in Quintus's hands. Showers of emerald and golden sparks poured off the magnificent creation.

It had curved tines embellished with emeralds and diamonds and small decorative carvings. The carvings and decorations were all simple and probably much less intricate than Quintus would have done if they'd had more time.

But even with a simple design, the crown was still breathtaking. The gems caught the light, casting a magical glow on the golden base and tines. The showers of sparks coming off the crown added to its extraordinary beauty.

The barrier enchantment didn't matter now. The fire didn't matter either. It didn't even matter that they couldn't open a door inside the vault because, soon enough, Quintus would have his magic back. Not only that, he'd have the added power from the crown of Crystalfall.

He'd probably throw one single enchantment that would defeat their enemies forever.

Mishti moved a little closer, eyeing the golden and emerald sparks. "Is that..." She gestured at them. "Is that a good thing?"

She had phrased her question positively, but the wavering of her voice suggested she feared the sparks would cause problems.

"It is a very good thing." Ludo lifted his lips in a grin. "The sparks mean the crown has chosen Quintus. They mean he is truly the rightful leader of Crystalfall, though we knew as much already."

"Oh." Mishti let out a breath that released a heavy weight from her shoulders. "I guess it's time then." She gestured toward the crown and glanced at Quintus.

His gaze fell to the crown, which he lifted slightly. He stared at the crown, then looked upward. Judging by the slant in his shoulders, Chloe guessed he felt a little awkward about crowning himself.

"Here." She held a hand out. "Let me."

Quintus's nerves had clearly overtaken him far more than she realized because he had completely forgotten to be angry with her. Instead, he just gave a short nod and pushed the crown into her hands.

She nearly lifted it and dropped it onto his head right then, but then another urge compelled her to wait for a moment. This moment needed a few words. Not many, since they had mortals desperately trying to break through their only protection right at that moment. But since the enchantment still held, it only seemed appropriate to say a little something.

Holding the crown higher, she took a deep breath. "Quintus, you are about to be crowned King of Crystalfall. I have known for a long while now that you possess qualities that will make you a great and fair ruler.

"You are loyal and fiercely protective. Your strong commitment to those you care about will lead you to keep this court safe and thriving. I have no doubt that you will not just be a great ruler. You will be the best."

She dared glance into his eyes and donned a careful smile. "Crystalfall is lucky to have you."

His expression remained even and unreadable, except for the lightest twitch at the corner of his lips. It wasn't much, but she'd take it.

Mishti and Ludo nodded solemnly in agreement.

It was time.

Rising to her tiptoes, Chloe lifted the crown higher.

Quintus was sober, but he seemed to finally accept that this was his birthright. He swallowed and lowered his head so it was easier for her to crown him.

Her breath hitched as she got closer. She found herself holding her breath as she placed the golden crown onto his head. It settled onto his hair easily. Her gaze darted around the room, waiting for a reaction.

But even though the crown sat in place, nothing happened. The sparks coming off it slowed to a light glittering.

Now she held her breath for an all-new reason. Maybe the crown just needed a moment. But even after a few beats, the crown still did nothing.

Was she wrong to expect a reaction? When Elora and Brannick got their crowns, there had been magical sparks and breezes, and the whole of Faerie seemed to glow.

None of that happened now. The crown simply sat on Quintus's head, beautiful and magnificent and unchanging.

At the very least, the crown should have adjusted and changed to become uniquely Quintus's.

Mishti opened her mouth, closed it, and then opened it again. She glanced around at the others. "Did it work?"

"No." Quintus's throat bulged with a swallow as he pulled the crown back into his hands.

Ludo shook his head in disbelief. "It should have worked. The showers of sparks reacted to your touch like they do for every true leader. The crown didn't react at all to Chloe. You are clearly a chosen leader."

"Maybe I was wrong about the ring being the fourth piece," Chloe offered, though even as she said it, she knew that wasn't true. The crown wouldn't have reacted at all if it had been made improperly.

"I know what happened." Quintus stood tall, confident. He wasn't sad, but he wasn't filled with joy either.

The others stared at him wearing identical expressions of confusion. When he stayed silent, they glanced at each other.

But the moment Quintus opened his mouth, they all turned to him again. He let out a sigh. "There is only one reason a chosen leader would not be given power after being crowned."

Even with a crackling fire behind them and mortals with daggers stabbing at the barrier enchantment, it still felt like the room was silent. Chloe, Mishti, and Ludo stared, their gazes growing more focused by the moment.

Quintus looked down at the crown in his hands. "There is only one explanation. The king of Crystalfall—my father—is still alive. The crown still belongs to him."

It took four whole heartbeats before the words sank in. When they did, Chloe gasped. If Quintus's father still lived, the crown would never give Quintus power. It wouldn't return the magic Quintus had lost.

As much as that truth hurt, an even more pressing one came snapping into focus. The snaps and fizzles of the enchantment had turned to cracks. The shimmering barrier started to flicker. Pulsing, the enchantment faded and started to disappear.

The mortals were about to break through. Chloe sucked in a breath, curling her hands into fists. The mortals were coming, and they had no way to stop them.

THE STORY CONTINUES

Find out what happens to Chloe and Quintus in Book 4,
Curse & Crystal Thorns.

*The king may be vile, but finding him
is their only chance to save the court.*

Curse & Crystal Thorns is available now!

ACKNOWLEDGMENTS

First, I want to thank you, reader, for exploring this magical world of Crystalfall with me. I truly hope you enjoyed this new, glittering court. If you have time, please consider leaving a review, which will help other readers discover this series.

I am deeply grateful to my two incredible editors, Deborah Spencer and Justin Greer. I had to push some deadlines we had set and they were both so accommodating and supportive of this book and me. Without my editors, this book would not have been published on time. As always, their invaluable advice and guidance helped shape this work into what it is today.

To my rockstar book cover designer, Angel Leya, thank you for always working with me! You are always happy to meet any challenge, even when I give you notes like, "Give me the blingiest dagger you can possibly create. Like, if Paris Hilton had a dagger, that's what this dagger should look like." And as always you took my notes and suggestions and created a book cover so much better than I ever could have imagined.

My sincerest appreciation goes out to my editorial reviewers, bookstagram team, and street team for their promotion and support. I can't say it enough how much it helps when you create a space for discussion about my books on social media. Without you, many readers might never had heard of me at all. You are the greatest!

Thank you to my best author buds, the Queens of the Quill, and the wonderful illustrator @berizart.

Finally, thank you to my husband who has always stood by my side, even after I've made mistakes. Thank you for believing in me and pushing me to be better. Now that the book is finished, I suppose I will do what you've repeatedly asked and let myself rest. But only for a little bit.

MORE FROM KAY L. MOODY

Want Elora and Brannick's story? Don't miss this related series!

Betray a prince. Conspire with a king. What could possibly go wrong?

THE FAE OF BITTER THORN

Start with the prequel novella, which you can download and read for free! Visit **kaylmoody.com/bitter** to get your copy.

You also might like Kay's previous series.

THE ELEMENTS OF KAMDARIA

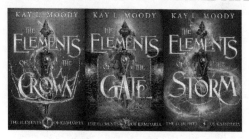

Chloe and Quintus Illustration (next page)
Artist: @berizart

DON'T MISS THE PREQUEL THAT STARTS ELORA'S STORY

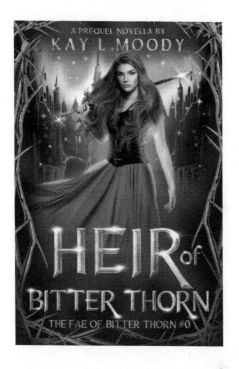

Visit **kaylmoody.com/bitter** to download the prequel

Heir of Bitter Thorn is a prequel to The Fae of Bitter Thorn. Discover how Elora got the mysterious scar on her hand, how Prince Brannick escaped Fairfrost, and why the two of them don't remember their first meeting.

Made in the USA
Columbia, SC
27 October 2024

45146034R00212